Shadow of Lies

Shadow of Lies

DONALD E. MC QUINN

TOR

A TOM DOHERTY ASSOCIATES BOOK

This is a work of fiction. All the characters and events portrayed in this book are fictional, and any resemblance to real people or incidents is purely coincidental.

SHADOW OF LIES

Copyright © 1985 by Donald E. McQuinn

First printing: August 1985

A TOR Book

Published by Tom Doherty Associates
8-10 West 36 Street
New York, N.Y. 10018

Cover art by Lee MacLeod

ISBN: 0-312-93726-1

Printed in the United States of America

For Ray Edinger, with thanks for his unfailing special trust and confidence.

For Zola Helen Ross, with thanks for direction and understanding.

A special note of appreciation to all the workers, past and present, who have done so much to make Woodland Park Zoo a sanctuary for such wonderful creatures as Nicholas and Alexandra, the snow leopards fictionalized in this novel.

CHAPTER 1

THE SNOW LEOPARD STIRRED, BLACK ROSETTES HARD-TEXTURED against the steel-gray coat. Although it was already mid-morning, overcast skies simulated a dawn hungering for its first taste of sunlight. Cage bars failed to blunt the cat's honed eyes that sought the mountain reaches imprinted on its memory. Rising, he arched his neck to test the heavy air, then shifted from one foreleg to the other in a limbering movement, preparing for a journey that would never occur.

The man on the bench in front of the cage remained absolutely still. It was a game he played with the silver-gray male leopard and its smaller mate. She, too, remained immobile, eyes glittering slits in a mask. That was part of the game. The man watched, and they pretended not to watch.

Martin Carmody was what the man called himself. He had light-brown hair, misted darker by the weather, and hazel eyes far too old for the unlined face. Compact, with broad shoulders, at first look he was overcostumed. The thick-soled walking shoes, twill trousers and glossy windbreaker seemed excessive, until one noticed they were well worn.

Carmody never considered using the name supplied the big male by the zoo, feeling this subversion created another strand in the braid that bound the two of them. He scoffed at the notion that the leopard thought of himself by a name, but was convinced he had a sense of being that transcended simple

9

physical sensation. When the leopard stretched, alternately tensing and relaxing in segments, the act emphasized Carmody's conviction. He believed the display was, in fact, a form of arrogance.

It pleased him. Arrogance was the child of capability.

Carmody smiled. The change of expression added little warmth to the stolid features. It was one of the few things about his personal appearance of which he was not completely aware.

The name Carmody was one of many. They were all good names, buttressed with superior paperwork. Acquiring an identity in the United States was ridiculously simple. Still, he was convinced a name carries power within itself. It was more than sounds or marks on paper. It was himself.

Carmody was very good at being different people, quite possibly the best in the world. When he considered his own skills, it rankled him that the male leopard was so impenetrable. When it bowed that incredibly graceful neck to nuzzle its mate, they were inviolate. A prisoner, the leopard rejected being an exhibit. Carmody had been present when particularly fatuous spectators disturbed the female. The male attended to her, courtly as any cavalier, never acknowledging the chattering humans.

A good man might bear up under similar imprisonment, Carmody thought. No man would handle it with equal *elan*. It would be necessary for the man to be very flexible in order to protect his character. He told himself that was reason. One adjusted, adapted.

The leopard refuted him by crystallizing its only personality.

Standing, Carmody walked to the rail between the sidewalk and the cage. The female stared at him, a two-second calculation before resuming her dozing attitude. The male continued to scan the distance, but Carmody caught the minute flick of the tail and smiled.

He glanced around to assure himself no one watched, then reached into the pocket of his jacket and pulled out two pieces of liver neatly packaged in plastic. Carefully unwrapping them, he returned the wrapping. He spoke, his voice a solid baritone, heavy in his chest. "See, liver today. That's

10

over a dollar's worth, you realize that?'' The female stared, no longer feigning disinterest. Carmody threw her the soft mass with a slinging, sidearm motion. She was on it in a blur, her coloration so blended to the rocks of the exercise area the granite itself seemed to have taken flight. The male jerked irritably, then burned a torch-bright stare at Carmody's chest.

"Just once I wish you'd look me straight in the eye,'' Carmody said. "Are you afraid of what I might learn, or of what you might learn?'' He laughed, the harshness of it swallowed by the moisture-laden park greenery. He lofted the second piece of liver past the female.

When it plopped on the cement deck, she tentatively considered a rush. At the male's slow turn, she made a dignified retreat to the rock ledge. The male padded forward, not stalking, merely careful, the smooth head tracing the outline of the meat while he nosed the entire surface. Then he flipped it over with a paw and repeated the process. A tremor in the throat barely betrayed the swallowing. With the food accepted, the eyes struck at the man's throat while muscles bulged at hips and shoulders, charges primed to explode.

"Ah, good!'' It was a sigh of pleasure. He leaned across the rail, stretched toward the wire. His legs trembled at the strain of keeping him in balance. "I love you, you murderous bastard,'' he said. The words unlocked his constrained features, allowed them to form a passionate yearning.

The leopard's muzzle opened red as a fresh wound. A reptilian sibilance wavered under the rumbling growl that poured from it.

"Yes, yes,'' Carmody said, "hate. I can wait.''

He turned from the snarling animal and walked away without looking back.

The end of summer had brought rain, as always. It weighted the air, trailed like threads from the clouds. Droplets spangled the trees, falling heavily after massing to sufficient size. Grass rippled with the full sheen of rough emerald. As Carmody neared the exit gate the rich humus smell of animals and plants broke under the pressure of exhaust fumes and oil-soaked concrete.

11

His car tires made a sound much like the undercurrent in the leopard's snarl as he left the parking lot.

Twenty minutes later he was shaking the water off his jacket before entering his small outdoor-equipment store. Gentle chiming filled the room at the opening of the door, issuing from a device that looked like a miniature banjo. It hung from the door frame. Movement disturbed dangling pithball mallets that stroked the strings. The chord seemed to come from a great distance and linger. The lone clerk, a pretty young blond, looked up and smiled a greeting. Immediately, however, her face fell.

"I'm going to miss that little doorbell more than anything else about this place, I think," she said.

Carmody said, "How could Chris Swenson not be attracted by something called a Swedish door chime?"

She made a face. "You bought it and put it there."

"I needed something to keep you awake."

"I'm going to miss everything here, even your teasing. This new girl better be good, or I'll, I'll—" A sufficient threat was beyond her, and they laughed together at the inadequacy. The residue of that enjoyment still lingered when the door opened once more. The woman standing there was as blond as Chris, but much smaller.

The newcomer said, "Mr. Carmody?" He barely had time to nod before she blurted, "I'm Elise Granger. Wally Jones sent me." Her blue eyes were anxious. "He said you were looking for a clerk."

Carmody walked toward her, extending a welcoming hand. "I am. Chris's getting married. She says they're moving away, but I think she's just planning to stay home and have babies."

Chris's indignant squawk chased some of the concern from Elise's face.

He was pleased by the firmness of her grip. Her smallness had troubled him. She was quite attractive, which was a sales plus for her work as a clerk, but it was an unacceptable drawback if he'd be needed to move every box or package. He led her back to his tiny office space.

"You're experienced?" he asked when they were seated.

12

"Oh, yes. In a sporting-goods store, too." The last was a hopeful thrust. Carmody smiled, unintentionally condescending.

"That's not exactly what I run here. We cater to serious runners, hikers, campers, and climbers."

Jaw set, she answered, "I asked Wally questions. I wouldn't apply for a job I couldn't handle."

"That's good. What do you know about my stock?"

"Not as much as I'd like, but I could learn. And I need a job."

"I suppose you're building up a premarital bank account, too?"

"I'm divorced." The words crackled.

As they discussed her work experience in detail, she displayed intelligence and motivation. He decided to take a chance on her physical strength and hire her.

Chris took her under her wing like the little mother she always brought to Carmody's mind.

The thought reintroduced Elise's divorced status. The insinuated toughness might be a newfound disguise. He watched the women interact. Elise was precise, a combination of grace and direct line. Questions were specific. Answers were filed with a sharp nod or drew another question.

When the phone rang they looked up only long enough to see that he was answering it.

"Carmody's Outdoor Supply."

"Is Mr. Carmody in?"

"Speaking. Can I help you?"

"Oh, Mr. Carmody. I'm told you can equip large parties."

"That's right. What'd you have in mind?"

"I have some friends coming to visit." The voice paused, as if readying itself. Carmody felt it, and straightened. "They are foreign guests. Six men and two women. And two young boys. Can you manage?"

The phone was suddenly very heavy. He had to lean his elbow on the counter and brace his wrist with the other hand. "Come in at your convenience. We'll arrange everything."

"Excellent." The receiver's metallic click ended the conversation. Carmody hung up gingerly. "I've got to go out for

13

a while," he said to the women. "I'll probably stay for lunch, so don't expect me back before one-thirty."

Chris's predictable expression was the same as when he'd teased her. He preferred Elise's restrained attentiveness. Chris waved good-bye.

Carmody walked to his car and drove away. After a few blocks, he could see Puget Sound. A breeze had combined with the sun to clear out the low overcast, leaving high, bulky clouds to create irregular masses of shade on the whitecapped surface. Between the darkened areas of gray and olive the sun polished the mixed hues to pearls and jade. A ferry churned out from under one of the shadows, the white hull practically incandescent in the change. It was lost to view behind the buildings of the city as the car proceeded downhill.

He drove mechanically, thinking of the phone call. It had been a gross oversight not to recognize the voice instantly. When possible reasons for the peremptory summons surfaced, he drove them from his mind. Whatever required an emergency meeting, Alex would explain.

Parking at the garage north of the Pike Place Market, he strolled to the market area. Crossing Virginia, he entered a building on his left where a tiny Vietnamese woman ran an over-the-counter restaurant. The site provided a superior viewing point and a choice of exit routes. It had the further advantage of being familiar, and he ached for anything suggesting normalcy. The exotic smells of *nuc maam* and cilantro, of steaming rice, all came on in assault. He was suddenly desperately hungry. Knowing it was a psychological reaction didn't help. He ordered *goi ga*, the mounded chicken salad with its crushed-peanut topping.

When he was finished, he left through the back door and walked the long flight of stairs up to the alley. From there he continued south, then downhill to the bank of craft stalls under their pale green protective shed. The cold weather had discouraged most business. Hardy sellers crouched behind their wares, eyeing passersby as fishermen watch bobbers, anxious for any tremor of interest.

At a door leading to a large outside deck, Carmody checked

his watch before stepping through. He walked to the rail, ignoring the speeding vehicles on the viaduct ahead and below, and the white-sprayed Sound beyond. Only the cold wind ruffling his hair stirred any interest. It found its way down the open collar of his shirt. Instead of buttoning up, he took a perverse pleasure in the relentless penetration. He was shivering when the man leaned on the rail next to him.

"It isn't like the country of endless wheat fields, is it?" he said, looking out at the roiled water.

Carmody half-turned to face him. "Is it necessary for us to exchange a silly parole, Alex? We know each other."

Alex smiled at him, and Carmody wondered how the man lasted. Anyone looking at that ingenuousness would be tempted to test the cunning behind it. There were innumerable stories about people who had given in to the temptation and how terribly they'd regretted it. Alex slapped his back and said, "Let's walk and talk. Down the stairs. And be careful. You know better than to use professional terms, especially our terms." Carmody accepted the rebuke without argument.

As they proceeded, Carmody studied the shorter man from the corner of his eye. Portly, well-padded by years of good food and drink, Alex was unchanging. More to the point, he was unremarkable. Anyone asked to describe him would do well to come up with anything more than a pleasant face with gray temples. He perched in the center of middle age like a bird on a branch. He would look exactly the same until one day he would simply fly away forever. Carmody tried to tell himself the image wasn't really morbid, but fanciful. In either case, he stopped inspecting Alex.

"This is better," Alex declared at the bottom of the wooden stairs. "You look good, Martin. Healthy. Still the outdoorsman, right?"

Carmody stopped abruptly. Alex, caught unaware, stumbled. Carmody said, "An emergency meeting to discuss *hobbies*?"

Sweat smeared Alex's rosebud upper lip and hairline. When he looked away from Carmody and faced the light, the dampness took on a greasy shine.

"We are caught in a dilemma." Alex tugged at Carmody's

arm to get him walking again. "There is a man who supplies us with information from his factory. The details are not necessary. What is important is that this man, on his own, has recruited a fellow worker."

Carmody made a sound of disbelief, and Alex grimaced, continuing, "Amateurs. Still, the new man is invaluable. Are you familiar with computers?"

Carmody shot him a hard stare.

"Of course. So. Scientists have reduced even the largest computers to incredibly small sizes through the use of supercooled circuits. I don't pretend to understand what's involved. The man improperly recruited is involved with a team project. Part of their work subjects certain compounds to immense pressures, and then the compounds react as if supercooled."

"You don't want me to handle this?"

"Of course! Who else?"

Carmody leaned toward Alex, who changed course immediately, rounding a convenient corner. Carmody followed. Alex talked on, obviously uncomfortable. "He's been transferred here from Denver. It happened before—"

Shock and fury blurred Carmody's words. "I won't do it. I can't deal with an agent here, where I live! Have you all gone mad?"

Alex refused to look at him. "I return home soon. I've taken risks for the Bureau that will be worth attention, possibly even promotion. I'll speak to someone then. But take no chances with them, Martin. Our lives are lonely enough, without separating ourselves further."

The warning only fueled his anger. "They're crazy, Alex! It violates everything I've established!"

"I know. Do you think I haven't fought with them? I even managed a trip to Washington, had a *dusha-dushi* with the people in charge." His face twisted, and Carmody wondered if it was because of his lapse into the Russian phrase for "soul-to-soul" or if he was physically expressing an opinion of their superiors. Alex continued, "The only time they give you a quick answer is when it's bad news. You control the new man, Martin."

16

"Shit!" Carmody drove a fist into a palm. Some tourists interrupted a conversation to stare, and Alex grinned embarrassed apology. He shepherded Carmody along under the waterfront's duel-level viaduct, away from the crowds. The traffic's roar thundered down on them in a torrent, while the hurtling wind from the Sound infused the noise with the smells of salt spray and garbage. Carmody walked head-down, wrapped in his own mental turmoil.

They'll ruin everything, he thought. The desk-bound bastards can't see beyond their own reputations.

Seven years. It rang in his head like a carillon. For what? A wife who'd forgotten everything except how to complain and two daughters who never knew him well enough to forget anything. A life of evasion and tension. Now he was expected to jeopardize what little freedom and accomplishment he could call his own.

They were abreast of the aquarium, and he looked back at the concrete steps that went crawling up to the marketplace. The staircase always made him think of an ancient castle keep. He drew his hand across his eyes to cancel his wandering thoughts.

Alex misinterpreted the gesture. He said, "It's an order." His hand settled gracelessly on Carmody's sleeve, then fell away. "This thing will use today's supercomputers as slaves! It will process hundreds of millions of instructions per *second*!"

Expressionless, Carmody said, "The Party already has more people than that responding to instructions every second. Unfortunately, the instructions come from morons."

"Don't make stupid jokes! This machine approaches true intelligence. Flawless logic, perfectly organized, untiring. It can win us complete victory!"

"There is no complete victory, ever. You want to risk my organization for a rumor of a dream."

Alex drew erect. "Your obsession with your own circumstances blinds you." He held his fists out in front of himself. "This man is no scientist. He is an administrator, a production analyst. He is involved in the development of the overall system, one that will select every target the Americans mean to destroy in our homeland, Martin. It will control the firing

17

of every missile, every decoy. If there is the need to change a target while a rocket is in flight, or as it is being readied, this machine will make the commands.''

"And we will have the same capability. Stalemate. The same as ever.''

Frowning, Alex lowered his fists, flexed the fingers. "Listen to me. Think. This man will know *where* this system is emplaced. He may even be sent to work on it himself. At the very least, we know exactly what the Americans have, and can duplicate it, as you said. But this man gives us *access*, the possibility of telling their devil's brain to think what *we* want it to think. Imagine the American president pressing that button and his missiles exploding in their silos or falling on his own cities. We will do more than make these bastards defenseless, we will make them commit suicide!''

Carmody stopped, staring out at a freighter being herded by a dogged tugboat.

Alex hammered at his point. "You will control the man who can give us the opportunity to destroy these people. Without this technology, we can't defend ourselves. With it alone, we merely continue to operate as usual. But with the technology and access to their use of it, they are in our hands. The men in the Square are determined to have the opportunity. The final triumph.''

Carmody smiled wearily. "Stirring oratory, my friend. And you may be right. Nevertheless, as my old grandmother said, when they make you eat shit, it doesn't help if they put sour cream on it first.''

Alex's mouth tightened in prim disapproval, the reflex of a puritan automatically acknowledging a god capable of instantly destroying those who mocked, a god so adamant in its demands of virtue it frequently destroyed everyone proximate to the suspected sin.

"We will make the Americans learn about eating shit. Get us what we must have. I'll support you any way I can.''

"You always have. But we work for idiots, Alex, and they grow worse.''

The disapproval was profound this time, and there was no

effort to soften it. Alex said, "We work for a cause. It never changes. And there is much to do." He stretched his pace, a trick of a few inches, but enough to pull him ahead. Carmody had to move quickly to catch up.

CHAPTER 2

THE SMALL OFFICE REEKED OF CIGAR SMOKE. IT WAS NOT THE aromatic, fat smell of good leaf, conjuring fantasies of leather chairs and expensive books. This was rank stuff, burned to clumps of gritty cinders that huddled in the desk ashtray like sun-bleached dog turds. A carved-stone nameplate declared that Robert J. Davis worked here.

The burly man in the visitor's chair surveyed his surroundings with a truculence so deeply ingrained it had the cast of permanence. Slashes of bitterness fanned out from the corners of his mouth. Similar runnels slanted diagonally across his forehead, tense grooves that finally plunged vertically between his eyes. Under that glower, his features were roughly masculine. Heavy brows shielded blue eyes above cheekbones sharp as blades. There was contempt in the hard gaze, as if the mind behind the expression was steeled against the present, waiting for a future it was determined to have. Eroded, abused, the face was a stark winter, jealously hoarding its power to rejuvenate.

His name was Steven Black, and he was obviously uncomfortable in his dark business suit. He exhaled noisily and reexamined the room for the fourth time.

A photograph on the wall drew Black's attention. He got out of his chair to inspect it more closely.

A group of men occupied the foreground, mantled in the

tailoring reserved for the sleek flesh of power. They were celebrating, their satisfied faces enjoying success and the appreciation of peers.

Two men stood apart. One of the pair was himself, younger. Hesitant fingers traced the belligerent set of his jaw while his shocked consciousness counted the few years since the picture was taken.

The man beside him was short and thin, his most remarkable feature an outsized head, ballooned further by masses of thick, wavy hair. The face canted forward, as though the eager skull would pull the body along.

Black and his companion smiled without the congratulatory flush gracing the others. Theirs was grim humor.

Black's lips barely parted to let words slide past. "Does it please you to look at this every day, to be reminded that I was the boss once and now you are? Still, it was a good case. Those were the days when we both used to resent the heavy hitters whooping it up over our bust."

The dull room absorbed the whisper, tucking it away with its other secrets.

Carefully, he tipped the frame away from the wall. Unfaded paint under the picture told him it had probably been in place for years. Still, it was a standard size, and it would be like Davis to hang a shot like that, just to remind him of friendlier times. He returned to his chair.

Black damned Davis for keeping him waiting. It was a transparent ploy. His first impulse had been to arrive late, just in case, but he'd decided to be absolutely punctual. That was the way Davis would remember him. The image could be helpful.

Amusement flickered in his eyes. He'd always considered himself calculating. Perhaps time and events had changed that to cunning. Or had that been the true characteristic all along?

He shook his head, throwing off introspection like a dog coming out of the water.

The door banged open. An older, barbered Davis hurried in, an out-thrust hand demanding greeting. His eye contact had the precision of surgery. Words bobbed in the wake of

21

his progress to the desk chair. "I'm glad you could come. I was afraid you'd cut yourself off from us entirely."

Black said, "I didn't do any cutting. Let's at least start off with truths and save the lies for important conversation, okay?"

Davis fumbled in his desk drawer for a cigar. Lighting it broke sentences into staccato bursts. "You weren't shanghaied to Seattle. It was a good place for you to cool off while the smoke cleared."

"Oh." Black paused until Davis looked up. "Important conversation already?"

Davis shuffled papers. "We think we have a lead on the man who caused all the trouble in the first place."

Black jerked in his chair. "You've identified him?"

"Nothing so rich. But we think we have a pattern. We may know where he lives." He got up to pace. "We go back a long way, Steve. I'm glad we can give you this one. We owe it to you."

Black felt the old fires growing. He chose words. "I like it where I am, trying to stay awake while I run name traces and exciting shit like that. You try to move me and I'll go right to the Chief."

"Your only hole card is a threat to quit. He'd take you up on it."

Black clenched his fists until the nails digging at his palms steadied him. "You're the one who said you owe me. I'm doing my job. Leave me alone."

"I'm giving you a chance to prove the system did you wrong, man!"

"Screw you. Where were you when they were after me with the knives, old friend?"

The silence in the tiny room elongated, became a mutually perceived challenge. Typewriters in other offices were a crude intrusion.

Davis broke off the staring match. He folded his arms across his chest. "Morris was your man. I saw him in Sacramento on a day his official report claimed he was working on a case for you in San Francisco. Should I have ignored that?"

22

Black pitched forward, grabbed the edge of the desk. Davis's hands moved in an involuntary defensive gesture. Black said, "You could have let me check it out, let *me* report it! Even when you knew they were checking on Morris— and me, God damn you!—you never said a fucking word."

"I was ordered—"

"I used to listen to you because I trusted you. I listened at the investigation because I had to."

Coolly, Davis retreated. He drummed on the desk with a pencil, the movement so rapid it was a rattling, yellow blur. "The man who doubled Morris never surfaced. We've never gotten close to him. Never thought we had, I should say. I want to show you something." Not looking back, he left the office. Ludicrously, Black found himself remembering a story about Queen Victoria, that whenever she decided to sit down, she sat, knowing someone would be behind her with a chair.

They walked a stark hall of bureaucratic beige and yellow. Open doors punctuated the sterile walls. Black lockstepped behind Davis, rigidly facing straight ahead. There were men in those flanking rooms who knew the counterintelligence sector chief who got burned. It was better not to see their stares.

Davis led the way into a computer facility. "The very best." His grand gesture managed to encompass the equipment and exclude the other men in the room.

Black stood transfixed by the hum, by the synapse flick of reels wrenched from repose to blurred action. A myriad lights blinked, the multiple eyes of a new creature that filled the room with its ionized exhalations.

He said, "Jesus, it's magnificent," with a sonorousness that deserved a cathedral.

Davis said, "One of the things we file is method-of-operation data. If we define a few aspects of an MO, in seconds we've got a printout identifying anyone who works that way, where, and what they go after."

"And you've got a hit between a current operation and the man who turned Morris." No longer awed, Black made the statement with certainty. "What data did you feed it? Where's the printout?"

23

"Let's go back to the office. I'll brief you."

When they arrived, Davis dumped a map on his desk, jabbing a pen at cities. "Los Angeles: communications technology. San Diego: laser research. Silicon Valley: computer technology. Elements of our research and development, techniques pioneered in those areas, are showing up in Eastern Bloc products."

Black sneered. "Who said their scientists are incompetent?"

"Not me." Davis sent a strained smile past the clenched cigar. "They scare me. But what attracted our attention was that some of these products had no history, like what antique dealers call a provenance."

"Make up your mind—technology or teapots, what's it going to be?"

Davis colored. "Let me put it this way. Imagine a Soviet lab working on an antitank missile that tracks by radar, okay? Suddenly, with no prior indication of interest, the same people, using a technique developed in San Diego, produce a heat-seeker."

"A back-check found leaks?"

"Our analysts concentrated on one technology, laser development, and developed some possible suspects. It seemed like a good chance to cooperate with the FBI types. I wanted to keep it in-house, but they've been getting nasty lately, reminding us it's illegal for us to pursue counterintelligence work in-country. I had to turn over the names."

"And?"

"They nailed a couple of people. We were allowed to participate."

"Anything worthwhile?"

"Not really. The agents were recruited long ago, utilized at low levels long enough to compromise them, then allowed to go to sleep for years. Since being reactivated, they get practically all their instructions by servicing dead drops, and that's almost the only connection with their control."

Black walked to Davis's side, staring at the map. His finger, curiously bent from an old break, traced a meandering course between the cities involved. "Someone talked to someone. You can't run agents in a vacuum. Who interrogated?"

24

"I did both of them. One stonewalled us good. He knew we had no real case. The other one came aboard right away. He was glad to have it over."

Black nodded. "Five gets you ten the control doesn't live near these places."

"Why do you say that?" Davis's eyes narrowed to a squint. Black remained engrossed in the map.

"Why should he? He'll live where there's no chance of being identified by any of his agents. From time to time he'll slip into town, service a drop—or service one loaded by a cut-out—and go home."

Davis reached to touch Black's shoulder, then, impaled on hostility, pulled his hand back to his side, unembarrassed. Black saw the pity in Davis's eyes, enlisting it to crush the apology in his throat.

"I want you to see something else," Davis said. He moved to a television set and its attached VCR, switching it on. "Every couple of months the source got phone calls setting up meetings." The TV picture that flashed onto the screen was a typical motel room, empty. "He swears the meetings were arranged by a man with a slight accent. The intercept on the uncooperative source caught one incoming phone call from a man with an accent. With no introduction, he asked if the person answering the phone had enjoyed his vacation. Naturally, our sonofabitch said the caller had a wrong number and hung up. *Fini*."

He paused, staring at the desk surface. Black waited, unintruding. Davis shivered out of his reminiscence.

"The guy actually at the meeting has no accent." A figure entered the TV scene. He stopped just inside the door, his face dead. A voice from the bathroom said, "Have a seat, Carl."

Davis stopped the tape. "Carl's the cooperative one. He's been hypnotized, several times, and this is a replication of his last meeting with a man he calls Marvin. Watch."

The image jittered to life. When the man was seated, a second man joined him, entering from the bathroom. He wore jeans, a sport shirt, moccasins, and oversized reflective sunglasses.

Davis said, "The set's really for our people. Carl sees it in his mind, but I wanted our men to see it, and Marvin, as well. Carl's the director, the actor and the camera, simultaneously. He can describe for us from each point of view."

Another voice filled the motel room, lifting the hair on Black's neck. "What are you thinking now? How does Marvin differ from your previous meeting with him?" Black realized it was the hypnotist, offstage.

The lips squirmed on the masklike features. "He doesn't trust me. Not anyone. He always looks a little bit different. He doesn't want me to be sure exactly what he really looks like. Before, he had a mustache and a bandage on his cheek."

"I want you to be the director now, Carl. You know the characters better than anyone. Tell me, is the man sitting on the bed afraid?"

"Very much." Carl could have been giving the time.

"Is Marvin the sort of character who'll go to the police and inform on Carl?"

"No. I see Marvin as a man against society. He fears the police. That makes him a greater danger to the man on the bed."

Davis stopped the film again. The frame caught Carl in close-up, mouth slightly open, gaze tunneling into space. A persistent shudder tugged at Black. Davis said, "Eerie, isn't it? It gets worse. I wanted you to be prepared."

The picture flashed to life and the voice said, "Let's talk to Carl. Tell me, Carl, do you like Marvin?"

At the change of perspective, Carl's voice altered, took on clearer timbre. "No."

"Why work for him, then?"

Fat half-moons of sweat stained Carl's armpits. He tripped on his first word, then continued forcefully. "Blackmail at first, but I didn't care, after a while. Marvin had a way of looking inside a man. He *wanted* me. I had to make him *like* me."

Carl's facial muscles twitched spasmodically, bending into fleeting expressions too quick to be identified with certainty. Black felt his own face twisting in sympathetic harmony, felt he was watching something raw and vulnerable being violated.

26

There was a slight movement from Carl, just within Black's peripheral vision. It distracted him, and he looked to see what it was, then recoiled. "He's getting a goddamned erection! They were lovers?"

Cigar jerking, Davis said, "No. It's a stress reaction."

From the television came the sounds of a hushed argument. The hypnotist said, "Rest, Carl. Think of the pleasant walk in the forest. Remember it." The anguish disappeared, wiped away.

The Marvin figure slouched to the washstand and sat down. Davis sent the tape whirring forward. When he stopped it, the angry hypnotist was saying, "—shortsighted. We have a chance to uncover motivations—"

For the first time, Black recognized Davis's recorded voice as he said, "You do that when he consents to it, and on your own time, Professor. My job is to capture his control. Get me identification."

"But—"

"*No*, goddammit! Get it!" Then, "You! Get off your ass and get back in position."

The man acting as Marvin moved quickly. The hypnotist reestablished his purchase on Carl, a new edge to his words. Black looked around, wishing there were a window. He heard a click and turned back to discover Davis frowning at a blank screen, muttering, "I hate that thing. I never should have turned it on. The hell with it." He dropped into his chair. "Carl's certain Marvin lives in the Northwest. He saw a label on a jacket once. Marvin comments about the rain where he lives. He's spoken of steelhead fishing. Better yet, Carl saw a tax tag on a pack of cigarettes. Hypnotic recall let him describe a Washington stamp."

Black raised his eyebrows. "That's it?"

Davis tented his fingers under his nose. The peculiar pose distorted his voice to an unpleasant facsimile of the hypnotist's. "That's all we have. Just so it's clear in your mind, I don't give a rat's ass how much you hate the assignment. Or me. In fact, I'm betting on it. This is the man who burned you. Before that, you were the best of us, Steve. No shit. Anyone'll tell you."

27

"You're giving me a chance to salvage my career?"

Black's sarcasm finally reached Davis. He dropped his hands to the arms of his chair, the knuckles white as porcelain. Patches of red, like blushes, surfaced in the centers.

"My son's hamster's got a better career ahead of him than you. You'll catch this guy because it's the only way you'll ever get even. That makes you the best weapon I've got. I only hope he doesn't screw you again, because this time we'll probably lose him for keeps."

Quietly, flexing broad shoulders, Black said, "I ought to kick your teeth out."

"Maybe you'll get a chance to try—*after* you've got our man."

"That's worth working for. I want to see the records."

"Three doors down. On the right. You're expected."

Black was gone no more than a minute before another man took his place. Davis remained bent over his papers until the new visitor had been seated long enough to change his position twice. When Davis finally raised his head in acknowledgment, the man smiled easily. "Keeping me waiting the way you kept Black waiting?"

"Sorry about that, Professor." Davis smiled, massaging his temples slowly.

"He's bigger than I realized. I'd think it'd be a disadvantage in your business. Tend to make him stand out." The Professor's voice invited response.

"Finding him in a crowd can be easier than it ought to be, maybe. It can be a mistake, too. There aren't many really lethal men, you know. Smarts, muscles, weapons—he was special. What do you think?"

"I think you can trust him."

"There's no question of that, for Christ's sake. Has he got the mental stamina, is he in control?"

"You're asking me if he'll hold off breaking until you're done with him."

Davis looked past the unfailing forgiveness of the face. The Professor had velvet features and eyes that stroked a listener while he considered an answer. He gave the impression of harboring understanding rather than possessing knowl-

28

edge. Davis knew it was how he hid a mind capable of pure practicality.

The Professor said, "You yourself told me about him—the investigation that terminated his ambitions, the wife who died, the trouble with his only daughter. You don't need me to tell you he's in agony. If he fails in this, it'll destroy him, certainly and utterly." He meshed his fingers and then splayed them outward in a silent explosion.

"He won't fail. It's too important to him."

The Professor's manner changed subtly. "I have to tell you, Bob, that's a very tenuous premise."

"This is one time I've got an edge on your textbooks and objectivity, my mind-twisting friend. I know him. He'll catch our man or die trying."

"Can you hear yourself?"

Davis smiled, a slash that exactly matched the one in the picture on the wall. The Professor turned away quickly.

"Don't be shy," Davis said. "You want to tell me I'll be the one who killed him. I don't need you for that, either. But what you don't understand is, I'm the last friend he has."

CHAPTER 3

Harry Summerton reached for the parking-ticket machine with a mumbled curse, jerking his hand back toward the warm interior of the car. His elbow struck the frame, and the paper fluttered to the wet road. Thoroughly angry now, he threw the door open and bent out to retrieve it. Gusts of breath whoofed through his nose at the exertion while fleshy lips worked in silent fury. Jamming the accelerator, he rushed at the tubular cement towers housing the ramps to the airport parking decks.

Immediately, he slowed, working his fingers on the wheel. Small muscles danced at the hinge of his jaw, and he inhaled deeply. He appeared relaxed when the car rolled into the dark maw and leaned left into the tightly curved steep grade.

Summerton seethed inwardly. Wade had promised protection, an uncluttered deal that required a minimum of effort and provided maximum security. Already there were what Wade called "procedural rearrangements," whatever that might mean.

He swung off the ramp and into the first parking slot available. It was a long walk to the terminal. He consoled himself by thinking of it as exercise.

No one else moved on the entire deck, although it was packed with cars. The discordance of distant jets and the retreating squeal of a solitary vehicle's tires on the ramp only emphasized dank loneliness.

A wind from the south hummed through the narrow rectangular windows. There was no honest winter's sharpness to it, although it penetrated Summerton's clothing easily. Chill wormed into his bones, and he hunched his shoulders. With elbows tucked into his sides and hands in his jacket pockets, he looked rolled up. His heels created echoing volleys that fled on the wind. Every gap between cars was an alleyway for a potential attacker. He edged to the center of the lane.

The glass-enclosed walkway to the terminal proper was escape. Summerton hurried through it and up the escalator to bathe in light, warmth, and color. After a moment, he proceeded to the small underground train that took him to the north satellite. Another escalator lifted him to the waiting room.

Fifteen minutes later, Ted Wade got off the plane from Los Angeles. When Summerton saw he'd come with his wife, he thought for a second he was going to be sick. He had to grip the back of a chair to steady himself. His welcome was brusque, a fact Wade either ignored or missed entirely.

"Harry!" Wade's thin hands were surprisingly strong, richly sprigged with heavy black hair. They wrapped around Summerton's pudgy, pink-tinted one with a hot, dry grappling that crammed his mind with images of tiny famished animals. He extricated himself and found a smile for the couple. Esther maintained an unresponsive coolness.

Wade was visibly excited. "Such a pleasure to see you! And such grand things building!" Glittering eyes scanned the crowd.

"It's good to see you again, Ted. And Esther's an unexpected bonus. Is everything all right in L.A.?"

Wade shot a quick glance at his wife. Esther looked past him to Summerton.

Tightened skin over Wade's cheekbones created hollows that drew large eyes into even greater prominence. "They aren't really happy with what I've done."

"Fools!" Esther's quiet venom shocked Summerton. Although they were barely acquainted, in his experience she

31

was a relatively plain-featured woman, artful with cosmetics and fashionable clothes but too haughty to be worth cultivating. This was unimagined fire.

"Now, sweetheart," Wade said.

Esther ignored him. "They were very harsh with Teddy. Initiative, any deviation from their imposed norm, threatens them." The words were delivered with imperative upper-class accents. "He was summoned to an extraordinary meeting with his contact and given to understand he'd committed a gross breach of security."

Summerton carefully put his hand on the chair again. He tore his gaze from Esther's vehemence and moved his face to within inches of Wade's.

"She knows everything!" It was an accusation.

Wade tried to back away, and Summerton grabbed his bicep. The muscle rolled across the bone, turning Wade's apprehension to pained defiance. "We're a team! I never do anything without talking it over with Esther!" Almost as an afterthought, he added, "People are staring."

Summerton released him. "What the hell difference does it make? Everyone knows what we're doing!"

"Melodrama, Harry." Esther chided gently, moving to link her arm with his. "We'll discuss this someplace warm and cozy, if we can find one in this dismal little town."

"Baggage?" Summerton distrusted himself to remain civil for more than one word. He led off.

"We're catching a plane back tonight." Wade hurried to stay abreast. "Esther has a literary meeting tomorrow morning."

"And you?"

"Oh, I have to be at work, of course."

"Of course."

"We're examining Faulkner." Esther gave his arm a confiding squeeze. She turned to look up at him, and her breast pressured his arm. "So obtuse. A brilliant primitive in some respects, don't you think?"

Summerton leaned away from the contact, directed his attention to Wade. "I haven't got time for this, you understand me? What's next, fucking cucumber sandwiches and Chablis on the patio?''

Without changing tone or stride, Esther said, ''Don't be such an asshole, darling. We know all about security.''

When they reached the parking deck, Wade stepped out into the cold and sniffed at the air. ''Ah, that's the smell of fall! You have to get out of L.A. for that.''

Esther said, ''It stinks. Cold rain and cars. You always see what you want to see instead of what's really there.''

Summerton bit back the urge to tell her Wade's marriage proved the latter point beyond argument. Instead, he said, ''The weather was quite nice through August, but the leaves are already turning.''

''How fascinatingly organic,'' Esther said, stopping. She hitched the collar of her thin jacket around her neck. ''Where's your car?''

''Near the end. The blue Chevy.''

''Has anyone shown any unusual interest in you since you got up here? Is there any chance your car's been wired?''

''Bugged? My car?'' Summerton bit back incipient babble. ''No way. I've got an alarm system on it.''

Almost smiling, Esther turned to her husband. ''We'll pretend to look for the car in the next aisle, Teddy. You work your way to his and whistle when you're ready, all right?''

''Got it.'' He moved away from them, working his way down the line. Esther nudged Summerton and they walked to the next row. He continued to watch Wade.

''I'm surprised you don't keep him on a leash,'' he said.

''Oh, I do.'' Her smile challenged and she tossed her head, turning away, pivoting so she seemed to float. The movement resolved her body into composite sensual curves. She threw a teasing glance at him over a tilted shoulder. Then she was walking away and the moment was past. It left him shaken, hungering, aware he'd been exposed to true magic.

They continued along the line of cars, their reflections distorted in flowing glass and chrome. He hid his smile at the convenient symbolism.

Wade was at his car, busying himself as if assuring it was the right one. Esther acted her part, frowning, searching.

Summerton wondered what chemistry could have put those two together, what night whispers convinced the complicated, disturbing woman that Wade was the man she must have. What was it about her that created a need for her, specifically, in Wade's world of computers and electronic paraphernalia? He shrugged, as much a gesture against the cold as the problem of winnowing human relationships. What mattered now was that they held his future in their hands.

It was a situation he would have to correct.

A sharp whistle snapped him out of his thoughts. Wade waved. "Is this it?" he called.

Summerton nodded. Esther hurried to him and they joined her husband. When Summerton reached for his keys, Wade stopped him, grinning broadly. Only then did Summerton realize his car was idling.

"Show-off," Esther said, laughing. She patted Wade's cheek and slid into the back seat. Summerton saw Wade in, then hurried behind the wheel. Backing out, he said, "Okay, how'd you do it?"

"Anything one man can build, another man can defeat," Wade said, unable to keep the pride from his voice. "The locks and alarms are really junk, you know. The only challenge is starting it without doing any damage. I could be faster if I wanted to be crude."

"Teddy's only crude when we're naked. Isn't that right, Teddy?"

Summerton looked up and Esther's lascivious grin struck at him in the rearview mirror. Wade chuckled scandalized delight.

The car filled with the silence of people hiding words while Summerton paid the attendant. Wade continued to grin. He looked directly to the front, tapping his kneecaps with wiry fingers bent in the textbook-pianist's position. As the car moved away from the booth, he bobbed his head from side to side in rhythm with his unheard song.

It was the last straw for Summerton.

"This whole thing's gone to shit." His voice hummed in

34

his ears, part of the noise of the engine. "You promised I'd be safe, said I'd be contacted weeks ago. I haven't been able to eat for three days, ever since you called me for this meeting. It's gone wrong, hasn't it? Everything's gone to shit. Well, I'm out."

They waited, unspeaking, until Summerton was forced to look away from the road. He chose to look at Wade, expecting some form of displeasure but unprepared for the cold hardness. Worse, there was something else, unidentifiable, but it made him flinch.

Wade said, "Nothing's gone wrong, Harry. Believe me. Get to the right, quickly. Take the first exit, then the next right onto the old highway. We're going up to the Marriott."

Summerton dodged a car, swept in front of a second. Clear of traffic, he twisted angrily toward Wade. The smaller man faced him with a tight smile and said, "That's where I called you from three days ago."

Esther said, "You see, darling? Teddy scouted everything."

Summerton said, "I could've done that. You didn't have to be so goddam clever."

Wade said, "You don't know how, yet. And security is something you do for yourself."

"You're saying you don't trust me."

"It's not that I don't trust you, it's that I do depend on me." They fell silent until Summerton pulled into the Marriott parking lot, Wade speaking only to give instructions. It was no more than thirty yards to the lobby entrance, and they covered the distance almost at a trot. Esther dabbed at rain-speckled clothes with distaste. "No wonder they build planes here—everyone wants to fly out."

Wade said, "There are tables in the atrium, down by the pool. We'll have lunch there." He fell behind Summerton, with no hint of deference. On the contrary, Summerton felt the smaller man used his greater bulk as a shield.

Esther complained about the weather until their orders were delivered. At a glance from Wade, she stopped talking and ate, watching the lunch crowd grow by twos and threes.

"It's taking longer than we expected for our friends to check you out." Wade's quiet voice was an instrument that

35

touched directly onto the brain. "You've lived in a lot of places, held a lot of jobs. It's harder to clear someone like that."

"Sorry." Sarcasm larded the word.

Wade accepted it with a tired smile. "Security," he said. "It's the keystone of this business."

"Business!" Summerton leaned forward. "It's spying, and it's too risky. I'm quitting."

Tapping his chest as if indicating a suit pocket, Wade said, "We have a contract. Signed." A sudden smile was unexpectedly understanding. "We knew the delay would have you on edge. That's why we wanted to see you."

Esther reached for Summerton's hand. "Never mind the contract. We don't have to think that way. Teddy fought for you, Harry, really fought. When he came home from his last meeting with the man we work with, he was absolutely exhausted." Her grip was an enfolding softness, her eyes welcoming. The contact reached through his concern, stirred the deepest part of his mind to prism colors of desire.

Esther said, "They've agreed to talk about more money, lots more. That means they really want you! Teddy got them to admit it." As she watched his lower lip retreat from its petulant outward thrust and the tip of his tongue dab it a quick swipe, she knew he was back under control.

He asked, "There's no emergency or anything?"

She took her hand from his, leaned closer to her husband. "The emergency is worldwide. We're fighting for survival, and you can help, more than you realize."

He looked at Wade, questioning, and she laughed, deep in her throat. "Oh, you say you're in it for the money, but we wouldn't have approached you if you hadn't responded correctly to Teddy's conversational gambits. We know you're philosophically with us, even if you're determined to avoid saying so."

Summerton grinned, almost shy. "I was about convinced he was a goddammed Communist at first, you know? 'Obligations to small nations,' peace offensives, unilateral disarmament. It took a while to be sure where he was coming from."

Her face hardened. "America must prove its integrity. There's no chance for world peace while this country persists with its secret, war-making technology."

He was tempted to bait her, but it would be foolhardy. He said, "If you're for peace, that's all that counts. You know I admire your dedication. But I've got to live, and that takes money."

Wade nodded. "No problem. But it'll be another few weeks before you're contacted. We're supposed to tell you that. As a gesture of good faith, there's this." Esther produced an envelope from her jacket pocket and slid it across the tabletop. Summerton realized the posture she'd held since leaning toward her husband assured that move would be almost impossible to detect. Wade went on, "Two thousand. A hell of a lot more than they ever gave me at first, incidentally."

"Inflation, darling—it affects us all. Another good reason to stop this insane arms funding." Esther stroked the back of her husband's neck. A breeze of envy touched Summerton. He folded the envelope's consoling bulk.

"You're not going to count it?" Wade's mock amazement lifted his eyebrows.

Summerton shrugged. "No need. See, I trust you."

"Ouch. I think we've just been had, Esther."

She laughed with him. "It's a good note on which to end this, I think. Are you satisfied now, Harry?"

"I really do trust you. We've got a deal."

Wade said, "I'm proud to have you with us." The approval switched to businesslike seriousness. "You leave first. We'll catch a ride with the hotel van."

"Please, Harry." The men turned at Esther's plea. She rose quickly. "I hate good-byes. I'm very bad at it. Just let me say I'm glad you're with us, too, and then please excuse me." She brushed Summerton's sleeve with her fingertips and was gone.

"We probably won't ever see each other again," Wade said. "It's a thought that troubles Esther more than she's able to admit. Sometimes I think she's too sensitive for this kind

37

of thing.'' Shaking off a frown, he extended his hot, dry hand.

Freeing himself, Summerton walked up the steps to the lobby and looked back. Wade was an indecipherable figure, any expression lost against the acid-blue stillness of the unoccupied swimming pool and the anxious green of indoor plants. Uncertainty made Summerton's departing wave awkward. Wade ignored it, and the unresponsiveness vastly enlarged the distance between them.

As soon as he was in his car, he yanked the envelope from his pocket and tore it open. A moonstone of saliva trembled in the center notch of his lower lip, threatening to drip onto the thumb that riffled the corners of fifty-dollar bills.

He permitted himself the first genuine smile of the day.

There really hadn't been any need to pretend to be afraid, but the possibility would make the contact easier to bargain with. Two grand! For nothing. Stupid bastards.

He backed the car out.

The smile died. Stupid people didn't last. Wade was a good example. If he wanted to pretend he didn't know he was working for the Russians, that was silly, but it wasn't stupid. His security precautions might be paranoid, but they worked. Whoever taught him was probably even better. It wasn't going to be easy to squeeze money out of that party, and underestimating him, whoever he was, was a bad start.

He sat up straighter, steering with taut precision.

When Esther returned, Wade rose and stepped away from the table. Taking her elbow, he led her up the steps toward the lobby. ''How'd it go?''

''Perfectly.'' She made a circular, inclusive gesture. ''He went to the car, counted the money—grinning like a fox in heat—and left.''

''And?''

Obviously anticipating the question, she flipped open her purse to reveal a small camera. ''Eight shots—front and profile, both.''

He kissed her ear. ''Poor Summerton. And after all our lecturing about security.''

Patting the purse, she said, "Our good security, sweetness. First, last, and always."

"And everyone trusts us. Isn't that a hoot?"

They were laughing gaily, arm in arm, as they strolled to the lobby and the plump sofa fronting the fireplace. They sat touching, holding hands, watching the pulsating flames, oranges and reds and yellows dividing only to blend in unending different hues. Every time the front door opened, a current of cold air surged across the mass, a black lash on the stricken sector. The flames reacted with a mad dancing that soon reclaimed the lost ground.

The Wades lost themselves in the display, her head on his shoulder.

A young woman employed in the sundries shop watched them, craning to peer past a shelf cluttered with glass objects and the sign declaring them made of genuine Mt. St. Helens volcanic ash. A wistful half-smile played over her face.

CHAPTER 4

THE CHIMING DOORBELL FAILED TO DISLODGE BLACK'S CONcentration from the televised boxing match. As usual, he watched with the volume off. Utterly silent, the minute figures circled and closed, punished each other with refined viciousness.

The unnatural distance from the reality of the thing bothered him. Distorted flesh, pain, and blood, without the sound of impact or the feral smells of battle somehow degraded the fighters. They shunned none of the brute truth of their business.

Nevertheless, the pompous stupidity of the announcer demanded the conditions.

Instinctively, he parodied the action with minute hand gestures and footwork that was little more than muscle tremor.

At the second chime from the door, he squirmed in the armchair. No one he wanted to see might be calling, and whoever was making the disturbance had no way of knowing he was home. Still, when the round ended, he rose grudgingly, attention fixed on the desperate cut-work in one corner while he moved to answer the door. It was an awkward progression through the dark living room. The single light on his end table, its brightness tightly confined by an opaque shade, gave little more than a tubular glare. The sparse illumination from the television set contributed unhelpful

40

flickering. Together they revealed bland furniture conventionally placed.

In the small entryway, he reached for the knob just as the chimes pealed again. He jerked the door open with swift irritability. An air current tugged at the skirt of the young woman standing there. She seemed to cringe while still erect. In the constant dusk of the hallway, her clothes were obscured, the jacket black and the skirt a large-patterned plaid of grays. Nevertheless, he registered everything with the acuity of a mind stressed to its limits. Consciously, he was absorbed by the pale oval face turned up to him.

The woman essayed the kind of crooked smile that is as intimate with fists as caresses. Her left hand rose to her breast, fumbling with a plastic zipper toggle as a nun might fondle a crucifix.

"Jane? Janie?" Black begged the woman to be his daughter.

"Hi, Dad." The words drifted, nearly inaudible. "How are you?"

It was a moment before he spoke. "I'm fine, Janie, just fine. Are you all right?" Distraction slurred the question as his eyes searched her, ignoring worn garments in an effort to see past them to sickness or injury.

Her smile brightened. Black was elated to see how the expression still crinkled the skin around her eyes, made them brighter, as though the act of smiling drew all the joy in her to one place.

She said, "I really am okay, Dad. A little tired."

He took her in his arms. "Come in, honey, come on in." Turning, keeping one arm around her, he ushered her into the apartment. "What a surprise!" He pulled her to him again, then held her at arm's length. "God, it's good to see you, Janie. I've missed you." He bustled distractedly, helping her off with the quilted jacket, getting her settled in a chair.

When he was seated in his armchair, there was a clumsy silence while confused smiles fenced across the room. He watched her hands plucking at her blouse cuffs. She centered herself on the cushion.

He cleared his throat, and she took it as a cue. "I've

41

wanted to come back for a long time. I didn't know how you'd be, you know?''

"You mean angry?''

She nodded, and he said, "Of course I'm angry, Janie.'' At her widening eyes, he added, "Not entirely at you. At myself, too. Lots of things. You can be angry without focusing on any one person. You can just be angry.''

Her laughter spiraled into the dim room, a razored coil of bitterness. "Tell me about it. I'm the one who ran away, remember?''

Laughter had been a child's happiness, long ago. This was an adult's covert tears. When a child had tears, they were vital, even if the reasons could be foolishly unimportant.

Daddy, my doll is broke.

Broke her arm, did she? Well, I can glue it back together. The line'll hardly show.

But I don't want any line! I want it to be right, just like it was!

Janie, it'll just be a little mark. We'll tell people she's a lady lion-tamer and a lion scratched her. Everyone'll be real impressed.

No! She doesn't want people to know, Daddy! Promise!

I promise I'll do the best I can, honey, but I have to tell you the truth.

She cried then. The doll spent more time on the shelf after that. The whole area around the glued juncture always stood out, because Janie never carried the doll without one hand protectively wrapped around the mended break.

The silence tried to reassert itself. He drove words into the void. "You must have had trouble finding me.''

One hand stopped fretting at her dress, made a slow, floating gesture. She tilted her head, breaking the eye contact he wanted to maintain. She spoke to a point somewhere between his nose and chest. "I wrote to the office address. Bob Davis had one of his people contact me and tell me where you were. Are. Whatever.''

He preempted her unspoken question. "Yes, I'm still with the government.''

She kept her gaze on her scuffed shoes. "I don't care, not

42

anymore. Not really. But I still can't accept what it is you do."

Offering the words as softly as bandages, he said, "Janie, you don't know what I do."

"Some sort of CIA spook shit. Spying on other Americans. Mom called you an outlaw. I remember. Mostly, she was scared to even think about it."

"Your mother was suffering. She said things."

Abruptly, Jane rose and walked to where the sofa was backed against the room's single window. She talked into the city lights. "Mom was never allowed to win, you know? Always second place. Second to your work, second to what she saw as my needs. Even the things she wanted in herself had to fight for second behind the goddammed booze!"

"What can I say to that? Do I defend myself? Her?"

Jane turned back to him. "It's been three years. I shouldn't have—"

Gruffly, he cut her off. "Not three. Two. And ten months." He shot a cuff ostentatiously to examine his watch. "And exactly two weeks. If anyone was to be counting."

She came to him, took the raised hand in hers.

"That's over," he said, and almost laughed at the huskiness in his voice. "You're sure you're okay?"

The question sent her back to her chair. The hem of her skirt swayed irregularly, and the thought that she might be limping frightened him. She sat down before he could be sure. "Not okay, Dad. Not really. I need to heal, I guess. It's a jungle out there." She managed a twisted grin for the tired line.

Cold touched his stomach. "Is there any trouble? Official trouble?"

Jane fixed him with a sharp, speculative look. "I'm not on the run from the law, no. The guy I was living with might look for me."

He turned away too late to hide the wince. The first direct challenge had been thrown and he'd broken under it. Defiance spiked her voice higher. "You won't talk about what you do, but I'm being honest. Don't lay any guilt trip on me. I'm the one being upfront."

43

"Of course you are." He leaned forward, elbows burrowed into the chair arms, hands cupped together in a bowl. "You were still a little girl when you left. I'd just started to think of you as growing up, edging into womanhood."

"No female on the street 'edges.' Nobody handles it alone. So there was always someone around to help me, and there was a price. I'm getting out of that while I'm still alive."

He said, "There's some of my junk in the second bedroom. We'll get started turning it into your room tonight. You live here as long as you want. Are you going to look for a job or finish school?"

Suddenly the prettiness that had been hers found its way out, and Black realized exactly how hard she'd become. She said, "School." Her hand moved, reaching inadequately. "You don't know how much I want just a high-school diploma, a decent job—just to live square."

A series of pecking nods got him past the tightness in his throat. "We'll have a glass of wine on it."

"Coffee for me, Dad. No booze. No grass. A whole new leaf. I bought a toothbrush on the way from the bus station. I've got twenty-eight bucks and change, some makeup, and these clothes. I'm just about Tap City."

"I knew you when all you had was a cute bare butt and a formula diet, young lady. And you squalled like a cat all night." The banter was easy, assured. "I'll get your coffee."

Alone, she examined the apartment.

So this was the way it was now. Home had never been like this. At this season home had been the warm fireplace and kids calling to organize a Hallowe'en party. The pictures on the wall at home were Mom's soft watercolors and the tangle of fluff she called a textile sculpture. Here was an ugly boat and a clown who looked as funny as terminal clap.

She sprang upright and her nostrils flared briefly. Folding one arm across her body, she gripped the opposite elbow and walked the room. The stride was tense, a drumbeat. She stopped next to her father's chair. The fingers of the free hand stroked the impression where he rested his head.

The furniture at home was always clean. Frequently new, for that matter. Mom dropped a lot of cigarettes and stuff.

Well, she had good reason to stay stoned. The son of a bitch used her, used both of them, wore his wife and kid like fucking ornaments.

People who get used learn. They get pretty crafty about using, themselves.

He never mentioned the funeral. By the time I got the word, she'd been buried for over a month. Anyhow, I was way the hell off in El Paso. Or Tucson. Someplace like that.

Light. That's what this place needs. It's as dark as any alley. One piss-ant lamp lit, for Christ's sake.

Echoing from the kitchen, the wine cork surrendered with a squeal and a hollow "poomp" that made her salivate wildly.

When he came in with her coffee and his wine, she was just coming out of the bathroom, running her tongue over fresh lipstick. He turned on the light at the end of the sofa. She smiled and sat next to it. Before he reached his own chair, she was well into a description of Louisiana's chicory-laced coffee and her first exposure to it. It was entertaining at first, a showcase for a mind that knew how to employ perception and observation in order to amuse. Directly, however, he saw the words as powdery motes, intended to dazzle while her interest ranged free elsewhere.

His gaze slipped past her to the window. An airplane crossed the distance, lights chipping the darkness, red and white. The back of her head was reflected in the glass. Long hair fell in a smooth, shining drop to a reverse curve at the end, a breaking wave frozen in place.

It was the exact shade of her mother's now, he decided, darker than before. The teenage gloss was gone, with its innumerable highlights, like sunlight penetrating raw honey. Replacing it was an adult luster of uniform richness.

Commenting when she paused, contributing anecdotes when it was his turn, he kept the conversation flowing. All the while, it limped in his ears, like a poem read in the wrong meter. It wasn't the tension. That was to be expected. This was torment compounded of distrust that wants to believe, of pain that wants to laugh, of reserve that wants to embrace. He and Jane had shared a love that broke. The shards lay

45

exposed between them, weapons they'd used to slash each other mercilessly, jagged edges still stained with anguish.

As she talked, her ploys became more apparent—minute pauses to select the evasions, precisely placed gestures that directed attention away from a revealing phrase, the bald change of subject at an uncomfortable question. Reason told him she couldn't be expected to open herself quickly.

The wounded thing that lived inside him snarled angry warning and demanded the protection of absolute truth.

At one point he tried to blame the entire problem on the image in the window. Seeing her like that, face on and facing away simultaneously, was a mine field. He broke free, indicating the empty wine glass. When he returned, they continued, touching nothing of consequence. He was half-pleased, half-startled, to realize she was as aware of the situation as he was. Their searching intellects became as observable as pivoting radars, filling the atmosphere with an invisible, immense energy. She stopped it with an abrupt gesture.

"We're playing games with each other, aren't we?"

"Yes. Two strangers pretending to be related. No, not related. Friends. That's worse."

She rose, then fell to her knees at the edge of his chair and leaned on his legs. "Let's make it a real beginning. You're different—I can tell. I want to be different, too. I want to be your friend, and mine, too."

Stroking her hair, he said, "That's the thing I've always wanted most in this world, Janie. Just that."

They remained so, her head pillowed against his thigh, until her breathing grew as steady as a sleeper's. However, when he called her name, she responded alertly.

"I've got to work tomorrow," he said. It was an apology.

She got up quickly. "I wasn't thinking. It's so good to unwind, just relax. I didn't keep you up too late, did I?"

"Not at all. This is my normal bedtime." Getting to his feet, he stretched luxuriously. "We're going to have to fit into each other's lives. If we start making unnecessary compromises, we'll be resenting each other in no time. There'll be enough necessary compromises."

For the next few minutes, they worked together in the

spare room, making the bed and moving things out of the way. Finished, they stood side by side in the door. A car horn blatted fuzzily from the street far below. Jane took his hand in hers. "I'm going to enjoy making this my room. I'm going to be happy."

"I'm already happy. You're here." He kissed the top of her head and was gone before she could do more than call a good night to his back.

He straightened up the kitchen, loading the dishwasher, setting places for the morning, swabbing off the counter. That done, he circled the living room, turning off the still-flickering, still-silent television and the lights. His hand was on his bedroom doorknob when he heard Jane's door open and, for no real reason, froze. She hurried through the darkness to the bathroom. For a moment he thought she was naked, but the bathroom light revealed a bra and panties. She stepped into the white glare, and then he saw the bruises. There were new ones, lushly purple, swollen like rotted fruit. Older examples were an intermediate bile green or dull brown.

Professionally, coldly, in the moment it took her to turn and close the door he noted that, as her face and neck were unmarked, so was she undamaged below the elbows and knees. Whoever worked her over had been very careful that regular street clothes hid his workmanship.

Shame roared in his ears when conscience reminded him it took a man of his experience to recognize the full significance of a beating calculated to punish a woman without detracting from her clothed beauty. When he heard water rushing in the shower, he escaped to his room.

He was sitting in a chair by the window, pajama-clad, when her door clicked shut and the bed squeaked under her weight.

He was still there hours later.

The lights of the city winked distant unconcern. In the office building down the block, a janitor moved solemnly between rows of desks. A chromed vacuum-cleaner wand swooped gleaming curves ahead of him in a modern sorcerer's rite.

Black addressed himself to the city, "Marvin, whatever

47

your real name is, wherever you're hiding, I'm coming. She needs me. You go down quick. And dirty, if it comes to that.''

His head sagged as if it would be too heavy for the waiting hands to control. His words dropped to a sibilant whisper. ''She didn't come to me because she wanted to. She's hiding. Why didn't she ask for my help? Couldn't she once have used the word 'home'? Can't she learn she doesn't have to lie to me?''

He went to the bed and turned down the covers. Lowering himself slowly, he lay with his hands behind his head, staring into the darkness in anticipation of a sleep he dreaded.

CHAPTER 5

COARSE FIBERS ERUPTED FROM THE SURFACE OF THE STIFF PAPER, giving it a woolly, rasping texture. When Carmody unfolded the letter, it crunched instead of crackling. The familiar, practical handwriting faithfully recorded the date. He wished Olga would forget, just once. Perhaps she took some perverse pleasure in reminding herself of the days draining from their lives. His own letters were studiously unnumbered. Occasionally he wondered if she noticed.

He read slowly, absorbing the straightforward minutiae. Nina wanted another pair of blue jeans. Two pair would be better. *Two pair? Did they eat the damned things? Did they think the diplomatic pouch existed only to keep the youthful asses of the Soviet Union wrapped in American denim?*

Zoya fell and scraped her knees. When she cried she was reminded that Daddy expected her to be brave while he was away. Zoya said she didn't even know her daddy, but she stopped crying immediately. Such a brave little girl! *Thank you, Olga, and congratulations. You've reminded me what a bastard I am and made yourself look very good to the others who read our mail.*

Rainy days. Sunny days. The end of summer, an unusually warm autumn. The imperialists were causing great anger among the peace-loving socialist nations, especially the Soviet Union, by arming the Afghan criminals hiding in Pakistan. *Interesting. Obviously there were more casualties than the government could deny.*

Zoya had decided she hated school. *Normal.* Nina was paying too much attention to the Vishniakov boy. *Normal. Who the hell is Vishniakov? More important, who is his father?* The sink still leaked and no one would come to fix it. *Normal.* "We miss you every day and love you and hope you will be home soon, your duty successfully accomplished. Your loving wife, Olga." *Normal. Over. Out.*

His unseeing eyes aimed out the window. The letter, its sparse treasure exhausted, remained clenched between two fingers. The stiff paper jutted outward in sharp wings, making the hand look like a shattered bird.

Zoya, nine years old. A mystic figure in photographs, growing larger without coming closer. Nina, a teenager. Do the memories of seven last until fourteen?

Seven years old. What could he remember of being seven? Only jumbled pictures, like a scrapbook thrown to the winds.

Father. Huge, brooding like the steppe he loved. Unless he was in one of his loud moods, which usually meant drunk. Full of laughter then, raucous bellows that could turn to brutal fury as quickly as summer's clouds turn black and dash lightning.

Mother. Afraid. What would a psychologist do with that association? How many psychologists grew up with a mother who saw a brother hanged and her own mother starve? And was wakened in the night to see the other brother dragged off to a camp, killed by his own government for an offense never named? Her love was an outgrowth of that fear, the love that understands every prickling implication of mortality.

What would Nina remember? Anything?

Coughing from the next room fragmented his thoughts. The view of his daughter trembled in his inner eye, and as he rose from the edge of the bed, he sorrowfully released the recollection of the small head pillowed on his shoulder. She moved in her sleep and sighed, trapping his soul with the gentle milk breath of infancy, thick as syrup in his nostrils.

Alex had the kindness to look uncomfortable when Carmody joined him in the living room. "Olga and the girls are well?"

"What other news would reach me?"

"Your attitude is deteriorating. Your mail isn't delayed or discarded."

"Merely read by unknown bastards."

Alex threw his hands in the air. "You're never satisfied! One minute all you care about is your security and the next you want the state to eliminate its safeguards! It has to be one or the other."

Carmody laughed. "I don't see how the state's need for security is quite as pressing as mine, but there's no point in arguing. We have more important things to discuss."

Glancing around nervously, Alex elaborately pantomimed the act of listening, eyebrows raised questioningly. Carmody waved the concern away. "There's no reason to wire my apartment. We can talk."

"We should have a safe house."

Carmody rolled his eyes heavenward. "What could be more compromising than for me to try to maintain another apartment, much less a house? Alex, I'm just another citizen."

"You can never be too careful. What if someone from here recognized you in California?"

"You can ask that? I go there on legitimate business. Our work is coordinated accordingly. It's your asshole friends—"

"I know, I know." Alex jerked out of his chair to walk to the bookshelf-lined wall. "I'm nervous, Martin. You will be very careful for a while, please. Until this ache in my bones goes away."

Carmody rose easily. "Aching bones? You antique, certainly your bones ache. You expect me to be careful until you're young again?" He smiled on his way into the kitchen.

Hurrying behind him, Alex said, "Don't make jokes. When I get this nervous, there's always a reason."

"Well, you know where the bathroom is."

Alex sniffed and stopped. Carmody knew the sound, knew his friend was pulling his face to prune-wrinkled disapproval. When Carmody returned with mugs of tea, Alex, back in his chair, accepted his without acknowledgment. Carmody sipped and sighed. "You can't have any more bad news for me. Spit out what's choking you."

Looking away, Alex said, "The new agent will have to be schooled in everything."

"Who will coach him?" Resignation inflated the words, created a drawl.

"This is a very high-priority operation, Martin. There is no time for niceties."

"My cover is being torn to shreds, seven years of work in jeopardy. Niceties, my friend?"

Both men were silent for a moment, hearing unforgettable voices from the past, men on their way to Kolyma, to Chernyakovsk. Weary voices, acknowledging betrayal, knowing it grew on trust in the climate of their world as naturally as humidity brought mildew to a rose. Shamefully, their world compounded even that misfortune. At Chernyakovsk or Kolyma, the rose would be judged insane and, if fortunate, be allowed to confess it was at fault for tempting its defiler.

Dismay stormed Alex's pudgy features. He had clearly been prepared for anything but that familiar, fatalistic disappointment.

"Martin, don't be this way! This work is the key to supremacy! We must match their technology. This new man gives us the chance to turn it against them. Think of a world with this country a stinking cinder, all these greedy bastards burned to soot. Everything we've ever dreamed will come true. They told me the *vlasti*—the biggest bosses of all—are behind this. I'll see you get anything you want!"

"Alex, please. Don't try to convince me. I'll do what I must do, but don't make me empty promises. You're as helpless as I am. They sing, and we dance. They'll kill us all."

For the next few minutes, each sought comfort in his own thoughts. Carmody held his mug in both hands, staring into the dark liquid.

Tea was safe. He could drink it the right way, hot as the devil's breath, bull-strong, sugar-sweet. People might question his taste, but no one thought of it as Russian.

Slurping sounds from Alex brought a smile to his face. For

all the older man's worries, not even he was willing to forgo the born-in-the-blood love affair with tea.

There were so few safe ways to reminisce on purpose. Constant danger lurked in the involuntary longing that might be triggered at any time. Once, a booth at a fair filled the air with such a nostalgic richness of *piroshki* it literally staggered him. Worse yet was the occasional burning homesickness. Olga's letters still had the capacity to generate one of those bouts. A snapshot of one of the girls signaled a week racked by moments of euphoria and hours of depression. He begged for pictures and damned his masochism. Photographs were rare, in any case. Olga took the camera with her infrequently on their outings. To her, the girls were simply there. She loved them, was a good mother, even spoiled them—and thought of them with placid acceptance.

In truth, that was Olga's strength. She accepted. Full to the brim with a peasant's avarice and ambition, when she was thwarted of an objective, she railed only loud enough and long enough to intimidate the victor out of the spoils. Failing that, she accepted. And made a new beginning.

Alex thumped his cup down on the end table. "I meet the new man tomorrow morning at ten. You will want to examine him?"

Carmody nodded. "What's your plan?"

"He will wait for me in front of a store in the University District. As soon as contact is made, we proceed a few yards to another store. It has a back door that exits onto a parking lot. My car will be there. Where would you suggest I take him?"

"To the city library, the reading area in the arts section. There are tables with chairs to the right as you come out of the elevator or from the stairwell. I'll be there ahead of you."

Rising, Alex said, "I know the place." With his hand on the doorknob, he said, "We know so many places, men like us. Have you ever dreamed of one of them?" The clack of the bolt hung in the room when he was gone.

It was the first time Carmody could remember Alex complaining. He hoped it would be the last. A sympathetic ear could be as destructive to self-discipline as a seditious mouth.

There was good reason for vigilance. Living was good here, a constant confrontation. At home, an apartment like his would be impossible for anyone except the *nachalstyo*, the bosses.

He lowered the cup abruptly. When had it become habitual to translate Russian to English? What did that signify?

The tea was discarded, absently left on the coffee table while he strode around the room, the heels of his palms pressed to his temples. He muttered to himself, the heavy Russian syllables like cream on his tongue. He spoke to Nina and Zoya, to Olga. He reported his activities to a faceless superior in the Square, conjuring memories of myriad lackluster offices, wallowing in their familiar drabness.

Stopping, he surveyed his apartment with loathing. Plastic. Glitter. Slim modern furniture, all elegance and taut curves, a sleek arrangement of occasional items that left no room for the keepsakes and junk that made a home of a place. Whatever beauty it had was obscured by an absolute lack of heart, or warmth, or something. Whatever was missing was the thing that defined human concern. He kicked the sofa hard enough to bounce it off the wall. The resonating boom warned him, and he settled back in the steel-and-vinyl rocker, bobbing furiously.

Waking the next morning, Carmody lay without moving, picking his way between the fires of yesterday's anger still smoldering in his mind. Shortly, he threw back the covers and rose. It was still dark and the room was frigid. He gritted his teeth and swung into the routine exercise program: ten push-ups, then, groaning at the contact with the cold floor, twenty-five quick sit-ups, followed by another set of push-ups. That done, he braced against the wall with one hand and executed one-legged knee bends before finishing with a dozen chin-ups on the bar mounted in the bathroom doorway.

After showering, he studied himself while he shaved, lulled by the satisfied buzz of the electric razor. It would be unfortunate if the new man—*the new man, he'd never even asked*

Alex to name him—was ever able to identify him as one of those present at today's session. At the same time, a public place was no situation for blatant disguise.

He selected a pair of plain-lensed glasses with heavy black rims to distract the eye from facial characteristics. A sweater-and-jacket combination added several pounds to his appearance and a cap, raked to the side, effectively concealed whether his hair was long or short. A pair of battered jogging shoes completed his costume. Examining himself in the full-length mirror on the bedroom door, he nodded his satisfaction.

At nine o'clock he called the store to tell Elise he'd be in late. She asked if he had any special instructions and when he said no, hung up with no further questions. Her unadorned capability pleased him so much he was whistling on the way to his car.

His good mood was reinforced by finding a parking place only a block from the library. With the time saved, he entered his security measures almost playfully. He hurried down the steep grade of Columbia to Third Avenue, turning right to Madison, where he entered the block-square bank building. Inside, he rode the elevator up one floor and got out in the glass box of the Fourth Avenue lobby. The library was now directly across the street, and he timed his exit to hit the traffic light exactly as it turned from "Walk" to "Don't Walk."

Seattle was the only city he knew where the signs made any difference. Here, people obeyed them, except for the students in the University District, who apparently found jaywalking a demonstration of intellectual accomplishment. He looked to see if he was followed, knowing he wouldn't be, and smiled at his dilemma if he actually did see someone and the party looked collegiate.

As he approached the steps to the front entrance, a movement down the block, an irregularity in the routine flow of traffic, jerked his head up. Before he actually identified the source, the first prickles of irritation warned him. He was sure he knew what he'd see. An anticipatory frown gouged his forehead.

Blacks, a young man and a woman on roller skates, swept

55

toward him through the pedestrians. Supple as reeds among the stolid walkers, their swaying transformed progress to dance, in keeping with the music howling from a portable stereo the man carried on his shoulder. The man caught Carmody's eye, and they evaluated the positions of the others on the sidewalk simultaneously. The skater smiled tacit understanding. If Carmody failed to give way, there would be a collision. The woman realized the same thing. She smiled as well.

In spite of a burning irritation, he was once again taken by the exotic dazzle of white teeth and eyes against dark features. Their faces always seemed the ultimate medium for expressing the inner being.

It was like them to assume he'd make room, he thought. It was something in their makeup that drove them to intrude, to be rude in any situation. They insisted on more room to express their childlike personalities, imposing on everyone with their bubbling voices, colors that hurt the eyes, and music that deafened while its gibberish either confused or offended.

Carmody waited until the last moment to step aside, actually contacting the man's shoulder, sending him on his way with his arms churning to hold his balance. Carmody looked back, and the man continued to smile at him. Carmody felt condescension in it, an assumption that the white man was probably a bit slow, a shade too clumsy to deal with the black's quickness.

He turned toward the curb, cleared his throat, and spat before moving to the library steps.

The couple continued to plague his thinking. They were only typical. Underprivileged in America, downtrodden throughout the world, they responded to freedom with excess.

Even in the Soviet Union, they clung to their own peculiar ethnic behavior, unwilling to become part of a society that wanted only to help them achieve the same standards as their teachers.

He admitted to himself that a mixed couple at home was an invitation to disaster, but most of that was rooted in the blacks' inability to comprehend deeper sentiments. Russian history had seen too many invaders help themselves to Russian women. It was only natural the men responded aggressively to trespassers, especially those so unmistakably different.

No one could deny they were much more socially integrated here. He reminded himself that this was true only of those who could be exploited as athletes or entertainers.

And yet they consistently rejected the one doctrine that offered true emancipation. There could be no greater evidence of their primitive perversity. African, American, French, or anything else, their rejection of the truth meant only that their accomplishments in Western culture were temporary measures that would collapse with everything around them.

At least he'd never had to work with one.

The thought that the new man could be one of them caught at his guts. He shook his head as he opened the door, forcing the idea away.

It took two escalators and a flight of stairs for him to reach the arts section on the fourth floor. He strolled past the librarian's desk and the hodgepodge of filing cabinets. The old veneered wooden ones drew him, just as the enameled shine of the newer ones blunted his high spirits by reminding him of his apartment. He continued on to the windows over the gardenlike entryway. A first spatter of rain strafed the sere, dead leaves swirling in the semienclosed area. Windblown water streaming down the decorative fountain swayed like molten metal.

Armed with a book of photographs of the Cascade Mountains, Carmody retreated to a reading table and waited. He loved the Cascades.

It was almost eleven when they arrived.

Alex looked as relaxed as a cow in a stall, Carmody thought, unless one watched properly. The eyes swept the room in hard arcs that missed nothing. Twice they paused, imperceptible blinks as quick as a camera shutter. Once was for Carmody, the other for a practically somnolent security guard.

Holding close to his man, Alex led the way beyond the

57

librarian's desk. In a while, Carmody wandered in the same direction.

He hoped the recruit would fail to notice Alex's telltale feet, never still, wanting desperately to get underway. Alex leaned forward, smile broadening. A hand cut a small gesture. He settled back, laughing, potbelly jiggling merrily. The feet pushed against the floor.

Carmody moved past them, turned down an aisle. Taking a book at random, he studied Alex's companion through an open space. There was nothing remarkable about him. Within an inch or so of his own height, quite a bit heavier. Too heavy, in fact. Some color to the skin, but no sign of weathering. No wedding ring. Ordinary clothes. Shoes that never saw polish, run-down at the heels.

Untidy, unconcerned about his body, but not necessarily careless or forgetful. Overall, not impressive.

It was a good thing there were Alexes in the world, the real sharks, the ones who smelled the blood trace from miles away. They were more than hunters. They didn't bag the game, they talked it into carrying them home, where they could have it slaughtered conveniently. This one smiled at Alex, an unpleasant, crooked thing of personal amusement that didn't care if it was shared. He rubbed thumb and forefinger together in the universal gesture for money, and even Alex was unable to hide a twitch of distaste.

Carmody sighed and headed for the exit. One took what one could get, and a man had no right to expect much of a traitor.

Alex watched over the top of his glasses as Carmody stepped through the elevator doors and disappeared. Suddenly very tired, he bent over to massage throbbing legs. Harry Summerton asked, "Is something wrong?"

Alex shook his head, straightening quickly. "An itch," he mumbled, and wondered why he bothered to lie. "There's something you must know, however, and I can't make it too clear. I've told you we allow no dangerous situations to develop, and it's true. We avoid them in several ways, all of which you'll be trained to use. Now you get your first lesson

58

in the most fundamental technique. It's called compartmentation, and it means no one knows any more than necessary
about anything.''

Fear pinched the corners of Harry's eyes. Alex's voice
turned soothing, fatherly. "We don't worry about anyone
asking you questions, of course. You're just another worker,
right? But we do worry about that slip of the tongue that
could embarrass someone else. So everyone is kept as iso-
lated as possible.''

"Sounds reasonable.''

"It is, I assure you. Very reasonable. It's why you can't
discuss your background with your instructor here. He's been
told you're from Denver. You must never, under any circumstances, let him learn otherwise.''

Harry frowned. "You and Wade have been talking a lot
about trusting each other. What the hell kind of trust is
that?''

"The best. You're protecting each other. He shouldn't ask
you any questions, but if he forgets, you're protecting him as
well as yourself, right?''

"Yeah, I can see that. But I still think—''

"Accept it,'' Alex interrupted smoothly. "It's a professional matter. Do I have your word?''

"Sure, why not?'' Harry grinned. "On top of everything
else, lying about where I worked last is pretty small shit, I
guess.''

Alex smiled back at him, trying to ignore the tearing
cramp in his leg.

CHAPTER 6

Gusting wind hammered the rain into slanting needles.
The climb from the parking lot to the office was steep
enough to make Black's knees ache, normally. This morning
the wind helped him as it swept uphill from the Sound and
hissed across the city's concrete and glass. His overcoat and
clothes were already damp through, with his car only three
blocks away and three more to walk. The wetness slipped
between the cells of his flesh and surrounded his bones.

Sometimes on the way to work, he noticed reflections of
himself in storefront windows, a heavy figure working uphill,
feet toed in, back bending at each step. Once he started to
analyze why he associated the image with machinery, but the
implications frightened him off. It was safer to stare at the
sidewalk.

Channeling buildings compressed the wind and increased
its velocity. Simultaneously, they combined with the low
clouds to confine the rush-hour's clamor in the same space.
There was no particularity in the noise. The wind, the rain,
and the clouds dulled everything to a sullen, ear-thudding
mush. It was a relief to turn into his side street, out of the
current.

Entering his building, he shrugged out of the coat and
hurried to catch the elevator. Overheated, packed, it steamed
with the aromatics of early morning white-collar life. Pride of

place belonged to the petite woman directly under his nose, her shampoo exuding an entire herbarium. By the time he exited past the press of bodies at his floor, she had contributed to a pleasant—and rather surprising, considering the hour—fantasy.

He was in an excellent mood as he plugged in the coffee maker and turned on the radio. Next, he spread a mass of paperwork across his desk, positioning photographs and a complicated line drawing. The photographs, of individual men, were attached to sheets of paper carrying brief biographical information. From each ran a different-colored line, converging in a box marked "Training." The lines diverged again, coursing to individual boxes marked "Employment." From there they joined once more at a larger, compartmented box. It said, "Vacations (Details, Appendix C)."

He dropped into the high-backed chair and leaned back, eyes closed. The long, narrow room, like a one-windowed cell, lent itself to concentration. The only other furniture was the coat tree, the chair on the other side of the desk and, behind him under the window, the small stand with its gurgling coffee maker and associated paraphernalia. The walls were bare above four-drawer, gray-steel cabinets ranking the walls like guards. Austerity shouted from the arrangement. On examination, however, the cabinets and the locks that held added steel security bars were the finest. Black's chair was quietly expensive, leather and walnut, the desk much nicer than any normally discovered in a minor government functionary's cell. What appeared to be Spartan was, instead, thoughtfully selected minimum equipment of maximum quality.

Straightening, Black tilted forward to shuffle through a loose-leaf folder. He read carefully for an hour, occasionally stopping to refill his coffee cup or to stare at the wall and silently mouth words, committing them to memory. When he finished the last page, he moved quickly to dial the phone.

"Janie, something's come up." The words were a shade too tightly bunched to match the chagrined tone. "I've got to leave town for a day or two. Yes, right away. You'll be okay for a couple of days, won't you? I'll be coming by to

61

pick up some clothes." He replaced the handset delicately. When a sudden spate of rain chimed on the window glass, he glared at it.

His next call confirmed an available seat on the ten-twenty flight to San Francisco.

Later, snugly strapped in, he looked at the few faces he could see, almost all determinedly self-contained, and thought to himself how little connection he felt with any of them. Usually he could empathize, but not during takeoff. It was a time he selfishly and helplessly reserved for close communion with a God he acknowledged infrequently. Once upon a time he told himself God understood his good intentions and didn't mind being ignored when things were going well. Later he told himself that calling on Him only in moments of stress was an economy for both of them. In the end, as his dreams spoiled, he was unable to deny either belief or disappointment and prayed when afraid, as now, with the guilt of a man gambling on a proposition that deserved better treatment.

He was in San Francisco shortly past noon. After renting a car, he made a short phone call and by one o'clock was having lunch with a thin, medium-height man who seemed constantly on the verge of smiling.

Black said, "You've done a damned good job, Will. This woman may be the lead. I reread your report again this morning. You just get better."

The man called Will acknowledged the praise by fluttering the fingers holding his beer glass. Black almost laughed at him. It was a familiar gesture, absolutely typical: message received and understood. Will was a watcher, an outrider who kept the target in sight while protecting the operation's flank. Everything about him, from his neutral clothes to his middle-of-the-road haircut, was understated to the point of near invisibility.

He said, "It's good to see you back in action, Steve. Been a long time between hunts. We've missed you." A hitch of his chin preceded his words, as if he would coax his audience closer. It was well he did, because his voice was devoid of resonance. Words born at his lips died within inches.

"When's the last time you saw her?"

62

"Nine-thirty last night. She came home from work, came out about six, drove a few blocks to the restaurant and bar where she usually goes to dinner when I've seen her go out at all, had her meal and a couple of drinks, and went home." It was all delivered with assurance.

Black grinned. "You scrawny bastard. What's she drink?"

"Vodka martini, rocks, before dinner. One white wine with, one after, at the bar. Rare roast beef, salad with Roquefort, no dessert. Put it on a Visa card. Calls the waitress Doris, the bartender Chuck. One pass from a guy at the bar. She eighty-sixed him."

"She got rid of him? How? You hear any of it? Is she easy to talk to?"

"Don't come on too strong. He did. A grinner, like. Full of smiles, suggestions—you know."

Glancing at his watch, Black said, "Okay. Tonight she gets off work at five. That gives me about three hours. Let's go over everything you know about her once more."

Will caught the waitress's eye, pointed at his empty beer glass, and started talking.

At four-forty-five, Black stepped into the small boutique. The heavy plate-glass door shut behind him, choking the howl of a distant ambulance to whining rumor. Perfumed air replaced the damp smog of the streets, and discreet lighting pulled the last nuance from the multitude of colors battling for his attention. A dark-haired woman approached him, her fashionably sweatered torso floating above crowded clothing racks and carousels. Unlike many tall women, she moved with a full stride, erect, sure of a femininity that blended beautiful facial features with athletic conditioning. When she smiled, Black felt cheated. It was a practiced fixture that stripped away the initial aura and left only the memory of thousands of other cold, impersonal evaluations. Her mouth opened and said, plastic-perfect, "Can I help you, sir?"

"My name's Black." He flashed an ID, complete with large seal and photograph, giving her just enough time to register those details. Her eyes, cornflower blue, wide open now, stayed with his hand as it swept the card holder back into his jacket pocket. He went on, "I'm with the IRS."

"Is there some problem? I pay an accountant—"

He stopped her with a reassuring smile. "Nothing to do with you at all. I think. You *are* the owner, Miss Madeline Hosmer?"

"That's me. 'Maddy's Place' is Madeline Hosmer. What's going on?" The smile was genuine now, even if touched by uncertainty, and the burnished vocal quality was gone, leaving a pleasing huskiness. Suddenly she was very real, more than a mannequin for her merchandise, infinitely more than: *SUBJECT is a thirty-year-old white American female, divorced, self-employed, lives alone* and on and on. Black felt the return of an almost-forgotten pain, an acidic burning at the back of his throat.

He took out a notebook and flipped through pages. "Five years ago you lived in Sunnydale? At two-oh-four Willis Avenue? With your husband, Mr. William Price?"

"Two out of three. *Former* husband."

"Right." He showed her a page in the book. "Do you recognize any of these names and addresses?"

A customer came in, the opening door creating a wash of sound that made them both start. When Maddy looked back to Black, he gave her a conspiratorial wink that touched off a tentative, answering smile.

It was a minute contact, but even the most fragile bonding was important.

"I've got an office back there," she said. "The two of us should just about fit." She called her departure to the lone clerk, leading Black away. In the office, she sat him in the chair and hipped up on the edge of the desk. From that vantage she looked down at him and went directly to the point. "Sure, I know some of those people. They were neighbors. The address told you that."

Black made a mark beside one of the names. "How about this couple, Miss Hosmer?"

"For God's sake, call me Maddy. I'm too old for that 'Miss' stuff. And if you call me ma'am, I'll belt you. Bill knew that pair better than I did. Politics. The three of them used to get together and pray for Fidel and Chairman Mao to have a baby, or something, you know? Flakes. What's the matter, they steal the Pentagon?''

"I don't think so. We want to talk to them about some tax matters.''

Laughter grew from her naturally, and Black found himself grinning. When she was finished, she said, "Ran out on you, did they? Ol' Guv gone hungry since they took off?''

"I certainly hope not. He needs his strength to lead and protect us.''

"Sure." She cocked her head, examining him. "How'd you come up with my name? I hardly knew them.''

He produced a carefully minimized frown. She must see him puzzled, not irritated. It was started too well to lose it all this early. He thumbed through the notebook, audibly muttering. When he had the right page, he made sure she could see the name printed at the top in large letters. As an extra touch, he ran a finger through the printed matter, as if unsure of himself. He continued to patter.

"I know I have that statement here somewhere. Too damned many people—ah! Here we go.'' He looked up into her impatience, closing the book. "One of the people on the list said you were good friends, as couples. The party intimated you might be willing to assist the husband, in particular.'' He cut his gaze away.

After staring at him for several seconds, Maddy threw back her head and laughed some more. "I saw the name in your book. That little wimp? If that's the best scoop you can get, I'm going to quit paying my taxes and let you try to catch me, too. Do I look like I'm going to fool around with a muppet?'' Brashness crept into her voice. The good musculature rearranged itself subtly, projecting the question physically. Through it all, the public character threatened to assert dominance and reject him.

"I never comment on a lady's taste in men.'' Sharply, as if irritated by his own lame try at humor, he cut the air with an edged hand. He said, "I'm sorry. See, this happens all the time. We're looking for someone, for leads, and we run across people too lazy to write poison-pen letters, but they'll smear everyone they can think of. Until we check out what we're told, we have to believe it. Now that I've met you, I know how to deal with the information"—he paused artfully, let her see him almost openly use the source's name—"this party gave me."

"Don't I have a right to know what she's telling the cops?" The front door opened again. A scrap of wrapping tissue on the floor leaped briefly in the quick draft.

"Hey, please. I'm not a cop. And please forget you ever saw that name in my notebook. But I'll tell you this much. I'm convinced the person who gave me the malicious information about you is trying to help the couple I'm looking for."

"Why? I mean, why me?"

It was a response he'd been afraid to hope for, one that avoided the major issue to center on what she perceived as a greater threat. Something was twisting inside her, hauling on the full lips until they were stretched taut.

"I'm going to take a chance with you, Miss Hosmer." She blinked at the formality. "I think you've been treated badly. If you assure me my information is all wrong, I can take steps to straighten out this matter."

"No." Instantly. "Don't do anything. All I care about is knowing exactly what she said about me. I don't want to see someone else in trouble."

And there it is, Black exulted. Someone *else*. No publicity, please. Just tell me if my secret's out.

"Well, there was the allegation about her husband. It had to do with an occasion when your own husband was out of town on business in Seattle."

"Good grief." Her relief was so profound she slumped. Her color came back, first in an excess almost like blushing, then resurging to a healthy glow. "Makes me quite the neighborhood *femme fatale*, doesn't she? We had some dogs around there, but I never thought of any of them as bitches. I guess you never know. Anyhow, it's a crock. I was straight as a string with my husband. That's a helluva lot more than he can say."

"Maddy!" The call came from the front of the store.

66

Maddy stuck her head out of the office to respond and was told it was past closing time. She told the clerk to go on home. When she turned, he got to his feet reluctantly.

"I won't keep you any longer, Maddy. I'll let this thing drop if you want, but it sticks in my throat."

Her hand started toward him, stopped. "I've lived alone a long time. Being talked about goes with the territory."

"I know the route. I've got a neighbor—a guy, can you believe it?—who watches me like a damn' hawk. Keeps stuffing religious tracts in my mailbox. Thinks I don't know who's doing it."

When he started past her, the hand found his arm. "You won't go after that woman, will you? It's not worth it, really."

He shook his head. "Not if you don't care. My job is to get the tax dodgers, not the liars and troublemakers. You and your husband—oops! former husband—aren't involved."

She dropped the contact, smiled at him. He said good-bye and left the office. When he reappeared in the doorway, moving with his customary silence, she was standing where he'd left her, tapping her fingers on the desk. She raised her eyebrows at his return, and he said, "I had lunch at a place a few blocks from here. Carter's. Would you have dinner there with me?"

"I eat there all the time! Will you tell me the name of the bitch?"

"No shop talk."

"Rats. Do you think you can loosen up enough to tell me your first name?"

"Steven Black, at your service. Steve, to friends. Even new ones." He managed a half-bow in the cramped quarters. She acknowledged it with a nod. "I'll meet you in the bar at six-thirty. Steve."

"I'll be waiting. Maddy."

For a first meeting, it had developed well. The divorce had scarred her. That by itself said nothing, but she was embarrassed about it. That was the weak point, where the knife would have to go so the secrets could rush out.

Outside, he dismantled the interview piece by piece and

67

reconstructed it, guaranteeing no word or gesture carried an overlooked significance. Only when he was satisfied with his inspection did he let his mind wander. It went directly to Maddy.

Getting information from her about that former husband without letting her realize she was supplying it was going to be one hell of a job, but the work area was superb. That counted for a lot.

The streetlights flashed alive, drawing his conscious attention to the gathering darkness and lowered temperature. It would be a good night to walk a few blocks, and the restaurant was close to her apartment building.

The tang of winter was crisp and sweet on his tongue, a sensation of apples. Without warning, the earlier acid taste returned, ruining it. Black pulled his coat collar tight, quickening his pace, heedless of the grumbling wake his passage left in the crowd.

CHAPTER 7

CARTER'S RESTAURANT WOULD BE AN ANACHRONISM IN MOST cities, but in San Francisco it was almost to be expected, and Black was delighted with it. He sat at the bar, savoring the eddying smells of food and drink, watching waitresses in uniforms instead of costumes serve dinner with quiet efficiency. No flaming brandy was borne aloft, nor was there an ostentatious cart loaded with salads or desserts. Background music encouraged, rather than drowned, conversation.

Maddy spotted him from the doorway and approached with the long-legged stride he'd already admired. She'd changed to a white-on-white blouse and dark skirt. A car coat draped across her shoulders was held together at the throat with a silver chain. He helped her remove it. She asked, "Been here long?"

"Maybe ten minutes. What'll you have?"

"Vodka martini, rocks. No olive, please." Black ordered it, making a mental note to twit Will for not mentioning the omitted garnish. The slight man was already seated at a table, picking his way through a salad. As always, the introspective smile was present, disappearing only as the mouth worked on food. He was sited to observe both the kitchen and front entrances.

Maddy took the first sip of her drink and faced Black. "Let's get the hard part out of the way. Are you married?"

"Not any more."

"Divorced?"

"No. An accident. A car." He mumbled it, clumsily, as always.

"Oh. I didn't know."

"Of course you didn't. Don't worry about it."

"It was thoughtless. I'm sorry."

"Don't be. It was a long time ago. And you had to ask. I don't picture you running with married men."

She turned away, tasting her drink before her lips carved out a hard smile. "It's happened. He said he was going to leave his wife. I told myself I'd give it a chance, and called that being honest."

"Everyone learns some lessons the hard way."

The smile acquired a hint of humor. "One of those smooth talkers, aren't you? Trying to play on my self-pity."

"That's me. Cunning."

They moved to a table, and the next few minutes were devoted to ordering. Maddy recommended the flounder and seemed pleased when he accepted her advice and ordered the wine in the same breath.

His control of the situation had already broken down at that point, he was to decide later. It came apart the moment she forced him to speak of his own deviousness. Even then, with no conscious awareness of harm already done, his thoughts had been wrenched backward almost two decades.

He was out of the snug restaurant, into the night of a cloud-spearing mountain in Laos. Fear and the unbelievably enervating cold of high-altitude tropics competed for the last of his strength. Ghosting mist concentrated in a huge drop on a branch above him and spilled down the back of his neck. He'd willed himself to silence then, as now, and the Pathet Lao patrol never suspected his presence. He'd killed his first man that night.

An impatient gesture, a quick rearrangement of her dinnerware, warned him he'd been quiet too long. He asked how she'd gotten involved in a clothing store.

"It's not a clothing store, it's a boutique." When he

70

nodded mutely, she laughed. "You don't know the difference, do you?"

"Okay, so what *is* the difference?"

"Nothing." Amusement degenerated to a deprecating smile. "Boutique has a classier sound and higher prices. It bothers me."

"Why the hell should it? You're not cheating anyone."

"Did you look at those price tags?"

"Someone else's turn to learn the hard way."

"Ah, that uncontrollable sympathetic streak again."

She was responding well, helping him build get-acquainted small talk, chatting on about working in her parents' store in a small town on the northern California coast.

He asked, "Are your parents still running the place? I'd think they'd welcome your help, maybe turn it over to you."

Tossing her head, she said, "I've become too citified, actually. Nostalgia talk, that's all." The skein of dark hair rested on her shoulder momentarily before tumbling back out of view.

The physical action before her statement excited him. It was like a fresh track pointing a direction. He said, "I grew up in a small town, too. It was a good time. We were a large family, and anyone around who wasn't blood kin was practically part of the family by mutual agreement. The kids ran in age-group packs, you know? You ate wherever you were playing when it came time to sit down to the table."

"Where was that?"

"Virginia. Little place no one ever heard of. Back up against the mountains. I miss it and wonder if I miss the place or the youth."

"I couldn't go back. I'd want everything to be exactly the way it was, even me. Especially me. Let the mistakes come."

"You didn't make as many as I did."

"They were gone quickly then. When you're a kid, if you make a fool of yourself, everyone teases you till you think you'll die, but in a couple of days someone else does something dumb and you're off the hook. Kids are cruel, but they forgive and forget. Adults forget how to forgive."

The waitress came with the salad, breaking the conversation at exactly the right place. Maddy's inner feelings were parading too broadly. Behind the lure of companionship tensed the polite sheen she wore to deal with strangers, waiting for him to advance too quickly. He remarked on the excellent salad dressing and gently, but firmly, restricted all dialogue to similar inconsequentials.

The technique drew her like a magnet. More and more comfortable, she spoke with less hesitation. Finished eating, they were enjoying their first sip of Drambuie when he asked how long she'd been divorced. It was a moment of considerable impact, and he tensed, ready to leap to safer ground if she balked.

"Three years." Black tensed at her suddenly lax facial muscles and slumped shoulders. He'd seen others sag exactly that way, just prior to confession. It was a sign that the mind was bent inward, had abandoned concern for appearance. Later, when the need to confess gave way to the need to be accepted as cleansed, the muscle tone would be reestablished and she would lean toward him. The inward-looking eyes would rediscover him. The self-directed mind would reach out for renewed, reinforced contact.

He would be waiting.

She said, "I tried going home, once."

"It didn't work?"

"God, I guess." She lowered her glass with a thump. "I'd been divorced almost exactly a year, you know? I was nervous about how people'd react."

"Because you were divorced? Who's that intolerant nowadays?"

"Intolerant?" She repeated the word, and he quickly sipped at the heavy liqueur to burn the blood-salt taste off his tongue.

"I was twenty years old when I married Bill," she continued, looking through him. "We knew each other in high school. He was two years ahead of me, into the anti-Vietnam demonstrations, student control of the school—all that. He went off to Berkeley like going to war. I just sort of drifted. Graduated, got a job in a bank here in San Francisco. I looked up one day and there he was, big as life. I dropped a roll of dimes and they went all over the floor. He went to another window while I cleaned them up, but he was in the next day and we made a date.'' Her hand moved in a slow, confused gesture. ''He was a mess, and I'd have passed up dinner with Robert Redford to sit in a bus depot with him.''

The confession was foundering on melancholy. Black leaned into it carefully, altering the course a few degrees. ''It must have been an exciting time.''

Nodding absently, Maddy said, ''A whole new world. Weird people, all leftovers from the sixties, full of hate, always talking about love. They didn't like me. Two years older, and he was father, big brother, and lover. Romantic. So we got married. He had a job, a good job.'' The last came defensively, a spark from embers dying. ''A technician, working on lasers. He still raised hell about politics, and I was glad of it, because I figured if he was that uptight about politicians, he wouldn't be scoping some other woman, you know?'' Her sudden laughter was the brilliance of shattering crystal. At the limit of his peripheral vision, Black saw Will's head pivot toward them. Concern flickered across the long face.

Black knew he could do nothing. The questions, the suggestions, had a finite limit. Now she must leap. He could not shove.

''I just knew something was going on. He was always restless, and it got worse, and then it got better. Too good.'' She paused, her courage faltering, searching his face for understanding interest. ''We had arguments. He was bored—with me, work, everything. Then, just like that, he mellowed out. I mean, instant Mr. Laid Back, and little presents, evenings out.''

He gambled on a question, hoping she was too caught up in her story to quit. ''How'd he explain the extra money?'' There had to be extra money. If she said there was none, the game was over.

''I never thought to ask. That should have been my first clue, right? Extra money, instead of less money. He had to be getting it from his friend.'' She gulped her drink and Black signaled for more. ''He picked me up after work one

73

day really high. Not drugged, either. Said he had to go away the following week and he'd be gone for a week. A seminar. I knew something was going on. I hired a detective to follow him.''

Something fell in the kitchen, a mangling of metal and dishes. Instinct shuttered her eyes, but psychological necessity denied the interruption. "The detective watched a guy meet Bill at the airport in Seattle. They went to a resort hotel together. I was already moved out when he came back.''

"You filed for divorce?''

She drew a pattern of waves on the tabletop with the wet glass. Anger struggled to dominate her features, losing out to hollow-eyed defeat. Black's memory saw a strobe-light recollection of the Laotian mountain night and the face of the surviving enemy patrol member.

She said, "My husband was cheating on me with a man. What the hell'd anybody do?'' Tears she refused to admit glossed her vision. "He could have at least argued.''

"Did he say who the other guy was?'' Questions were safe now. It was over.

"I couldn't do it.''

"Couldn't do what?''

"I never told him about the detective, never said I knew it was a man. I just said he better not give me trouble with the divorce.'' Still skidding the glass in a monotony of sloping vees, she studied his face. "He wanted everything 'civil.' His word. He said a lot of excitement would destroy his life. And maybe mine. The way he said it, I believed him, Steve.''

"You never told him you knew about his lover?''

"Not after what he said.''

"Then you never told me, either.'' Her eyes widened, and Black said, "I'm glad you'd talk to me. It's nice to feel you've been a help to someone, even if it's just listening.''

She smiled and her shoulders pulled back. "I do feel better.'' Placing a hand on his was an act of almost virginal shyness. He rolled his palm upward, squeezed. Then she was patting her hair, saying, "I'll be back in a minute.'' She rose smoothly and made her way to the rest room.

Rolling the stem of the empty glass between finger and thumb, he envisioned her husband spinning in it, scratching at the smooth surface.

It was working out, it was a make. Her husband was one of the pictures on his chart. He had been recruited, and the "seminar" was where he got his training. A relief close to euphoria poured through him, honey in his veins.

Will was still in place, nursing a drink. The prearranged signal for him to call it a night was for Black to massage his right shoulder. The slim figure was leaving as Maddy returned to the table.

She said, "I shouldn't have left. I almost didn't come back. What I did—laying all that on you—I'm sorry."

"I wish I could do more. I hope I helped."

Once again she touched his hand. "You really did. Sometimes a person just has to talk, don't they? I don't tell everyone my troubles, Steve, I really don't."

He burlesqued indignation. "I thought I built up an image of trustworthiness and Old World chivalry."

Color seeped upward from her collar. Black was so intent on the blush he almost missed her next sentence.

"I won't lie to you. I don't know you well enough to really trust you. But I *wanted* to tell you about Bill. Why would that be?"

The direct guilelessness of the question stabbed at him. He said, "I must have a face that invites confidence."

"No." She shook her head then, embarrassed, and giggled. "Oh, that's not coming out right. I mean, it's not inviting confidence. You look like maybe you already know half the story, like you've heard so many secrets another one won't make any difference."

"That's an interesting observation."

"It must be your job. Investigating, and all." She embellished the comment with a peculiar fillip, both hands raised as if in prayer, but separated by several inches. The sudden shadows moving over the whiteness of her blouse reminded him of Jane's bruises. "There's something—like you've had troubles, too."

"We all have."

75

"I know. Your wife—" The sentence had no end.

"That happened. It's over. But I am worried about my daughter. She ran away, before her mother died. She's come back. I'm not sure I can do her any good." His words had a strained discordance, as if another voice imitated his. There was no reason to prolong this meeting.

"And I've been leaning on you with my troubles! Oh, God, Steve, can you ever forgive me?"

"Will there be anything else, sir?" The chipper tones snapped Black and Maddy upright. He paid in a fluster, helping Maddy with her coat, ushering her outside as if escaping.

Neon, red as blood, blue as sapphire, golden yellow, stained the fogged darkness, claimed the dark spaces between streetlights. Around each lamp post an island of brightness resisted the smaller, more colorful signs. None of it added warmth to the night, and Black and Maddy drew close. Sometimes they touched, but the sensitivity of their relationship forced them apart in an exaggerated conflict of unconcern and awareness. As they walked, he told of Jane, of her growing up, her school, and lastly, her collapse under the weight of parental discord.

"I don't know what I could have done differently," he was saying just as she put her hand on his elbow, directing him toward her apartment building. They shunned the lobby, standing outside, as if the conversation wanted night for its backdrop. "Even if I'd quit work and stayed home all the time, the drinking would have gone on. And it was the fighting over the drinking that drove Jane away from both of us."

"Maybe some things just happen, maybe there isn't always someone at fault."

Moving as if capturing a bird, he put his hands on her shoulders. "Have you looked at your own troubles that way?"

"I'm starting to. The talk tonight helped. I wish I could be as much help to you." She turned her head away from the light spilling out of the lobby. "That pretty much says it about me, doesn't it? Almost good enough."

The increased pressure of his hands brought her face around

76

to meet his look. "You're cheating yourself out of a good life and someone out of a good woman. You gave up on yourself too easily."

Stepping back, she studied him frankly, the eyes sharp enough to measure inside and out. He was thoroughly uncomfortable before she spoke. "You're a strange man. All evening I've told you things because I wanted to. Because I felt you were pulling things out of me, too. I can tell you're not just on the make. So why do I feel like that's all I know about you? Oh, sure, I know a bit about your wife and your daughter. But you know something? You never mentioned your wife's name. Not once. You told me you were born in Virginia—that's all. The town against the mountains, right? No details. And you watch and listen. Deep, past anything I said, like you were seeing nerves and hearing thoughts."

She walked to the door, unlocked it. Poised in the opening, she considered her next statement, then said, "You're one damned attractive man, Steve, and I'm grateful for a special evening, but you scare hell out of me."

For a moment neither moved. He said, "Geraldine."

"What?"

He saw her hand tighten on the door. "My wife's name was Geraldine. I called her Dina."

"Oh. I didn't—"

"Maybe we'll see each other again. Maybe we can talk about the things that scare both of us."

"Maybe."

The night enfolded him almost instantly, his shambling gait eerily quick. He never saw her broken-off wave or the brittle disappointment mar her face as she continued into the lobby. Neither did he see the thin bit of darkness detach itself from the wall across the street and keep pace with his departure. Those things escaped Black, as did the sight of Will dropping off his trail at the first all-night store they passed, where he huddled out of the chill in the phone booth and made a very businesslike call.

77

CHAPTER 8

LIKE AN ARTERY AND ITS COMPLEMENTARY VEIN, THE TWIN levels of the north-south traffic viaduct pulse between the city and the Sound that nourishes it. Carmody, on his way to Green Lake in blue running suit and green windbreaker, merged his car into the early morning northbound rush. Once part of it, his thoughts drifted to the walk with Alex under the viaduct's swooping arches. He remembered the raw wind and how it abraded his nerves while Alex warned him that his own people were jeopardizing his entire net.

He forced his attention to the scenery.

To his left, the southernmost peaks of the Olympic mountains clawed through the clouds and into sunlight. The range fascinated him. He saw it as beautiful, accessible, but strangely repellent. Hiking in the Cascades was no easier than in the Olympics, but the latter tolerated men with barely contained violence. It is the shortest single mountain chain in the United States, a wall running the length of the Olympic Peninsula, snowcapped, immensely creased by hidden valleys. On the western slope, precipitation is measured in feet.

Carmody told himself, and others, it was the rain that kept him away.

The forests of the Olympics are dark, silent, cloaked with moss and ferns that devour sound the way desert sands drink water. They frightened him in a way he could never admit.

The primeval silence stripped away his carefully constructed defenses with the cruelty of ripping the shell from a turtle and revealed his awesome aloneness.

He had camped in the Olympics twice. The second time was to prove the dread he couldn't cast off during the first trip was a fluke. It wasn't.

The beauty of the early sunlight dispelled such troublesome thoughts as it touched clustered rounds of cumulus. Alive with roses, golds, and creams, the lush curves appeared to glow from within, imitating robust flesh.

Carmody checked his watch and cursed. There would be hardly any time for visiting the leopard after the meeting.

The need to deal with an asset so close to his own base required increased personal thoroughness, not less. He told himself to relax, turning on the radio, punching buttons until he found soothing music. Vague aches surrendered in shoulders, lower back, the calves of his legs. He concentrated harder, proud of controlling his body.

Envisioning the forthcoming conversation, Carmody saw himself handling it easily, as usual. This one would also go exactly by the rules.

Contact should always reassure the asset.

He patted the envelope in the pocket of the windbreaker. Money would reassure the man. Americans understood money.

A new voice blared out of the radio, selling cars. Carmody smiled at the coincidence, punched buttons until music again filled the car.

As soon as he was parked and outside, he ran. Wind from his motion combined with a sharp breeze, stroking his face to tingling sensitivity. Good smells rode the air. The loam and leaves of the approaching park's grounds mixed with the darker, thick scent of the gray-green lake and its spangling of whitecaps. Unconcerned ducks bobbed on them with aplomb. A group of three swirled out of the northern sky and dove for the water, landing with arrowing splashes. After short social comment with the established group, they went about their business.

There were relatively few people in the park. Carmody complimented himself. Those present in this weather would

79

be dedicated to their own pursuits and unlikely to notice or interfere with anyone else.

He smiled inwardly at the people doing warm-ups prior to exercising. Animals knew—a chase, a stalk, must originate in the mind, not in trembling, uncertain muscles. The body must obey, not dictate. At the moment of striking, there was no time to stretch or cut poetic figures in the air.

Carmody ran. Pitty-pat joggers blocking his way irritated him. He watched his feet, a technique that helped him set a pace as well as preparing a pathway into the recesses of his brain. The bright-blue running shoes flicked in and out of his vision, the metronomic white trim like winking eyes.

Logic and reason drew back, cold, poised. From deep in the subconscious, other thinking leaped to life, soared unimpeded. Wild, instinctive, the ideas reminded him of fingerholds beckoning from a rock face. The excitement came from knowing their truth waited for your test, your discovery. Were they pure or treacherous? Life and death intersected at each one.

His best thinking usually came toward the end of the run, when he was so tired he felt he could drop and sleep without moving. Ideas came to him then with a precision and clarity that sometimes sent a bolt of sheer joy through his nerves.

The sight of the man on the bench created a very different sensation. It settled in his solar plexus, trying to pull his heart into his stomach, threatening to collapse his lungs. Unbidden, his feet slowed to the detested jogger's pace, degenerated further to a shuffle.

Alex watched him approach with a smile, a ghastly caricature. He surreptitiously patted the seat next to him. Carmody pretended to massage a leg. He limped to sit beside his friend. "What the hell are you doing here?"

"I am going home."

Carmody thought he would choke. Such glorious words, what wonderful news! And Alex stared past his clenched, liver-spotted old hands at the earth as if it waited for him. Slowly, dragging out the word, the older man repeated, "Home." Despair moaned in the single syllable.

"Is it an emergency, Alex? Do I have time to warn my assets?"

Puzzlement clouded Alex's face before he grasped the significance of the question. "You're in no danger, Martin. Only me." He looked around quickly. "Not real danger, you understand. I didn't mean that at all. I have nothing to fear."

"Then why are you here? Are you out of your mind? I'm to meet Summerton in thirty minutes just the other side of this lake."

Pulling himself upright, Alex spoke with dignity. "There is something you must know."

"Then tell me and get away from here!" A sudden thought struck Carmody. "Am I compromised? Is that why you must leave?"

"No, no. I was betrayed. A *zhid*, Martin, a dirty Jew! An operation in San Francisco, purely commercial, nothing to do with you." He slumped forward, staring between the fists again. "I bought from him in good faith, didn't even ask him to smuggle the things out—arranged everything myself—and he was informing the FBI every minute." Alex's voice dropped to a hoarse whisper. "You can't trust them. I've known that all my life, and now! A *zhid* trick, and I'm done!"

"Me, Alex, damn you! What is my status? Why did you come here?"

"The FBI is after me, Martin. I am being ordered home. You know what that means." Desperation danced at the back of Alex's eyes.

Carmody resisted the urge to shout. "Tell me what you came for, Alex, please. Then go!" The smaller man looked away. Carmody added, "If you've given me a bad apple with this Summerton, I won't see all my work ruined, Alex. I'll make a report."

The effect on Alex was electric. He jerked violently. His voice steadied. "There's no danger to you. You will continue as you have. I merely wished to say good-bye."

"You took a chance like this? Have you lost your mind?"

"Perhaps." Alex rose, knees cracking. "I saw myself naked for the first time, my friend. My first thought was of the things that will soon happen to me. The second thought was that perhaps I could spare you a similar experience. Maybe I am crazy.''

"Ah, an early morning chat!"

Vibrant with power, the grating voice spoke Russian. Carmody and Alex turned their heads as if both were mounted on a single shaft.

Taking the last few steps to stop directly in front of them was a small man, shorter than Alex. Thin lips bent in a smiling bow under a pepper-and-salt mustache. Fierce blue eyes turned the expression into a grotesque artifice. The face was capped by short, tightly curled gray hair. Carmody memorized the features automatically. Malice surrounded the man, tangible as heat. Mutually massaging hands declared a boiling impatience for challenge, an opportunity to prove authority. When he licked his lips the strident red of the tongue was like a warning that the words must be afforded rapt attention. He said, "We have never met, Martin Carmody. My name is Nicolai Bunin. I have the honor of being Alex's replacement. What has he been telling you?"

The question voided Alex's presence. Nicolai steadfastly refused to look in his direction. Carmody noticed how Nicolai's discarded smile let his lips pull inward, puckered as if drawn tight by a string. His gaze broke when Carmody met it, and sensing a minor psychological advantage, Carmody spoke hurriedly into the gap. "We were saying good-bye. Alex has been an immeasurable help." He had no idea why he failed to mention Summerton.

"Yes." Nicolai's smile returned. It was apparent the broken eye contact was no more than a habit. His mantle of authority was undiminished. "We shall all miss him. He told you he was compromised?"

Boldly, Carmody said, "Yes, he did. Now I fear for my own cover. Why must we stand around this way?"

Nicolai shrugged. "The Americans have no idea where he is. He is not completely incompetent."

"He was betrayed. It could happen to anyone."

"Anyone foolish enough to trust a Jew."

Heat moved up Carmody's neck in waves. "We deal with whatever we must."

"Deal. Not trust. What he did was stupid."

Alex made a mewing sound of protest. At Nicolai's stare, he turned away, visibly shaking. Suddenly Carmody shared Alex's anguish. Alex was strong, ferocious in his dedication. The entire KGB knew him as a ruthless fighter. To play with him, to speak of him as already sentenced, was obscene. Carmody's fury spiked his words. "You have no right to speak to my friend that way, comrade—"

Grabbing Carmody's loose jacket, Nicolai pulled. The baggy garment stretched ludicrously, further enraging the little man. "Listen to me, *comrade*. I have one mission in this rotten country, and that is to see our collection upgraded. Your supercomputer access is first priority. Now I must deal with this failure. He was instructed to remain in place, but he ran here. To you." He looked past Carmody and toward the road, nodding sharply. Turning, Carmody watched the dark-blue van approach. There were vans at home, too. Ordinary, sometimes painted as commercial vehicles, the better to disguise their mission.

Nevertheless, when one of them approached, a man knew what it meant.

Alex groaned audibly and took a step back. Dropping Carmody's jacket, Nicolai took Alex's hand in both of his, clamping the taller man's forearm to his side with his own. To the casual observer, he was helping a man taken ill. In truth, one of Alex's fingers was folded under his hand and back on itself. The stressed joint sent a current of pain up the arm that paralyzed resistance. Sweat coursed from his thick sideburns, traced the jawbone.

Two large men in coveralls exited from the van and walked swiftly toward the trio. Nicolai hurried Alex along, looking past him, anticipating Carmody's protest. When he glared, Carmody felt words shatter in his throat.

Wordlessly, the two newcomers braced the now wild-eyed Alex between them. Carmody turned away. His friend's expression was too familiar.

Arrest, to those who knew the KGB intimately, was a private horror. When a man became part of the organization, did what it required of him, he submitted to a knowledge of human frailty few among the living are cursed to bear. Each morning dawned with the same question: Do I go today? Any unexpected change triggered the same response. Once a man knew the cells, the camps, even the sweetest slumber harbored retching nightmare.

When the van door clattered open it was a signal for Alex to scream his awareness. He opened his mouth, and Nicolai broke the finger with the greasy pop of a baked chicken wing. The intended scream became an agonized exhalation that carried an acceptance bordering on relief, as though the commencement of punishment signified the end of uncertainty.

Carmody's stomach heaved, but he kept his eyes averted.

Nicolai was saying, "Control yourself, comrade! You are hysterical! You are endangering your friend's work, his goals!"

Carmody heard Alex grunting as he hoisted himself inside, heard the scuffling of other feet, nimble, businesslike.

A skater swooped past with a huge, howling radio cradled in his arms. A cyclist hurried by barely twenty yards away, his beard billowing in the wind. Neither man paid any attention to the activity at the van.

"Martin!" Alex called. "Martin!"

Lifting his eyes, Carmody saw Alex standing in the door clad only in trousers and undershirt, his other clothes on the floor. One of the pair in coveralls stood next to him. The manic thought came to Carmody that Alex looked like some bourgeois ready for his TV baseball, except for the glittering hypodermic dimpling his bicep. Already he was canting his head, trying to adjust eyesight crumbling under the strength of the injection.

"Summerton," he mumbled. It sounded like "summer'n." Then, dry-mouthed, chewing furiously, he struggled to add more. The door closed in front of that contorted image. The van moved away and Carmody bit the inside of his lip, willing himself to believe the thud he heard was the closing door.

Nicolai was still beside him, surveying the area easily, only the darting blue eyes revealing the professionalism of his search. "Look at them," he murmured. "We have removed a man from their midst, and they continue their

84

aimless, circling pursuit of good health. They are as sightless as moths around a flame. Amazing!''

At Carmody's silence, he looked at the taller man coldly. "Do not judge me, comrade. He compromised his position, then he deserted his assigned post to come here. Things could have gone harder for him."

"And probably will."

"How old are you?"

It was an unexpected question. Carmody stammered. "Thirty-two."

Walking toward the lake, the small figure drew Carmody along. Switching to accented English, Nicolai said, "You were born in peace, grew up in peace. Men like me are responsible for that. I'm sixty-three. I lived through Russia's destruction and helped rebuild her until we are the most powerful nation in the history of the world." Thrusting a hand at the heaving lake, he frowned as if irritated when the water continued to move at the wind's bidding. A duck paddled forward and veered off when it realized the gesture failed to include thrown food.

Nicolai continued, "The only thing between us and continuing peace, the peace we have enjoyed during your lifetime, is this nation of corrupt pigs."

"I'll do everything I can—"

"You will get what I want." Nicolai talked through Carmody's voice without bothering to look away from the water.

Alex's terrified face swam back into Carmody's mind. Alex, swept away like the tumbling clouds. If he could be so easily eliminated, what chance did anyone have? Alex's image burst apart, leaving him empty and ashamed.

Continuing, Nicolai said, "Alex postponed your meeting with the new asset. It is scheduled for tomorrow, exactly the same as today. I will contact you soon." Turning abruptly, he walked away, chin high, shoulders squared, in a tin-soldier stride that should have been ludicrous.

A small car pulled out of a side street across the boulevard and stopped for him. Carmody watched until it was out of sight. For lack of anything better, he decided to continue around the lake and was startled to find how urgently his lungs sucked at the air.

For once the flashing pattern of his feet had no steadying effect. No coherent thoughts would form. Desperately, he conjugated verbs, only to produce imagery that led down unwanted paths. Fear plucked at him then, giggled and asked if he was completely satisfied of his sanity. Abandoning words, he sought solace in numbers, mumbling multiplication tables in time with the pounding pace.

A man on a bicycle swerved around him, leaning dangerously. To Carmody, the liquid sound of the tires became Alex's cry when his finger snapped.

He leaned forward into a punishing sprint, racing for his car. Reaching it, he flung himself onto the seat and slumped over the wheel, gasping for breath, swallowing the urge to vomit.

Only when he was able to sit up did he recognize the envelope on the seat next to him as a new letter from Olga. There was writing on the back, an unknown hand that crabbed across the paper. It said, "I neglected to give you this. I hope all is well with your family. N."

CHAPTER 9

THE COPY MACHINE RUMBLED CONTENTEDLY AS IT DEALT WITH the material Summerton fed it. Intense light spilled from under the pad holding flat the original paper, a conspiratorial wink to accompany the mechanical sigh following each duplication. The counting gauge ticked importantly at each completed assignment. Integrated, conforming, irreplaceable and perpetually redundant, the entire mechanism ran with idiot precision.

Summerton's fear-sensitized touch recognized the different texture of the next page.

An unbound document was stacked in front of him, the text down in the way the machine accepted material. Randomly sandwiched among the pages of legitimate work were some pages giving results of experiments on the transmission capacities of stressed alloys. They were classified secret. Summerton had no reason to deal with the subject, and no one was allowed to reproduce any of the material.

Summerton was earning his spy's wages.

He slipped the illicit paper under the pad, pushed the "Print" button, and gripped the edge of the machine. Claws of tension picked at his nerves, making his skin twitch visibly. He jammed his hands in his pockets just as the damning copy oozed into the holding tray, text up. It took two bumbling tries to get it out of the tray and turned over on the pile of finished copy. The original caught under a metal guard, almost tearing. When his suddenly dead fingers failed to hold the paper, it fell free of the guard as if mocking his terrified clumsiness.

Three more pages, he told himself, wishing he had held the total number to four instead of six. Copying four was safer. It was simple arithmetic. Six took longer. There wasn't any more money in taking the greater risk.

Martin had never hinted at the stress of actually stealing information. The closest he'd ever come to it was his flat refusal to even discuss any name for himself except Martin. That should have been enough of a clue in itself. All the professorial crap about avoiding surveillance, not talking on the phone, never holding anything incriminating longer than necessary—that was bullshit. Why hadn't he talked about something to help a man's nerves? Because it was a scam to make life safe for Martin, and the hell with everyone else, that was why. He was no different than any other boss.

Reducing the number of pages per effort only increased the number of efforts.

The thought reestablished his hand tremors. The third of the forbidden pages went under the pad.

"What're you copying, Summerton?" The voice numbed his body. His head threatened to explode, and he knew if he looked inside his skull he'd see the trapped brain seething in blind demand for survival.

The voice repeated the question, louder. It was the department supervisor's. Summerton realized his paralysis was being misinterpreted.

"Some work stuff." Without turning, he displayed the folder at head level. "That much to go. In a hurry?"

"I can wait. Let me know when you're done, okay?"

"Sure." The smoothness of his voice elated him. A smile tugged at the corners of his mouth. He wanted to spin around and grip the other man by the shoulders and explain what a tremendous performance he'd just witnessed.

Unimaginably, horribly, the speaker was standing beside him.

"This thing's been acting up again," he said. Summerton stared back, mute. Once more, his silence was credited to the natural problem of hearing over the machine's noise. The man went on, his very calmness threatening to undermine the last of Summerton's tottering stability. "The contrast varies for no reason. Damned nuisance."

There were ten pages left. Two were classified. One look would be all the supervisor needed. Summerton twisted the contrast-control knob. "Shoot a page through. See what happens."

Dreamlike, Summerton watched his hands strip the top sheet from the stack. Now, when he needed it, his touch refused to identify textural differences between legitimate papers and contraband. The supervisor was following every move.

The heavy rubber pad covered the new piece. Illumination leaped out, pinioned Summerton's hands. The first millimeter of copy paper eased into the reception basket.

I'll make a run for the parking lot. Martin'll protect me. It's all his fault, anyway. And it's his ass, too.

The copy was harmless. Bile raced up Summerton's throat. He swallowed scalding bitterness that sent tears to his eyes.

The supervisor said, "Looks good to me. Go ahead and finish."

"Just be a minute." Summerton lifted the pad, standing with it upraised, hoping his frozen smile wasn't as grotesque as it felt.

When the man was safely around the corner, Summerton looked at the next page. *Experiment results.*

At quitting time, the six duplicates folded into a packet that hardly stretched a shirt pocket.

On the way out, he deliberately sought the man from whom he'd borrowed the original, reveling in the covert daring.

"Hi, Rex. Ready for inspection?" Heartiness boomed in the words, and he clutched Rex by the arm momentarily. The slight figure jerked, surprised by such bluff camaraderie, mustering a thin smile that barely rearranged his full beard.

Answering Summerton, he pointed with his chin at the security man behind his desk. "What's the fucking point? He's not allowed to search anyone, and who's going to tell him they're carrying any of this so-called classified shit? It's ridiculous."

Summerton grinned and winked. "Be like me, stay away from the super-spook stuff."

"That's exactly it." The faint smile disappeared in its thicket of whiskers like a shy bird. "You know as much about what I'm working on as I do, but just because your name's not on some stupid access list, nobody asks you a goddam thing."

"Don't be so defensive. It's not like they questioned you."

"They better not!" Rex altered course, headed for the security man, arms pistoning belligerently.

The uniformed officer tried a friendly nod before resignedly acknowledging the impervious hostility. "Taking any work home with you, Mr. Harris?" The question was flat, with a pause prior to the name, as if an internal program spoke the set piece.

Summerton smiled to himself. Sheep were more adventurous.

Rex was chewing strands of mustache when Summerton rejoined him. "See? Every evening, the same shit. 'Taking anything home?' " The mimicry was viciously accurate. "Someday I will, just for the hell of it. What can they do?"

"Throw you in jail, for one thing." Muscles tightened in Summerton's back. "The President himself gets a progress report on this work almost every day. Anything that important deserves security. Don't be impatient with the guard."

"Bullshit. He could find a real job if he wanted to."

They were outside by then, two young executive-scientists, the new theocracy. The cold geometry of their temple rejected the misted softness of lowering night. Precise windows fractured the darkness with square brilliance while the glow from the parking-lot standards scored the building's squat modernity.

Summerton gestured, a graceless shooing action. "Look at this. A few minutes after five, and it's dark. This is what makes me miss Colorado the most."

"Colorado? Your resume says you came here from southern California."

Summerton faked a cough as an excuse to bring up a hand that touched his pocket. The papers, the miserable goddammed papers were on his mind, *in* his mind.

"I lived in Colorado before. I was thinking more of the cold darkness, I guess. Is that a Freudian slip?"

"Who knows? It's cold—that's a given. Want to swing by my place for a drink? Marge can fix something to eat."

Summerton winced. He despised Rex's tiny apartment, decorated in Upwardly Mobile, a melange of furnishings that could have come as-is from the pages of any homemaker's magazine. What it lacked in character it made up for in Disneyesque cleanliness not even an active three-year-old daughter could completely disrupt. The wife was to specifications—wholesomely young matron, hostess-inquisitive. On Summerton's single previous visit, the three of them babbled at him constantly through a meal he would forever recollect as unpalatable organic pap. Not satisfied to force it on him, Rex and Marge rhapsodized appreciation for its taste and nutrition. After dinner, the child, like a uniquely mobile golden flower, played quietly in the middle of the room while the conversation ranged from high interest rates to Rex's stories about his maltreatment in the army.

Safely on his way home, Summerton swore the stench of middle-class kitsch had permeated his clothes. He determined to forget the wife's name as quickly as possible and was delighted to find he'd already forgotten the child's.

He told himself he would never forgive Martin for requiring him to demean himself to such a degree.

Martin had interrogated him about the other employees until he came up with Rex's name. Then he directed Summerton's approach to the dissatisfied, carping little scientist in a series of training sessions that were more like confrontations. The precise conduct required of him made Summerton feel reduced to a surrogate, grafted with Martin's senses. When each meeting ended, he had the impression he could only control his own thoughts after the door closed behind him.

91

An excellent example was the need to pretend a liking for Rex while in Martin's presence. The memory of the insipid family evening helped, supplied a spiced vindictiveness to offset the saccharine arrogance of their contentment.

And Martin could blame himself for the slip that produced Colorado instead of California.

Not for Martin, playing up to some self-centered sonofabitch with access to secrets. Nossir, not good old Martin. A fucking oracle, looking wise and pronouncing things good or bad. Let him put up with somebody like Rex for a while and see how disciplined he kept his mind. It was dealing with Rex that caused the slip of the tongue, and it was Martin's choice to cultivate Rex. It was Martin's own fault.

"Have you got time?" The repeated suggestion jerked Summerton back to the present.

"Wish I did, buddy. Made other arrangements. Maybe one night next week."

"Good grief, today's Friday, isn't it? You've got something laid on for the whole weekend?"

Mugging, Summerton laughed. Rex shook his head, the beard hiding an expression that could have been rueful or admiring. He said, "You single guys," a neutral phrase that died before it exposed any definable feeling.

Summerton said, "Us social butterflies don't really know true contentment. Wife, home, family—"

Sharply, Rex's voice cut across the humor. "Marriage is important. Today's people don't have any sense of commitment."

"Ah, you're getting too deep for me. Serious matters bore me." Summerton allowed himself a rich laugh at the duplicity of the thrust, enjoying the secret wall that denied Rex access to the irony of the conversation.

It was amazing, he thought, how a basically stupid man could be so well-positioned in the company. Then he changed his mind. It was only typical. Rex was a standard model, a numbnuts who'd work till he dropped and kiss ass for the privilege. The really bright people, the ones with some pride, wouldn't deal with corporate sucking up. They got dumped on and the clods got promotions. Well, there were always wheels within wheels.

They parted with mutual wishes for a good weekend. Summerton's sense of well-being dimmed slightly at the sight of his car. It was another indication of Martin's galling intrusion into his private life. With what Martin was paying and his company salary, he could easily afford something sportier, but no, good old Martin insisted on a low profile.

The car started easily, untroubled by the damp in the air. He leaned back to outwait the after-work traffic rush. His mind drifted to Esther Wade. He caught himself thinking of her more and more, and he wondered if the radical change in his own life hadn't affected his deepest perceptions. After knowing the woman for years and finding her completely uninteresting, she had become, simply, The Woman. All the rest were judged against her. What puzzled Summerton was that in half his fantasies he humbled her, debased her. The remainder saw him accepting the abuse. No, not accepting. Enjoying.

Nothing like that had ever happened before, nor did daylight fantasizing ever generate the latter image. Dreaming did, and he always woke churning with guilt and shame.

He sat upright again and joined the stragglers headed for the exit. In twenty minutes he was in the library. A self-sealing plastic bag from the glove compartment now held the folded papers. After dawdling through his book selection, he returned to the parking lot, shortcutting across the planted median separating the rows of vehicles. Before reaching his car, he dropped the book and bent to pick it up. A quick movement slipped the plastic envelope under a large rock.

Martin had been full of praise on learning how Summerton cleansed himself of incriminating evidence while waiting for the chance to pass it on.

As his departing headlights illuminated the hiding place, Summerton smiled to himself. It was all so easy, if one used one's head. Martin made a monumental project out of each teaching point. Obviously, he did it simply because that was his job, his reason for existence. There was probably a psychological explanation, perhaps something reflecting a primitive territoriality.

For a moment, he considered building an analytical profile of Martin, but abandoned the notion as quickly as it had come. The man was skilled, determined, but functionally limited. Beneath all the one-dimensional crap was more one-dimensional crap.

By the time he reached his apartment, all that remained of the afternoon's excitement was the dregs of adrenaline, rendering his movements brisk, but imprecise. He almost scraped a fender pulling into his parking slot. Standing in the shower, reconstructing the scene in the copying room, he could regenerate no more of that fear than a shadow's brief darkening. Pulse beats registered no appreciable change, even when he closed his eyes and concentrated on the mind-jarring thud of his heart when the supervisor spoke to him.

Toweling, he watched his mist-softened reflection in the door's long mirror.

A touch more weight than necessary, but nothing good clothes didn't remedy. He said, "By the time the old threads are off, it's too late for them to be concerned about a little extra beef, right?" The image laughed at the wit.

He decided to prowl the massive Southcenter shopping complex. Lots of women hung out down there, not to mention the hookers who worked the motels, hotels, and restaurants along the stretch of old US 99 adjacent to the airport. The latter was a desperate consideration, but it was dependable.

The restaurant he chose was large. The interior made him think of old movies. Art nouveau curves and angles gleamed richness a nuance short of decadence. The disturbing, brittle gaiety of a generation he'd never known winked from buffed copper and polished wood.

The crowd was still thin, early arrivals claiming ground, sizing up newcomers. He watched two reasonably attractive women sitting at a table check him out with shoppers' eyes, accurate to the inch, the ounce, the penny. When he found a bar stool and turned their way, they were oblivious.

The game was on.

One of them had a date, a lanky man, nondescript except for arms and legs that got in his way no matter how he folded them. Summerton was relieved to see he was with the better-looking of the two. She would be solicitous of her friend, anxious to see she didn't have to spend the evening alone.

The unescorted woman left. Her friend leaned across the table to speak earnestly to her date. He moved to order drinks at the bar, standing immediately next to Summerton. There was a wait for service.

"They ought to have more help," the stranger said with good humor. "You could die of thirst."

Summerton agreed. "If I'd known it was going to be like this, I'd have stayed in Bellevue and saved some gas."

"You live there?"

"Live and work. Felt like going somewhere different, you know?"

The lanky man nodded. "What kind of work you in?"

"Electronic stuff—product design." Impressive without being stuffy or threatening. A good fisherman understood chumming.

The man got his drinks and left.

From that point, it was well-scripted farce. At the next round of drinks, Summerton asked if the other girl was waiting for anyone. That formality out of the way, he asked if he might join them.

Their names were Patty, who was with Ron, and Debbie, who said she was going with a guy who was in Alaska on business. Faint challenge pinged, a false note that drew Summerton with the tug of addiction. Lies meant defensiveness, vulnerability. He almost smiled, thinking how well he knew all about that, immediately reminding himself that he was different by several orders of magnitude. In his case, lies were aggressive. The lies of others parried the truth. His thrust at it. It was such a beautiful perception it pained him to forgo mentioning it.

The conversation was swift, a drumroll of hard, brief sentences. Subjects were examined superficially and quickly discarded. There was constant physical movement. Debbie's favorite technique was to lean forward, full breasts threateningly close to the tall glass holding her drink, and then throw herself back into her chair as she delivered the final line. If the comment was meant to be humorous, she primed her listeners with a surprisingly clear, sweet laugh. Seriousness occasioned a short toss of her head that tumbled thick hair like storm-blown wheat.

Youthful prettiness clung to her features, expertly frescoed by cosmetics. Still, the patterns of the future were there, delicate signals Summerton read eagerly. At full attention (a rare moment in itself), her facial muscles realxed. Mouth and eyelids drooped. Laughing vivacity became the gaunt bewilderment of a woman struggling to understand the train of empty days that had brought her to this place that was neither goal or ending. It was not a look of hopelessness, but rather an assumption of similar, unending disappointments.

Summerton flowed with the group interplay, carefully balancing deference against the necessity to establish a positive image in Debbie's eyes.

Time passed quickly and people filled the bar, curdled the air with smoke and voices. Summerton leaned close to Debbie with calculated intimacy. She didn't encourage or reject him. Her scent mixed perfume and wine, sweet, exciting and erotic.

Pursuit became less a game and more a need.

Dinner was Mexican, the place a short distance down the same boulevard. Ron suggested they walk, and Patty led him out front, discreetly allowing Summerton and Debbie to lag behind.

It was practically inevitable they go dancing afterward, another step in the standardized sexual progression underway. They traveled to the airport strip in both cars, Patty with Ron, Debbie now firmly with Summerton. As the night inched toward the morning hours, Debbie's dancing altered. Her hips swayed more provocatively, her shoulders twisted more forcefully, the taut material of her blouse swelled outward at the thrust of her breasts. Her eyes sought his, heavy with sensual suggestion, but there was a strange, elusive background as well.

Uncertainty troubled him for the first time.

He dismissed it when Ron suggested they change partners for a dance. Patty took the opportunity to assure him Debbie really liked him. Did he like her, too?

He did, very much. He couldn't get over his good luck.

Patty glowed with accomplishment. Back at the table, the women excused themselves. Debbie looked different as they returned, and when she sat down, her color was high. The women giggled at each other, accumulated wine pitching the laughter upward. It wasn't until Summerton bent to speak to Debbie and she turned, leaning into him, that he realized she was no longer wearing her bra.

Again, cautiously, Summerton moved against her, giving no clue of his awareness of the contact. She watched his face intently, the same disturbing strangeness flickering across her eyes. Pressure in Summerton's groin overruled his second attempt to read that look.

Less than an hour later, he took her home. Patty insisted on one last consultation with her friend, and Summerton spent the few minutes with Ron, mentally gnashing his teeth. The whole thing was a scene from the junior prom. Finally, with a motherly pat on Debbie's shoulder that sent a chill up Summerton's spine, Patty let her go.

There was no discussion when he parked the car or when they made their way to her apartment elevator. On the way up to her floor, they talked of Ron and Patty. Inside, they faltered until Debbie suggested a glass of wine, and then they were seated on the sofa, the stereo adjusted to whisper the melody while the rhythm thumped insinuation. When she complained about tired feet, he slipped her shoes off and massaged her soles.

She smiled down at him. "My luck. I meet all the guys with fetishes."

He laughed softly. "You ain't seen nothing yet, baby."

Feigning shock, she drew back the foot, a motion that lifted her skirt to reveal a white thigh. Summerton perched on the sofa beside her, one hand on the backrest while he reached for the buttoned blouse with the other. He said, "I don't have a fetish," and when she gave him an arch look, added, "I have *all* of them."

The buttons released easily and he pushed the material aside as each unfastened, so the globes of her breasts were revealed in stages. His blood surged as the nipples came into view, dusky red. Each hand claimed its own, fondling, and he bent to them, kissing first one, then the other, testing the softness with teasing bites. Debbie's hand was busy with his belt. Unable to unfasten it with one hand and unable to get at him with the other, she made small, frustrated sounds. In response, Summerton scooped her off the sofa and carried her to the bedroom.

They undressed each other in a clumsy frenzy, thrown clothes mottling the darkness. Her lovemaking startled and delighted him with its wholehearted lust until the words came. She crooned first, mouth distorted as though she intended to whistle, but then she cried out for more, for love. The word became a chant as she clawed and arched, impaling herself, absorbing him as if his being could fill the void in her.

Too aroused to consider stopping, the litany nevertheless gave Summerton a feeling of being stained. Physical sensation continued to burn him with delights, but came as once removed. He listened to his own hoarse vocalizations, noted the spasmodic thrusts of his climax.

When he was spent, he lay exhausted until she complained of his weight. He rolled away, flat on his back, eyes on the ceiling. He was still like that when she silently returned from the bathroom. She avoided touching him until he took her in his arms again. At that, she twisted to face him, burying her face against his chest, the sobs breaking free unrestrained. He couldn't understand her reaction, but spoke nervous reassurances anyhow. In a little while she stopped.

"I love you," she said, and waited. When it became clear no response was coming, she exhaled. The warm breath flowed across his chest and made him think of blood.

Sleep came immediately.

Confusion burst in his brain when the lights blazed on.

Dazed, dazzled, for a terrified moment he had no idea where he was and staggered out of the bed into a wall. Naked, he was confronted by Debbie. She clutched a short robe around herself, face distorted with rage. She threw one of his shoes at him.

"Get out," she said, body trembling as violently as her voice. "You miserable sonofabitch, get out before I scream rape. *Get out!*"

He dodged the other shoe, scrambled into his underwear, stepped into his trousers. Struggling, he missed his shirt when she threw it at him and it fluttered down over his head. She mouthed obscenities at him in a steady monotone throughout. At last, with his trousers secure, socks, shoes, and shirt in hand, he straightened and attempted dignity.

"What's wrong with you? What did I do?" The whine of it grated on his ears.

"You used me! My body! In my own fucking bed!"

"I didn't—"

Her voice rose, threatened to become a scream. "Esther!" She made a face, repeated the name in a moaning parody, then, "In my bed! 'Esther, you're the woman. Esther!' You *bastard*! Get out! *Get out!*"

She stormed behind him to the door, slamming it when he was gone. He was leaning against the hall wall, getting his shoes on, when it opened again. "I'm glad you didn't get away before I could tell you, you creep—I was so horny I thought I was ready for anything, but you're the worst, man! You're nothing, a potbellied, dead fuck!"

The door boomed again, counterpoint for two others opening cautiously. Tousled male heads peered out at him, one down the hall, graying, with a conspicuously displayed handgun. The other was immediately adjacent to Debbie's apartment, younger, openly amused. The gray head surveyed him, unblinking, and withdrew. The younger one continued to watch, breaking into a chuckle as Summerton stalked to the elevator, stuffing his shirt in his trousers.

He ripped the car out of the parking slot, tires screeching. Stopping abruptly, he reversed, backing up until he was reasonably sure he was under her window, where he leaned on the horn and bellowed at the top of his lungs. Then he sped away, head back, howling. It wasn't until he was out of the lot he realized he was beating on the dashboard so hard the instruments were behaving erratically and the noise from his throat sounded embarrassingly like pain.

CHAPTER 10

"NOBODY'S PERFECT," BLACK SAID, UNAWARE OF DAVIS'S smile at the cliché. No humor was intended. He ignored the other man, staring at the gleaming facade of the computer.

Davis said, "Of course he's not. You'll catch him."

"I know." Black continued to look straight ahead. "But every day costs. The sonofabitch is there somewhere, running his net, hurting us." A sweeping gesture indicated the machinery, rather than the wintry world outside.

"I can't spare anyone—"

"Manpower won't get him. I need a break. A link."

"You need rest."

"Later. After."

Authority flowed into Davis's voice. "Go back to Seattle. Other people need this goddammed computer too, you know." He was unprepared for the desperation in Black's look.

"Let me run a few more analyses, okay? I'll be finished today."

"You said that Monday. It's Thursday. You trying for liar of the week?"

Counterfeit amusement touched Black's features. "I'm checking out that KGB Major we burned just before the holidays. We've got a pretty good book on him. If he was part of our man's operation, maybe I can get a picture, some connection—"

"The rest of the day, Steve. That's it." Davis turned on his heel and left.

Black typed information into the system. He used the standard touch system, but slowly. Thick fingers worked in a steady march, stopping only when he consulted notes in a loose-leaf notebook. Finally, he closed his eyes and leaned back in the chair. When he webbed his hands above his head and stretched, the knuckles popped.

He waited, thinking.

Originally, he called his target Major Leskov, as he was officially identified. Slowly, however, as he sifted through the mountain of reports concerning the man, he began to think of him as Major. Later, without even noticing the change, he was using the name Alex, as the man called himself.

The sheer bulk of data was almost overwhelming. People contacted by Alex were interviewed. FBI surveillance reports noted everything, even the use of a park drinking fountain. To a critical reader, the details would be ludicrous. To Black, repetitive use of that fountain might indicate a signal, or use of the fountain itself as a drop site. There were subjective reports, generated by desk clerks and neighbors. If Alex showed an interest in a particular product, overseas informants were questioned to determine who bought the item, who shipped it, who picked it up. Alex would have been flattered and dismayed by such attention. So would many of the people he dealt with.

Identified as KGB as soon as he entered the country, Alex had never been tied to any specific net. He spotted surveillants by seeking out lonely areas for his walks, then lost them, if necessary, with the apparently innocuous stunts of a polished performer. There was nothing remarkable about him. He favored dark suits, dark beer, X-rated movies, and public transportation. His cover as a member of a San Francisco-based trade mission necessitated a great deal of travel. Black was certain Alex was a liaison man, a high-level cut-out acting as personal contact for at least one resident.

It was a singular clumsiness, quite uncharacteristic, that blew him. Black reexamined the hard facts. Stripped of jargon, it was a sad outline. Alex was seduced, offered a deal

102

on the newest computer chips available. The seller came to him direct, refused to deal with anyone else.

Poor Alex! He wanted so hard to believe his faith would protect him against all evils. It's what gets all of us, eventually. Not the cynicism, the loneliness, the depravity. In the end, we choke on our catechism.

Looking at the clock, flexing his shoulders, Black pulled himself back to specifics. Interdicted, Alex would be replaced. The man was of no consequence, even when the report of his rough departure, escorted, boded ill for his future.

The chill of that observation make Black wonder if there was some flaw in his own makeup, an inability to react properly to other people.

He rejected that concept. There were relationships in his life, genuine ones.

Not good ones.

The thought was a spark, burning where it touched.

He slumped, aging. Craggy features softened, as though uncertainty weakened the very bone structure.

Had he truly driven his wife to her bottle? Was her drunkenness an honest search for solace because she knew she was as separate from her husband as he was from his quarry? And what of the breakdown between himself and his daughter? What if the thing he felt for her wasn't really love, but nothing more than one more instance of this excruciating ability to worm into another human being without being affected by the contact? What if he had no capacity for affection, only a studied intelligence that observed others, defined their needs, and created proper forms of behavior?

Berating himself for letting his mind wander, he opened his eyes and bent toward the terminal, fingertips massaging his temples, and gratefully filled his nostrils with the stabilizing smells of hot plastic and baked paint. He straightened and entered instructions for the machine to provide him comparative lists.

Through the sparkling green letters on their velvet blackness, he followed Alexei Leskov on all known trips. He matched surveillance reports of those trips with informant and communications intercept information, looking for anything that tied Alex to the mysterious Marvin.

Tedium threatened to overwhelm him. Alex had been an extremely careful—or useless—man.

The discovery came late in the day, at normal quitting time. Slamming file drawers and closing doors, shouted invitations and good-byes, all subsided to the shuffle of departing feet and more-restrained conversation. A minor resurgence of sound signaled the settling-in of the much smaller night crew. None of it meant anything to Black.

He had his link.

Time would verify it, but he was satisfied.

The computer had examined and categorized every scrap of information in every surveillance and informant's report dealing with Alex.

Buried in all the activity was a pattern.

Approximately every sixty days, Alex made a circuit of Southern California. He never stayed at the same motel twice in succession, and clearly avoided visiting any single one too frequently. Living his cover, he always had legitimate contacts to make. On one circuit—Black was already categorizing them as "A" trips and "B" trips—he made all his telephone calls from his room, as a normal businessman. He hustled around and visited people.

That was an "A" trip.

On a "B" trip, he made far fewer calls from his room. There were others, however. The FBI surveillance carefully noted a technique of using pay phones at a considerable distance from his lodgings. Apparently selected at random. In one city there might be only one such call. There were never more than two. All were made in the evening. No recipient had ever been identified. "B" trips also saw Alex spending more time sightseeing and simply lounging around the motel premises. He spoke to no one except as courtesy demanded, but scrupulously avoided any indication of evasion. He made advance reservations no more than one day ahead, never staying more than twenty-four hours.

It fit. The witness—*what the hell was his name? Carl? Right.* Carl said the meeting with the agent-handler was laid on by a middleman. That would be Alex, who also did the legwork. And he'd provide countersurveillance or any other backstopping necessary.

Now the field digging could get underway. Did Alex make reservations for the agent-handler's room? Would anyone recognize Alex? If so, could he describe a companion?

A check of everyone who arrived the same day as Alex might turn up something.

Black groaned aloud. One site chosen on three occasions was the Disneyland Hotel. The number of people who stayed there at the same time as Alex was too immense to contemplate, and if Alex was indeed the middleman arranging Marvin's meetings with his agents, any one of those guests might be an agent.

Black groaned again, holding his head in his hands.

Slowly, tentatively, he moved to shut down as a rich grin broke free across his face.

He warned himself there were many steps and many problems waiting to disprove this minor find—if it was a find.

The grin remained in place as he left.

By the time he reached his bedroom, he knew he'd reveal nothing to Davis the next morning.

The decision troubled him so much he couldn't sleep. Nothing like this had ever happened to him before. Inexplicably, his whole being was rejecting his past experience, demanding complete independence.

It frightened him.

His profession taught him to take advantage of the human desire to create routine. When you broke a man's standard behavior, you knocked him off balance as surely as if you'd struck him. This decision to act outside the confines of accepted guidelines was a radical change in his own performance that put his own balance awry, and there was no identifiable reason for it.

When he'd been falsely damned because one of his men went wrong, there was no change in his style. There was a complete stop, not a change. This was different.

He no longer liked Davis or wanted to be liked by him, but

he didn't distrust him. He certainly didn't harbor any fantasies about capturing Marvin singlehanded.

Or did he?

Was that it, a childish urge to "make things right," to show everyone, including poor Dina, that he could do it, that he wasn't a failure?

And if I fail?

In the morning, Davis bluntly searched Black's features for an indication of success or failure and finally gave up. "So?" he demanded.

"Nothing special. I'll be checking around, trying to get a handle on suspected industrial leaks. Unless I see solid evidence, I'm going to assume he's not actively pursuing military information. Marvin's a high-tech specialist. The men you interrogated are so politically naive they're pitiful. Most of his assets probably think they're involved in industrial espionage. Good fun, just like screwing around in class back at old Washwater High."

"That's what you said Monday. You spent the week here and that's all the progress you've got for me?"

"That's about it."

Davis's hostility electrified the small room. "Now I go upstairs to explain a wasted fortune in computer time." He burst out of the chair, leaned across the desk. "Maybe you've forgotten what being in charge is like. I told you this one was yours, but I can afford you for only so long, Steve. I'm sorry, but there it is."

"Fish or cut bait?"

"Exactly."

"I'd tell you the same thing if I was in your place."

"I know."

"No problem then, right? Anyhow, I'll get him."

Black searched the thin face, dreading a sign that Davis was suspicious, had somehow penetrated the easy manner and discovered the confusion. When Davis frowned, he braced himself to tell more lies. Instead, the smaller man was placating. "I didn't mean to drop on you, Steve. We're very close

106

to something very big. As badly as I want you to break it, it's more important that it not be fumbled."

"Hell, I know that. A little more time, Bob, and I'll put his head on your wall."

Davis grimaced. "From you, that's not funny."

They both smiled. Black almost laughed out loud at the two of them. Like gladiators, they were incapable of watching any man without seeking the slowed arm, the halt leg. Worse, they were equally sensitive to the careless word, the nervous stammer.

Davis reached to touch Black's shoulder in a gesture that was really a salute. He said, "I really want you to get this one, Steve. It's personal."

Black raised his eyebrows and waited. Davis went on, "You weren't the only one hurt, understand. Oh, you took the hard fall, all right, but the section lost its best man. And I lost a friend." Turning suddenly, he walked to the wall and busily straightened a picture. "Don't worry about bringing him in, Steve. I mean, legally we're not supposed to be doing any of this. But if you have to ice him, I've got to be in on it so we're all singing the same song when the questions start."

"I'll let you know."

Davis waited until he saw Black had no more to say, then said, "I don't know how you do it. You make it sound like buying a morning paper."

"It's not the sort of thing you let yourself get emotional about."

" 'Don't let yourself?' How do you avoid it?"

Black savored the irony of his response. "I have other things on my mind."

Davis waved his hands. "Enough. I shouldn't have brought it up. Let's talk commonplace. How's Jane getting along? Did you two have a good holiday season?"

"Pretty good. She's picking up some junior-college courses and working part time. It's been rough on her."

"Hard subjects, or is the job a hard one?"

Black shook his head. "Neither, actually. She's bored. I guess that's the best way to put it. She got used to no set

107

hours, no responsibilities—everything geared to the simplest kind of gratification, you know? Now if she stays up late for a movie, she hurts the next day in class. And there's waiting for payday, days off, appointments. Life's not the carefree drift it used to be.''

"Crashed back into the real world, has she?''

"Pretty much.''

He answered the rest of Davis's harmless questions with carefully composed phrases. His newly discovered lead was a stone in his stomach, and he desperately needed solitude. More than anything, there was the need to understand himself. Mercifully, the conversation finally ended. It was an act of moral courage to walk away at a natural pace.

From the parking lot, he went directly to the airport, where he turned in the rental car and bought a ticket for Seattle. He dozed fitfully on the leg to San Francisco, dreaming chaotically. Wakened to fasten his seat belt, he looked out the window and immediately identified Maddy's neighborhood. On landing, he startled the stewardess by declaring his decision to get off and continue on to Seattle some other time. Then he rented a car and was on his way to the boutique.

Maddy saw him as he entered, and surprise flared in her eyes before her expression settled to evaluation. It jarred Black. For the second time that day someone he liked was measuring him. This occasion was particularly galling. Unlike Davis, she operated from standards he couldn't identify with certainty. Worse, she had no right.

Her hands were poised on the sunlit countertop, the brilliance accentuating tense, bridged fingers. Black noted her palms were forced against the edge of the glass so hard it pressured deep grooves in the flesh. Her face remained completely under control.

He said, "I was on my way to Seattle and I decided I wasn't going through this city without seeing you.''

"Just like that?''

"Just like.'' His smile failed. She looked past him to watch her clerk move some blouses. The hangers clashed on the rack. "I don't like surprises all that much.''

He said, "I'm sorry. I should've called."

Time drained out of Black, left flat emptiness. As he turned away, she said, "Are you really passing through?"

"I was back East. I had a layover, so I told them I'd catch a later plane. It's not important."

She looked away again, busying herself with some receipts. "I thought you might call during the holidays, or send a card, or something."

"I meant to. I almost forgot Christmas. Would have, but my daughter reminded me."

"Forgot Christmas?"

"I've sort of let it get away from me the past few years. Me and Scrooge."

She sighed, then was suddenly furious. "Dammit, I was lonely! I wanted to talk to somebody, and you didn't call!"

"I wish I had."

"I thought about you, about what you said when you were here. You were kind."

"I thought about you too." It was all coming out wrong again, lumps of noise. "Maybe that's why I didn't call."

"Does that mean something?"

He laughed bitterly. "Damned if I know. Must be pretty wise, huh?"

She smiled. He said, "Can you take a break? Give me a chance to apologize?"

In answer, she pulled a cloak from a clothes tree, calling to the assistant to watch the store. She preceded him outside, where the wind caught her hair, flaring it across the dark green of her rippling cape. He wondered if she'd ever been on a sailboat, wondered if she enjoyed good music and solitude.

For the first block they walked arm in arm, making neutral small talk. Waiting for a traffic light, she looked at him sideways, half-pleased with herself and half-shy. She asked, "Have you noticed anything different about me?" and he racked his mind for an appropriate answer. In the end, he said, "No. What did I miss?"

She laughed, tugging at his arm when the light changed.

"Nothing you can look at, I hope. I'm enrolled in assertiveness training."

"And what have you learned?"

"You were right. I've been cheating myself. No more, though. I made mistakes and I'll make more, but each one's a lesson." She grew serious. "I enjoy myself, Steve. I feel good about me."

"You should. You're a very accomplished lady."

"Woman. Accomplished woman."

He grinned at her. "We seem to have a jargon block here. I understand your references, but you don't know about mine. I mean, I know you well enough to know you're a lady, but I'm not able to say much about your being a woman. Sad, but true."

"Male-chauvinist differentiating! Lady, hell!" She jabbed a thumb in his ribs and his ensuing squawk turned heads. He glared, but she was already studying a shop window as though nothing had happened. When she faced him again, her smile dripped insincerity. "That's what happens when you make assumptions about us assertive types."

"I'll remember. And I owe you."

They laughed about that, and as Maddy's break stretched out to an hour's stroll, it seemed to Black nothing could put an end to the laughter. The power she was finding in herself was the thing he'd sensed, an ability to come back. It made him feel good.

And then she asked why he was back East.

Entire speeches flashed through his mind, discarded in the seconds before he must answer. The opportunity to tell her the truth would never be better, but that required confessing the original lie.

The battle was lost before it properly started. A few brief sentences satisfied her and left him feeling slick with the sweat-stink of fear, which was absurd in itself. Nevertheless, he concerned himself more with his reaction to the lie than the commission of it.

They closed the store together, sending the clerk on her way early, earning an appreciative, if leering, good-bye. From the store they went to Maddy's apartment. It was an

110

odd sort of journey, full of companionable moments suddenly staggered by a nervous laugh or a comment so completely out of context it grated. Both knew the cause, but neither knew exactly how to stop what was happening. The relationship had acquired a hurtling momentum, dragging them along, forcing them to define issues too quickly.

They stalked her living room with the wary precision of strangers meeting on strange ground. Black examined it quickly, seeing nothing surprising. Her taste ran to contemporary and her expenditures to mid-priced items. The furniture had the minor scars of normal use, but everything was clearly well-maintained and neat. Color was Maddy's strong point, used with verve. Touches of bright yellows and reds added warmth to the primary scheme of blues and shaded whites.

He refused a drink, accepted coffee. While she prepared it, he stood by the window, watching the throbbing, traffic-jammed streets. Buildings dimmed steadily in the lowering sun, and as office-window lights blinked off in hundreds, Black got an impression of a retreating day devouring man-made energy as it left. Little sound reached Maddy's floor. What did was more like surf shuddering through muscle to the brain.

She brought the coffee and stood beside him while they drank. He said, "My plane's in an hour and a half." The statement was rigidly neutral.

"Good," she said, and at his quick look, went on, "I want you to stay, Steve, I really do. But not yet. Please, try to understand."

"No problem. I want to be sure, too."

Suddenly she was grinning, a taunting look. "I knew it all along. That old chauvinist male-chivalry stuff."

"Well, I'll be damned." He turned and searched carefully for something stable to hold his cup and saucer, then faced her again. Concern and impudence warred in her expression. He said, "I owe you one. Now I'll collect on it, and that one, too."

She backed away. "Don't make me spill my coffee!"

"To hell with your coffee."

111

"Steve!" It was a squall, forced higher as she bent to get rid of the endangered cup.

When he caught her and pulled her to him, she returned his kiss with a fire that threatened to destroy their earlier agreement. Then she broke away, staying within his arms and pressing her cheek to his chest. "I let you catch me only so the noise wouldn't upset the neighbors," she said.

"Let's hear it for the neighbors." The crown of her head was just under his chin, and he buried his face in her hair as he spoke. He tilted her head back and kissed her again. His hands slid down her back, spanned firm buttocks with increasing pressure. She pushed against him, stepped back with graceless haste. "You better go, Steve. I have to think."

Tightness in his throat warned him not to trust his voice. He nodded, then said, "I'm going. And I hope you'll be thinking about what I'm thinking about right now."

When he looked, she was coloring, and he laughed. She made a face, feigning irritation. "I don't know how to get in touch with you," she said. "I called our local IRS office and told them you were an investigator, and they said they didn't have any way of finding you."

"You asked them how to find me?"

"I shouldn't have, huh?"

"Did they ask who I was checking out?"

She looked away. "I wouldn't tell them. I didn't want my name mixed up in it."

The hand reaching for his pen was shaking. He took the pad from beside her phone and wrote two numbers. "Home and office," he explained, copying her number on a separate sheet and putting it in his pocket. "I'll call you tomorrow evening, okay?"

"I'll be here."

"Not eating at Carter's?"

She came to him and put her arms around him. "That's our place. They'll have to wait till you're in town. How's that for sophomoric?"

"Perfect." When she lifted her face, he kissed her one last time, softly, before pushing her out to arm's length. "Now or never, Maddy. I really better get going."

Head resting against his bicep, she walked him to the door. As it was closing, she framed her face between it and the jamb. "Look out, bad guys," she said, teasing, "the good guy's coming."

He managed to keep smiling until he was out of sight.

CHAPTER 11

Black STEPPED INTO THE TINY ANTEROOM OF HIS APARTMENT before realizing something was wrong.

In one swift movement, he was back in the hall, poised, waiting for his senses to identify what caused the warning that still crept across the flesh of his back.

No sound came from the room, no telltale scrape against the wall, no footstep. Anyone in there knew enough to be patient. He moved back inside, pressed against the wall.

Smells. There was the heavy masculinity of his own life. Jane's more delicate presence was there as well, familiar now. A discordant scent cut across the accepted ones. Like a color, it was a mixture of hues and tones, defying instant identification. Fundamentally, it was male. A stranger.

Jane had entertained a male guest. There was nothing wrong in that. In fact, it was a very good sign, a mark of adjustment.

Yet he was irritable, thin voltage touching his perceptions. His advance was cautious.

When he saw the living room, his first thought was of struggle, but it faded immediately. Clothes draped the furniture, other apparel spread bright colors across the carpet. It was a fantasy garden of disarray, the soiled accumulation of days. Even as disgust overwhelmed him, he caught the acridity of marijuana. An empty bottle of his dessert wine lay on its side by the sofa.

114

Preoccupation with concern for Jane had blinded him to the male clothing. Angrily, he wondered if the oversight wasn't more deeply revealing than anything else. The things were in plain view. Could eyes refuse to acknowledge what emotions didn't want to deal with? Even if that were true, how could he have denied the greasy sexual musk hovering in the room?

He strode to the window, angrily threw it open to a pale cold that absorbed the suggestive warmth and scoured it clean. Eventually it also drew his pain, left only harsh memories of nights when each sleepless minute brought imagined variations of this scene. He'd damned himself then, wondered what sort of man pictured his daughter in such circumstances, prayed for release from the self-torment. Neither prayers or curses diminished the horror.

He shivered and closed the window, then circled the room, kicking Jane's clothes toward the bedroom, the rest into another pile. When he had to use his hands, as in picking up the empty bottle, he used the tips of forefinger and thumb. He washed his hands and was walking toward his chair when he heard the key in the lock.

Jane's voice preceded her. "Didn't I tell you the town's a graveyard?"

Male laughter answered. Then she was in the room, startled. Her companion blundered in behind. He was very tall and thin, with wide shoulders that bloomed out of his neck as a horizontal bar. When he half-turned to shut the door, Black noted that the joint of arm and shoulder was no more than a bony knot. The frontal view was deceptive. In profile, the man was shallow, a rickety fraud. Light hair framed a long face presently racing through interchanges of deference, arrogance, and fear.

A familiar pity welled in Black. It was an irresistible question for him: What could such a man have been, given other circumstances?

Jane broke the silence. "Well, welcome home, Dad. I'd like you to meet Richie. Richie, this is Dad." Black ignored the taunt in her words. Seductively, experience whispered how easily Richie would break.

115

"Hello. Have you known Jane long?" His hand jerked at his side, a reflex toward a handshake he couldn't complete.

Richie didn't notice, too involved exchanging a histrionic glance with Jane. "We used to hang out, yeah. We were close. Really." Jane laughed, collaborating.

Black asked, "Will you be in town long?"

"Depends. I got no job here. Nowhere else, either." Having determined Black's complaisance, he was warming to his situation, playing to Jane, passing his words through Black to her knowledge of their genuine meaning. His posture altered from cautious poise to hip-shot assurance. Jane reached for his hand, and Black turned on his heel and walked to his chair.

The couple sat on the sofa. Behind them, a single cloud hung in the window and framed their faces with gentle white abstraction.

Black waited for one of them to speak, knowing Jane would understand what he was doing and hate it.

"I see you straightened up the room," she said. "We left in sort of a hurry."

"Had to rush off, I imagine."

"Naw," Richie said, "we just got tired of sitting here, you know? We should have stayed. We went to a park, right? Shit, man—the *park?*" He rolled his eyes at the hopelessness of it.

"We're very outdoorsy here in the Northwest," Jane said. "Dad even owns a boat."

"Hey, all right!" Animation lit up Richie's face, exposed the ruined youthfulness for a moment. "How fast is it, man?"

"Maybe eight knots. It's a sailboat."

"Oh."

Jane said, "We wanted to talk to you about a job for Richie. Maybe you know someone who's hiring?"

"Not right offhand. I can ask around."

"I can't handle anything heavy," Richie put in quickly. "I mean, like I parked cars for this restaurant in L.A. and that was okay, but I got like asthma or something. My lungs are all fucked up."

"Asthma? From parking cars?"

Jane said, "That's not what he meant. He's *got* asthma."

Black said, "I'll keep an eye out for something light."

"I told Richie he could stay here until he finds a job."

Control sagging dangerously, Black said, "You were wrong."

Jane's face was glad with challenge. "I know this is your apartment, but if I'm going to live here, I can't be a prisoner. I don't tell you how to live."

" 'How' has nothing to do with it. We're discussing 'where.' "

She rose with a grace that wrenched his heart, and he almost missed what she was saying. "What do you think living here's like? You're gone most of the time. When you're here, it's one long goddammed lecture." At his attempted protest, she gestured angrily. "Oh, you're too smart to preach. You just come on with heart-to-heart bullshit about school and hard work. And the nights! Climbing the walls all alone in bed while you sit out here watching some asshole suck up to Johnny Carson. Christ!"

Gesturing weakly at Richie, Black said, "Look, Janie, this isn't the time or place for this."

Richie grinned. "Don't worry about me. I'll just go have a beer while you all talk." He swaggered into the kitchen.

Slowly, almost ponderously, Black rose. His face looked curiously relaxed, although his eyes were hard with concentration. Jane's belligerence collapsed and she rushed to get between her father and the kitchen entry. Both hands on Black's chest, she faced him while trying to talk over her shoulder.

"Rich! Richie! You stay in there till I call for you, hear?"

Black allowed himself to be stopped, let her press him back to his chair. He was seated in it when Richie stepped out of the kitchen, a bottle of beer held in front of him like a scepter. His smile was condescending. "You and Jane decide what's best for you all, Steve. I can find us a place, if you don't want to share." He glanced around the apartment. "It won't be this nice—we're more used to rats and roaches, like—but where she lives is up to you, you know? See you."

117

He was gulping from the bottle on his way out, and the thump of the empty hitting the hall floor was as derisive as laughter. A moment later, Jane rounded on Black.

"You were going to hit him, weren't you?"

He nodded, knowing the question required no answer.

"You looked like you could kill him. I've seen that look."

"Where?" There was a stranger speaking from inside his daughter. He had to know more about her.

"Around. It's a bad look. I know about you now. More than I ever did."

"You're being dramatic. The point is, he was interfering in a family matter."

"He's family. When I was on the street, scared and alone, he took care of me."

"There was no reason for you to be on the street."

"The hell there wasn't! You think I'm going to spend my life like Mom, washing stained underwear, drinking my way through a million soap operas? Bullshit!"

"What you're doing is better? Running around with Richie? What d'you need with that?" His gesture indicated a world somewhere below where they stood.

She lit a cigarette, going through the ritual crisply. "That's real life, where the excitement is, where the *fun* is. All this other shit is fairy tales." She tossed her head. "Look, everybody says we're going to get nuked pretty soon anyhow, right? And there's no fucking work, even if you wanted it, you know? The world's shot, man. Richie knows how to laugh, how to have a good time. He knows how to make me have a good time."

Quietly, as if reminding herself rather than informing him, she went on, "You live alone. I've never seen a friend of yours come through that door. Mom got smashed because she couldn't talk to anybody. For all the talk about work ethic and character and education and on and on and on, what've you got? Nothing. Not a fucking thing but being lonely."

"It was difficult, having friends, when your mother was the way she was. I got used to being alone."

Bitter laughter cut at him. "I remember how much we

118

were alone. You spent a lot of time away. Pretty convenient, huh?''

''That's not true. My work—''

She cut him off. ''Look, we're talking about Richie living here. Either he moves in or I move out, it's as simple as that.''

Black sighed. ''If that's the way you see it.''

He had no way of knowing if her instant anger was genuine or affected. ''You're damned right that's the way I see it! I'm *alive*! Look at yourself! A job you can't talk about with a fucking government everybody hates. You don't really care who I sleep with or where, as long as it doesn't screw up your precious fucking job.''

''Please, Janie—that kind of language. It—''

''That's the way human beings talk! Can't you understand anything? I'm a living human being! Richie's a living human being! You're not! You're a fucking zombie!''

''I'll talk the situation over with Richie,'' Black said.

''There's nothing to talk about. He moves in or I move out.''

''That's clearly the most likely option. But you've got your school and I've got my own hours I need to myself. When we find work for Richie, he'll have his schedule, too. We have to talk about the best arrangement for all of us.''

Her eyes sought assurance in his. Seconds passed. He said, ''Go after him. I'll talk it out with him right now. We don't want any attitudes hardening. Catch him.''

Still suspicious, she edged back, twisting suddenly to run out the door.

Day's last light slipped through the window to form luminous tracery at the edges of the room's shadows. In his winged easy chair, he could have been backed into the earth-dark of an infantryman's fighting hole.

He considered his options.

The simplest solution would be to kill him. Knowing it was impossible, Black nevertheless savored the idea. The man lived in an environment where sudden death was far more common than lingering illness. No police force would consider his disappearance noteworthy. But Jane would shout the world down. No matter how cleverly the thing was done—even a perfectly arranged accident—she'd know.

Her excitement would generate an investigation. It'd be degrading to stand trial for eliminating such a nothing.

Black prowled the room, a black bulk against the lighter walls, the only sound the scuff of his shoes on the carpet.

There had been other men. They represented a tyranny capable of liquidating millions of lives, one that would happily crush a Richie, but they offered up no one more detestable. And they believed with a fierce conviction a man could honor. There was pride in hunting them.

He eased back into the chair. His weight forced air from deep in the upholstery in a prolonged sigh.

Jane returned with Richie a little while later. They sat on the sofa again, side by side in the soft light of the end-table lamp. Black deliberately remained in the dark of his chair. He said, "I think we both agree the important thing here is Jane's happiness, right, Richie?"

Unaccustomed to inclusion, Richie was a beat late agreeing. "Yeah. Like, we'll be out late a lot, you know? We'll need our own key." He beamed at his contribution.

Black headed for the door. "Come on, I'll buy you a drink and we'll settle this whole thing, the two men."

Jane said, "I'm coming."

Richie stood. "Let it go. He wants to help. I'm going to help him do it."

"He's too smart! He'll lay some scam on you."

Richie's eyes narrowed, the full lips thinned in a grimace. She paled and stepped back.

Black's hand squeezed the doorknob. It occurred to him that injuries and slights were Richie's debits and credits, the accountancy of a life so impoverished its avarice extended no farther than revenge.

The men left, exchanging small talk until they were in the dim bar down the street. Black called for a couple of beers as he led the way past the only other pair of customers, selecting a booth that offered privacy.

Richie accepted his drink with a smug satisfaction that brought a broad smile to the older man.

Black said, "I didn't know Jane was in touch with you."

Richie winked. "Called the day you went back East. Said she was lonesome."

"I thought you looked her up."

Pulling a face, Richie shook his head before drinking.

Black went on. "Well, then, I guess she really needs your company. Did she ever tell you what business I'm in?"

"Never said much. Some kind of government cop, right?"

"Some kind."

Richie leaned back in the booth, grinning across the scarred table. He rotated the bottle on the surface, making a rumbling noise. "Wild, man. I mean, a guy gets in a little trouble, be real handy if his old lady could put in a word where it'd help. You probably even know when the heat's coming down. Like narcs, and all, right?"

"Jane knows that's impossible."

Richie drained the remaining beer and waved for two more with a grin at Black. "Wrong, Dad. She feels the same way about cops everybody else does, so she'd sure as shit hate to see her own dear old dad let her man take a fall. You understand what I'm saying?"

Black paid for the beer, frowning. "I can't have her hurt. Can we shake on that, man-to-man?"

The answering grin left no doubt of Richie's contempt. Nevertheless, he went along.

Black reached with both of his hands to clasp Richie's, gently but quickly turning it so the palm was parallel to the tabletop. Both of Black's thumbs braced on the back of the offered hand, the fingers curved into the palm. Lifting the enfolded hand and leaning forward automatically lowered Richie's elbow to the tabletop and closed the forearm toward the shoulder, so the entire limb looked like a shadow-play swan. It happened with such smooth speed the younger man never thought to resist until it was too late. Black bent the hand down and back in one of the simpler, agonizing, techniques of jujitsu.

The searing pain jerked Richie's head back in an instinctive retreat, and then he was struggling to rise. The table restrained him as effectively as a colonial stock. When his

121

thighs thumped the solid wood, Black increased the pressure. "Sit down, you son of a bitch," he said, moderating the tone and speaking deliberately, "and don't scream, or I'll break this wrist and then the other one."

Richie reached to release himself and Black's thumbs depressed perhaps an eighth of an inch. The sallow face exploded with silent anguish, circular eyes glittering, red lips drawn in a snarl. The free hand flew upward, fingers splayed in a plea for Black to stop.

Bent over the table, smiling, the larger man could have been making a point in reasonable discussion. He said, "You pimp bastard. I can't do anything about you and Jane because she'd just take off after you, so you be nice to her. Give her, or me, any shit and this'll be like ice cream." He gave the wrist a tiny twitch, jerking a whimper from Richie. The staring eyes brimmed tears. Black went on. "You find a place to sleep. Don't mess up her life more than you have. When she gets tired of you, get out. You understand what I'm saying?" He savagely parodied the younger man's phrase.

"Yes! Jesus, man, don't break it, please!"

Black let him go, continuing to lean forward. Richie fell back as far as he could, massaging the wrist. Black told him, "I've got too much on my mind to fool with you, boy. Do what I want and I won't hurt you. And believe, there's no place you can run where my friends won't hunt you down for me. Now finish your beer and we'll leave." He hoisted his own and drank. When the younger man shook his head negatively, Black merely frowned and Richie quickly took a tentative sip.

"Don't dawdle." Black chided, exaggerating, as with a child.

Richie took a long pull and Black smiled. "See? Just do what you're told."

When they entered the apartment, Jane needed one look to know something drastic had happened. She turned on her father. "What'd you do to him? What's wrong?"

"Nothing. We agreed I need some privacy and you have to study. He can visit any time, of course. It was a difficult decision, but we feel it's best. Right, Richie?"

122

Richie nodded without meeting his gaze. Jane fumed. "He's my fucking lover! He doesn't 'visit!' "

"Shut up!" Richie shouted and raised a hand in an automatic gesture, only to drop it as quickly after a sidelong glance at Black. "We agreed, okay? Keep your fucking mouth out of it!"

Jane's shrill scorn was practically a scream. "That's it! You give me shit, but you can't stand up to him! Jesus Christ, Richie, he's *old*!" She walked toward the bedroom, unbuttoning her blouse, exposing her breasts. "Come on. You want it now? What can he do? He can't do shit!"

Richie wadded his fists, face twisted with rage. He spun away to storm out the door.

Jane leveled cold eyes at her father. "I'll get you for this." Her voice was strained, but she refastened the buttons with sure fingers. "You're like all big men, like all frigging cops. Just because Richie's not strong, you fuck him over."

Carefully, Black said, "It wouldn't have worked, having him live here. He agreed. You can see him any time, Janie. You know I wouldn't do anything to hurt you."

"Hurt? You think hurt comes with muscles. It doesn't. You wait, me and Richie'll show you."

"You'll stay here?"

"Goddam right, *Dad*. I saw Richie. If I move out, he'll just send me back to keep you from dumping on him."

"Don't be this way. Please. I love you. All I want is for you to give yourself a chance."

She laughed at him before disappearing into her room.

CHAPTER 12

WILL STEPPED INTO THE SMALL OFFICE, SCANNED THE CHART on the wall, and pursed his lips in a silent whistle. Black smiled at the compliment.

"Ain't it a dandy?" he said. "Now all I have to do is make sense of it."

"Do you have that much time before they retire you?"

Black chuckled. "The way Bob Davis talks, they'll retire me if I don't."

Taking off his raincoat, Will shook it, creating his own small storm before hanging it up. "It was raining in Frisco, too," he said. "Thought you'd like to know."

"I appreciate you making the trip. Just remember to bitch about our weather when you go back."

"You people still think you can hold out everyone who wants to move here?"

"We try." Black moved to the chart. "I think I've learned something. Maybe important."

"Good!" The unusual enthusiasm called Black's attention from the chart, and Will explained. "Davis is very tense about this one."

Black made a sound in his chest, then, "Look at this thing." The diagram now featured new boxes connected to the previous illustration by solid black lines. Each new square carried the name of a hotel or motel and the name ALEX in large letters. Under that, in precise, small print, Black had hand-lettered dates, also in black. Most of the boxes showed nothing else, but a select few carried other small-print names and dates in red.

The bright color drew Will. He ran a tentative finger across the data as if reading braille.

Black said, "The black print shows the dates Alex stayed in each of those motels. I haven't had much time. I've concentrated on the smaller places."

"Why them?"

"Hoping to get lucky. I can handle several small ones in the time it'll take to do one big one."

Will shook his head. "If he's meeting people, he'll make them register under cover names."

"I'm betting people break the rule. Are you paying cash for your room here?"

"I see. Sooner or later, someone decides that kind of security's unnecessary and goes back to credit cards."

"Exactly."

"And these red entries are people who were there on at least one occasion when our Alex visited?"

Instead of answering right away, Black stepped to the window. A crow on a rooftop across the street started at his sudden appearance. It cursed him violently, bobbing in time with its harsh cawing. Satisfied, the bird ruffled its feathers and preened briefly before swaggering along the parapet.

Turning from it, Black said, "My luck doesn't run that good. Most of it's sure to be simple coincidence—you know, some salesman stays there every time he has business in that area and happened to be there when Alex was. I need help checking those red names and addresses."

"I don't know, Steve." Will bent over Black's desk as he spoke, scribbling a note. It said, "Outside."

Black said, "Walk along with me and I'll go over what I've got in mind. The air'll do us good."

"Air? Fish should breathe air so wet." He moved to the coat rack. "Understand, I'd like to help, but I've got my own chores."

Black shrugged into a long leather jacket and ushered him

out. They didn't speak until they were a good half-block from the building entrance. Then Black said, "Okay, Will," and the thin man winced.

Without looking at Black, he said, "You don't have any idea what's going on, do you?"

"I guess not."

"That's it? You 'guess not?' "

"Are you going to tell me, or do we dance?" Black accompanied the words with a down-curving smile. He led Will to a plaza featuring an immense Henry Moore sculpture mounted on stubby posts in a shallow, rectangular pond. The slow, thick curves blunted the misted wind. Black positioned Will with his back to the piece, keeping himself facing away from the glass walls of the bank building. Again, he said, "Are you going to tell me?"

Will said, "That KGB Major, the one you call Alex? I'm the one who burned him. The fake buyer that turned him over to the FBI is my man. It was an Agency operation all the way."

Droplets quivered on the metal behind him, tiny, impatient glints from a compound eye. When they found the strength, they joined forces and skittered downward in impromptu streams.

Sarcasm tinted Black's response. "Congratulations. Why was it done?"

"There was a lot of conflict building up—jealousy—you know how it is. He was doing a good job for his side. Four or five agencies were getting anxious to bust him, but nobody had a decent case. Davis told our own bosses, the upstairs people, we should build a case around him before some asshole scared him off. They had me set up a singlehanded deal, something Alex'd get a medal for, if it was real. Our people let the Bureau know, and they set up the fall."

"It was Davis's idea to burn Alex?"

Will shrugged. "His idea. I don't know who made the decision, okay?"

"What're you telling me?"

"Don't get upset. Davis wants to move up, Steve. I told you."

126

"So what's the point, Will, the eternal bottom line?"

Sighing hugely, Will looked past Black at the beckoning warmth inside the glassed lobby. When the larger man smiled down at him, Will spread his hands in surrender. He chose not to remove them from his overcoat pockets, and the black garment flapped in a sudden gust of wind. He said, "You're not going to get much help catching Marvin for a while. It's the jealousy thing again. If you nail Marvin now, and he confirms what you've learned about Alex, a lot of people are going to look like jerks. How'd you like to tell a Senator your men followed Alex for a couple of years and didn't get zip-shit? And then someone else checks his act for a few weeks and figures out the guy's servicing a major Soviet illegal?"

"When do they expect to move on Marvin, then?"

"Davis wants Alex's replacement completely in charge. That way, when we take Marvin, nobody's going to even remember Alex. The connection can be swept under the rug."

"It was just expedient? Davis making points upstairs?"

"Same as always. Name of the game."

"I almost feel sorry for Marvin. First Alex goes, and when we roll up the net, we'll get the new liaison man, too. Moscow will be unhappy. But letting Marvin continue to operate is stupid, Will. He's collecting information we can't afford to lose."

"Davis is convinced we put a temporary stop to Marvin's operation by picking up Alex. The bosses are willing to bet his way's right."

"He didn't use to be that kind of a son of a bitch."

"It's not all his fault, remember. Alex was an approved burn, no cowboy job. And it gets us a million brownie points with the FBI."

Abruptly, Black moved toward the sidewalk. Pressure on Will's unresisting arm brought him along. Their lost conversation was underscored by the sigh of tires and an infrequent horn. It was lunchtime now, and the sidewalks blossomed with umbrellas. Two girls approached, heads encapsulated in long-ribbed, clear plastic versions. They talked and laughed from inside the sheltered environments, free hands gesturing gracefully. The more vivacious of the two wore a dark-blue sweater and much lighter jeans. Black wondered if she had ever seen a Portuguese man-of-war, the clear-and-blue jellyfish of warm seas.

When the numbers around them had thinned out, Black asked, "Is my office bugged?"

"I don't think so."

"You were just being careful, right?"

Will looked at him sharply. "Don't get pissed. No way does Davis find out I'm doing you any off-the-record favors."

"Are you, Will? Are you doing me favors?"

"I'm here. I'll go back to Frisco with your info and get some name-traces moving."

"I can do name-traces by phone from my office. I need to know who really stayed in those rooms. I can't slow down. There's too much involved now." Black spoke quite softly, but Will's expression altered, turned wary. His eyes never left the larger man.

"Look, Steve, it's all in his lap. He's the one who told you to get Marvin."

"That's the point. He told me if I didn't get Marvin fast enough, he'd take it away from me. Now he wants me to go slow."

"You've seen changes before. It's politics."

"You think I ever stop thinking about politics? After what happened to me before? Why else would I feel like this thing's going to end up falling exclusively on me?"

"I said I'd help."

"I'm going to burn Marvin, Will. Davis can do anything he wants, but I'm doing my job. You came up here off the record. Go home that way."

Black wished he'd phrased the ultimatum with more tact. Will continued beside him, withdrawn, heels popping the sidewalk. After they'd walked a while, Black apologized, then blurted, "Goddammit, Will, I *need* this. I was dying and didn't even realize it."

"I was afraid you'd just get mad and quit."

Black stared in amazement. "Quit?"

"Look, everybody knows they pushed you into this back-water to rust away. You sulked so long you almost did, too. And I'll tell you something else—I think Davis hopes you'll tell him to stuff the case."

"He wakes me up to tell me to go back to sleep? Like hell I will."

"Watch your ass, hear? This is a greasy one." His head snapped around at Black's unexpected laughter.

"God, they use us. What fucking puppets we must look like."

"Sometimes I wonder why we take it."

"Who knows? It's not the money, and God knows there's no glory. It must be the friends you make along the way." He gestured to their left. "How long since you had Thai cooking?"

"Years. And we've walked a mile or more. Let's eat."

"It's a couple of blocks to my car. We'll drive." They exchanged small talk about mutual friends for the fifteen minutes it took to get in the car to travel out Elliott to the foot of Queen Anne Hill.

The tiny restaurant could have been lifted directly from Bangkok. The tables were packed side by side, covered by plain white tablecloths. Each one featured a bud vase with a brilliant stem of small orchids. Pictures and posters decorated the walls, and to the far left, behind the counter, a small altar gleamed from a shelf high against the ceiling.

Will smiled broadly. "Leave it to you to find places like this. I was hungry until I smelled the air in here. Now I'm starving."

The waitress took their order, very carefully pointing out the pepper-heat of her food was measured in star ratings, from a mild one star to a sizzling five. When both men ordered the full five, she looked dubious, then repeated the system and made them repeat their desire to be scorched. When she was gone, Will asked, "How's Janie doing? Enjoying school?"

Black studied the tabletop. "An old boyfriend showed up. I'm not too happy about it. He's a bad influence."

"I'm sorry."

"Jane and I can handle it. We're communicating better."

"Let me know if he makes trouble." Will looked out the window at the busy street, his peculiarly quiet voice placing words in the air. "He could become a nuisance. I'll have it taken care of."

The waitress returned with lunch and they fell silent. When Black was free to speak again, he said, "If I need help, I'll call. But, for Christ's sake, don't say anything to Davis. If he thinks my personal problems are getting in the way—" He let the sentence die of its own implications.

Will nodded. "I understand you not wanting me involved in this thing with your daughter, Steve, but I offered to help with the Marvin matter because I don't think you can handle it all alone. Are you sure you want to try?"

"If Davis is working a slowdown and I make too much progress in California, he's going to know you helped." Will gestured, and Black ignored it. "I didn't want this job. Now you couldn't pry me off. I learned, Will. No matter how much it takes to stay alive, being dead is worse. I won't go back, and I won't take the chance of getting you in trouble with me."

Will said, "It's a job, Steve. Like laying bricks."

"It's more than that. And if it wasn't, it'd make no difference. I'm a worker. I do my job."

"Fine. Job—not crusade."

Black laughed shortly. "Cynical bastard. You make it sound like a four-letter word."

" 'Fool' is a four-letter word. Don't swap being one kind for another, okay?"

"Bet on me."

Will pushed away his plate, dabbed at his lips with a napkin. "Well, no matter what happens, I had the best meal I've enjoyed in a long time. I'll be dealing with those chilis for days. Remember what I said—if you need anything at all, holler. I'll be there."

"I know that."

"Good." He rose. "Thanks for the lunch." His ghosting smile flicked on and off. "Jet-setter. Fly to Seattle for lunch, then back to the Bay area." He shook Black's hand. "Be careful."

130

Black fished hurriedly for his wallet as soon as Will cleared the door. He dropped an untidy wad of bills on the table and watched through the curtained window as Will flagged a taxi.

Once the smaller man was safely out of sight, Black trotted to his car, speeding out the viaduct to the airport, hoping Will would do exactly as he'd said he would.

Parking, he ran across the enclosed skywalk from the parking tower. This was Will's specialty, he reminded himself, sliding into place behind a family headed in the right direction. Crowds were no distraction to the thin man. Once he gripped a subject with those unfathomable eyes, it was as if that person was alone on the earth. If he was looking for surveillance, the game was probably over already.

Black broke away from the group, turning into one of the concourse shops. From there he could see the banked phones. There was no way to be sure Will would be making a phone call or that he'd use the phones closest to the counter of the airline that issued his ticket. Waiting, feeling more foolish and conspicuous by the moment, Black admitted he had no definitive reason for suspicion. Still, all morning long, nothing seemed in balance. There was a feeling of hidden forces shouldering for position.

Suddenly, Will was there. Black shivered, realizing he had no idea which direction he'd come from. He was just *there,* sitting at one of the telephones. He spoke briefly and hung up. Black willed him to get up, to move away, but he sat, staring at the instrument until it rang. He snatched it out of the cradle, and Black's mouth went dry.

One of Davis's control techniques was a required telephone report at the earliest opportunity. It was degrading, a time-check of the most blatant kind. It assured no field man had enough free time to conduct any independent moves. And he insisted you call him, give him your number, and he called back. It made sure you were where you claimed to be. It was abnormal precaution, technique reserved for the most sensitive situations. And Black could only guess at the conversation.

*   *   *

Will said, "He's hooked. Everything's working exactly as you anticipated." He listened, then, "Yes, I'm sure. But there's one potential problem. Jane's boyfriend is here." Another pause. "He says he can handle it. Either way, I'm out. I only tailed him because I was worried about him. He's okay now. Or he will be, if you'll leave him alone."

Whatever was said next produced an amazing burst of color in Will's cheeks, two almost perfectly circular red spots. On the pale face, so clear of expression, they had the contrast of clown makeup. They were still there when he spoke a last time. "Yes, I understand. Thank you very much, *sir*." He slammed the receiver back in place, glaring at it. Then, "Fuck you, Davis. You push too hard. Maybe once too often."

Black watched Will leave. He felt empty, broken. Worse than the betrayal was the sense of exposure, a revelation of his appearance in the eyes of others. Davis, condescending, unable to trust. Will, a friend—a former friend—listening, confiding, reporting.

Straps of pain, as clear in his mind's view as if the skin had been flayed from the muscles, stretched from each eye to the juncture of spine and skull. Another discomfort, a strange rhythmic closure and release in his throat, worked in harmony with the beat of his heart. He concentrated on it, using it to stand off the crushing stricture in his skull.

He was on the walkway, leaning against one of the girders of the structure, absently aware of the traffic on the street below, when he saw his reflection in the glass. It was a frightening visage, a beaten man uninterested in his own defeat. He snarled at it with a vehemence that electrified a young woman headed into the terminal. She scooped up her toddler and practically ran to the escalator.

Black walked to his car.

CHAPTER 13

THE ENERGY OF THE FALLS SHUDDERED THROUGH THE CEMENT deck of the observation platform.

Carmody marveled at the power necessary to create that sensation. The falls were at least two hundred meters from where he stood. Masses of rock split the river into two distinct throats at the drop-off point, one much narrower than the other. Both constricted their portion of the water, turned the cold, flat green to a whitewater rush. The split streams were close enough to blend into one flow as they dropped, which pleased Carmody, corrected a situation that might have diminished the spectacle.

He decided it would be impressive enough in any case, with a drop of about seventy meters.

Oddly, the river's name had the sound of softer scenery. He rolled it across his tongue slowly, "Snoqualmie," letting the exotic vowels expand and linger, fill his mouth with a thick sweetness like chocolate.

Yes, it was a name for the lower stretches, where it turned more accepting, sympathetic. Here was continual ferocity.

Bending reluctantly, the stream fell in a headlong dive to the pool below, breaking into shining vees that pulled away from each other. They made Carmody think of gleaming claws attacking the waiting boulders. The cliff itself curved in a natural amphitheater, the wall randomly marred by rockfall scars. Some were huge craters like whorled thumbprints. Other slides created shallow benches in the surface, and plants colonized the skimpy soil lodged on them. The lively, verdant slashes accentuated the impassive gray with an impressionist's strokes. Far up on the most distant section clung a patch of moss, a vivid, cold yellow-green.

Clouds of mist boiled up at the point of impact, their delicacy contrasting with the tumult. Masses of it fled downstream, slipping away across the pool's surface. Some was trapped, spiraling upward to expire against the cliff face.

The viewing platform extended outward from a flank of the cliff. Wind gusted through the open area between roof and deck, whisking away any warmth from the sun. Nicolai was the only other person present. He stood behind Carmody, stiffly erect, maintaining a full body-length between himself and the safety railing. When Carmody looked over his shoulder, the older man shifted irritably, throwing a meaningful glance toward solid ground. Sighing, Carmody retreated until he was next to him. "We have at least ten minutes before our reservations at the restaurant," he said.

Nicolai took a step backward. "We will not be eating."

Carmody kept his expression impassive. "Not?"

Another backward step and Nicolai was turning, moving to the steps in his ludicrous toy-soldier posture. Carmody followed and, on safe ground, Nicolai faced him again. "Someone might see us," he said. "We can speak here. You should know better than to arrange a *treff* in a place where everyone comes only to stare."

It had been months—no, years—since Carmody had heard a meeting referred to by that term. It was archaic. So was Nicolai, for all that. A dinosaur, too stupid to know his life span had passed. Carmody looked away, not wanting the contempt that pulled at his features to break free. His gaze wandered to the restaurant, perched on the cliff's edge overlooking the falls, and he understood that Nicolai's aversion was to the location rather than to public view. He gestured down the sloping macadam walkway. "There is a bench at the end of the path," he said, moving away. "No one can approach without our being aware. We can speak safely."

134

Nicolai kept to the right of the prepared surface, canted to the side as if the fence on his left didn't exist. Strain pulled the thin face tight, puckering the lips into a rosebud of irritability.

From the bench, the canyon was hidden from view, with only the top of the falls visible. The thunder from below was distant, actually soothing. Swallows hurtled up from under the lip of the cliff, chittering darts of emerald and ivory. Their maneuvers laced the sky.

"You have fallen behind," Nicolai said. "The computer-technology operation should be finished. Instead, you ask for this meeting."

"There has been a problem. I decided it was necessary to inform you in detail."

"Problems must be eliminated."

It was exactly the phrase Carmody anticipated. For a moment, the accuracy of his insight was frightening, as if he had seen into the mind of the other man. On consideration, however, he understood that someone had seen into Nicolai's mind long ago, explored all its cracks and crannies and turned it to use, farmed it as wild earth is tamed to wheat. His thoughts, no matter their number, were precisely like everyone else's. Or everyone he cared about, in any case.

The sliver of understanding brought a touch of sorrow. Nicolai was undoubtedly a good man, but under an obligation created by the world, not his fault. If a man was unfeeling, one could hate him. But when the state pointed out the necessity for unfeelingness and the man shouldered that burden faithfully, one owed him consideration. Even respect.

Enemies surrounded Russia, waiting to strangle her. Those who would save her measured today's sacrifice against tomorrow's existence. Ruthlessness was a necessity and, it followed, a virtue. Weakness was the unforgivable vice. If Nicolai's thought processes were rigidly programmed and if he was harsh, that was as it should be. He was at war. The world allowed no other way.

Of course, Carmody told himself, he himself was partially at fault for the latest friction between them. He should have foreseen a possible collapse of the computer experiments.

That would have allowed a proper slack in the operation plan. A delay such as this could have taken place and no one higher up the chain would have been the wiser. Nicolai would have accepted the time frame without question, understanding the routine cushion. He knew the system. Now they both faced disapproval.

Still, no matter who was running the experiments, Harry Summerton said the new data promised to solve all the previous problems.

"Our delay is no fault of our operation. The experiments were flawed. We are still in position."

Nicolai's answer crackled. "Damn position! I forwarded what you gave me! Do you think the *nachalstvo* care about position? They have been made to look like fools!"

Carmody twisted awkwardly, assuring there was no one in the brush behind them. Nicolai watched him with uncompromising fury. Carmody said, "Please, don't use our language. You must speak English."

Nicolai sneered. "You said this place was safe. It's your responsibility. If I want to say *nachalstvo* instead of 'bosses,' I will. Don't lecture me."

Carmody wondered exactly how powerful Nicolai's connections at the Square might be. He said, "We are supplying information our superiors know is not available otherwise. They'll be patient."

"No." Nicolai looked away to smile. "Not us, comrade. You're the one who needs their patience."

"I don't understand."

"You still think of me as doing your friend's job. I am not. You might as well know you are under suspicion."

The judgment was delivered offhandedly, a comment about the weather, the condition of the roses, the unfortunate bus schedule.

Judgment. Alex left in disgrace. Alex had been liaison for Carmody.

What was it Grandmother said? *"We put our hand to the dead and think we are touching them, but they neither know nor care. It is they who touch us, who give us the silent lesson of fear."*

Nicolai continued to examine the uppermost part of the falls, apparently pleased with the view. "Your friend was a good man, once. I concede that. But his exposure to this decadence ruined him."

"Don't talk foolishness! I am suspected of what?"

"There are no specific charges, but we must examine everything he touched. You understand that."

"Like hell I do! What do you mean, everything? You're not thinking of my net?"

"He knew about every one of your agents."

"No. You're wrong. He only made appointments, provided security."

"Security? From a man who compromised himself? And wasn't it part of his 'security' function to see that no agent was followed to the meeting place, made no contacts after leaving? Didn't he see everyone of your people several times?"

"Of course. Who else was there? I had to rely on someone, and you sent him here, not me!" Carmody heard himself damning his friend and burned with shame.

Grandmother said, "They neither know nor care—"
I know! I care!

The admission released the fire of ideas in Carmody's brain. It was exquisite pain, enough to block the cruelty shining from Nicolai's profile, enough to blunt the terror of accusation.

He saw his life in this alien place. Hours of apprehension were summed up in split-second wavering images, a montage of instant reminiscences. One instance persisted.

He saw himself in pointless and unavoidable conversation with a uniformed policeman while leaning against a phone booth he'd just marked to indicate the unloading of a dead drop. In the mind-picture, the dark uniform blurred, losing and gaining focus like an object at the bottom of a swift stream. The color melted into the sky while ice-blue eyes smiled and expanded until there was no face, no sky, no time. There was nothing but the eyes, and the man who called himself Carmody was being absorbed by them.

He thrust the fantasy away, said, "Alex would never identify my sources."

137

Nicolai swiveled to face him. The movement lifted his right foot, leaving only the toe in contact with the earth. He looked coiled. "All your sources will sleep until this Summerton operation is in hand and can be transferred to another control. If Summerton is a double agent or a provocateur, you are the only one who will fall into his grasp. Be assured, we will not be as careless with your net as you have been."

"Because Alex was tricked doesn't mean my net is compromised. Furthermore, I wasn't involved in any way with the incident that," he paused, searching for just the right phrase, but when nothing would come, had to blurt out, "got him in trouble."

Nicolai grinned at the extended delay. He said, "Remember, his so-called deal was clandestine from the start. The Jew who destroyed him would have insisted on some indication of professionalism before getting involved."

"Well, certainly! We know it was all arranged. Jew or not, the contact was a professional."

"Exactly. We must assume Alex compromised his actual position in this country. We know absolutely that he trusted a Jew. He never even had him investigated. This is the man who was your security."

He looked past Carmody and made an inarticulate sound of warning.

A young woman and a girl approached. The red-haired child, no more than five years old, skipped with excitement, alternately racing off the path to study the mowed grass and then hurrying back to cling to the woven wire fence to peer at the crashing falls. Her fascination with both subjects excited Carmody. The spectrum of life was all one to her, infinite in its variety, individual in its beauty.

His heart filled with love. There was no other word to describe the feeling. It went beyond affection, yet he knew it wasn't love for the child, alone. There was a yearning for what the girl symbolized, a view of life that he had held at one time, and that had escaped.

Swiftly, he amended the thought. The view hadn't escaped; it had been put aside, stored. Like a kite in an attic, to take it out and look at it in bleak winter is to think of a complete experience. Still, bright color and rustling material can only regenerate memory bits. Nothing but reality can hope to recreate the experience.

He saw the child as a symbol, and he ached because he couldn't fully understand her significance.

His obvious interest alarmed the young mother, who moved closer to her daughter. Trapped, Carmody had only one way out. There was no chance to pretend nothing had happened. He smiled broadly at the woman. "I wish my two had stayed at that age. They enjoy everything so much then."

Tension ebbed in her face, a slight smile softened it. She was an attractive woman, casual in jeans and blouse, dark hair short in contrast to the coppery waves bouncing down the child's back. She said, "She's impossible to keep up with."

"I'm sure." Still smiling, he looked away, giving her a chance to retreat. She spoke softly, a mother's half-command, half-offer, and when he turned back, they were walking hand in hand toward the parking lot. The child peeked over her shoulder at him for a second. A chill touched between his shoulders at the sobriety of the tiny features. It made him wonder if she understood her role as failed messenger.

Nicolai said, "That woman will remember us forever."

Carmody refused to argue the matter. "Exactly what do you intend to do about this suspicion directed at me?"

"Do? Nothing. I am instructed to review your friend's activities. Moscow will decide what other steps to take. We'll go back to the city now." Nicolai got to his feet. "There's nothing to talk about here."

Falling in with him, Carmody said, "You still don't know about the situation I wanted to discuss."

"In the car."

"As you wish." Carmody stopped, looking back at the falls for one last time. Near where the river exited the pool, a couple sat on a boulder. Lovers gleaming in the sun, they typified the people drawn here as if by psychic magnet. Too minute to be clearly identified against the distance and vast terrain, they were still part of the scene. They belonged in it.

Suddenly, he was afraid. This land, with its spaces that fell

139

in on one, this landscape of clear views tainted by unexpected dark whispers, had the power to enfold a man, absorb his soul.

He pulled his gaze from the couple to the valley beyond. New leaves were forming on the trees, translucent, gold-green as cats' eyes. A breeze shuffled through part of the forest, setting myriad points of light dancing and beckoning in an exuberance of budding life that was almost lewd.

He hurried to the car, where Nicolai waited impatiently, cigarette smoke boiling out the window next to him. As soon as Carmody was behind the wheel, he said, "Tell me what you wish to have reported."

"Summerton has learned that work continues on the experiments. They know where the errors are and are correcting them."

"Good. It is not as bad as I thought. You have only to copy this new material."

It startled Carmody to hear Nicolai making jokes. He looked at him quickly prior to laughing, which was fortunate, because Nicolai was not smiling. In reaction to his near-error, Carmody was abrupt. "You're not even trying to understand."

"What did you say?"

"My agent has access to papers, and he has to steal them. He's not involved with the actual experiments. The work—"

"Excuses! Listen to me! We have given worthless data to our scientists. They will attempt to use it. They will fail, and they will complain to their friends in the government. Our entire organization will be doubted. Can you understand the significance of that? No one must be allowed to question us!"

"What right have they to complain? If our scientists are so brilliant, why must we steal from American scientists?"

Nicolai was very still. "That is dangerous talk, comrade."

Carmody swallowed. "I'm not finished. In your report, tell our people I will proceed with my operation. But I'll personally beat hell out of anyone I find interfering with it. Tell them."

"You'll make yourself a lot of trouble. Think about it." The tone was darkly suggestive.

"I have. I do what I must. The *rodina* comes first. They can only kill me."

In the quiet aftermath, Carmody started the car. A strange lightheadedness swept him, strong enough to override his embarrassment at speaking Russian. It was the only proper tongue for "motherland," and that was the word that had to be used. Nicolai had to understand. All the talk about trouble for the scientists, loss of prestige for the committee—those things could see a man off to the camps, could literally kill a man, but they were external forces, as capricious as the ancient gods were supposed to be. A man owed it to himself to try to be honest inside. Above all, a man did what the *rodina* needed. That was first.

Nicolai said, "What do you mean, they can only kill you?"

"I will do my duty. If it's decided I've done something wrong, they'll punish me. I accept that. But if I fail my country, whether I'm punished or not, I can't accept that."

The small man seemed to draw inside himself. For long miles, he sat looking straight ahead, oblivious to magnificent scenery, passing traffic, or roadside distractions, focused on a spot directly above the horizon. Fine-boned hands lay palm-up in his lap, the fingers limply curled, like the hands of certain statues of the Buddha. When he moved, at long last, it was with an old man's slow, generous concern for stiff joints. He twisted in his seat, faced Carmody.

"You think your life is hard. It is. Russian life has always been hard. That is why you will succeed. It makes me glad to see you still have a Russian heart." His right hand moved in a gentle sweep. "I will leave you for a while, and return to San Francisco."

The simple phrase had the ring of a reprieve. Carmody heard it very clearly.

CHAPTER 14

DROPS OF SWEAT TICKLED HARRY SUMMERTON'S ARMPITS. Resisting the urge to scratch, he continued to stare at the receding skyline of the city as the ferry drew out into the Sound. He wished the place would disappear, sink below the horizon, so he might never have to look at it again.

The weight of the envelope in his jacket pocket was like an anvil.

He cursed Martin, working himself into such a state his lips moved with the words, a silent caressing, almost kisses. He luxuriated in the obscenities. Imagination twisted the Sound's heaving waters and blunt clouds, pregnant with another spring storm, into replicas of Martin's writhing form. The face he pictured was in an agony of pain and horror.

A sound like a muffled sneeze startled him, and he turned quickly, catching two girls, barely in their teens, watching him, convulsed by furtive giggling. Discovered, they hurried away forward, into the semienclosed observation deck.

His face burned. He glared back out the window, chewing on his lower lip. There was a rough spot there, the result of the nervous habit. He'd been warned often that many cancers start that way. It frightened him when he thought about it.

Fear was his daily portion now, he reflected bitterly. It was difficult to remember a time when he was without it. With the new experiments in progress, Martin was more demanding than ever. And as if that wasn't enough, he'd also practically broken off all personal contact with a weak lecture about "operational safety."

Naturally, he explained the use of what he called a dead drop was for "mutual safety."

Both terms, to Martin, meant someone else taking all the chances.

Summerton smiled wryly, oblivious to the delight the expression afforded the continuing observation of the girls.

He'd thought it through, many times, and was convinced it was far more dangerous to put something in a dead drop than it was to take something out. When a person picked up something and kept it, that was accepted as natural. The casual watcher might even assume the person was only retrieving something of his own. The worst reaction would be mild curiosity.

On the other hand, if people suspected a person of trying to hide something, they watched closely. They felt they were in on a secret, and no one could resist that. Even if a spectator assumed the object being hidden was trash, it was abnormal to hide trash. *Ergo,* anything being hidden was cause for suspicion.

He risked his very life getting the information and carrying it around. And who sat back and waited as long as he wanted, until he was certain of safety before moving? The man responsible for the whole scheme.

It wasn't fair. It never was. No matter how hard he tried to make allowances, to be easy to get along with, people always took advantage. If the police caught him, would Martin rush to his defense? Like hell! Martin would just let him go to jail, and he'd never even *be* in this situation if it weren't for him.

Thoughts of arrest made Summerton remember he was to be constantly observant, sensitive to any indication of interest in his activities.

The girls, seeing his head swivel, hastily averted their gaze, feigning rapt interest in an overtaken sailboat.

He went inside, where the barnlike expanse of the ferry lounge reassured him. There was an intense humanity confined there, protected from the chill spring winds. The smell was unique, a mingling of warm bodies, paint, and the iron bite of salt air. Through all of it ran the cloying taint of fuel oil.

Taking a seat, leaning his head against the window, Summerton hoped to be lulled into a nap by the easy movement of the vessel. His mind refused to let go of his worries.

It was ridiculous to have to travel all the way to Bremerton to drop off material. And dangerous. After all, Bremerton was near the Trident submarine base. What area could be more sensitive, more closely observed? Still, Martin insisted a foot passenger on the ferry had good countersurveillance opportunity, that weekend travelers were in too festive a mood to pay attention to anyone in particular, and that the town's road network provided a choice of entry and exit routes. He had been very patient in his explanations, flattering Summerton by telling him that soon he'd have enough experience to pick his own drops.

It was all an obvious sop. The reason for using Bremerton was to get the transfer point the hell out of Seattle, away from Martin's own base. And the touch about alternate routes was the crowning irony. The simple bastard on foot returned on the ferry, or not at all. If there was trouble, Good Old Martin would be in a car, able to leave at high speed in any direction he wanted.

Martin's trouble was his assumption that everyone else was stupid. That, and the equally incorrect assumption that he was in total command of all aspects of the operation. Within his profession, that was undoubtedly true. Summerton smiled. It was time to start showing Harry Summerton's importance.

There was no time for that now, he reprimanded himself, rising as he did.

Buying a cup of coffee took only a minute, and then he strolled out onto the weather deck. To the south, sunlight bolted through breaks in the clouds in angled colonnades. Beyond them, Mt. Rainier rose into a clear sky, unperturbed, uninvolved. The darkening weather tumbling from the north would soon blot out the broken cover, shroud even the

144

immensity of the mountain. Swirling gusts slapped at Summerton's clothes, punishing him for getting in their way.

Drinking from the cup proved to be something of a challenge. Wind plucked at the liquid when Summerton tilted it, sending alternating tendrils of hot and cold across his upper lip. He avoided most of the problem by turning his back and hunching over like a miser with his hoard.

Making his way to the observation enclosure forward, he got his first glimpse of the dock. Impatience surged at the sight. There was something in him that actually enjoyed this part of the business. As unjust as Martin's techniques were, Summerton had to confess to himself that he was thrilled anew at each step of his clandestine life. At times, he felt a sadness for the wasted years of the old Harry Summerton. The new one was so much more exciting.

Blank-faced strangers passed without seeing, intent on their small matters, never realizing the man beside them had their future in his pocket. If he waved the envelope under their ignorant noses, they still wouldn't understand. That was the way they were, all of them. A man of genuine daring stood right there among them, and all they knew was that it was time to get in line.

Sudden deceleration broke his train of thought as the ferry nudged into the funnel-shaped array of pilings flanking the dock. Screws rumbling in reverse churned the water, lacing the ice-green with swirls of bubbles. The pilings leaned and groaned under the weight of the vessel. Creosote fumes mixed with the clean sea smell of the disturbed water. In moments, the car engines started, blanketing everything with their noise and exhaust.

Laughing, chattering, the off-loading crowd engulfed him on the foot ramp leading ashore, most of them bicyclers and walkers hopefully gambling on the uncertain spring weather. A couple passed him, arm in arm, the young man's free hand holding a mylar dragon kite. They laughed, and the man's eyes lifted momentarily to meet Summerton's before moving on.

It was only a few blocks to the restaurant where he would get rid of the envelope. Reluctance mingled with relief at the

145

thought. Without the envelope, he was only another passer-by.

He consoled himself by imagining the expression on Martin's face and the faces of Martin's superiors when they realized Harry Summerton was rewriting his role.

The necessary booth was available when Summerton stepped through the door. He settled in easily.

As Martin said, any dead drop had its advantages and disadvantages. Placing or retrieving material in a restaurant booth was simple, unless the place was crowded. That was why the actual drop took place between lunch and dinner.

Working quickly, watching the lone waitress, he tore off a strip of double-backed tape from the roll in his pocket, attached it to the envelope, and stuck it against the underside of the table.

Now Summerton's job was done, except for placing the signal to let Martin know the material was there. The only possible danger was something unforeseeable. People do strange things. It wouldn't be unheard-of for someone to feel under the tabletop and discover the envelope.

Martin's problem, Summerton thought, allowing himself a smile. Let the old pro spy-master worry about it. Harry Summerton had done his job to perfection, and if anything went wrong now, no one could blame him.

When the waitress came to take his order, he was feeling expansive. He ordered the largest steak she could find in the kitchen. As an afterthought, he told her to bring him a beer as well, and to keep them coming until he told her to stop.

The second bottle thumped on the table just as the two girls from the ferry angled into his view. Shielded by the waitress's body, Summerton watched their giggling progress to a booth diagonally across the room from his own. They were accompanied by a uniformed sailor, a mere boy. He made a show of seating the girls, one on each bench, then cozied up against the taller of the two. Their position made it impossible for Summerton to avoid them, and as soon as the waitress moved, the action drew the girl's eye. She recognized him instantly. Leaning toward the other girl, she grasped the sailor's hand. Her entire face worked along with the

146

heavily lipsticked mouth. The second girl bent her body in an impossible curve to stare at Summerton. Then she spun back, and they were inches apart, communicating in a buzz of whispers and laughter.

The sailor listened easily, amused eyes flicking from them to Summerton and back. He still had his hat on, the stark white of it crisp against the bland, round features. Ugly, Summerton decided, his single notable characteristic a flourishing case of acne.

There was more to his meal than expected, and he gestured for another bottle of beer to wash it down. The trio continued to watch him, talking among themselves. The sailor was the most irritating. He reveled in his masculine role, muttering an occasional remark that never failed to touch off squealing amusement. Summerton wished he could see under the table, absolutely certain he'd find the sailor's leg rubbing the girl's from calf to buttock.

She pulled the sailor's head to hers, saying something with her mouth touching his ear. The sailor rolled his eyes to look at Summerton and threw back his head and laughed out loud.

Fury built in Summerton's stomach, shrinking it around the just-finished meal. Tighter and tighter it squeezed, until he felt he'd be ill before he could get to his feet. Then, suddenly, he was icily calm, the hard, logical part of his mind in total control of his being. His shoulders pulled back, throwing his chest forward, and his chin rose.

He aimed a full look at the sailor, directly into his eyes, following that with a sure, practiced smile. He let the piercing, sophisticated gaze slide away to rest on the middle distance. The boy fell silent at that, as Summerton knew he must.

Poor young fool, full of counterfeit power. How embarrassed, how absolutely awestruck you'd be if you could understand anything of my secrets! I know things you never will.

The tension drained from his stomach, allowing the meal to fill him with warmth. Downing the last swallow of beer, he strolled to the counter, where the waitress stood poised at the cash register. He overtipped, gesturing away the surprised thanks. Outside, he pretended to decide which way to go, using the act to check on the three youngsters. He could only see the sailor and his girl. It was enough. They were conversing seriously.

Nodding slightly as he stepped off, Summerton said to himself, "Not surprising. The boy's at least smart enough to realize *something* touched him. He's probably trying to explain to that adolescent bitch. Waste of time."

Walking back to the ferry dock, he watched his progress in the glass storefronts, smiling inwardly at his swagger. Ought to be ashamed, he chided himself good-naturedly. Impressing a dumb sailor wasn't anything to get excited about. Nevertheless, it felt good.

It was only honest to admit it, and he was proud of himself for facing the fact.

A slight frown, not much more than a penciling of lines, crossed his forehead. He wished he could impress Martin similarly.

He brightened almost immediately. There was no need. Martin already knew of the new power. It was impossible for him to be unaware of it. The wonder was he'd been self-contained enough to avoid any indication of that awareness.

Summerton thought about that for a minute. Yes, he was certain of it—there had been an increased warmth, a *camaraderie* in their last meetings.

Damn, Martin was sly! Quite a man. A fellow professional, intelligent in his own right. When he heard his prize agent wanted to put their relationship on a more equal-to-equal basis, he'd probably be delighted. He'd never admit it, of course, because he was management and he'd know the next demand would be for more money. He'd resist as a matter of form.

They'd argue back and forth, a real shouting match. It'd be great fun, almost like one of the old movies, the kind where they had two really strong characters competing. Men like himself and Martin would see it that way, almost play it for laughs. One hell of a relationship would grow out of it.

148

That's the way it always went—the closest male bonds ripened in the heat of an honest argument.

Martin was probably looking for some such issue right now.

CHAPTER 15

CARMODY WATCHED ELISE DEAL WITH THE CUSTOMERS, A young couple. Her technique fascinated him. She leaned toward them gently as she explained the construction of a running shoe. When she pulled the shoe back, their eyes remained on it and he thought of children gripped by sleight-of-hand. The woman looked up momentarily and Elise was waiting in honest anticipation of helping. Putting down the shoe, she picked up a different model, less expensive. Bluntly, she told the other woman the second example was practically identical. The man looked up sharply, and Elise moved away while they talked.

The scene pleased Carmody. Elise was a natural merchant, selling to whatever psychological need she discovered. Nevertheless, she saw herself as guiding her customers. As a businessman, he applauded her. Satisfied customers were return customers.

More than that, however, he liked her sure instinct for interaction. He experienced it daily. There was seldom any need to explain to her. It was as if she understood the underlying intent, as well as the spoken directions. More to the point, she anticipated. Not in the sense that she intruded, but she had a habit of suggesting he take a break within moments of his own acknowledgment of weariness. Sometimes she would silently appear with a cup of coffee or a sandwich, invariably so closely in tune with his thoughts that he'd come to accept the small offerings with a curious apprehension that blended tense discomfort with a warm gratitude. The only comparable thing in his life was the wild exhilaration of boyhood raids on fruit trees, when discovery was as much a part of the game as the heart-thudding stalk through the night. That was innocent danger, wonderful excitement. The idea that she saw into his mind was ludicrous, but her performance was so nearly psychic it carried the same pleasurably stimulating artificial peril.

Genuine fear insinuated itself through all those moments with Elise, however. Her sudden appearances outwardly concerned only the needs of the business day, but a terrible suspicion crept through his mind that she had some instinctive awareness of the forest-darkness of his soul and was slowly mapping its paths.

Watching her had become more than a matter of supervision.

For the first time in his career, Carmody was afraid of an identifiable presence.

Over the years, he'd learned that every sharp look was not an attempt to penetrate cover and that traffic violations weren't ruses to initiate an identity check. Nevertheless, his palms still grew clammy when some garrulous fool pressed him about his invented childhood.

He protected himself by drifting through the smothering mass of *them,* rarely considering any as individuals. Attempts at familiarity, no matter how pleasant, triggered something in him much like nausea.

Swift dizziness struck as he thought of it. His hand on the counter tingled.

He concentrated on the couple, filled himself with a proper attitude, and sneered inwardly at their typical American bourgeois arrogance. Buying specially constructed running shoes, as if they were world-class competitors! Consumption for its own sake.

The customers left with their packages, and the ingenuous pleasure in Elise's look after them forced him to admit his moral outrage was self-delusion. She stood with one hand on the credit-card impression machine with a proprietary air.

151

Turning unexpectedly, she caught his open entertainment. Instead of being embarrassed, she shared his amusement. Perversely, that triggered a return of his previous irritation, and he groaned inwardly, recognizing brute contrariness as simple nervousness.

Elise said, "What're you staring like that for? I'm making you rich."

A delicious yearning for real conversation filled him, threatened to erupt through his skin. He nodded, sought the proper light tone. "You give new meaning to the words 'free enterprise.' "

"No 'free' to it. The things I want cost money, and this is the only way I've got to get it." She gave him an arch look and added, "Not only not free, I can be downright expensive."

Carmody would have sworn she gave an extra move, a sort of hitch with her hips as she turned away, and there was no question but that she looked back at him over her shoulder and grinned.

A warm urgency swept from his groin up through his guts. *This couldn't happen!*

He closed his eyes, thought of Olga. The image sighed, pouted, shattered like ice. He built another picture, Olga in their bed, warm, her breasts exposed as her arms reached in passionate welcome.

It was a wife he'd never seen, and the picture altered, created another person.

Firm, round breasts rose in place of Olga's aggressively conical thrusts. The new ones were milk-white against skin washed darker by spring's richer sun. Roseate nipples crested wide, pink aureoles, filling him with the sorrowed memory of button-hard mahogany nubs. The fantasy figure shifted, faced him with small shoulders square on, unlike the half-turned implied refusal that was Olga's usual pose. His eye coursed the sun-marked lines above and below the breasts again, translating them to subtle notice of even greater, still-hidden, wonders.

Gleaming hair fell in golden cascade beside the column of the throat. He fought against lifting his eyes to the features, certain of who he would see. Twisting logic played with his mind, told him his fantasies were harmless if they didn't actually identify anyone. He could imagine Elise's body. He must not picture her welcoming smile.

Elise spoke from a foot away, almost touching him. "You're in a mood again, aren't you?"

"I guess I am." He turned quickly. "What do you mean, 'again'?"

"You've been like this before. Irritable, but you hide it. I appreciate it."

"Appreciate it?"

She gestured. "This is a small place. It'd be rough being closed in here all day with a grouch. You try to keep it to yourself, and I appreciate it."

"You watch me that closely, then?" He cursed his leaden reflexes. He had no control over the conversation, no initiative at all.

"Not exactly," she said. She cut her eyes away, then resumed her level gaze. "We're together a lot. There isn't much to do when there aren't any customers."

He smiled. "And I thought I was the one doing all the secret observing." Her laughter was shy, well-reined. He went on, "I keep to myself. I'm not used to being noticed. What else have you seen?"

"Not much. Where are you from?"

"Minnesota. Why?"

She made a face. "I invented a whole background for you. You ruined it right away. I had you coming from Chicago."

"Really? Why?"

Raising a hand, she traced lines in the air an inch or so from his face. Lacking her touch on his skin, he felt it in his blood. She said, "Cheekbones. Eyes. I knew a girl from Chicago. Her dad was from someplace in Russia, you know? Where the Cossacks came from, she said. Anyhow, he had the same bones, and all."

Keeping her at a distance might be difficult. It might even be more dangerous, more intriguing to her, if he tried.

Is it that, or do I really want her to know me?

She was waiting, puzzlement growing at his delay. Carmody listened carefully for any telltale vocal stress as he answered,

"No Cossacks in our family. Just English and American shopkeepers. Dull."

Shaking her head, she disagreed. "Never try to kid someone about her own problem." At his glance, she added hurriedly, "Look, I know loneliness when I see it. And I know what it's like to be lonely because you won't take another chance on being hurt."

Words leaped from his lips. "I like being alone. Some of us value privacy."

Elise set her chin and met his eyes. "Play it any way you want. I didn't ask you any questions."

He forced a laugh. "That's true. You surprised me. I didn't think I was that transparent."

"Hardly transparent. All I can tell you is what I said—you keep away from other people by choice. I certainly wouldn't want to guess why."

"What's your own reason?"

Her eyes wavered before firming once more. "Good intentions, bad selection. I thought I was in love."

After a moment, Carmody said, "No," and ignored her quick tension, continuing. "You wouldn't make a mistake about that. You were in love. He wasn't."

"That's one hell of a leap to a conclusion."

"Maybe. Are you telling me I'm wrong?"

"No. I can't say that." She turned, made as if to walk away. He touched her shoulder. She faced him again. He said, "Make you a deal—you don't try to see through me, I won't try to see into you, okay?"

She smiled acceptance, and he said, "Just so we don't have to pry at each other, why don't we shut this place down, go have lunch, and get better acquainted?"

"I'd like that."

He caught the almost infinitesimal pause before she spoke. It made him want to laugh. If she thought talking with a man was taking a chance, how would she live with risk at his level?

The telephone rang as he reached for the door.

Nicolai. It was his call, as scheduled. Carmody checked his watch. Punctual to the minute.

It would be nothing. More stupid questions about progress with Summerton, as though Carmody needed prodding.

Elise moved away to answer it.

"Leave it alone!" She turned startled eyes on him, hand in midair above the receiver. He said, "We've earned some time of our own. Let's go." He pulled her from the counter, almost roughly. She took it as play, laughing like a child.

Conversation stumbled back and forth between them while he drove, mundane things about eating preferences, tastes in movies, sports. Each smiled a lot, hiding behind enthusiasms. They ate in a small, bright sandwich shop.

Afterward, as they headed for the car, Carmody said, "We've got some time, and it's a pretty day. Would you like to drive up to Volunteer Park and see what's going on at the museum?"

"Oh, yes!" There was no doubting her enthusiasm. "I haven't been there for months. Are you sure you can keep the store closed that long?"

He laughed. "The bosses always have the time."

In a matter of minutes, they were parked in front of the building. Elise seemed to expand in the glare of its white modernism. As they entered, Carmody watched her remaining tensions slip away, replaced by an open eagerness that drew him closer.

In the wing to the left was a Japanese painting, multiple panels spanning several feet. The subject was crows, dozens of them, velvet-black, caught in individual flying and feeding postures against a bold, gilded background. The work defied reality and forced the eye to accept this synthesis. It filled the room with windstorm activity.

Elise studied it in rapt silence for a full minute. Carmody watched her, comparing. The frozen swirl of the painting reminded him of the economy of her own movements. He touched her arm again, and she turned to him, still caught up in the piece. "I love that," she said. "Wouldn't it be marvelous to have something like that in your home, where you could sit and look at it whenever you wanted?"

"You'd get used to it," he said, joking. "Pretty soon you wouldn't even see it."

She shook her head. "Never." She linked her arm in his, leading him on. "I can't imagine why I haven't been back here for so long. It's wonderful."

"I didn't know you enjoyed art so much."

"We've never talked about it. It wouldn't make much difference if we did. I don't know anything about it."

"Half the people who say they do are lying. And the other half aren't sure if they are or not."

"What a cynic! Really down on the whole human race, aren't you?"

"Yes." The confession came too easily. "I wouldn't put it quite that strongly, but there's a lot of truth in what you say."

She studied him for a moment before turning back to the display cases. "Maybe your way's better."

"Meaning you want to think the best of people, but you keep remembering how much you believed in the man who hurt you."

Her chin came up a fraction of an inch. She continued to examine a selection of Chinese ceramics. "You said you wouldn't try to look inside."

"It was a bad bargain. Knowing about you is more important than I wanted to admit."

Without her tiny nod, he would have thought she hadn't heard him. They moved past the displays. Carmody was distracted from the museum's treasures by their own reflections in the protective glass. He wondered if any archaeologist ever unearthed anything so unrewarding as the set features of the two people mirrored there.

Breaking the silence, Elise said, "Maybe it'd be better if we promised each other to *really* listen. Most of us don't, you know? We hang in, waiting for someone to shut up so we can say what we're thinking. We don't pay attention."

He took her hand. "If we can do that, if we can hear each other—" He let the sentence trail off.

Her eyes were unable to hide wary relief. He had the feeling of holding a hand-tamed bird, a wild thing essaying acceptance rather than trust.

The man called Martin Carmody smiled for her. He was a

156

good creation, a plain man, with a plain name. He understood stability, the comfort of solid rules. Elise's instincts cried for surety, certainty—and offered sympathy. She could never take without giving.

Martin Carmody was on good, safe ground.

"How long were you married?" he asked.

"Four years. We lived together for almost two years before that. We wanted to be sure." Her laughter sawed the air, drawing covert attention from two passing women. Carmody steered her toward the front door, walking slowly. Elise accepted the new direction, continued talking. "As soon as we were married—legally—he expected me to start having babies. I told him I wasn't ready, I had things I wanted to do first. That's when he started hitting me."

They stepped into the daylight as she said it, the almost expressionless statement baldly incongruous in the soft afternoon.

Carmody said, "Why do you think he changed?"

Elise made a small throwing gesture. "I thought we got a marriage license. He thought he paid for a title, a pink slip."

"What were the things you wanted to do?"

"Wrong tense—want, not wanted. And I'll do them, too. See things. The Grand Canyon. New York. I want to swim in the Atlantic Ocean." Childishly enthusiastic, she took his arm in hers, hugged it to her. "Someday, when I have kids, I want to tell them I swam in both oceans, way out, so far I couldn't see land."

"You're crazy." He laughed, her warming pleasure overflowing into him. "Why so far out?"

"To make it something special. And I want to walk on the Appalachian Trail and eat at Antoine's in New Orleans."

"You won't have time for having those children."

"I will. I need it, Martin. I don't think I'm asking for so much, really. And I'm working for it."

They were across the street from the museum by then, standing by the huge Noguchi sculpture. Black polished stone, it throbbed in the heat, a massive irregular sun, pierced

157

through its center to frame city, sky, Sound, and the distant Olympics.

Elise said, "You haven't told me anything about yourself."

"There isn't much to tell. My wife found another man."

She reached up to cover his hand with hers. "I'm sorry."

"Yeah."

What could she know now of loneliness? The presumption of the thing wrenched his stomach, threatened to explode out onto the ground.

Yet, as it did, he knew there was no need to bring her pain. They could truly help each other.

As long as the world allowed, he'd be all the things she needed, be the man she needed.

But if that man was Martin Carmody, who was he? What did he want?

CHAPTER 16

Maddy irritably turned on the stereo. Candy notes, heavy with blunt harmonies, poured from the speakers. Her mood wanted more than that, and she spun the tuning knob until she found something classical. It played exactly to her frame of mind, darkly solemn.

Dropping into a chair, she glared at the telephone.

Steve might call. He might not.

And she wanted him to call.

If he did, she knew she'd handle it badly.

And if he didn't, she'd have to call him.

Merely acknowledging the possibility tightened her shoulder muscles, threatened to pull her into a slump. She resisted it, sat straighter. Still concentrating on the telephone, she spoke aloud. "Damn you, Steve Black! I am a single woman. A human being with my own mind and abilities. I spent a bundle to learn how to face up to that fact and enjoy myself. Don't you dare make me feel like I have to be afraid to be honest."

Confidence swelled in her.

Another, silent voice filled the room, a simpering, coy presence. It said, You'll be telling him you *like* him. He'll *know*.

She spoke aloud again, crushing the inner argument. "So he knows! So what? My God!"

Next week was her one chance for a vacation. It would be wasted if it wasn't spent near him.

A delicious weakness swept through her as she considered the sensual difference between "near him" and the more accurate "with him." Her mind didn't run to imaginative erotica, but there was a magnetism to him she no longer wanted to deny. And that was the problem with the phone call. How to tell him she wanted to visit him in Seattle? Being attracted to the man didn't mean automatically inviting herself into his bed.

The serious mental picture suddenly twisted, went all askew. She found herself laughing, almost embarrassed, as she continued her solitary conversation. "If the silly bastard had good sense, he'd have asked me to bed long ago. Poor innocent! How's he to know there's a semicrazed modern American woman prowling her apartment, calling him names because she's afraid to phone him?"

It was a stinging, dark humor that turned hurtful as quickly as it appeared. Her next image was of Steve, put off by aggressiveness, mouthing soft, trite good-byes as he sprinted for safety.

She rose abruptly, moving to the kitchen with a deepening sense of frustration, a conviction that nothing was going to go right. The lid slipped off the coffee pot as she poured herself a fresh cup, sending a stream of hot liquid across the counter and onto the floor. Spatters hit her ankles and she yelled, more in fright than actual pain.

"Damn! *God*damn!" She lowered the cup to the counter, grabbed paper towels to clean up the steaming mess, repeating herself. "Damn. *Damn!*"

The phone rang. She flung the wet towels at the wastebasket, frowning at the sodden splat of the miss. When she picked up the handset, she paused long enough to take a deep breath and brush back her hair. Then, calmly, she said, "Hello?" letting her voice rise on the last syllable. The word became greeting, question, and conditional invitation.

An unformed, childlike soprano said, "Mrs. Hosmer?" and without waiting for an answer, plunged ahead. "This is

160

Meg, and I'm with Ready Eddie's Rug and Carpet Cleaners. We're having our big quarterly special—"

"I'm not interested. Sorry."

"O-kay. Thanks anyway. Have a nice day."

Hanging up, Maddy noted the time. Nice day, hell—it was nearly eight. Little chance of Steve calling. She remembered the spilled coffee with a start, hurrying back into the kitchen.

She was almost finished when the phone rang again. She answered icily.

"Are you okay?" Worry rushed Steve's question.

"Oh, it's you." Her face warmed.

"Yeah. Listen, if you're expecting another call or something, I can call back."

"No, it's all right. I was just— Oh, the hell with it, it's too long a story. How are you?"

"Fine. Just fine." He sounded as if the repetition was his own reassurance. "Things are pretty quiet. What's new down there?"

Maddy asked about Jane, anxious to get that out of the way quickly. As she feared, the subject brought up his defenses. Sometimes the slightest reference to his work had the same effect, only worse. It frightened Maddy when it happened, made her think he was willing himself out of contact, pulling back into himself. He answered briefly. "Jane's fine."

She said, "When are you coming back down this way?"

"I wish I knew. I'm trying to work out a trip, one that'll keep me in town for a few days."

"Don't you ever get any time off?"

"Oh, sure, but it wouldn't be easy just now." The reserve was there instantly. Originally, she'd thought it was a form of modesty, but that notion waned quickly. Then she wondered if he deflected investigation because his work was sensitive. That carried the pleasant tingle of vague mystery, maybe a hint of danger. Eventually, when she was alone, the echoes of their conversations had convinced her neither impression was true. It startled and hurt her to concede that he walled her off.

"Are you there?"

161

Flustered, Maddy said, "Yes, sure. I was just thinking."

"How about you? Could you manage a trip up this way? A long weekend, or something?"

She knew she should say yes. What came out was, "I don't know, Steve. The business—"

I could bite my tongue off. Why did I say that?

"You've got people there. Let them run it for a day or two."

"I suppose I could. I'm awfully tired." *Dear God, it's a reflex!*

"So give yourself a break. The weatherman says we're in for a taste of early summer. It's beautiful now, warm."

"It'll rain."

"Good for the complexion. When'll you get here?"

"I couldn't possibly leave for a week. But what about your job? If I come up there, you'll just be going to work."

"We'll have the weekend, and I'll make some free time as long as you're in town. How long can you stay?"

"Three days—four at the most."

"That's great, Maddy! You like sailing?"

She had to laugh at his enthusiasm. "I've never tried it."

"You'll love it. When will you get here?"

"I'll call you. I have to make reservations."

"Leave the room to me. I know just the place for you. Close enough so I can get to you quick and far enough so you don't have to worry about me breathing down your neck all the time."

"My goodness—sailing, heavy breathing, the whole works." She laughed, and he echoed it.

This was the way it should be, she told herself. She was shocked by her pleasure at the anticipation in his voice. They hung up only after he determined she'd be home for another call the next night.

She sat at her vanity and lingered over her preparations for bed, brushing her hair while her eyes remained fixed on a distant point. Steve was far more rugged than handsome. Thank God it wasn't his looks that appealed to her, she thought. Her first husband had been exciting to look at, and that was his one good mark. Steve had a quality, something

162

like a capability. He tried to understand what was going on *inside*.

She thought about it, and the hair stirred on her arms.

He drew you with those eyes, looked into you and pulled your words, your thoughts, your life right up to the surface. It was a penetration more total than sex, but he'd never made her feel he was demanding surrender, or violating her. While that link held, she was part of what was happening to him. They were a single entity. The rest of the world was excluded.

She sat bolt upright. There it was again, "excluded." He could exclude the world. He was one who would weave a woman into his life, into his personality. What about her own need for retreat, her own walls?

The steeled woman who called herself Maddy remembered how the girl who had been Madeline died at being excluded. It took a long time to come to terms with the need for survival and need to permit vulnerability. The woman had learned to respond to her own wants, to bend to those of a man and still spring back. Was there room in Steve's probing look for that kind of woman? Or would he smother her, demand that she surrender the force that made her an individual?

She was a long time falling asleep.

When she saw him waiting at the end of the ramp connecting plane and terminal, she reminded herself that she was in Seattle for a vacation. This was no husband-hunt.

He greeted her clumsily, unsure if he should embrace her, nervous about kissing her. She stepped up to him, putting herself inside the round of his arms, kissed him on the cheek. He held her a split second longer and a bit tighter than mere greeting required. He stepped back, hands on her shoulders, and her worries evaporated at the straightforward delight in his eyes.

He said, "It's good to see you! Welcome to Seattle. How was your trip? Everything okay? I told you I'd arrange a warm spell." He took her arm while she told him everything was fine. He laughed happily, leading her away. They chatted through the wait at the baggage rondel and during the walk across the skybridge to the parking lot. Driving away, he pointed out Mt. Rainier. "First thing in the morning, we'll drive up to Paradise Lodge, spend the day getting you acquainted with our mountain."

"You share ownership, do you?"

"That's the way everyone sees it. 'Ours.' "

He gave her the full guided tour on the drive to town, naming the more prominent Olympic peaks as they came into view on the left, identifying some of the logos on the aircraft parked outside Boeing's huge facility. Then they were in the city, turning off the freeway that slashed through the buildings like a canyon riverbed. They climbed a steep hill to an older hotel. Maddy was less than enthusiastic until she was inside. She turned wide eyes to Steve.

"This has to have been restored! They couldn't have kept it like this since it was built!"

"I thought you'd like it." He shifted her luggage to one hand, put the other arm around her. "Nice, isn't it?"

She searched for a word. "It's opulent! What a darling place!" While he took care of booking her in, she drifted through the lobby, savoring it. Her practiced eye inspected everything, enjoying the rich materials, the polished wood. She breathed deeply, tasting the full-bodied air of the place.

In her room, she went directly to the window. She tensed as Black joined her and put his arm around her. She spoke without taking her eyes from the view. "I'd never have found this hotel. If anything else on this trip is as nice as this, I may hate you for talking me into coming up here."

"I'll try to make it up to you."

She gave him her best raised eyebrow and said, "If we're going mountaineering tomorrow, what've you got for us today?"

"A ride around the area," he said, indicating the door. "The lake, the floating bridge—the arboretum is beautiful now—all that stuff."

They were at the door on their way out when he suddenly whirled and faced her, catching her totally unaware. He took her in his arms and kissed her. It spoke of powerful yearning held in check only by an equal restraint. He was gentle, and under it pulsed a maleness that filled her with a fear she cherished. Then he released her, stepped back.

He said, "I couldn't wait. I've dreamed of it."

She swallowed before speaking, knowing her voice would tremble anyhow. "Me too. But we have to be careful, Steve. Please."

Hands raised, palms toward her, he said, "That's why I waited until we were on our way out. I didn't think doing it as soon as we came in was all that safe."

Ducking past him, she grinned from the hall. "Come on, then."

He did, turning to check the lock, and she thought that if he tended to be overpowering, it was only natural. He was, after all, as bulky as a bear, a wonderful combination of strength and tenderness. She hurried on down the hall without waiting for him to catch the swift change in her color.

Maddy lived through that day and the next in a state of almost fevered awareness, knowing that some of the impressions coming to her would necessarily be forgotten. She wanted to hoard it all. She caught herself thinking in phrases, playing with words as she scanned a tumble of mountains or the crash of a waterfall, trying to construct sentences that would commit each sight and sound to memory. And Steve was ever-present, enjoying through her. No one had ever treated her quite that way. Antique phrases came to her. "Catered to," she thought, and "being courted." As with the kiss in the hotel room and the others that followed, his actions continued to carry a sad aftertaste of rigid constraint. The desire to test the fires beneath the will picked at her.

Sunday night they ate dinner in a lakefront restaurant that shouldered its way out over the water. An almost palpable smell of burning alder and cooking salmon extended into the surrounding neighborhood, a selling technique beyond any advertiser's skill. It poured through the open car windows and captured Maddy. She was famished by the time she crossed the threshold. Luck was with them, and they sat next to a window, where they had an unobstructed view of the boat traffic. To the right gleamed the city, and on the left the arching mass of a highway bridge looked down on them. As the darkness thickened, the various lights took on more urgency.

After dinner, they sat in the bar. Conversation struggled, limped back and forth. In the end, it was Steve who broached the issue.

"We're going to have to do something about us, Maddy. I can't get away to visit you often enough. I need you nearby."

Nodding, she kept her eyes on an approaching cruiser. Jeweled green and red running lights framed the gaping rectangular eye of the cabin. Silver-speckled wake curled from the bow.

Steve went on, "We've got something important going. How do we keep from losing it?"

The words cut. She thought, I thought my life had that importance once. I still want it, to share days and nights of being in love, to experience the wholeness of being a woman without suffering the humiliation of being used and discarded. But how do I tell a man like Steve a thing like that without either frightening him away or putting an unbearable obligation on him?

He would ask her to move to Seattle. She was sure of it, and her head swam with being wanted and being asked to abandon everything she'd built.

She sipped her drink. "Could you get transferred to the Bay area?"

"I won't even have control of my weekends for a long time."

"Your work load can't be that heavy."

"It's the way things come up. When there's a break, I have to move on it."

"I don't understand. These 'things' aren't all running away, are they? What's so damned urgent?"

He looked away from her. "That's not the issue. We are. It's this simple—I can't get to San Francisco to see you often, and I want to be able to see you all the time."

"I've got a business, Steve. I broke my back putting it together. I've got a goddammed *clientele,* man, just like the big stores. You can't see what you're asking?"

"Yes, I can." His eyes sought hers. Wounded by what he saw, he lowered his gaze to his drink. "Maybe, when

166

this is over—" The unfinished sentence dangled between them.

Maddy said, "When what's over?" and wished she'd choked on the words. A muscle under Steve's left eye jerked. It stopped as soon as he spoke. "The case I'm working on presently. It's nothing important." He gestured for the check. "How about a moonlight ride on the ferry to Bremerton and back, and I'll take you sailing tomorrow?"

Waiting until he was pocketing the credit receipt, she said, "I don't want to go on the ferry tonight, Steve. I'm too tired to enjoy it. Where's your boat?"

"South of town, about forty-five minutes' drive. Place called Des Moines."

"Can we see it tonight?"

"Sure. Not much to it. Just a thirty-four-footer. She's no big-time yacht, understand."

"Sounds yacht-y to me. I've never been on a sailboat in my life."

He stopped, the open restaurant door forgotten in his hand. "Not even once?"

"Cross my heart." She laughed at his expression, then laughed harder when another couple took advantage of his holding the door, walking past with grins. She took his arm. "I've been in a couple of motorboats, but never been sailing. My mother warned me about sailors."

He squeezed the arm against his side. "I'll try to live up to the reputation."

At the Des Moines marina, Steve led Maddy through the gate and out onto the dock. There was only one other vessel being tended to, far removed from them. Maddy was impressed by the size of his boat.

"You said it wasn't a yacht! It looks like the *Queen Mary*! The little mast in the back looks like a tree, and the big one goes up to the sky!" The slim hull caught a wave and bowed as if acknowledging her excitement. It continued to roll easily, like a good horse waiting to be unreined. Rigging slapped, and a fender crushed against the dock, exhaling a long, impatient sigh. Maddy reached to grab Steve's shoulder.

"Can we go inside?"

Indulgently, he said, "We can go aboard. Then we'll go below. Can you remember that?"

She was already stripping off her high heels, clambering over the side. "You know what you can do with your dumb sailor lingo, too. Boats are all 'she,' and us girls understand each other without that stuff."

He followed her. In the dim light of the marina, she moved from point to point as much by touch as by sight, her hands lingering, trailing over the mast, lines, and fittings. She even bent to run fingers across the deck before returning to Steve.

"She's a darling, Steve, just wonderful! So smooth and neat! I can hardly wait to go out!"

"I'm glad you like her. She's called *White Music*."

Her laughter stopped, cut off by a suddenly startled expression. "Oh, yes. How'd you think of that?"

He shrugged. "She's white. I like music." He gestured. "She's packed with stereo stuff. I like to go out, turn it up, and listen."

"I want to see."

Showing her how to work the hatch, he led her below, then put a record on the turntable. The first sound was a blow, a tremendous flourish of trumpets. He turned it down quickly, apologizing. "I forgot how loud I had it going last time out." The music, soft now, was heavy in the cabin. Maddy sat on the couch, looking and listening. When Steve suddenly appeared in front of her with a glass of wine, she accepted it with an absent smile. After a while, she stirred as if waking, and moving quickly to him, stared into his eyes. "You love this boat, don't you?"

"I guess I do. Yes. She keeps my head from blowing up."

She put her hand to his cheekbone, fingers stroking his temple. "I envy you. I truly do. I wish I had a place to hide."

For an instant, he was gone, and she watched him come back into his eyes with a feeling of triumph. She went on, "Are you allowed to go sailing at night?"

"Would you like to?"

"Very much."

Silently, he moved past her and up onto the deck. She

heard his shoes thump on the deck by the wheel as he took them off and dropped them. The engine started, growled heavily to life under her, settled to work with steady, animal-like heartbeats. When she stuck her head out the hatch, he was casting off the last line, shoving off, and she climbed up to be beside him. He jumped aboard, hurrying to the controls, backing into the slip channel. As soon as they were clear of the jetty, he hoisted sails and cut the engine.

Maddy was sure there was nothing finer. The cool darkness swept through her hair, stroked her clothing to her body. On shore, the lights of homes and automobiles fought the dark. She laughed out loud at the foolishness, the waste of it. The night, the blackness, were to be enjoyed. She turned her attention to the water, watched the bow splinter the reflections of stars with headlong carelessness.

"Where to, Captain? The South Seas? The Gold Coast? Fabled India?"

"I'll settle for this. That's all the romance I need."

She kissed his cheek. "When you say it, it is romance, buddy, and you better watch it or you'll get yourself in a heap of trouble."

"You scare me to death."

From behind, she wrapped her arms around him. "I'm glad I came up here, Steve. I haven't been this happy since—" She paused. "I can't remember *ever* being this happy."

He covered her linked hands with one of his. "I'm glad, Maddy."

For the better part of an hour they cruised, the only sounds the eager hull against the water, the sough of wind across canvas.

Steve pointed at the bulking mass ahead. "Blake Island," he said. "The whole island's a park. The only way to reach it's by boat." He altered course, heeling over a few degrees. Maddy clung to him, peering around. At the increased angle of the deck under her, her confidence in her circumstances altered as well. The land became a threat, blacker than the night, tensed above her. A glance to the right gave quick reassurance, the spangled lights of the mainland. Peculiarly, she was pulled back to the island. Her initial fright receded,

169

leaving curiosity, a wondering that wanted to press into that darkness and know it. When she looked again at the vivid lights, they contrasted with the timeless stars overhead as infant babble raised against ancient hymns.

Suddenly, Steve twisted the wheel, and the boat rose sharply at the bow. Before she understood what was happening, he disengaged her hands and scuttled forward busying himself at something.

"What's wrong? What's happening?"

"Nothing." His voice was calm. "I'm stopping her for a bit." The sail collapsed with a coarse whisper of disappointment. The boat continued to bob, but with decreasing moment. Steve continued to work for a minute, and she heard the splash of the anchor and the sibilance of line paying out. It seemed completely unremarkable to be able to identify the sounds with such certainty, although she'd never heard them before. "Come sit with me," he called to her, stretching out, back against the mast.

She did, pretending to sulk. "You scared me. Why didn't you tell me you were stopping?"

"Wanted to scare you. Remind you you're in me power out here. Pirates, buccaneers, all that."

Maddy knew she was supposed to respond with something light. They would sit here for a while, admiring the view, sensing the heavy depths beneath them, listening for the splash of feeding fish. Not once would either of them speak of what was becoming a force to separate them.

She decided against it.

"I don't want to go back tonight." The precision of her voice amazed her. "Let's stay on the boat." Her head dropped to rest on his shoulder. She hadn't really thought of doing that.

His arm moved behind her. He said, "You don't have to do this, Maddy."

"I know that. Maybe we shouldn't. I don't know. But what we're doing is stupid, and it's getting worse. We're two people with a lot of problems, but each other isn't one of them. Being together without sharing what we have, what we

170

need—it's pretending we don't know each other, or we don't care about each other. That's obscene."

He shifted, intruding himself between her and the shore, the bulk of him blocking the lights. In the darkness, his face was dim, the eyes no more than a vague gleam. He lifted her chin, kissed her. It lingered, and soon she felt his hand drift across her breast, as light and slow as the swells moving the boat. Her breath altered to sharp, quick inhalations, and she pulled her face away from his, eyes drawn to the thick fingers at the tiny buttons of her blouse. They moved with a magician's smooth dexterity, yet impatience and need racked her as though he deliberately tantalized. Each touch of his hands sent new waves of heat pulsing through her veins. Her mouth and lips were dry, unconcerned parties to the small sounds she made.

His breath was as strained as hers, she noted distantly, and then a hand at the small of her back lifted her buttocks from the deck with almost effortless ease. His movements were different now, a physical, tactile urgency that leaped from him like electricity. She heard him brush her clothes away, and he put both arms under her, preparing to pick her up, and she gripped his biceps.

"No." The word was faint as breath in her own ears, and she repeated it. "No. Here."

Wordlessly, he lowered her, then straightened. Indistinct against the moon-dark night, he loomed hugely, legs spread against the rolling motion of the hull as he undressed. He brought his feet together to drop his trousers. In that moment, he formed a wedge, a living statement of penetration, pale against the sky. The burst of fear in her stomach was immediately swallowed by an exultant anticipation she neither understood or questioned. Then, with no conscious awareness of his having moved, she was helping him, guiding him, and he was inside her.

When he lay next to her, spent, she rested on her side within the curve of his arm. He'd held her close for a while, a hand stroking her, trying to stay awake to talk. He'd lasted a few minutes. Now he was solidly unconscious, breathing steadily, unaware of her examination. The warm breeze tugged

171

at his forelock, drawing it back and forth across his forehead. She brushed it smooth again, then lowered her head softly to his chest. The heart thudding against her ear was calming.

Their sex had been unlike anything she'd imagined, but it went beyond physical enjoyment, and now that she could think in a leisurely, relaxed manner, the simple truth of that awed her.

She knew too little about him and had the frightening feeling he meant it to be that way. Still, she cared for him, about him. In spite of his reticence about himself, he cared for her. She knew it, felt it, as surely as the winter-bound wall knows the sun. It would be that way with them, warming and protecting them. It couldn't be a matter of guarding psychological territories, of warring over rights and obligations. They'd have something that belonged to two people who belonged to each other, each multiplying the strength and pleasure of the partner.

That was the way it was supposed to be.

CHAPTER 17

WILL SMILED AT THE MAN BEHIND THE COUNTER. "YOU been managing this motel long?"

"If you're a cop, you already know I own it. If you ain't a cop, you're wasting my time." The face spoke of a lifetime of failed opportunities. Bored, watery eyes measured Will through wire-rimmed glasses. Antagonism projected from the blank features without altering a single wrinkle. Will considered looking away, but changed his mind. At least the face was alive. The lobby was a plastic repetition. For Will, places like this not only failed individuality, but somewhere along the line they'd ceased to exist. It took a conscious effort to remember one, to render a true image from the crushing sameness. On the other hand, the names and faces he dealt with never escaped him.

He put a large black briefcase on the counter and displayed private-investigator credentials. "I'm not looking for anything that'll make trouble for you. Another horny husband, that's all." From the case, he showed the clerk a glossy of Alex. It was an artfully retouched surveillance shot. Alex would never have recognized the tuxedo whimsically provided by a bored darkroom expert. Will said, "Here's the guy I'm checking out. We think he's been coming here for a long time."

"We?" Only the clerk's lips moved.

"His wife and me." Will smiled broadly, leaned an elbow on the counter. "She's generous. There's money in it."

"How much?"

"If you can show me when and where he stayed here, I can find twenty-five bucks for you."

Dentures flashed in a snarling smile that made Will think of an abused dog. "That don't get you a look at the fire-escape plan."

Controlling a quick surge of excitement, Will said, "Hey, no offense, man. I'm just looking for a number, you know? Let's try fifty, okay?"

"Two hundred."

"To check cards? How do I know he was even here?"

"Don't try to shit me. I've as much as said he was. You want more, it costs two hundred."

"I don't carry that kind of cash."

The plastic teeth flashed again. "You think I take fucking Visa? Come back when you got it."

Opening the door to the searing sun, Will turned. "I have to know about *all* his visits here." Wordlessly, the clerk rubbed thumb and forefinger together.

Waves of heat rippled off the sidewalk and tickled Will's nose. For a moment, he thought he'd have to sneeze, and he damned the Bay-area weather that demanded warm clothes in the morning and cooked a man in them in the afternoon. His earlier excitement returned, displaced the physical discomfort. If this lead was as good as it felt, Black's case would have a momentum no one could stop. All the footsie about who got medals would be shoved aside.

He performed the correct ritual at the bank machine and pocketed the bills. They made an interesting wad. He smiled grimly. Why would the clerk risk so much for so little? Two hundred was a nice number, but the man had sold his entire future.

From now on, any time Will asked, he'd answer.

Going on the take was like losing virginity, Will told himself yet again. You only lost it one way and it never came back. Sometimes he felt sorry for people so stunted they'd sell any aspect of their lives if the price was right.

174

Occasionally he saw himself in a parallel situation. He traded in confidences, privacies, covert observations. There was no denying it. Still, he told himself, he worked for principle as well as a salary. And his real quarry were professionals, as dedicated as he was.

When he reentered the motel lobby, a reedlike man with a matching voice was checking in. His wife stood behind him as if ready to push if he faltered. She ignored the squalling baby in her arms. The clerk glared past the father at the child. Will waited patiently, apparently lost in study of the parking lot. The family was barely outside when the clerk exploded. "Cheap bastards! Sucking for a minimum rate, goddam kid blowing snot all over."

Will fanned the bills like playing cards. "Show me the records. And I need some privacy."

"No kidding." The clerk scooped the money. "The office is back here." He slouched, one shoulder ahead of the other. The bent body suggested muscle and bone twisted by a furious mind that warped everything it touched. When he gestured at the filing cabinet, he looked beyond, through the dirty window to the growling boulevard traffic a few yards distant. He said, "Called himself Allard. You got fifteen minutes. But I'll tell you right now, he always come alone, left alone. No funny business. I think you pissed away your money."

"Maybe. How come you remember him so well?"

The clerk bristled. "I remember him, that's all."

"You remember all your repeaters?"

"He was here enough. I told you." The eyes behind the glasses skittered like small bright beetles in a bottle. "He don't mean nothing to me." He tossed his head, a comically coltish move.

"You're lying." The easy flow, the insistent confidentiality, dropped away. Will's voice was naked stone. "We'll talk about that later. Close the door when you leave."

The clerk mustered a final piece of bravado. "Fifteen minutes, buddy. That's it."

"When I'm done. You understand? *I* tell *you*. You want to complain, call a cop. Now get out."

175

The man hesitated until Will took a half-step his way, then scuttled backward out of the room. An afterthought brought him to an abrupt stop, and he reached back to pull the door shut.

Alone, Will pulled Black's list of dates from his pocket and started flicking through the registration cards. At the first appearance of Alex's alias, he allowed himself a heavy sigh and a momentary pause. Then, from the briefcase, he took a slim-legged tripod and set it up. The apex of the triangle was about five feet above the floor. He attached a tiny camera, aimed straight down. A weighted chain from the tripod gave him a center, and he measured off a square from that point, indicating the corners with thumbtacks. Returning to the files, he pulled all the registration cards with Alex's date of arrival. Positioning as many as would fit in the square, he photographed them, then repeated the process until all were copied. He did the same thing for the days immediately before and after Alex's arrival as well.

He returned the cards and looked at the list again, making a face. Alex had liked this motel. Will resignedly dug into the files.

In the lobby, the clerk dialed a number at his switchboard. After the second ring, he muttered under his breath, stealing a glance at the office door. A voice interrupted him.

"Alliance Answering Service."

"I've got a message for Mr. Arthur King. Tell him to call Ed Slidell. He knows the number."

"Thank you. Mr. Arthur King is to call Ed Slidell—is that correct, sir?"

"That's it." He hung up in the middle of a rote thank-you.

When the communications assistant brought the note to Nicolai, he stared at it and frowned. Finally, shifting the gaze to the man, he asked, "Exactly why are you bothering me?"

The man swallowed loudly. "Comrade Leskov arranged a communications link with certain people. They were instructed to call the Alliance Answering Service and ask for a particular name. It was a way for people to report to him if something important came to their attention. Comrade Leskov instructed us to contact the answering service every hour for messages.''

"Leskov never mentioned such a thing to me."

"Perhaps he had no time—" The explanation stopped abruptly.

Nicolai let him dangle a few seconds, watched the breath rate increase. "Leskov was a fool, but he did some things acceptably. What does this message mean, precisely?"

It took another gulp for the man to answer. "A man named Edwin Slidell owns a motel that Comrade Leskov used as a meeting site for a resident—who, I do not know—and the resident's agents. Slidell was instructed to call the Alliance service and ask for Mr. Arthur King if anyone asked about Comrade Leskov. When staying at Slidell's motel, Comrade Leskov used the name Allard."

"And Slidell has called?"

"Yes."

"And I am to return the call. Does Slidell belong to us?"

"No. According to Comrade Leskov's communication plan, Slidell knows only that he will be paid for informing 'Mr. Allard' that someone has asked questions about him."

Rising quickly, Nicolai said, "Give me the number. Is there anything else I should know?"

"The call is to be returned from a randomly selected pay phone, using the name 'Mr. Allard' as identification. That is all Comrade Leskov's communication plan says, comrade."

Nicolai pressed the button on his desk intercom. "Have Ivan meet me in front of the building. We will use the small Ford." He straightened to face the communications assistant. His eyes burned up at the younger man, and his voice hummed with anger. "You called Leskov and me 'comrade' in the same sentence. If you choose to call the traitor Leskov by an honorific, I can only make note of the fact. But if you associate my name with his again, I will make you regret it." He brushed past.

Twenty minutes later Slidell's phone rang. At the sound of the familiar accent, a smile started across his face, quickly giving way to a nervous frown. The name was right, but this

177

voice was sharper. Threat lurked in the words. Slidell said, "I've been waiting for your call," and cocked his head in intense concentration.

Nicolai said, "I returned it as soon as I got word from my answering service. You have a message for me?"

Slidell knew it wasn't the man who called himself Allard. He said, "You're not Allard. Who are you?" The pouring silence from the phone frightened him. He told himself he was being foolish. His eyes searched the parking lot, regardless.

"Mr. Allard has been transferred. I hold his position now," Nicolai said.

"Oh." Just his luck, Slidell thought. A chance to make a few bucks and blow the whistle on that smart-assed peeper at the same time, and it was turning to shit.

Speaking into the pause, Nicolai said, "Mr. Allard would still be interested to know what questions were asked. I am authorized to pay."

"Hey, all right," Slidell said, then, slyly, "What would it be worth to see the guy who's doing the asking?"

"Double the original figure." Nicolai responded instantly, but the threat hidden in the voice was suddenly dominant. Slidell's notion of demanding more burned to ashes at the sound.

"Did Allard tell you the name of my place?"

"I have it."

"Well, the guy's here now. Maybe you can catch him before he leaves."

"I will try."

"So how do I know if you saw him? I mean, you said you'd give me twice the money, but what if—?"

Nicolai cut him off. "You will get your money in any case, Mr. Slidell. Trust me. But first, listen. Be sure this man does not leave for at least five minutes. When he does, come outside with him. As he walks away, pretend to adjust a button on your shirt. Is that clear?"

"That's all?"

"I will contact you again. Your money will be delivered by messenger." Nicolai hung up, gesturing his car to him. Getting in, he told the driver, "I was right to come here. Pull

178

into the shopping center ahead of us. It is directly across the boulevard from the motel. We will watch from there. Have the camera ready.''

When Will told Slidell he wanted to talk to him out front, he made one of the major mistakes of his life. He compounded the error beyond repair by attributing Slidell's preoccupation with a shirt button to nervousness. He told Slidell, ''I may be back.''

Slidell bared his teeth again. ''Don't bother.''

Will laughed easily. ''You'll learn to love me. I'll see you're well paid.''

''Forget it. There's too much aggravation.''

''Maybe right now. But you think about it. Be seeing you.''

As soon as he turned away from Slidell's awkward figure, Will felt the observation. It took all his strength to resist searching for it. Instead, he snapped his fingers ostentatiously and returned to Slidell, grinning broadly, hand extended. Nonplussed, Slidell accepted it, looking bleak.

''Who did you tell I was here?'' The light in Will's eyes shouted at Slidell to forget the artificial smile.

''Nobody. Christ, man, they'd bust my ass for letting you fuck around in my registrations! What're you talking about?'' He glanced about wildly before Will's pressure on the hand stopped him.

''Don't!'' Will said. ''Get back inside!'' Slidell hurried away.

It was a blow-out. Will was certain he was under surveillance. The taste of it coated his tongue. Hypersensitive, he registered the heat waves stroking his face. The brick facade of the motel suddenly loomed in his vision, the jagged pores in the clay like fresh scars. He walked to his car, started it, maneuvered onto the boulevard.

Now was the time to see them. This was where the hunter had to make a move, to pursue. He toyed with the idea of simply losing them, discarding it immediately.

A car pulled out of the shopping center, a blue Ford Escort, moving quickly.

There were two figures in the front seat. In the glare of the sun from behind, it could have been two men, two women, two boys. Chewing his lip, Will turned off the boulevard. If the car was following him, he had to get rid of that sunshine, identify the passengers.

The car continued straight ahead.

Residences lined the street, smug homes with thermopane eyes that watched, unconcerned. No car followed his.

He stopped at the curb, opening the hood. Inch by inch, he inspected the car. Nothing was attached to it. A car came down the street and he tensed, waiting. It passed, neither the young housewife or her grade-school daughter favoring him with a glance.

Getting back inside, he squeezed the steering wheel. There had been someone. He knew it.

A woman peered nervously out her picture window at him. He drove away.

Nicolai was beating an impatient tattoo on his desk when Ivan entered the office. He greeted the driver coldly. "How long can it take to develop film and look through our picture files? Do we know so many American agents it takes hours to look at their faces? Is it so difficult to find out who owns a car in this country?"

"A great many more people own cars here, comrade."

"I am not interested in excuses, especially stupid economic slanders. Report."

"The man is not in our files. The car is registered to William Walters. He is a private investigator."

"That is his cover, you mean."

"It is a legitimate business."

Nicolai's thin lips crept upward. "You have an interesting wit sometimes, Ivan." The thin smile left a lingering pall. "Obviously, the man is counterintelligence. His cover is unimportant. I want to talk to Slidell."

Nicolai called from the same phone booth he'd used earlier. Slidell's fearful objection to a meeting amused him almost as much as the man's greedy reconsideration when payment was discussed.

Nicolai directed Ivan to go get Slidell and drive around until he was certain there was no surveillance. Then he would deliver him to Nicolai in the cocktail lounge of the shopping center's restaurant.

When Ivan arrived with Slidell, they sat in a booth. Nicolai remained at the bar.

Slidell's nervous eyes worked constantly, even during the compulsive polishing of his glasses, when it was obvious he saw nothing without them. Watching in the bar mirror, Nicolai understood that each time the man bent forward across the table, he was impatiently asking when the meeting would get underway. Certain they were unobserved, Nicolai waited anyhow. It would be good for Ivan to contend with this crippled fool, he told himself. The entire staff had grown sloppy—following Leskov's example, probably—and several strict lessons were in order.

He caught a questioning glance from Ivan and seethed inwardly, deliberately frowning in response. Checking his watch, he decided to let them wait another full two minutes before joining them.

As he slipped into the booth across from Slidell, he said, "Mr. Allard asked me to find out what the private investigator said today."

Slidell dropped his ignored attempt to shake hands, picking up his drink instead. He stared at the glass, thrust his chin out. "I took good care of Allard, or whatever his name is. You tell him that. The guy wanted to know all about him. I told him Allard was only there a couple times. Made him wait while I pulled the registration cards, both times. That was so you could get here to see him." He winked.

"What else did he ask you?"

"That's it."

Nicolai nodded. "How did he identify Mr. Allard? Did he describe him, did he know exactly what date he stayed in your establishment?"

"He had a picture. Allard in a tuxedo."

It startled Nicolai before it occurred to him that such decadence only fit the pattern he'd already seen. "He asked no questions about Mr. Allard's activities?"

181

Slidell looked from the drink to Nicolai. He squinted, eyes cunning. "The guy said Allard's wife wanted evidence for a divorce. That's bullshit."

"Oh?"

"Oh?" Slidell mocked Nicolai, raising his brows. "Everybody thinks Ed Slidell's some kind of dumb, fucking tool. Well, he's not. Allard didn't screw around in my place, or I'd of known it. He was a businessman, a foreigner. So are you. I think you guys are into some sort of industrial spying. I read about it all the time."

"True, we are from another country, but we are legitimate businessmen, I assure you."

Slidell gestured widely. "I don't give a rat's ass. We're talkin' about making money, man. And I can help you guys."

Nicolai almost said, "Oh?" again, but caught himself. "How can you help us?"

"Listen, when the FBI gets on your case, they stay on it. I can jockey a few records, stall them whenever they come around." When Nicolai's dead eyes failed to brighten, Slidell added, "Or I could help them. Take your pick."

"Ah." Nicolai congratulated himself for waiting. The man was as predictable as arithmetic. "You think we should pay you for your silence, is that correct?"

"That's it, buddy."

Leaning closer, Nicolai closed his mind to the stink washing out of Slidell's lungs. "Perhaps you can help us. Sometimes we need a safe place to meet, you understand?"

"No sweat." Slidell waved the drink, spilled some, drained the rest. Ivan ordered another. Slidell thanked him, then, "Fix you up anytime. Comfort and conveniences. All of 'em, if you get my drift?" He leered at the waitress as she put his drink on the table, then guffawed for his hosts' benefit. He poured the whiskey down, unaware of the trickle sliding from the corner of his mouth. It gathered in a pendant drop at his chin. Belatedly, he swiped at it with the back of his hand.

Nicolai got to his feet. "We will be in touch with you. It

182

would be better if we discussed business in a more private place."

"Gotcha." Slidell winked as he rose. While Ivan took care of the bill, Nicolai walked him to the door and watched him cross the boulevard to his motel.

Back in their car, Nicolai signaled Ivan to drive, then stared at the lights flashing past, unspeaking, for a full fifteen minutes. Finally, Ivan said, "Will we really continue to use that man, comrade?"

"Yes," Nicolai said, enjoying Ivan's consternation from the corner of his eye. "He is exactly what I need. Unlike some people, I make use of everything the enemy provides me. Our entire organization here is a disgrace. Decadence has infected you all. Leskov has endangered one of our most vital nets. I shall right those wrongs. With one blow, I will remind our people of their proper function and make all our residents and their entire apparatus aware of our strong arm once again."

Ivan said, "I didn't realize the situation had gotten so bad, comrade. I, for one—"

"You are not as bad as most. That's why I intend to work with you first, allow you to lead the way, with me, in the repairs I must accomplish."

"I appreciate it, comrade. Can I ask what you mean to do?"

"We are going to show our people and the American fools that we get what we are supposed to get and that we protect our people."

The car wavered as Ivan cut his eyes to Nicolai. The small, taut face was as cold as ever. He said, "A large order, comrade. It will take stern measures."

Nicolai agreed, nodding briskly. "The precise word. Stern. You asked if I meant to use Slidell, and I said yes. I also mean to use the counterintelligence man. They will be my examples. You will kill them."

CHAPTER 18

THE SUN PICKED AT THE REMAINS OF THE NIGHT, BRINGING reluctant colors and life to the new day. Sitting up, Will leaned against the headboard, hoarding his own darkness. Silent, he watched as shapes in the room altered from obscurity to familiar objects. Outside, where it was brighter yet, a bird flipped across open spaces in the avocado tree. On each new perch, it busily pecked at the bark for a moment before stopping to raise a trilling cheer at having survived another night. Will wished he knew what kind it was. Bobbie would like hearing about it.

He looked down at her hair spread across the pillow, framing the plain, honest face. Even now, with her features blurred in the softness of sleep, he reveled in what he saw there. In truth, the bone structure was no better than average, the complexion a triumph of unguents over dry skin. Nose and lips were good, the arch of dark brows perfect. It was easier to be objective when her eyes were closed. When they looked into his they filled him with a love so overwhelming he sometimes literally expected it to buckle his knees.

He was glad he hadn't disturbed her with his restlessness. Uncertainty always made him sleep poorly. Not stress, he thought, pride forcing the reminder.

It was that meeting with Slidell. It started there.

Bobbie changed her position, rolling so slowly he followed

the movement of individual muscles, saw the insect-wing tremor of her eyelids.

His mind jerked away from her, from good things.

The awful feeling of exposure grew in his bowels, drained life from the sunshine. Words like presentiment and premonition nibbled at his reason. He told himself it was ridiculous, which failed to affect the dread. He hoped—indeed, expected—oncoming daylight would free him, as it exalted the bird still singing outside his window. Now that notion was destroyed.

Once more, he reassured himself of the impenetrability of his cover. He *was* a private investigator. Whoever followed him might have managed to get the car license and a snapshot—no more. If they pursued their investigation, they would find nothing to tell them he was anything except what he claimed to be.

The argument was pointless. Whoever they were, they knew he was looking for Alex.

Bobbie moved again, frowned in her sleep.

At least the people backstopping Alex weren't crazies, the vindictive spouses or dopers the private-investigation business turned up. No one would phone threats on Bobbie or the kids.

There was a moment's comfort in that thought, but then he considered his own situation. Alex obviously considered his use of Slidell's motel sensitive enough to warrant a warning link between himself and Slidell. More to the point, Alex's people still considered the connection important enough to respond to that warning, despite Alex's departure in disgrace.

Will levered himself upright. Bobbie muttered an indistinct question. Positioning himself between her and the dresser, he opened the top drawer silently and eased the blunt 9mm automatic from its holster. He released the magazine, checked the chamber and barrel. Slipping the magazine back into the grip, he pushed gently until it caught with its characteristic cold snick.

"What are you doing with that thing?"

He slumped at the sound of Bobbie's fully awakened voice. He said, "I don't believe you. You can sleep through

185

anything, but if one of the kids sniffs or I pick up this piece, you're awake and on top of us. How do you do it?''

"Fear. I worry about *all* my kids." When he turned she wore the characteristic grin she used to screen genuine worry. The lips curved properly, but they were tight, thin. It was the only time she professed amusement without exposing her teeth.

She dropped her head back on the pillow. "Why are you fooling with it?"

"It goes with the territory, honey. You know that. We agreed a long time ago to leave it at that."

"You never left my bed to play with the damned thing."

"Get your children off to school and I'll show you playing."

Laughing, she got to her feet. "I won't even get them fed before you're telling me you're late for work. Just don't exhaust yourself today and we'll see what you're made of after they go to bed tonight."

"You got a deal, lady."

She swept past him on her way to the bathroom.

Putting on trousers and undershirt, he made the trip to the kitchen and started the toast, turning on the small television, idly swapping channels. An alarm clock whanged to life down the hall and died abruptly. He smiled. Exactly like their mother, both his daughters were convinced early morning was a plot. He walked down the hall and pounded on their door.

"We're up, Dad! You don't have to break it!" Kathy, always quickest to respond.

"Should I come in and check?"

"No! I'm not dressed!" Krista, always the second, but improved, answer. A great team.

When he got back to the kitchen, Bobbie was there, busy. He kissed the back of her neck and was rewarded with a murmur of pleased surprise. He continued on to wash up and finish dressing.

Breakfast was the usual mad scene. Afterwards, the girls raced out, shrieking good-byes over their shoulders.

Silence crowded in, filling their absence. Bobbie broke it. "What's the occasion?"

186

He pretended he didn't understand. "Occasion?"

"Don't stall. The gun. Why?"

"I was awake, so I was just checking—"

"That's not so! You're wearing it! Why?"

Appalled, he pulled the coat aside. "After what I paid for this suit, the piece shows? That's disgraceful."

She placed her elbows on the counter and lowered her fists onto the surface. He smiled weakly, saying. "It's a little security thing."

"VIP protection?"

"Something like that."

She sniffed. "Worse than kids, all of you. Secrets. Guns. I hate that damned gun."

"Have I ever used it? Even drawn it?"

"How would I know? All I know is, you wouldn't be out there with yours if you didn't think someone else is carrying one just like it."

"You make it sound like my fault."

"I don't mean to. But I wish you had a different job." Her jaw jutted, then, defiantly, "*Jobs*."

He got to his feet. "You're breaking your promise."

Moving with quick grace, she rushed to put her arms around him, clung to him. "You're not a 'gun' man. You'd wait for the other guy to shoot first or some dumb thing."

"You think I'm headed for the OK Corral? The piece is required sometimes, that's all."

"You're sure?" Her contrition filled him with shame. He said, "I'll try to get home early." She hugged him closer, a momentary desperation. When she stepped back, she visibly composed a smile. He kissed her at the door, each tasting the other's fear while projecting strength. Will walked to the car wondering how it had come to pass that their honesty was practiced schizophrenia. United, they savaged any challenge to what they chose to call truth.

Perhaps, he thought, there was a measure of salvation in the free admission they were outside normalcy.

Starting the car, he decided it was no one's problem but their own, and they handled it perfectly.

Unable to see any pursuit, incapable of shedding the feeling it was there, he abandoned himself to antisurveillance maneuvers. Logic and training dictated against it, and he acknowledged the weakness of his actions.

In the morning rush hour, the behavior was particularly stupid, and he drew more attention to himself than he'd suffered at any point in his life. The last stunt, a squealing U-turn that sent him racing back up a hill, nearly ended in a head-on collision. He pulled to a stop at the curb, trembling. After regaining control, he drove directly to the parking lot under the building housing his office.

The day was a lost war, an exhausting succession of deferred decisions, detached responses. He refused all calls, instructing his two assistants and the secretary to answer for him with the message that he would call back. When a call was for him, their eyes sought him out, and in their looks he saw accusation, pity, an entire panoply of suspicion. He tried to imagine their reaction on learning that Will Walters was far more—and far less—than they ever guessed. What would they say when they learned his "personal cases" were directed at foreign intelligence efforts?

He was certain no one could link his undercover counterintelligence work to any agency. No one would genuinely believe the government's plausible denial, but it was unassailable. He imagined the propaganda scenario. The Soviets would hang tough, remind everyone Alex was an official representative, not only allowed to travel around and meet people, but encouraged by the American government to do so. They'd sing the glories of peaceful trade. In the end, the familiar cooler heads in the media would prevail, apologizing for yet another American zealot's vulgar obsession with nonexistent Soviet espionage. They would declare the American was obviously CIA but staunchly reject speculation that Alex was KGB, citing lack of evidence.

By day's end, Will puzzled over his enemy's lack of activity. The license number of the car had undoubtedly been traced before breakfast. By ten o'clock, a good organization would know as much about Will as could be discovered without mounting a full-scale surveillance. The fact that no one had made any waves suggested the surveillance might be already underway, or was under consideration.

A long-term close observation would reveal his contacts, areas of interest, personnel under investigation. Worse than compromising himself, he could be used as a window onto other operations, compromising many others.

It was time to bail out.

Knowing Black would be in his office working late, Will made no effort to join the mass exodus from his office building. If he was being watched, he could spot the opposition much more easily if there were fewer people around. The lobby was empty when he got off the elevator, and he left by the side door, strolling several blocks before entering a small bar.

No one followed him.

The telephone was shielded in a wooden cubby, the once-varnished surface scarred with names, numbers, and contemporary cultural comments. Will hunched forward, hovering over the mouthpiece. He covered the ear away from the phone with his free hand to shut out the crowd noise and made a person-to-person collect call. He identified himself as Harlan Evinrude. Black accepted the charges, said, "Problems?"

"I think I'm burned."

Black said, "Had to happen someday, right? How'll you explain to mother?"

"Mother'll never know, exactly. I'll just explain I got spooked. I got some brownie points saved up."

"Sure. Did you learn anything I can use?"

The disinterest troubled Will. He put it down to his own nerves. "I sent you some stuff you'll find interesting. There's a picture of the guy who fingered me. You may want to talk to him eventually."

"Depend on it. Thanks."

Will said, "Take care," and Black hung up without saying good-bye.

The number of customers was a bit smaller already, and Will elected to sit at the bar. He paid for a beer and nursed it for perhaps ten minutes. Davis's arrival was punctual. He slid onto the stool next to Will and said, "So how'd your first day working for Black go yesterday? Find anything?"

Will nodded. "More than we bargained for. I'm burned."

Davis's only sign of surprise was an almost imperceptible forward thrust of the thin neck holding the outsized head. He said, "Tell me about it."

Will was impressed. No one else in the business would have so coolly resisted the urge to scan everyone in sight. Few would have ignored the opportunity to ask Will if he thought he was under surveillance presently. Davis simply assumed Will would have aborted the meeting if there was the slightest chance of compromise. It rankled Will to discover he was gratified by the confidence. He said, "I'm glad it happened. You have to know that, up front. I hated lying to Steve. It's pointless."

Davis stared, waiting. Will shrugged. "I found a place Alex used for a meeting site. It's a motel. The manager burned me. I'm pretty sure they took pictures of me and my company car."

"Pretty sure?"

"They didn't send me proofs for approval, Bob. But I know the bastard made me, and there was someone around when he did it. Don't ask me how I know, I *know*."

Only the bartender's request for his order broke Davis's gaze. He called for whiskey, straight up, finishing it in a quick gulp before speaking. Looking into the emptied glass, he said, "Call Black and tell him what you've told me. Tell him you're dumping everything, going strictly civilian."

"I already did."

Davis nodded. "Good. Continue to be careful. There's a new man on the scene, a real commissar." Twirling the glass, he went on, "I'm sorry I had to hold out on you. I appreciate your help with this thing." Either he caught some movement by Will or he anticipated a statement, because he raised a peremptory hand. "You think I had you set up Leskov—the guy you and Black call Alex—for my own purposes. I don't deny my ambitions, Will. But Alex had to go because he was too good, and because jerking things around should create cracks where we can stick in a wedge or

190

two. I want this 'resident' of his, this Marvin. I'm setting Black on him because he's the guy who damned near destroyed Black himself, years ago.''

"That's all fine, so far. But why all the backstage bullshit? Why not just tell Steve what's going on?"

Davis sighed. "Think about it. Remember who blew the whistle on Black's compromised man? You think Black's going to help me help himself? He'll work himself to death to prove the outfit—and I—did him wrong, and he'll do anything to catch Marvin. But if he thinks I'm moving things around, he'll dive back in his hole and maybe never come out again." He paused, looked Will in the eye, then returned his gaze to the glass in his hand. "He was emotionally mined out, you know? All he had left for me to work with was hate.''

Will turned to his own glass, thinking over Davis's argument. When he spoke, the words were directed at his folded hands on the bar, much as Davis aimed his at the unresponding whiskey glass. The conversation wanted no glance or movement that might be misinterpreted. Neither man could afford to let the other see the other truths and other thoughts that no one must ever grasp. "Steve told me pretty much the same thing. About being dead, I mean. Said he was alive now. That was when I told him you wanted the operation slowed down.''

"Now you see why I did it? Just hearing himself say the operation's important to him makes it more so, understand?'' A corner of his lip twitched. "And it gives him all the more reason to prove what a bastard I am.''

"It's not right. He needs friends more than he needs to be kicked.''

"You're wrong. Black can't accept real friendship from any of us now. Not yet. He sees himself as a failure, a member of the team who let us all down. Once he proves to himself he's as good as we know he is, he'll be willing to be our friend again.''

Sliding off the bar stool, Will wedged himself between it and the bar. The position allowed him to look directly at Davis's face and made it practically impossible for Davis to

191

avoid looking at him. Will said, "I hear you saying you want to help Steve, and I believe you mean it. But I've got to wonder about the other side of that coin, you know? I knew—hell, everybody knows—about you and Steve and the investigation. Did you ever think maybe you're using Steve to haul your own ass out of the fire? You talk about giving him a chance to save himself. I have to wonder what happens if he misses, 'cause he's saving you, too, isn't he? He's the only hope you've got to lay a few of your own ghosts, God damn you."

Davis's smile cracked across his face. A fierce light flickered in his eyes but was smothered instantly. Gently, he said, "You really are always there, aren't you? You come out of nowhere, like a damned dart." He turned away, looked at the door. "He mustn't miss. You've already seen it—if he goes under—" He abandoned the thought.

Reluctantly, he turned to seek Will's understanding. The slim figure was exiting through a side door. For a brief moment, he considered running after him, but it made little difference if Will pretended to misunderstand. He knew. He didn't want to face it.

Who could blame him? No one wanted to admit he was balanced between worlds, half shadow, half light. Reality was just another word to play with.

CHAPTER 19

"YOU LOOK TIRED." ELISE SPOKE FROM THE OFFICE doorway. Carmody admired her beauty and still asked himself if she deliberately posed.

He damned himself for the question. Lately he was overanalyzing everything. He said, "My eyes are burning. This paperwork is killing."

"Can I help?"

"One-man operation."

"Turn it over to me. A woman can manage it in half the time."

"You think that's funny." His crooked grin belied the growl.

"Actually, it's kind of sad." She slipped away quickly, trailing laughter. When he walked into the store, she was dealing with a customer. After she was finished, he said, "We haven't had lunch together for a while. Join me today?"

She frowned ruefully. "I can't. I'm supposed to meet someone."

"Oh. And tomorrow I'm tied up. What if I pick you up around eleven on Sunday and we spend the day?"

"You're tempting me." She thought a moment, then surrendered to the idea with a freedom of mind that filled him with envy.

* * *

At nine o'clock on Saturday morning, Carmody was in the arboretum of the University. Diamond-hard sunlight gripped the trees and shrubs. People moved slowly, languorous. Carmody had the sensation they were all in the hand of a power that might choose any moment to immobilize them completely.

The thought conjured up Nicolai in his mind, reminded him of the little man's increasing aura of mystery, like an evil child with a secret.

Carmody set his jaw, determined to demand time off, if only a week. He wondered what Elise might think of such an idea.

He stopped walking and lowered his camera bag to the ground and checked his watch. Summerton was due in fifteen minutes, exactly. He wondered if he would be on time.

The man was unfathomable. Greedy, but he tried hard to earn his money. He exuded a veritable stench of deceit, and yet he executed every task assigned him in more than workmanlike fashion. In fact, Carmody conceded irritably, one of the most unlikable things about Harry Summerton was that his production was excellent.

Adjusting camera and tripod, Carmody focused on a cluster of rhododendron blossoms. Translucent pink petals faded to white at the outer limits of each flower, while small dashes of near-purple accented the throats. He almost lost track of the time.

Apparently aimless, Summerton strolled into view from up the hill. He stopped to admire several plants, inspected a sunbather, always edging closer to Carmody. Punctual to within seconds, he stopped beside him. "Lovely flowers," he said. "What film are you using?"

"I prefer Ektachrome," Carmody answered, without looking up.

Summerton responded, "Me too, although I've heard rumors about a new film that does better on reds."

Carmody remained bent over. "What did you want to see me about?"

Summerton smiled. Something in the expression struck hard at Carmody's warning centers. He straightened quickly.

Summerton said, "I've been promoted. By my company, that is."

Then Carmody understood what made the smile troublesome. Summerton sensed advantage. The subtle expression change revealed a mind searching for a place to strike. The bare suggestion of challenge fueled a searing rage in Carmody. He barely restrained it, feigning boredom. "Meaning?"

"I'm going to be part of the design unit. The tests are almost finished. We're going to create the working machine."

"Why were you selected? How did it happen?"

Summerton's tongue painted a nervous circle across the lips. "You don't seem very pleased."

Carmody backtracked rapidly. Summerton was a weapon, to be used to greatest effect. *No personalities.* "Of course I'm happy. The company's only confirming what we've known for a long time. But I have to be honest with you, Harry. My first concern is for our work. As it was, you had access with minimum security scrutiny."

"I thought of that, but when I considered the advantages, I had to apply for the position. It's design planning, my special area. Look, from this it's a small step to specific programs and actual locations of military and industrial sites."

Military sites. Alex's dream. It would be Nicolai's triumph.

Carmody packed his camera equipment and walked away. He knew Summerton would follow. Indeed, he had to make Summerton aware of his command, make the fat fool know in his very blood that confrontation with his control was unthinkable.

He directed his thoughts at his joints, at the muscles straining to reflect the turmoil of his emotions. It required only a few steps for him to eliminate the problem. When he smiled at his companion, it was no different than usual. He attributed the flurry of light in Summerton's eyes to the sun penetrating the leaves.

He said, "You mustn't be too concerned with improving on what you've already accomplished, Harry. We're very satisfied with your work. Our greatest worry is that you'll take a chance, do something unnecessary."

"All I've been able to produce so far is the end product of

195

the experiments. I know what that means to your people—they have to back-engineer everything we send them. I can give them the whole process now.''

"Back-engineer? I don't know the term." Carmody led the way from the wide meadowlike walk into a dark pathway.

Animatedly, Summerton explained. "Your people know what McKay's been doing, but the only way they can determine *why* we're doing it is to feel their way back through the whole experiment. Most of the time they're guessing. I can offer involvement, Martin. You'll be watching every step while we develop the new defense computer facility. His stuff will be the core. It'll control every capability and plan this country has. I can tell you every move they make." He paused, looked around dramatically. "I'll tell you something else. Without that information, your people don't stand a chance. One of the fundamental components of the defense mix is an antimissile system that *works*. I haven't actually seen it, but they're sure of it. Even if you move without warning, they'll snuff you."

Carmody turned away, feeling the blood drain from his face. His hands grew cold, and he saw Moscow in ruins, a smoking rubble. The picture was hazy. What replaced it was a flash of light that froze his daughters in mid-stride, and when the light was gone, so were they.

Alex had been more right than he knew. Nicolai truly understood. These people must be destroyed before they acquired such power. Summerton provided the key to survival.

The image of the children slashed across his vision again, and he winced.

He considered the weapon he must use to protect them. Harry Summerton offered up his country's heart like a dog fetching a stick, seeing no significance to his actions except his own future. Carmody swallowed before speaking, then said, "You may have assured world peace, Harry. My people will know how to respond. I'm lucky to be the first to congratulate you."

"I want to do what's best for us as a team. I trust you. You'll see I'm taken care of."

The trite venality left a sour taste at the back of Carmody's throat. He moved off slowly to his preselected site, edging away from Summerton's determined closeness.

A cropped meadow sloped down to the distant boulevard, its turf irregularly spiked by slim trees. Tufts of shade circled each one. Carmody sat down with his back pressed against a trunk, artfully safe from any possible covered approach.

For a moment, the irony teased him. Only openness afforded the sure privacy his business demanded.

He said, "Of course you'll be rewarded. Still, the magnitude of it goes beyond money."

A breeze riffled the hillside, carrying a rough tang of grass heating under the sun. Summerton's greasy voice droning away forced him to ignore that smell, and he was shocked to realize he was forming a genuine hatred for the man.

Summerton was saying, "It's not just the money, Martin. I genuinely admire your oganization."

"I'm glad to hear it. As I said—"

"You people know how to get things done. You understand the true value of things." Summerton swung his gaze away from Carmody to the distant boulevard and followed the progress of a top-down convertible. It was canary-yellow, as sharp as the sunshine.

Carmody watched the glittering eyes track the vehicle. Summerton continued, "We all work to secure ourselves a future, and there's none in what I'm doing for you."

Carmody opened his mouth to object, but Summerton talked on. "I know I have to continue to advance with this project or lose my value to you. That's a very limited future."

The probing smile was back, the window into the ambition behind the bargaining.

Carefully, Carmody put together an answer. "That's not true, Harry. If we have to deactivate you for a while, it's a security matter, not a fiscal one. You said yourself, we understand the value of things. We're not going to lose a man like you."

Shaking his head, Summerton exhaled laughter in silent gusts. He faced Carmody. "Are you telling me I'd stay on your payroll if I couldn't produce for you?"

"Absolutely."

The laughter acquired sound, rapped out in harsh staccato. "Bullshit, Martin. You're really good, my friend. I don't mind. Hell, man, if you're not good, my ass is dead, right? But save it for the suckers. I'm giving you more than you ever hoped for. And more to come. I expect a whole lot in exchange."

"We consider ourselves your friends, not your employers. Your contract with us is a lifetime matter."

"Sure. And if the money stops, I take my contract to a lawyer and complain I'm being cheated out of my espionage checks. Your fucking contract's not worth shit to me. Try to blackmail me with it, you'll find out it's not worth shit to you, either."

Carmody sighed. "What can I do to reassure you?"

"Guarantee that when I'm ready to bail out, I'm set for life. Assure I'll be protected if someone fucks up." Moving with startling quickness, Summerton thrust his face within inches of Carmody's. His eyes were suddenly fearful, belying the bravado in his voice. "I'm used to being alone, you understand? I know how to protect myself. You treat me right and I'll bring you people material that'll make your heads spin. Try to fuck me over, and you'll find the FBI in your lunch."

Carmody turned away, unable to bear Summerton's sweating visage. The unpredictable swing from potential opponent to demanding servitor rolled in his stomach like a soured meal. "Let me think a minute. I don't want any misinterpretations when I answer you. There's too much at stake."

Summerton held his position for a moment, then grudgingly twisted away.

As he considered words, Carmody also examined his view of Summerton. The answer to handling him was simplicity itself, he decided, although the actual accomplishment offered severe problems. The Summertons of the world were the ultimate test. To penetrate a mind so intent on self-preservation, to bend it to *his* will, was the pinnacle of recruitment. It was not a perversion or a diversion, but a creation.

Carmody berated himself. He should have seen the possibility at the outset. Summerton learned well, and resisted the lessons while he did. Outwardly despising direction and control as weakness, his soul cried for nothing less than possession. The single truth in Harry Summerton was the unassailable refuge—*"It wasn't my fault."*

Harry Summerton was a parasite, seeking an indestructible, all-forgiving host.

He needed only a point of entry.

The organism would create one for him.

Carmody smiled.

Strangely, having lifted that screen, Carmody found it impossible to concentrate further on Summerton. The scent of danger and infection lingered only as troublesome nuisances. His mind drifted, undisciplined. A figure moved in the distance, small to the point of nonidentification, but there was that in the walk, in the style of the movement, that said female.

And his sole concern became his appointment with Elise.

It was half-past ten. If he hurried, he would be only a few minutes late.

On his feet, he looked down at Summerton's puzzled features. He said, "I'll call you. You know we have special programs for unique individuals. I'll recommend you. Keep up the good work."

Summerton struggled to his feet, grunting harshly. He clutched at Carmody's arm, who shrugged off the contact but waited. Summerton said, "You can't just walk off now."

Carmody sidled away. "Harry, I have plans that'll make you happy beyond your imaginings, but I have to get approval. It's time for bargaining, and the less you know, the less you'll worry." He caught himself just before saying "Trust me," and finished, "I'll take care of everything."

"Where are you going now? What's so important? God damn it, Martin, I need to *talk*!" His voice reached a dangerous level.

Carmody said, "I've got another meeting." He recovered some of the distance he'd put between them. "I'll call tomorrow. You understand. Look, you're a professional. You and

I, Harry—we know this is a tough business. If we're going to be a good team, we have to back each other up."

Visibly calming, Harry finally nodded. "I'm okay. Sure, okay. Do what you have to do, Marty. Just be sure you call tomorrow, right?"

"Right. I'll call your place. You know which pay phone to go to, once you hang up at your apartment?"

"I'm a professional, remember?"

"Sorry. Force of habit. You've done better than I ever anticipated, Harry. I'm still getting used to it. Excuse me."

"Sure, Marty. I hope your other meeting goes well."

"Thanks."

The last Carmody saw of Summerton, he was grinning and waving good-bye.

As soon as Carmody was out of sight, Summerton's features moved, the changes imperceptible in themselves, until the cheerful smile was changed to fawning supplication. Summerton felt the flow of tension and relaxation create a pattern he couldn't identify. For a moment it was like wearing another's face, and he imagined himself looking in a mirror, staring at an alien fear through his own eyes.

His skin was suddenly hot. Raising a shielding hand to his forehead, he moved onto a path between towering rhododendrons, eagerly submerging in the shade. Overhead, the green cover robbed the sun of its sting. Small filtered shafts could only dance harmlessly across the rich loam at his feet. He stepped through them, on them, with impunity. Walking to his car, he thought how eagerly people in this climate exposed themselves to summer's newly arrived sun without considering the power hidden in it. Then he laughed. He knew about power. All kinds.

Carmody took his eye off the road to glance at Elise. He wondered exactly how she saw him. The vagrant thought made him smile. How easily he'd been able to dismiss Summerton from his mind, how quickly he'd driven to her apartment! The schoolboy excitement of it was comical. But it was wonderfully comical. He couldn't remember ever feeling so free. Their eyes met. They exchanged smiles, and once again Carmody marveled at the ease of it. No hidden meanings were exchanged, no sexual signals warmed the air between them.

And yet there was a sexuality there. It was building in him, and it was dangerous, and he cherished it.

She said, "There's a place to turn off up here, an old logging road. It's a good place to hunt for agates."

He teased her. "You spend a lot of time in the woods on dates?"

"What a rotten mind. Come on, let's look."

"Why not?" He swung across the highway onto a dirt road at her instruction. A few hundred yards farther, they were beside a clear, rushing stream. He said, "Am I looking for anyplace special?"

"No. Stop anywhere along here."

He found a level spot, and she was out of the car as soon as it stopped. In jeans and khaki shirt, bright red bandanna highlighting the golden hair, she stretched and inhaled with the unself-conscious exuberance of a child, reaching out to the strength of the land and pulling it to her. Trotting across the road, she maneuvered across the tops of the massive boulders down to the creek bank with careless agility. He followed at a somewhat less breakneck pace. When he reached the gravel bar where she waited, she hugged him, breaking away to gesture, laughing. "This is my kind of country, Martin. I hate the city."

"You never mentioned it."

A frown etched her forehead, disappearing as rapidly as it came. "Talking about it while I'm there only makes it worse." She stepped out into the stream, still wearing her lightweight hiking shoes. At his expression, she said, "I used to go barefoot, but we've got so many beer bottles in the streams now you can lose a foot if you're not careful."

Carmody sat to unlace his boots. "I can get a foot sewed up cheaper than I can these damned things. I'll take a chance." Draping them around his neck, he rolled up his trousers and stepped off into knee-deep water. He yelped at the icy shock, and Elise laughed. "Big outdoorsman, can't take a little chilly water."

201

"Chilly? Cold as hell is what we're talking, lady."

Stopping suddenly, she pulled up a sleeve and plunged an arm in the water beyond the elbow. Straightening, she held up an irregular white object about three inches across. "First one!" She tossed it to him. White swirls penetrated the glassy agate, like crystallized smoke in frozen air. Carmody turned it over and over, admiring the changing views presented by each new angle. It dried quickly, turning opaque and dull without moisture to smooth the surface.

A splash interrupted him as Elise pitched another, smaller pebble at his feet. He hurried to join her, and they searched in earnest, shouting at each new find like gold panners, until one of Carmody's boots was loaded. They sat on the bank and sorted out the stones, arguing happily over which was the prettiest and who found it. When he suggested they hike up onto the high ground, she insisted they return their hoard. As they scattered the hoard back into the creek, he commented on the folly of soaking and freezing to find something only to throw it away. She scolded him for his materialism, and his laughter pleased her, but she looked at him quizzically when it continued far longer than the small joke warranted.

There was no trail to follow up into the timber. Carmody asked Elise if she minded. She reminded him that people disappeared in those mountains, and he laughed.

It took little time for them to crest the first ridge. That was always a magical moment for Carmody. Even when he had a map and description of the country, there was nothing like breaking clear of an uphill climb to look on new ground. No guidebook ever suggested the thrill of country seen for the first time.

This crest belonged to a spur. They were almost in the center of a flat stretch, perhaps one hundred yards long, no more than ten yards across. To the left, the spur continued up to join a longer, more massive ridge. To the right, it trailed off toward the highway. Carmody spared that direction the slightest glance, lip curling at the iron growl of distant traffic. Elise saw the expression and struck off toward the rising slope. Carmody fell in beside her.

The grade was unusually gentle, the forest floor relatively

uncluttered. Nevertheless, both soon wore the soft gleam of perspiration. At the juncture of spur and ridge, they climbed a very steep pitch for a few yards. Carmody pressed ahead, offering a hand back to Elise. She accepted it, taking his greater strength as a handy fact, letting go when it was unnecessary. They arrived at the top of the ridge together. Elise gave a small cry of pleased delight at the suddenly revealed view, and Carmody reached to take her hand in his.

A small, forested valley spread out below them, accented by the glittering blue eye of a lake. Two peaks thrust higher than the rest of the looming walls around the valley, making Carmody think of beckoning arms.

Without a word or look for Elise, he started down the hill toward the gentle undulations of the valley floor. She followed, her amusement tempered by the awareness that the things that affected him most could exclude her instantly. Angling to the right, they intersected a creek, surprisingly large at this altitude. It bumbled headlong ahead of them.

Carmody moved with more than deliberate slowness. Every few yards he stopped, checking his back trail for landmarks to help him on the way out before peering around the trees to his front for a view of the lake. Breaking free of a particularly thick tangle of brush, they were suddenly at the edge of a clearing. Immediately before them was a litter of massive tree trunks, all lying in the same direction, downed by an immense wind of years past. The huge logs were rotting now, some of them living nurseries, sprouting new, eager growth along their length. Beyond them lay the lake, still distant but attainable now. Carmody stopped as if struck, then hurriedly clambered up on one of the trunks. Pulling Elise up beside him, he held onto her hand, squeezing it almost to the threshold of pain.

"What is this place?" he asked, and then before she could possibly answer, he whirled on her. "No! I don't want to know. I don't want it named. It's my place. Mine." He faced her, leaning over her, shoulders pitched forward, chin tucked in. The attitude slanted his whole appearance, made him look poised to attack. The normally mobile features were stilled, the deep eyes impenetrable.

Fright touched the base of Elise's neck, an awareness of desperate intensity. It dawned on her that the strength she admired was equally a capacity for violence.

He said, "Our valley."

"The Martin-Elise Valley?" She made a jibe of it, raising her voice over the thudding roar of the creek.

He responded sincerely. "No name. Just 'The Valley.' "

She gestured widely, still trying for a lighter side to the moment. "You'll have to be more original than that. We've got hundreds of valleys."

"But this one is the best. A thing like this, if you tell its name to someone, they know about it, might find it. No, this is ours. The Valley."

Quieter now, he stood more relaxed, although the same evasive quality pinched the corners of his eyes.

Sorrowfully, she understood her earlier insight was correct. From greatest elation to cruelest depression, she would never touch more than the edges of his character. She looked into those controlled eyes, so determinedly unconfiding, and the sadness she felt for herself wilted under a terrible certainty.

Where she had faint hope of communion, he had no hope of expression.

CHAPTER 20

THE HOURS SPENT EXPLORING THE VALLEY PASSED SWIFTLY. Shade creeping up the eastern slopes caught Carmody by surprise. To the west, the valley walls were already dark.

"We better get moving," he said to Elise. "There's not much daylight left."

"And look at that." She pointed at the northern peaks. Sullen clouds boiled into the gap from a gray sky. To the south, white cumulus caught the sun and glowed rich flame colors.

Carmody and Elise struck out for their point of entry to the valley. The clouds advanced steadily, muttering thunder, and the lowering sun stole the light from the forest. In spite of their fast pace, the ridge seemed to keep its distance. The dropping temperature failed to prevent sweat collecting at Carmody's hairline. When he stole a glance at Elise, her face was drawn. Wisps of hair that had blown free earlier in the day were now unsightly straggles glued to her skin. He offered her a hand over a fallen branch and she managed a smile.

They finally reached the stream. Glancing over his shoulder, he saw the storm against the peaks, the two highest disappearing into the first clouds. The growing wind set the trees to cracking and sighing.

It was the message he heard consistently in the dank green

of the Olympics, and it had come to haunt him here in his Cascades. He shook his head, told himself he always felt this way during storms in the mountains. It was the time his skills were held up in front of him and ridiculed.

Elise clutched at his shirt from behind. "Do we have to go so fast? It's a rainstorm, not a tornado, after all." The words came in gusts, and answering her own question, she slumped to the ground, leaning back against a tree.

He dropped beside her. "I wasn't thinking," he said. "It won't hurt if we get wet. I'm sorry I tired you out."

"Oh, I want to hurry," she said, gulping air, "but I don't want to end up exhausted."

"What?"

"I've got a surprise. Tell you back at the car."

"Tell me now!"

She shook her head, dabbing with the bandanna at the same time. "Wait."

A hissing noise broke in on their conversation, and they both faced back down the valley, where the last rays of the sun glazed the western peaks. Cutting through the ragged crests, an almost horizontal golden light intercepted the first columns of rain. Glowing, shifting patterns of color and intensity transformed the ordinary storm into a disturbingly different phenomenon. Elise put her hand on his shoulder and pushed to her feet. "Let's go."

Carmody set out in front. The stream took on a new sound, as menacing as the rain. It snarled now, rocks battering together along its bed, like the gnashing of giant teeth.

They reached the upper slope where the trees thinned out. He took Elise's hand and hooked it over his belt, then drove uphill off the balls of his feet. Behind them the rain and the moan of the wind grew ever louder.

The ridge was at hand. From there, it was downhill.

Lightning blasted in the distance as they stepped onto the crest. Sagging against the seamed bark of a fir, they looked back. The twin towers of the far rampart softened, wavered, and were absorbed into the devouring clouds.

Elise turned her attention to Carmody, touched by the feelings that emanated from him. "Marty, don't be so down!

The valley's not gone, it's just full of bad weather. It'll be even prettier the next time.''

His answering smile was weak. "You think so?"

She took his arm, squeezed it. "Certainly. It needs the rain. Even if we don't. And we've still got some ground to cover, or we're going to get wet.''

"Right." He scanned the sky. "I think we can slow down a little, though. The wind seems to be falling off.''

When they arrived at the car, it was fully dark, the merest glow to the west indicating where the sun rested beyond the horizon. Only then did she speak, wonder in her voice.

"Will you just look at that sky? All that hell and damnation to chase us home, and there're *stars* coming out now.''

"Perverse," he said, and she cocked her head to the side, waiting. He went on, "Weather in the mountains—it's always treacherous.''

"Good word." She held sweaty arms out, inspected herself. "I'm so wet I might as well have let the rain catch me.''

He rounded on her quickly, stern. "Never take a chance with weather. This country will lull you. You get a bit wet, you hurry a little too much, the first thing you know, you're dying of hypothermia. Forget the lightning. That plain, ordinary rain can kill you.''

She started to get in the car, stopped, spoke to him across the roof. "Listen, you're going to think I'm crazy, but I was ready to believe that damned storm was actually chasing us, and now—'' She gestured helplessly at the clear sky directly overhead.

He slid in behind the wheel. "You're right. I do think you're crazy.''

The car started with reassuring ease, the headlights picking up a foraging doe. Carmody and Elise sat motionless as the animal daintily picked its way to the edge of the illumination and disappeared into the dark. Elise sighed. "That was nice. A good end to the trip.''

Moving down the rutted road, Carmody smiled over at her. "I'm glad you liked it. It *has* been a good day.''

"It's not over yet, if you'd like to hear some good music tonight. That's my surprise.''

"Like what?"

"A club. They always have good music. We can get something to eat on the way back, shower, and catch the last part of the evening. It's my treat. If you want to."

"It's a great idea. Neither of us'll be able to move tomorrow."

"That's my plan—do it all today, and tomorrow's Loaf City."

"That's the way it's done. Prior planning. You have to have it." For some reason, the drift of conversation brought Harry Summerton to mind, the first he'd thought of him since leaving the arboretum. It struck him as very funny.

The drive to town was uneventful, marked by a stop for a box of chicken to eat on the road. He dropped her at her apartment and returned to his own to clean up. When he called for her, she was ready and waiting.

Carmody found it hard to picture her as she had been on the mountainside, exhausted, sweaty, bedraggled. Sleek in wine-red jacket and trousers, her step was vivacious as she swept into the car, full of anticipation and laughter.

The club was in the Pioneer Square section of the city. Once the hub of the city's life, it deteriorated for decades before being rediscovered. Reclamation had swept through the solid, ornate buildings like the fire that once razed the entire town. The more-determined Skid Road derelicts— the name dated back to the time when logs were literally skidded down to the waterfront on what was now Yesler Way— kept a tenuous grip on their old turf. They tolerated the cleanliness and orderliness with studied indifference, secretly overjoyed by the shoals of panhandle-able newcomers.

Carmody disliked the entire area intensely.

The preservation of buildings of little historic value was ludicrous in his view. Worse, the monuments were mere shells. Everything in them was modern, another example of the West's veritable love affair with sham. Blatantly commercial, slickly consumer-oriented, they offended his sight.

More, he despised the street people, their filth, their language, their self-pitying—or bullying—beggary. A nation with pride would never allow such people to exist. He marveled that such wasted men weren't scoured from society's view and put to work for their own good.

Like cats that single out the house guest who most dislikes cats, the panhandlers invariably found Carmody.

Now Elise intended to take him there. He set his jaw and drove.

He parked the car opposite a park, leading Elise warily past the snoring, laughing, shouting residents.

The pressure of his arm holding hers to his side amused her. She regarded the locals as more raffish than dangerous, men too concerned with themselves to make trouble. In moments of truth, they could strike viciously at the world that so terribly used them, but for the most part they slipped through life with heedless momentum. To Elise, they were unfortunate. If they were to blame for their own situation, that was even more unfortunate. She hoped society would find a way to care for them and avoided them as a matter of basic caution, as one looks out for traffic.

Seriousness was replaced by an immediate delight as they entered the club. The aura of the crowd enveloped her. She blended in with the mass that was sufficiently packed together for an enforced conviviality, but that pressed no one to immobility. More, the music was inspired. Jazz sped through the rising smoke, skimmed across the subdued hum of conversation with the delicacy of leaves breasting stream water. Captivated, Elise worked close to the musicians, attention riveted to their playing. She was unaware of Carmody ordering drinks. Once the number ended, she saw the distaste in his face.

"You don't like it." She made it a hurt accusation.

He shook his head, leaned closer. "The music's not my favorite, but a little's okay. I don't like crowds."

"I'm sorry, Marty. I love jazz, and it's always best like this—live music, lively people, all together. Because I love it so much, I just assumed you would."

"Don't worry about it. You enjoy yourself. It'll make me feel good just watching you. I mean it."

"You're sure?" She put her hand on his arm.

"I'm sure."

209

She smiled her appreciation, turning away as the music started again.

In truth, he found the music confusing, an assault of sound, each note struggling for primacy. Equally true was his determination to see her enjoy herself. It was a small price to pay, when her presence brought him such pleasure.

He admitted that now. He wanted her near.

But this place was almost more than he could bear.

The music was bad enough, but the *crowd*. So many blacks. To be expected. Loud. Crude.

The weight of people, close to him, any of them able to study him at leisure, memorize features, movements.

Unconscious reflex responded to the crescendo of the music's ending chords. He was smiling at Elise when she faced him again and picked up her drink. She studied him over the rim of the glass while applause rose and fell. The group leader went into an introduction of the next piece.

She said, "You're not enjoying yourself, are you?"

She'd caught something in his attitude, his feelings. It was important to learn what it was. "I like being with you. That's the truth. But I don't like this place."

Riotous laughter exploded off to the side, a high-spirited shriek, quickly joined by deeper, rolling amusement. He glanced that way, and when he looked back, Elise was putting down her glass. Her smooth features, silvered by the dim light, were a study in controlled tension.

"I want to go now," she said.

"There's no reason to go. Not so soon, anyway."

She shook her head. "No. I think we ought to leave now." She pushed her chair back, quickly getting to her feet to lead the way.

There was a statue not far outside the door, a metal impressionistic piece that crouched just inside the circle of light from the club. Elise walked directly to it and put a hand on it, turning to face Carmody.

"Suppose you tell me what you're so uptight about?"

"Have I said anything?"

"You don't have to. I can tell."

It was the thing he feared. "What did I do?"

"How do I know? Something. The way you smile. It wasn't really you." She waved, the gesture as weak as her answer. "Whatever. You're steamed. Why?"

The way he smiled? "I didn't realize I looked so different."

"Not that different, dammit! You're evading me!"

He moved toward the parking lot, farther into the night. She pursued him. He said, "Everybody has a blind spot. We can't help it."

"It certainly wasn't just the music." She was beside him, looking up at him.

There was sweat on his upper lip, a painted stripe to mark his lies. She actually believed that the shallow foolishness of blacks was an expression of life. Ridiculous. But the thought of arguing with her and angering her was unimaginable. Another reason, something real. "Crowds. I get panicked. I can handle it, usually."

A bottle broke somewhere, chiming shrill discordance. Elise ignored it. "Why didn't you tell me? I didn't realize. I wouldn't have minded."

His muscles slacked a bit. "I wanted you to have a good evening. I thought I could make myself forget the crowd if you were there."

She stopped. They were directly under one of the clustered globular street lights. It turned her hair into a gilded helmet. "I like being with you, too, Marty, but it embarrasses me for you to do something like that. If we're going to get along, we have to talk. I want to know what you feel. I hope you'll try to understand me when I can't enjoy something you like. Can't people give each other that much truth, at least?"

He pivoted away on the cobbled surface. Something metallic grated underfoot. He said, "I misjudged you very much. I'm really sorry. I didn't trust plain honesty." The smooth words left a trail on his tongue. He felt as if he'd just been sick.

"Oh, God, Marty." Elise put her hand on his arm. "Please, don't do that to me again. I value you too much. Let's trust each other."

He turned quickly, took her hand between his, squeezed as he lifted it so the back of his own rested against her cheek.

Bending at the waist, he kissed her gently. Straightening, he noted her mouth was still pursed, her eyes still closed. She opened them sleepily, and he said, "I can't promise I'll always be exactly the man you want me to be, Elise. I have to be what I am. But I'll trust you. I hope you'll trust me."

She said, "I do," and linked arms with him, resuming the walk to the car.

He said, "Come with me. To my home."

She paused before answering, long enough for the arrhythmic mingling of their footsteps to set Carmody's teeth on edge. When she spoke, she twisted her head to glance at him, the movement stiff and reluctant. Nevertheless, she said, "I want to. I meant what I said."

It was all a matter of control, he told himself, exactly as he'd been taught. Control one's self, control the circumstances, control the conversation, control the subject. When one accomplished those tasks, the desired outcome of any meeting was inevitable.

It never failed.

Men might fail. Principles were inviolate.

That was a known truth.

And he felt dishonored.

CHAPTER 21

Black woke, as he always did, with the snap of an internal switch. On this occasion, he stared at the hotel wallpaper for a second before allowing himself to slip back to self-indulgent comfort. Closing his eyes, he let his other senses bask in Maddy's presence.

Suddenly uneasy, he sat up, turning as he did.

Her side of the bed was empty.

He rose silently, ignoring his nudity, and hurried to the bathroom. A discarded towel, water on the shower curtain, and still-wet soap showed she had already been there and gone. He absently wrapped himself in the towel and backed away, puzzled. Her suitcase was still on the floor of the closet.

Moving to the sliding-glass balcony door, he shook his head in relieved amusement at the sight of her. She grasped the rail, feet spread, like a sailor at the helm. Windswept hair streamed over her shoulders, tossing restlessly across her back. The skirt of the long robe swayed in its own slower pattern, the stark white of it brilliant against the blue-green of the Sound.

She saw him from the corner of her eye and faced him. Taking in his costume, she arched an eyebrow and smiled questioningly.

He opened the door. "I didn't hear a thing." He gestured in the direction of the bathroom.

"I think that's a compliment." She chuckled and moved to him, tracing his cheekbones with a finger.

He grinned, kissed her forehead. "Absolutely."

Her smile faded and she stepped back. "I really ought to hate you. This is the third weekend in the past five that I've schlepped up here to stay with you. My business is in big trouble."

"I keep telling you—dump it. Move up here."

Walking back to the rail, she spoke over her shoulder. " 'Whither thou goest,' and all that? Come on, Steve."

"There's nothing I can do about it."

Cold anger flared in her quick look and stiff turn away. Fetching his robe from the closet, he switched on the beeper attached to his belt. It sounded off instantly. Sitting on the edge of the bed, he dialed, made his connection. "Black."

"Steve? Bob Davis. I've got some information that might help you. Republic has a twelve forty-six arrival there, flight-number nine-twelve. Can you meet me?"

"I'll be there."

Maddy was standing beside him when he hung up. "Business?"

"Always."

She squeezed his shoulder. "I'm sorry I was bitchy. When it's time for me to go home, I start feeling sorry for myself."

He wrestled her to the bed, braced himself over her with an arm on each side. "Maybe I won't let you go home. I'll keep you a prisoner right here, ply you with wine and cheese from room service, make mad love to you night and day."

"Scratch the sissy food, make it three squares a day, and we may have a deal."

Flopping beside her, he buried his face in the soft, scented curvature between her jaw and shoulder. He said, "I love you, Maddy. Will you marry me?"

The silence in the room was so complete his ear against her throat registered the drumming rush of arterial blood. She said, "I want to, Steve. But there's too much I'm not sure about." The words came to him as speech through one ear and as a tactile impression through the other, simultaneously.

214

Mind and body acted as receptacle for mind and body. He wished he could stay there forever.

"We can work out the details."

"Details?" There was no amusement in her laughter. She rose, moved to an easy chair while he sat up. "Besides the detail of whether we live in Seattle or San Francisco, there's the detail of your daughter."

"She's certainly not going to live with us."

"Wherever that might be. That's not the point, anyhow. Do you realize I've never met her? And I've never seen your apartment. I feel like a hooker, Steve. I fly into town and we roll in the hay for a few hours, then—"

"Hold it." He leaned forward, massively coiled. "I wouldn't hear anyone else say that. We're not doing anything wrong."

"Then why do we hide from your daughter? Your neighbors?"

He laughed, truly amused. "Listen, my neighbors don't know if I'm alive or dead from one month to the next." Then, sobering, "You wouldn't like Jane. And she'd hate you."

"Why?"

"She's having problems. I told you her mother was an alcoholic. Jane blamed me, and she ran away. Her mother died, so she blames me for that, and for the fact she wasn't there when it happened. We're trying to put the pieces back together, and it's rough work. She'd see you as her mother's replacement, and she's too hostile to handle that any way except violently."

"We're going to have to meet sooner or later."

He got to his feet, headed for the bathroom. She was always surprised by how much larger he looked with his clothes off. He said, "Maybe not. I wouldn't be surprised to see her take off."

"You've got to stop her! How old is she?"

"Nineteen. Been on her own for three years. She's way beyond me telling her she has to stay home. Don't trouble yourself about her, please. Think about what I asked you."

The noise of the shower precluded any answer, and Maddy acknowledged she had none anyhow.

Steve was more intricate than complex, she decided. Things meshed in his mind, like the animations of engines they showed on television. What seemed like junk clattering around was really each piece supporting all the others.

What you had to do was grab one thought and listen and watch until you found out where it joined onto another, and another, until they formed a sort of structure. He wouldn't tell you everything you asked, but there was honesty in everything he said or did.

She made up her mind to tell him she'd marry him. She loved him. It was as simple as that. Being with him was the best she'd ever felt in her life, and she didn't want to be away from him.

She clutched at the balcony railing, realizing what was happening to her, knowing she'd doled out controlled reactions for so long that an uncompromising decision was frightening.

He was behind her, fully clothed, before she was aware the shower was off. When she discovered him, she fell into his arms. He laughed pleased surprise. "What brought this on?"

"I thought it over."

He understood instantly, tilted her head back to study her face. "You decided? You will?"

"Whenever you say. The sooner, the better."

He kissed her, pressing her dangerously against the balcony rail in his enthusiasm.

They parted, and both said, "About my business," in chorus, and laughed until they could hardly stand. He regained control first. "I'm meeting my boss this afternoon. I'll tell him I have to be transferred. He'll squeal, but he'll go for it if I insist."

She shook her head. "No. If you leave here, you'll lose your daughter for sure. It'll be good for me to make a complete break. The store's just a thing. I'll start another."

He said, "There are things about my business—about me— that I can't tell you, Maddy. But when this thing I'm on right now is over, I'll be able to tell you a lot more."

"If you're not ashamed of your work, I'm not worried. And if you were—" She looked away. "I love you. I don't

216

know what I'd do." The tone of the last sentence was a lament.

Putting his arms around her again, he held her closely, tenderly. "I'll make you happy, Maddy. I promise."

There was nothing she wanted to say in return. To hold him, to stay in his embrace—that was enough.

There was a plane to catch, and her stomach reminded her there was a belated breakfast to attend to. She allowed herself a last deep breath, the air redolent of scrubbed maleness. She spoke without moving her head from his chest, enjoying the muzzy, bedtime sound of the words against his shirt. "I have to go, Steve. I'll miss my plane." She giggled. "God, how *ordinary*!"

He said, "We'll put an end to that soon. We'll catch planes together, go places together."

She kissed him before slipping away. "Not for a while. No more hotel rooms, not even nice ones."

They were folding clothes into their small bags, side by side on the bed, when the knock came at the door. He looked at her quizzically. "You call room service while I was showering?"

She shook her head, and her throat caught at the instant chill in his manner. Puzzlement increased at the way he stood well away from the door, and her, before gruffly asking who was there.

"Open up. It's just me."

Intuitively, Maddy knew it was Jane Black.

Steve froze. A small vein like a chalked blue line throbbed down his neck.

The voice wheedled. "Come on, Dad. I know you're in there."

Maddy glanced from Steve's immobility to the door, wishing the voice away, hating herself for doing so.

That's his child out there, a young woman who knows hurt as clearly as I do. I can't let myself dislike her. I mustn't!

Black threw one pained look at Maddy before reaching for the door. As he did, Jane spoke again, "Hurry up, Dad. You and your girlfriend aren't at it already this morning, are you?"

217

Maddy thought she heard smothered laughter. She almost gasped when Steve flung the door open and the man beside Jane was exactly what she had imagined. Jane strode into the room. Following her, the man's eyes wandered from shrewd focus to infinity. Maddy realized he was drugged. She put on a smile for Jane's extended hand.

Jane said, "I don't know your name. My father keeps his women separated."

"My name's Maddy. Steve's told me good things about you. I hope we can be friends."

"Maddy. Cute." Jane settled into a chair. A hard look brought the man with her to her side. She cocked her head toward him. "This is Richie. My man. Part-time pimp, full-time head. Right now he's so junked up he can fart in color. Right, poopsie?" She chubbied Richie's cheek and he smiled loosely. Jane continued. "Richie wouldn't have nothing to do with my dad unless he was bombed, you know? Daddy gets off on beating up people like Richie. And my mother. Daddy never said good things about me. You're as full of shit as he is."

Anger burned Maddy's throat, her cheeks. She started to rise.

Black stepped between her and his daughter. "You've embarrassed everyone, Jane. You can leave now."

She smiled, and Maddy was amazed to see how young it made her, how girl-pretty. "You're the one who preaches truth is beauty. Is it possible there's a touch of hypocrisy there? Could it be?"

"Please. Don't make trouble."

"Ah, trouble." Bending sharply, she peeked around Black, spoke to Maddy. "Did he tell you he's very heavy into stopping trouble?"

Sly assurance oozed from the question, and Maddy remembered Steve's earlier statement about things he couldn't tell her. She said, "What he told me is between us."

Jane burlesqued surprised approval, looking up at Black. "Very good, Dad! This one's tough. Maybe she'll wear better than Mom. How's she hold her liquor?"

Black's left foot slid forward toward his daughter. The left

218

shoulder dropped, and the massive right fist drew back ponderously. Maddy remembered the locomotives of her girlhood, the action of slabbed-steel driving rods as the train started.

Jane's head pressed against the back of the chair.

Abruptly, Black was backing up, rage ebbing from his features, leaving surprised fear in its stead. He blinked only when his back hit the wall.

Jane's voice quivered as she moved in her chair. "See, Dad? When somebody's not afraid of you, you don't have anything left. Now we can talk."

Maddy inhaled, a catch in her chest the first awareness she'd been holding her breath. She wanted to scream at the girl, warn her about the burning void left by destroyed love. The moment when she might have spoken came and went, and her silence remained as a foul taste in her mouth.

Continuing, Jane said, "I've got a deal for you, 'cause Richie and I have to get away from here."

Black shook his head. "If he's in trouble with the law, there's no way I can help you."

"Fuck the law. Look, I told Richie he was moving in, you know? And he goes, 'Not me. That asshole'll kill me,' and I go, 'You just be there. I'll take care of it.' So he gets a load, okay? Only he scammed the dealer, and now him and his friends are looking for him."

"So Richie gets lumps. I'm supposed to care?"

"Nobody thought you would. But I figure if you drop a couple of grand on us—call it my dowry, right?—we don't tell the newspapers your office is a fucking front. And I don't give your girlfriend details about how you killed my mother." For Maddy, she flashed a simpering smile. "Not with a gun, sweetie. With a bottle. And lies. Only he knows which came first."

Black said, "That's all you've got?" and Maddy refused to look toward that cold voice.

Jane said, "It's enough."

"Tell Maddy anything you want. But you make trouble for me in my business, and you'll have me and *my* friends looking for Richie." He moved away from the wall, lowered

219

his face to within inches of hers. "Since you were born, my life was geared to making your life a good one. It didn't work. I loved your mother. That didn't work. My professional life fell apart. I wanted to die, Janie. The only thing I've ever *wanted* to kill was myself, and by the grace of God, I failed at that, too. Then Maddy came along. Then I found a purpose in my work. Between those two things, I've got a world to live in. You think I'm going to let you squander it on this piece of dirt?" He straightened. "Get out."

Richie started quickly, but Jane pulled him back, her jaw set. "You'd really contract him out, wouldn't you? You're just what I always thought." Turning to Maddy, she said, "I wasn't kidding about my mother. What'd he say his job is?"

Exhausted, Maddy could only shake her head.

Jane sneered. "Jesus, what a wimp. Okay, listen. He's some kind of super-cop, you know? Only he works against his own people. He's so proud of his job, and all he is, is a motherfucking informer!"

Maddy looked at Black, back in his position at the wall. He stood with his arms folded across his chest, face blank. Her expression was question enough, and he said, "I lied to you. I didn't want to. I was going to tell you the truth."

"Shit!" Stretching the word to two syllables, Jane responded with grating amusement. "Pick whatever lie you like. When that one gets old, he'll have another one waiting."

Maddy ignored her. "Why?"

He moved a shoulder. It could have been a shrug. "I can't tell you. Not yet. Not here."

"Aw, he's telling her he trusts her, but not us. That's what really good screwing'll get you, Richie. Maybe—"

Later, Maddy would reflect that she never saw Black move. One instant he was stolidly watching Jane, and the next he had her by the arm, on tiptoe in front of the chair. Richie cowered in his chair, whimpering. Jane spat in her father's face. The frothy mass dribbled down his cheek to the curve of his jaw before he carefully drew his handkerchief with his free hand and wiped it away. Dropping the soiled cloth, he walked her toward the door her feet barely scuffling the carpet. She made no attempt to resist. Their eyes blazed at each other until he released her. Rubbing her arm, erasing him from her presence without another glance, she called Richie. He scuttled for the hall, stopping as if clubbed at Black's one-word order to wait.

"Remember, Richie, not a word about me to anyone. Ever. Or I come for you. Not her. You."

Richie's face melted under the enormity of the sentence. He opened his mouth to protest, and Black shook his head, then said, "Take out the garbage, Janie," and smiled.

The door closed and Black turned. Maddy's head threatened to split at the sight of his face. Until that moment she had believed she understood the depth of his pain. Surely the gate-keepers of hell smiled like that when they welcomed suicides, she thought.

And if he'd never met her, maybe none of it would have happened.

Rather than run from the idea, she examined it, decided it was specious. If it wasn't, it still made no difference. No stupid guilt problem was going to affect her opinion of him. The issue was truth.

She said, "You weren't interested in my husband's taxes. You were checking on his politics."

"In a sense."

"Good answer. Were my answers funny? I mean, me sitting there pouring my guts out. Did I make you laugh?"

"You know better."

"No, not really. Why did you do it?"

"He did some illegal business with some people."

"You are a cop, then."

He spread his hands, palms up, like a man about to produce a coin from behind a child's ear. Only the earnestness of his eyes kept Maddy from breaking into laughter. He said, "I do counterintelligence work. Your husband was involved in espionage. For what it's worth to you, he's not anymore. And I knew he didn't leave you because he's gay. I wanted to tell you, Maddy. I swear to God I'd have told you when it's over, but I couldn't. I'm trying to catch the man he worked for." An edge crept into his voice. "While I'm being so goddammed honest, you might as well know I'd tell you

221

nothing now, if I could avoid it. It's not wise for you to know some of this.''

"What are you, FBI? And why lie about it?''

"I'm not FBI. I'm CIA. Counterintelligence. It's illegal for us to operate in this country.''

Frowning, she spoke almost to herself. "What she said's true. You are a spy.''

"If you like.'' He moved to the bed, closed his suitcase. "You can criticize what I do, but if the men we hunt have their way, there won't be anything left of the U.S. to debate about.''

She got to her feet. "You'd kill Richie for talking. Would you kill me, too?''

He picked up the bag. "I have to leave.'' Looking at the floor, contemplative, he said, "I love you, Maddy. Whatever I am, whatever I've done, whatever I might do, nothing will ever change that. I know how much that means to me. You're going to have to decide if it means anything to you.''

She was alone, the blank white door impassive.

One summer, when she was a girl, they went on vacation and Mom forgot and left an open scrapbook on top of the air conditioner. When they got back, the sun had washed out all the pictures on those two pages, left nothing but accusing, square white eyes against the black paper. Except for one, in the upper corner, where it escaped most of the light. Amid all the memories stolen from those pages, no one ever identified the solitary, faded, remaining figure. It was just somebody with his back to the camera.

CHAPTER 22

MADDY HAD NO IDEA HOW LONG SHE'D BEEN SITTING IN THE same position when the maid opened the door. Small, dark, the woman stopped open-mouthed. Fluttering embarrassment, stammering, she explained she'd been told the room was vacant. Maddy rose quickly, stifling a wince at joints too long immobile.

"It's okay," she said, finding a smile. "I'm leaving right now."

The woman's nervousness subsided slightly. "There's no need to hurry. When they said your husband already paid, I took it to mean you were both gone. I'm sure sorry."

"It's okay," Maddy repeated, feeling foolish. She picked up her bag. "The room's full of mistakes today, honey. It must be something in the water."

The bravado felt good, like a straight shot, but it faded just as quickly. By the time she was at the elevator, her mind was in turmoil again. She no longer wanted breakfast. The only prospect facing her was to catch a cab and sit around the airport for an hour until plane time. On asking, she found the desk willing to safeguard her bag, and decided to spend the hour exploring.

Outside, she walked to the waterfront tourist trolley stop. The motorman's bell clanged as it started its run, and crossing an intersection triggered the railroad gate and its accompanying bell. The two brazen tones entangled each other, wonderfully complex in their sliding harmonics.

She tried to join in the festive spirit of the other passengers, but instead grew more and more depressed.

Swinging down off the steps of the clattering machine, she was surprised to discover the hearty aroma of fresh-cooked seafood coming from a nearby open-air counter, spurring hunger. She ordered fish and chips, and smiled to herself at the thought that this was, technically, breakfast. A bench beside the building provided a sunny spot to enjoy her meal.

As she ate, she thought. Regardless of the tension between herself and Steve, they would work that out to mutual satisfaction. They were adults, accustomed to accommodating to workaday stresses. Jane had fallen out of that habit. Her answer to trouble was to run.

Maddy dropped the paper utensils and napkin in a trash can and walked. She knew about running, how the first step started you gaining on new problems without ever increasing your distance from the first one. Jane was on the first step, and forcing her father, her only real hope, to abandon her.

She frowned, striding past a fountain made of huge angular cement beams. Sheets of water transformed them to shimmering crystal. The splashing sound literally pulled her closer, offered a screen against the discord of the street.

She wished she could contact Steve and tell him how much she wanted to speak to Jane.

But Jane would be gone long before she could reach him. And there was no way to find her.

Or was there? Hurrying, she was back at the hotel quickly. The desk clerk smiled, swung her bag back up on the counter when he recognized her. She thanked him, then, "My husband paid for our room before he left, but he didn't tell me if he was using a check, a credit card, or what. I have to keep the books straight. Would you mind letting me see how he handled it?"

"Of course, Mrs. Black. Just a minute." In seconds he cheerfully displayed the check, with its home address and phone number. Minutes later she had changed her return reservation to a later flight and was in a cab on her way to his place.

After knocking on the apartment door several times, Maddy was ready to leave when she was certain she heard noise on the other side. Looking down, she saw shadow disturb the faint line of light at the bottom of the door. Positioning herself directly in front of the optical peephole, she said, "It's me, Jane. I'm alone."

Cracking the door cautiously, Jane examined as much of the hall as possible before opening it further. She stared hostility at Maddy. "What the hell do you want? He's not here."

"I came to see you."

Jane grinned crookedly. "You want to do stepmother, is that it? Cookies and milk? Make my little troubles blow away? Get out of here!" She pushed on the door and Maddy braced against her.

"Give up, bitch! Go away!"

Straining, Maddy said, "You've got to listen!"

Jane let go with such suddenness Maddy nearly tumbled into the room. Jane slammed the door behind her, locked it. "So say something," she said, throwing herself on the sofa. "When Richie gets back, we're gone."

Maddy nodded, smoothed her hair. She felt disheveled, violated by Jane's stare. She stammered, finally got the words straight. "I know the trouble in the hotel was strictly between you and your father, but—"

Jane was on her feet. "Right. It's none of your fucking business."

Working to keep calm, Maddy said, "Steve's a fine man, Jane. I can't believe he really hurt your mother. I know he certainly never meant to."

For a few seconds, Jane looked at Maddy with narrow-eyed speculation, then sat down as quickly as she'd risen. "He likes you, does he?" she asked, and without waiting for an answer, went on. "He sent you here?"

"No." Maddy permitted herself a smile in the hope she was making contact. She was further encouraged when Jane returned it, and she hurried on. "This is just between us.

225

He's got something to see to, and he thinks I'm on my way back to San Francisco. I just had to talk to you. Whatever the trouble is between you, you can't shut him out of your life. Or let him shut you out.''

Jane lifted a languid arm to the back of the sofa, glancing at her watch as it passed. "You really like him, don't you?"

"Very much."

A swift darkness marred the old-young face and was gone. A sharp coldness touched Maddy's mind. It puzzled her, since Jane appeared even friendlier than before.

"How'd you meet my father?"

"He was looking for someone I used to know. My name came up."

"His business is like that." The sarcasm crackled.

Maddy said, "Don't be too harsh, Jane. These things are necessary."

The younger woman's eyes flashed and her lips parted, but the retort was stillborn. Instead, she put on a tightly neutral expression and peeked at her watch. She said, "We won't argue. How long have you known him?"

"Only a few months. But it's you I'm concerned about. Look, Jane, I cut myself off once—no contact with my parents, old friends, old locations. It's hell. I'm sure Richie's great company, but a person needs more than just one other person. You both need other people, other things. Sooner or later, everyone needs someone else's strength and love. Don't throw away your father's love because his strength wants to overpower you. Keep a distance between you, if you have to, but not a distance you can't cross when you need each other.''

"Richie's plenty for me."

"And you're both running. Alone together." She leaned forward, demanding Jane's full attention. "You know you're the strong one. What if he starts to come apart, decides all his troubles are your fault? Who do you turn to? Don't do this to yourself, Jane. Don't do it to Steve!"

Pale, mechanically stiff, Jane rose. "I'll make us some coffee," she said. Her look at her watch was undisguised, and Maddy hurried to her feet. "I've stayed too long. I only

226

came to say what I've said." She moved to pass Jane, headed for the door, and when the girl put a hand on her arm, Maddy reached to touch it. She said, "Think about what I've told you, please."

The hand on her arm tightened. "Stay a few more minutes. Just a little longer."

The dark insinuation that corrupted Jane's face earlier now surfaced in her voice. The hair stirred at the back of Maddy's neck. Her polite exit became a need to get away. She pulled against the restraining grip. "I really have a plane to catch. I've said everything I can. I'm not very eloquent."

"Sure you are." Jane was sweetly insistent. "I love listening to you, I really do. I'll just be a minute. You go on and sit down."

"No, really." It sprang from her mouth, unbidden. More trite babble rushed after it. "I'll be late. I know you have things to do." The fingers taloned into her flesh as Jane heaved back on the arm. Maddy's confusion thickened to a formless dread. She knew she was heartbeats away from panic.

The door swung open, freezing them in their strained attitudes. Richie stared at them in open wonder. Jane hurried to him, pushing the door closed behind him. "Where the hell have you been?"

"A couple guys were watching the pawn shop. I had to wait till they left. What's the deal with her?" He jerked his chin at Maddy.

Jane slipped on the chain lock, shot the dead bolt. "She's telling me what a good dude my old man is."

He grunted. "Son of a bitch. I hope he gets cancer."

Maddy said, "I'm leaving now."

Leaning back against the door, Jane said, "Not yet. You had your turn. Now it's mine." When Richie shot her a quizzical frown, she said, "He gets something to remember us by."

Richie said, "What is this shit?"

"Kick her ass."

"Do *what*?"

"Kick her ass! I want him to see her hurt!"

In the bright silence that followed, no one moved. The first clear thought to work through Maddy's amazement was an incredulous awareness that she knew exactly what Jane would look like in old age. Her order to Richie warped her face into sere, exaggerated shapes. Wrinkles absorbed the smooth cheeks, pinched the eyes back into the skull. Lips wrenched into a prune-textured lump, and the chin fell back, quivering.

Maddy forced her feet to carry her forward. Richie stepped aside.

Jane screamed at him. "You gutless son of a bitch! You worked me over enough! Now do it to her!"

Maddy ignored her, ignored the wadded, pounding knot that used to be her stomach. She concentrated on the door. Sanctuary.

There was no pain from the first blow. The door receded, rising up and to the right, changing places with the ceiling. Only when worn carpet cords scraped her cheek did she realize she was on the floor. An approaching foot moved with sluggish speed, but when she tried to avoid it, her head was even slower. This time the pain was instantaneous, overwhelming. She screamed.

In the distance, Richie said, "Shit! Shut her up!" Another explosion rocked through her body, this one slightly below her breasts. It snuffed her breath as quickly as a child blows out a birthday candle. She writhed, strained for air.

Jane said, "Perfect! You knocked the fucking wind out of her. Now work her over!"

"Somebody must have heard her! We're splitting!"

"Not until I'm ready, asshole! Do it!"

"Jesus!" Fright and resignation warred in the single word.

Maddy lost track of the blows, tossed on waves of pain. Her paralyzed diaphragm suddenly relaxed, allowing her to breathe. She tried to cry for help, but only weak grunts came out, stained with blood and saliva. Hopelessness released the tears pain failed to generate. They ran down her cheeks.

The beating stopped. Richie's labored breathing rasped overhead. Hands grabbed her shoulders, flipped her onto her back. She tried to scream again when the ends of broken ribs

228

ground across each other. The feeling of her panties being pulled off overrode even that pain, and she struggled to prevent this newest horror. Jane's backhanded slap drove her head against the carpet.

"Fuck her," Jane said, clamping Maddy's head between her knees while holding the weakly flailing arms at the elbows.

Richie said, "You're crazy! We don't have time!"

Calmly, Jane said, "If anyone was coming, they'd be here by now. I want that no-good bastard to know his little darling can get fucked just like the rest of us. Get it on."

Blearily, seeing him through the remaining slit of a swelling eye, Maddy watched Richie's tense apprehension give way to a lip-licking preoccupation with her exposed body. He said, "Maybe you're right," and thumbed open his fly.

Outrage seized Maddy, a desire to punish these people, to inflict pain on them. Lunging forward, she yanked her head free. Jane moved with her right hand to force her back, and Maddy sank her teeth into it. She caught Jane's thumb at the bottom joint, and she attacked it with the fury of desperation. Things severed, popped and crackled. The sound of Jane's agony was music. Maddy shook her head like a dog killing a rat, and the scream ululated wildly.

Richie grabbed her shoulders, but Maddy held on, telling herself she must until help arrived. Jane's pounding on her back was no problem. She knew she'd lost when Richie twisted her arm up behind her back. She let go and tried to roll away from the pain.

Jane continued to wail. Richie's sympathetic murmurings grew increasingly short and nervous. When the knocking on the door started, he whispered hoarsely, "Goddammit, you finally did it! Come on, we've got to run!"

Hazily, Maddy saw him grab Jane and tow her, stumbling, behind him. Jane cradled the torn hand against her body. Letting go of her, Richie flung open the apartment door, bowling past the middle-aged couple standing there. He fled without a backward glance for Jane. She ran after him, her dwindling cries filling the hall with strange, dying echoes.

The couple crept into the room, cautious as mice. Maddy

was already struggling to open her purse. The woman gasped. "My God, what have they done to you?"

The man said, "Call Medic One," and hurried to Maddy as the woman picked up the phone. He put his hands under her arms to steady her, and Maddy resisted, fumbling to produce the paper with Steve's phone number. She pointed at it. Blood dripped on the white surface, three thick drops, like a pawnbroker's symbol.

The woman said, "They're on the way." Then, in a hushed aside, "Will she live?"

Maggie slumped onto her side. She decided she didn't hurt enough to be dying. Then she wondered if that might not be the way it worked—the pain died along with you.

She rolled her eyes, found the man. He faced his wife, shaking his head, his mouth bent downward in a tight, sad curve.

CHAPTER 23

DAVIS STRETCHED LUXURIOUSLY IN THE CHAIR, HIS CONTENTED groan resonating in Black's tiny office. He said, "I'm not going to ask you to pursue this thing in L.A. until we're reasonably certain it's a Soviet pitch and a lead to Marvin. Meanwhile, I don't want you distracted." He got to his feet. "That's about it. The only thing we've got in this area is a possible fabricator. Came up in a routine background check. The guy's paperwork's perfect, but an interviewee said he's caught him saying he's from California and correcting himself, changing it to Colorado. Excitement abounds." He shrugged.

The phone rang. Davis grimaced around his cigar. "Take it, will you? That's the third time."

"The hell with it. You're the only one who can chew me for not answering my phone, and you're here."

"You're in an odd mood. What's going on?"

"Nothing, for Christ's sake." Black snatched up the handset. "Hello!"

He leaned heavily on the desk. The thick body surrendered like a candle in the sun. "How is she?" After a pause, he said, "How'd it happen?" and suddenly sat bolt upright. "*My* apartment?"

Davis moved to his side, so that when Black said, "I'll be right there," and hung up, he was there to put his hand on Black's shoulder.

"Easy," he said quietly. "I've seen you like this. You're not going anywhere until I hear what's coming down."

Black rose through Davis's restraining touch as if unaware of it. "Whoever did it to her got away."

"Oh, Christ, Steve. Jane? Is she all right?"

Dumping the work papers in a filing cabinet, Black shook his head. He handed Davis his briefcase and brushed past him, saying, "Madeline Hosmer. I met her in Frisco, checking out leads from those Marvin contacts. Somebody assaulted her. In my apartment."

Davis swallowed questions he could ask later. "They have a suspect?"

"What? Oh. No, of course not. That's why we're going to the hospital."

"Certainly." Davis dabbed fine sweat from his upper lip, fell in with Black's half-trot. He cursed to himself, consigning both victim and assailant to the farthest reaches of hell's foulest corner.

The entire operation, strung together as neatly as a Broadway production, dangling in space. Someone'll burn for that. No one told me about a woman, damn them. And damn him. All those years, sitting alone in that dump of an apartment, and now, when he's finally coming back to life, some broad gets mauled and he's on the edge of diving back into his hole. I'd like to belt her myself.

He warned himself that he was indulging in self-pity, that it could be destructive. At best, it was useless.

Black drove at little more than average speed. Davis watched him maneuver through traffic, judging inches unerringly, swooping into gaps that seemed impossible. The controlled face was unreadable. Still, he was enraged. Davis wondered how he gave off such a clear signal. Only the flickering eyes hinted of tension, and that could have been the fault of traffic.

At the hospital desk, Davis half-smiled at the matronly, gray-haired woman looking fearlessly up at Black, whose question was almost murmuring soft. The woman gave him Maddy's room number. Polite thanks trailed over his shoulder as he moved away to the elevator. Davis followed.

232

Black stopped outside the room, suddenly irresolute, transformed from an object of danger to a large, uncertain man. He said, "What can I tell her, Bob? What do I do?"

Davis surprised himself. "I think it might be a good idea if you told her you love her."

"Does it show that much?"

"Yeah, it really does. Sometime you'll have to tell me how this all happened without me getting any idea it was going on."

"I guess I ought to go in." He remained unmoving.

"I guess so."

Black looked away. "I don't know if I can handle it."

"You have to. She needs help."

The uncertain expression fell in on itself, and Black leaned his forehead against the slick, disinterested wall. "Jesus. I can't stop thinking Jane had something to do with this. I'm sure of it. What can I say to Maddy?"

A nurse appeared in the door. She was a slim black woman, elegant in crisp white. She touched Black's arm, and he straightened quickly. Her words were quick, like notes in bird song. She said, "Your voice is very distinctive, Mr. Black. She knows you're out here. You'd better come in." Black considered her for another two heartbeats, then nodded briskly, moving past her.

Pulling a chair to the bedside, he took Maddy's hand in his. He tried to blot out the bruises, the sausage-swollen lips, the discolored mounds of flesh heaped over the eyes. A string of sutures marched along her jawbone. In his mind's eye he saw the wound as it must have looked. Now the neat black stitches accused him, a doctor's scorecard of her man's failure to protect her.

Her hand closed on his, soft, hot, the fingers moving in disjointed confusion, each one independent of the others. He said, "I'm sorry, Maddy. I never should have asked you to come up here."

An increase in the strength of her grip stopped him. Slowly, painfully, she moved her head in a negative arc. The smashed lips parted slowly, and she frowned at the pain. The nurse hurried to the other side of the bed in a sibilance of immaculate white polyester. Contradicting wisps of perfumed soap and disinfectant eddied behind her. She touched Maddy's other hand.

"Don't try to talk, honey," she said, the musical voice soothing. "He has to say something, and he's just acting like a man. You hurry and get well. We'll educate him."

Muscles moved in Maddy's face. Black told himself she was trying to smile. The nurse caught his eye, cocked her head at the door. He nodded.

To Maddy, he said, "She's right about you getting well. We'll count the days you're here as lost time, you hear? We'll make it up, I promise. I have to leave now so you can rest." He leaned over her, kissed her temple. "I love you."

When he straightened, a tear was materializing at the outer limit of the slit marking her ravaged eye. He gently placed her hand on the bed.

He waited for the nurse at the central station down the hall. Davis took up a position at the ward entrance, far enough to afford Black privacy, close enough to be at hand if needed.

When the nurse approached, Black asked, "What's the prognosis?"

She smiled. "She's going to be just fine. It looks lots worse than it really is." Then seriously, "Dr. Johan's on the floor. He'll give you the details. But there's no major damage."

Dr. Johan proved to be a compact, businesslike young man whose sympathetic brown eyes belied almost brusque mannerisms. He detailed the damage in swift, precise language, and predicted complete recovery.

When he was gone, the nurse reappeared at Black's side. She fidgeted for a moment before speaking. "Mr. Black, do you think she knew whoever did this?" Hurrying, she went on, "I see victims a lot. I think someone meant to hurt her, to punish her. I'm only asking so we can try to screen visitors." She looked away. "Things like this— I hate to say it, but it's usually somebody pretty close."

"You're very kind. And brave. You're sticking your neck out, asking that kind of question, and I appreciate it. Yes, I think she knows who it was. They won't be troubling her.

She's just a message to them, and she's served her purpose. I think that's worse than a punishment, don't you?''

The nurse was about to answer him, when she looked up into his face. Whatever she meant to say died then. She turned away before Black moved to rejoin Davis.

In the elevator, Davis ran a hand through his hair, eliminating the expensive styling, while he watched Black from the corner of his eye. They were in the parking lot before Black spoke. He leaned on the roof of the car, talking across it to the shorter man. "Quit peeking at me, Bob. Get your lecture out of the way.''

"I don't have a lecture." Davis bristled. "All I have is a statement. There's no way Jane could have done that.''

Black said, "Her boyfriend. You won't mind if I run you out to the airport and leave you to fend for yourself?''

Underway, he continued, "This is when I'm supposed to throw up my hands and wonder where I went wrong. Fuck that." He scowled an unanswered challenge at Davis, then went on. "Dina chose to drink her way out of a world she didn't want to look at. Jane's so-called goddammed rebellion's the same thing, a fucking foot race to oblivion. I *did* try, Bob. I did my best. I'll be damned if I'll destroy myself because they did.''

"I'm glad to hear it. Now I have to wonder what you're going to do about the man who attacked Maddy.''

"I'm making up my mind.''

"Let me help. I've got an interest in this, you know. You're my friend, first off, but nailing Marvin's my major concern. If I can't depend on you for that, I've got to make some kind of move, Steve.''

Black nodded. The conversation stopped.

When this was over, he decided, he'd take Maddy on a trip. By the time she felt up to it, fall would be scouting down from the mountains in the evenings, anxious to make its move. She'd need sunshine and rest. Maybe Hawaii. Maybe someplace far, far away from everything, someplace tropical and exotic.

He could use rest himself. If Davis or anybody else begrudged him the time, they could stick the whole damned thing. There were other ways to make a living.

Jane and Richie were free.

The thought was in his mind without warning, without reason, displacing everything else.

That was ridiculous. Freedom without goals, without pride, without honor—that was aimlessness. No one could exist that way without guilt or the uncomprehending fury that grows from life without purpose.

Davis said, "We're only a few minutes from the airport, Steve. There's no need for you to come in with me. Call me in the morning, okay?"

"Sure."

"Good. Look, the last thing I need is half your mind on business and the other half wondering about the guy who did this thing. I know you blame yourself for Maddy being up here, but that's just dumb. At the same time, I know how personally you're going to take this."

"You're goddamned right I take it personally. Jesus Christ, Bob, they did that to her because they're pissed off at me!"

"Nobody can blame you. Least of all me. I leaned on you pretty hard to run the Marvin investigation."

"Don't you start up. First you tell me none of this is my fault, then you tell me it's yours. Bullshit."

"No, I mean it. You don't deserve what's happened, and she sure as hell doesn't."

Black frowned, unanswering, and Davis continued. "The real irony is that she's not involved. We're the ones making war—she's the one who got hurt. It makes you wonder if there's any point in any of it."

Black worked the car past off-loading vehicles, grabbed a spot at the curb. Laying an arm across the back of the seat, he twisted to look directly at his companion. "It's because she's hurt that there *has* to be a point. What happened wasn't because I'm chasing some KGB bastard, but because I happened to meet her while I was after him and I've got a child who's a vicious—ahh!" He waved it all away with an angry growl. "The hell with it. Marvin cost her her first husband and brought me sniffing around. Now she's hurt because I

236

talked her into getting involved with me. I know exactly what I'm doing in here." He tapped his head. "I'm blaming my enemy for my problems. And I can't help it. The son of a bitch *is* responsible. Maybe I did neglect Dina and Jane because of him and his goddamned kind. If it wasn't for him, she'd be sitting in her store right now."

"So? What're you telling me?"

"I want Marvin as much as I want Richie. Different meal, same hunger. I'm telling you so you won't get in my way, Bob. Don't fool with me, and don't let anyone else."

"Promise me you won't kill Marvin."

"Hell, no. I will before I'll let him hurt anyone or escape, but I'm not going to cowboy the bastard. I'm not that crazy."

"What if this Richie shows up?"

"Merry Christmas. He'll survive it. Look, don't worry. I know the priorities. Marvin first. I promise."

Davis opened the door, uncoiled onto the sidewalk. "Be honest with me, Steve. Back off if you want. Just don't short me. Marvin's important, and he's good. We can't afford less than our best shot."

"What color ribbon you want around him?"

Grinning, Davis extended a hand, shaking Black's. "You don't know how glad I am to hear you back in business, my friend. I was really worried."

Black threw him a salute and a crooked grin, then eased into traffic. The grin altered, went from deprecating to sardonic. He talked to himself. "I know you're glad I'm back in business. I know you're using me. What I can't figure out is if I'm deliberately using you, or if you're playing me along. Something terrible's going on inside all of us. God help me, Bob, I wouldn't stop if I could. I wish I knew what I'll be when it's over, though."

CHAPTER 24

Talking to Nicolai's cold resistance was like talking to a snake, even to the eyes that blinked without losing their focus. His presence turned the nondescript motel room into a dank interrogation cell, forced Carmody's mind to reject the laundered air and wallow instead in remembered stinks of mildewed cement, urine, and cabbage.

"The man is unstable, Nicolai. Promise him anything, then use him to steal everything he can get in one fast operation. After that, we can send him home."

Nicolai tented his fingers, lowering his chin to rest on them. "He is in place, unsuspected. He has produced invaluable data. He has improved his position in the company and therefore his value to us. You say we should dispose of him. What am I to think?" He speared the larger man with a look.

Desperate, Carmody said, "Think of being called to the Square to explain the loss of the most productive espionage operation in this country, comrade."

Nicolai's upper lip curled. "I am in no danger of being questioned, *comrade*. I am not proposing the elimination of the largest jewel in this vaunted network."

"Summerton jeopardizes me and everyone I deal with." Carmody gritted his teeth at the surly, childish tone of his voice.

"We are in a business of extraordinary risk. Some more

238

than others." Nicolai looked up and bubbled a mysterious laughter he quickly swallowed.

Carmody leaned back in his chair. For some reason, Nicolai found him wanting, distrusted him. Life now would be a constant test. Carmody had seen similar situations, created it for others. Now it was his turn.

Sweat like ice tickled his armpits. It stank, rank as any beast's.

Nicolai said, "There was a man in Sweden, many years ago, who posed the same problem as Summerton. We made him a colonel, promised him eventual transfer to the Soviet Union with pension and privileges."

"And he was captured. He told them everything he knew."

"Never mind. Is that the sort of thing Summerton would like?"

"I can't be sure."

"Meet him again. Find out."

"All right. Yes, I think it's what he'd like."

Nicolai baited him. "You wouldn't want a meeting? To reassure yourself?"

Carmody glared openly, not caring. "He will accept such an arrangement. I'm certain."

"I accept your judgment. Now, we need a proper location to impress him. As quickly as possible."

The room closed in on Carmody. "For whom?"

"All of us—me, him, and you, of course. After all, you're his uncle."

"No! He was assigned to me. I use him, that's all. I didn't spot him, didn't recruit him, nothing!"

"You're sweating," Nicolai observed. He angled forward. The sarcastic manner was gone, wiped away by a workman's close attention to his task.

Carmody said, "Certainly I'm sweating. I've put as much distance between me and that bastard as I can, and now you want to actually trust him. This scheme is dangerous."

After a short pause, Nicolai said, "You young people have no sense of our history at all. We have spoiled you, stifled you with peace. What is that thing they wrap the babies with? Yes, *kosinka*. You are mummified in your *kosinka*. Warm,

239

safe, helpless. In my time, we had nothing, you understand? We beat the Hitlerites, but we were bled white. Only Stalin had the foresight to see the West, ready to kick our broken bodies, and he *attacked!* How he drove us! The capitalists and their Jew bankers ran from us. We talked sweetness and peace to the weak to isolate our enemies, then destroyed them. At home, every day for us was a new *chistka*. Every day, a purge. Those left were pure flame.''

He stopped abruptly, walked to the window, turning a shade too slowly to hide the distaste sweeping his face. When he resumed, he kept his back to Carmody. ''These people are divided, each cares only for his own convenience. If we show them resistance is dangerous, they'll collapse.'' He whirled, an accusing finger aimed at Carmody. ''You worry about being arrested. What will they do to you? Refuse sugar for your tea? Make you read the Bible? Pah! We lived with danger because our goal was great. In my day we stole *factories* from these idiots, ripped entire railroads from the ground, moved them to the motherland.''

Suddenly confidential, he sat down across from Carmody. ''This pile of shit is ready to topple. We increase the pace of operations, punishing whoever interferes, while our friends discredit our enemies. Each step makes the next easier. Fear eats at resolve. Lack of resolve breeds uncertainty. Uncertainty creates more fear.''

''And your first shot in this war is to involve us even further with a moron?''

The placid answering smile troubled Carmody more than the little man's naked ferocity. ''Just do as you're told. All will be well.''

Lassitude oozed through Carmody's veins. There was nothing to be done but cooperate. Nicolai had spoken the single commandment that ruled all things: Do as you're told. He heard himself agreeing to manage the meeting, even pictured calling the hotel for a reservation, arranging a celebration dinner. Another part of his mind thought of Nicolai's purges, those times he spoke of with such fond reminiscence.

Those times.

Mother's brother was swallowed during those times. Father drank himself into a stupor at every opportunity, cursing the Germans for killing so many Russians and letting Stalin live.

Nicolai finished his instructions a few minutes before ten. At eleven o'clock he left for the airport and San Francisco.

Back in his apartment, whiskey in hand, Carmody could remember absolutely nothing of the drive home.

Elise answered his telephone call sleepily. When he suggested that he come over she responded with pleased, happy laughter that was as welcoming as it was indulgent. She said she'd be waiting and hung up.

The chill clouding his heart began to dissipate.

Delight burst onto Summerton's features as he entered the hotel suite. Carmody sat stiffly on the sofa, waiting, and Summerton favored him with an abstracted nod on his way to examine the luxurious bathroom. Emerging, he stood looking up the curving stairs to the upper level. He said, "Shit, man, it's just like a movie, you know? Look at this place!"

"Yes." Carmody reminded himself he must be more than civil. "We thought you'd appreciate it."

"We?" Summerton was alarmed.

Carmody smiled disarmingly. "I'm introducing you to a particular friend of mine today."

"He knows?"

"Everything." Carmody fitted a laugh to the smile, engaging.

"Your boss?" Summerton asked, moving to the bar, and Carmody damned his presumption and his perception.

"Yes. He knows the bureaucracies of the world better than they know themselves."

"Meaning what?"

"Meaning you can live anywhere you like, quite pleasantly, when you're finished working for us—or if the opposition becomes interested in you."

"Goddammit, Martin, you promised me everything was safe." The self-indulgent face puckered, infuriating Carmody.

"You were taught how to make it as safe as possible. No one promised you anything!"

241

Summerton blinked rapidly. "I'm sorry. This is a pretty big event for me. I'm nervous."

"That's okay, Harry. So am I. We don't extend this sort of treatment to many people. I'm proud to be part of it." He poured himself a tumbler of bourbon and downed a relieving swallow before returning to his seat.

Summerton was at the window, his hands behind his back. Carmody reexamined the room. The opulence made him uncomfortable because he liked it. Knowing he need only pick up the phone and the concierge would produce the finest food, the best wines, a selection of clothes, show tickets—anything the city had to offer—embarrassed and charmed him.

At the knock on the door, he hurried to admit Nicolai. He watched the small, bright shoes in their brisk pace across the carpet and thought of rats. Acting the perfect host, he introduced him to Summerton.

"Martin," Nicolai said, bubbling heartiness, gesturing like a circus clown, "make a drink for me and our friend. This is a festive event."

Carmody obeyed, aware of Summerton's amused glance.

Rejoining them, Carmody downed half of his fresh drink, letting the spreading heat weigh down anger. He reminded himself to think of the mission. Whatever the fools projected, Carmody had to protect his net and his mission. All the rest was unimportant.

Nicolai was saying, "Your work has been praised in the highest offices, Harry. I'm privileged to offer you a considerable increase in your payments, retroactive to three months ago."

Summerton smiled smugly for Carmody as Nicolai busied himself in his briefcase. Carmody returned it with delicious malice, knowing what was coming. Nicolai produced a sheet of heavy vellum that rustled importantly as it pulled free. He slapped it down on the coffee table. "There. Read."

For a moment the cheery public-relations facade slipped, revealing the imperious martinet.

Carmody was gratified to see concern tug at Summerton's eyes. Nicolai clapped Summerton on the back as he read. "A handsome figure, Harry, and you're worth every cent. I only wish we could avoid this administrative foolishness of banking it. I fought to get you access, but some things are unarguable.''

Summerton grunted.

Smoothly, Nicolai continued. ''Everything's indexed, to account for inflation, naturally. That brings us to this paragraph, 'Transportation and shipment of personal goods to location chosen.' When you're finished working for us, you tell us where you'd like to retire. Everything you own will be shipped at our expense. And the house purchase allowance is also indexed.''

He stopped to sip his drink and observe the effect of his review. Summerton's gaze swept between the amount promised and the paragraph about retirement in greedy arcs.

Nicolai ventured a tight grin for Carmody, then returned to the attack. ''What is retirement age in your company, Harry? Sixty-five? With us, it's a matter of mutual convenience. It could be as soon as next year.'' Summerton's tongue darted across his lips, and Nicolai's voice dropped to a murmur. ''Obviously, we benefit by what you provide, and your earnings potential increases every year we're in active partnership. But we also understand pressure. I imagine you'd like to retire to some nice waterfront home, perhaps in the San Juans?''

Summerton looked up sharply, then out the window at the lengthening afternoon shadows. ''Not me. It'll cost you a ton when I bail out. I'll be on my way where the bananas grow, friend—Hawaii, Tahiti, Jamaica, Brazil.'' Carmody nearly laughed out loud at Nicolai's flush of indignation.

''Not Cuba?'' Nicolai's brittle question sang malice.

Oblivious, Summerton guffawed. ''Volunteer to cut sugar cane for El Supremo? Bullshit.''

Nicolai turned away stiffly. ''Would you pour me a little more of that Scotch, Martin? Thank you.'' The hand that blindly extended the glass trembled.

By the time Carmody returned, the conversation was amicable again, Summerton outlining the areas of research his company felt most worthy of attention. Carmody interrupted.

"You're talking as if the McKay experiments are essentially completed."

"The theoretical work's done. Setting up the testing machinery for the new alloys is going to take time. But in effect, yes, the work's done."

"When will the new computers be ready to perform?"

Summerton's offensive grin failed to disturb Nicolai, and Carmody silently congratulated him for grace under pressure. Summerton said, "Not for quite a while, but yesterday I was assigned to the team evaluating the emplacement-facility plans. It'll eventually be in a tunnel under a mountain in the North Cascades. I'll be in on every step of the development, and when it's in working order, I'll be right there with it."

"You're a treasure," Nicolai enthused, "a marvel! Martin, it's time!" Before Carmody could speak, he pointed at the briefcase. "The manila folder. Give it to me."

Cursing under his breath, Carmody searched for the folder, pulled it free.

It's so idiotically dangerous and so unnecessary! he wanted to shout. Summerton was already satisfied. Helpless, he gave the papers to Nicolai, who broke out the crackling bond with a flourish. He read in Russian, the richness of the language cheated by the tight northern accent. Carmody twisted his face into what he could only hope was a warm smile.

It went amazingly well. Summerton clowned his inability to understand. Nicolai went through the entire speech, flinging gestures and letting his voice range from whisper to hearty pronouncement. Then he did it again, in English, and this time his needle-sharp eyes poked at Summerton. When it was over, Summerton's eyes were round and protruding.

He said, "Me? A colonel? A lifetime appointment?"

"It is the least we can do," Nicolai said.

Summerton rose awkwardly, made his way to the window with unsure steps. Nicolai hurriedly downed his drink and snapped his fingers for Carmody to refill the glass. They both waited for the next move from the slump-shouldered figure silhouetted against the lingering dusk.

"No one ever did anything like this for me," he said. He walked back to the bar, poured himself a drink, hoisted it in a toast to his companions. "To belonging. To our friendship and our goals."

Nicolai stood to drink with him, allowing himself a triumphant smile.

Disaster surrounded Carmody, a thin mist coating his skin like dead sweat. His mind refused to relinquish the image of Summerton in the hands of FBI agents—and in the background, himself, his arms pinioned by KGB enforcers, while Nicolai watched.

Nicolai ordered dinner from room service. Carmody ate mechanically. Beneath the table talk of cooperation and companionship, his mind prowled nervously, worrying over a future suddenly grown more hazardous than reason required.

What was it Nicolai had said earlier? Something about spying being more dangerous for some than for others.

The waiter reappeared, wheeled out the remains of the dinner.

It was just nine o'clock when the small man rose, pomposity magnified by drinking. "I leave now. I have a plane to catch. Harry follows in a few minutes. Martin stays here." His natural abrasiveness scraped at the veneer of the evening.

Summerton approached him, eyes wet with emotion. He embraced the neat figure, rumpling his clothes, and said, "It's taken all my life to find a friend like you. I'll never let you down." Releasing Nicolai, he moved to clasp Carmody's hand between his own, and said, "You made it all possible. We're going to be a great team, a force."

Carmody said, "I'm looking forward to it."

Nicolai was already leaving, arms punching into uncooperative topcoat sleeves. It took him two tries to open the door, and he left without further word.

Summerton turned from watching him. "I'll never be able to thank you enough." Emotion thickened his speech.

"You're too modest, but if you want to thank us, the way to do it is to keep supplying us with the material only you can provide."

"Trust me."

Carmody steered him out. "More than that, my friend, we depend on you. Take care of yourself." He closed the door behind him, leaning against the reassuring solidity. It took several seconds for him to find the strength to straighten up. When he did, he went immediately to the telephone.

When Elise answered, he said, "Are you in bed yet?"

She laughed. "If that's an invitation, it's one of your less-subtle ones. No, I watched television, wondering why I had to be home alone, and I'm just cleaning up the kitchen."

"I'm at the Weston."

"What?"

"I'm alone, too. Sitting here in a huge suite. Got late check-out privileges. Interesting?"

"What are you doing there? You're alone?"

"Very. Can you come? We have the place to ourselves."

"I'd feel awful, Marty. I mean, walking through the lobby at this time of night, asking for your room—everybody's going to know."

"Meet me in the Shampers Bar."

"You still haven't told me why you're there."

"A business deal. Don't worry about it, it's deductible. Please, Elise, come down. I need you."

"Oh." The silent wait that followed drained his breath. He would argue no more, knowing he couldn't maintain routine conversation after the sudden, unintentional admission.

"Give me a few minutes to change."

"I'll be waiting."

She entered from the main lobby, using the stairs that led to the bar. Carmody's table overlooked them, and he rose at her approach. Soft light from fanciful chandeliers touched the gloss of her hair, making it more silken than ever. Her black skirt and deep-blue blouse were accentuated by the neutral colors of the room. He knew he would dream of her movement on those steps for the rest of his life.

They talked for a while, inconsequentials about her neighbors, the shop's requirements. After a glass of wine, he took her hand in his and they left.

Elise stopped a yard into the suite, lowered her shoulder bag, and leaned against the wall to inspect her surroundings carefully. More than simply looking, she was *feeling* what

246

she saw. She said, "I don't like this place, Marty. What happened here?"

He managed to scoff. "You think you're psychic? I had a business talk with a couple of guys."

"It's got nothing to do with spirits." She faced him. "I can feel through you, Marty. I can't tell what's bothering you, but I know when something is. I think something happened here, and it makes the place unfriendly to me." She waved, encompassing everything. "I've never been in anything this luxurious in my life, and I may not again, but I think you had a bad experience here."

Making a joke of it, he said, "You shouldn't tell a man how well you see inside him."

She ignored the humor, wrapped her arms around him. "Marty, I worry about you. You said you needed me."

Unyielding, he stood with his arms at his sides, looking out the window. Down in the harbor on a ship, a welding arc flashed. The diamond-hard light sped across the city to prick at his eyes.

She said, "It wasn't really about the store, was it?"

"No." The trick to living with lies was to tell as few as possible, and marry those few to the truth. "A different business. From the past. They—the people who were here—want me to go back."

She turned up her face to ask the inevitable question, but he was waiting. He kissed her, then spoke with their lips making tender contact. "I said I'm staying here. Okay?"

"Okay." She kissed him, and their tongues initiated a different conversation. It was Carmody who broke off, turning her so they both looked down at the city. He said, "It's all ours tonight. The lights, the secret dark places, everything. Tonight we rule the city, because it can't touch us."

Her head settled against his chest, and he stroked upward from her waist, traced the curving line of torso to breasts. He cupped one of them, pressing gently, before fumbling at the buttons of her blouse.

Elise pulled away. "I brought something," she said. "I'll call you." She retrieved the shoulder bag and went into the bedroom, closing the door behind her.

Carmody darkened the room and returned to the window. His eyes were drawn to the ship, where the hard blue light spoke to him once again, then stopped. He was still staring at the vessel when he heard the door click.

The city's illumination gave all the detail he needed. She wore a pale negligee, a gauzelike thing that flowed from her shoulders to the floor. He stood transfixed, unsure if he saw her body or an imagined beauty beyond reality. The lift of her breasts was undeniable, but the darkness between them that emphasized their fullness might easily have been a trick of shadows. The suggestion of further shading just below her hips might have been the juncture of legs and body, or an image created entirely of desire. He crossed the room to her, swept her into his arms.

It was almost noon when they left, which gave Nicolai only a few minutes to slip into the room and retrieve the voice-activated miniature tape recorders he'd attached to the underside of the coffee table and the headboard of the bed.

CHAPTER 25

WILL WALTERS STEPPED OUT OF THE ELEVATOR INTO THE underground parking garage and stopped.

At least two nights out of every week, regardless of the time, the feeling of being watched grabbed him exactly at that point.

Yanking off coat and tie, he surveyed the ranked cars. There were two people leaving, a woman who'd been around the building for years and a man he recognized from a law office on his own floor. It was always that way. Identifiable people. Harmless.

But the sensation of scrutiny was irresistible.

They were writing a book on him, getting his pattern.

He was convinced the operation was one man, two at the most. The temptation to imagine their appearance whined in his ears. It had started when the surveillance was in its second week. That was when he saw the little blue Ford again. It was too far away for license-plate identification and moved off instantly when he stared at it, but he was certain it was the one from outside Slidell's motel.

A great weight slipped from him. He wasn't burned out. The stalking existed. Reprieved, his mind started reaching out, felt its way through the passing crowds. No one was unsuspected. Did that man stare an instant too long? Who was that hurrying around the corner? How many green Mustangs could a man see in one day? Faces, scenes, inched through his consciousness to no purpose, elongating each day's unimportant seconds to infuriating hours.

Now, bending into his car, his face twisted in a strained smile. He told himself he might not have been crazy before, but he soon would be if this foolishness didn't stop.

Once clear of the garage, he circled blocks and cut traffic lights for a little while, without urgency. He elected to take the long route, but he knew he was free, and that was almost as bad as knowing he wasn't.

The whole operation had a ragged texture, an on-again, off-again eccentricity. If it was a KGB attempt to do a book on him, there should be a team, the whole thing should be reasonably constant. This had the smell of a couple of cowboys working on their own. Guys like that could do dumb things.

Bobbie waited for him at the door, as she always did these days, to make him go directly to the bedroom and put the gun away before she'd let him kiss the girls. Or her. Will didn't really mind. He hated the way she drew up inside herself whenever she felt the cold bulk of it.

This evening, as soon as the weapon was in the drawer, she was in his arms. He put lightness in his voice. "What's all this about?"

"You've lost weight. You carry that damned gun all the time. I want us to leave here, go somewhere, anywhere. Run away from whatever's doing this to you."

"Nobody's doing anything to me."

She jerked her head back to stare up at him. "Don't do that, Will. For God's sake, don't do that, not on top of everything else. I couldn't stand it if you started lying out loud."

"How can we go anywhere? What about the girls' school?"

"A week. It wouldn't be such a big thing. We could leave on a Friday afternoon, be back the next Thursday night." Her fingers kneaded his bicep, as beseeching as her eyes.

"I'll see what I can do."

She kissed him quickly. "That's wonderful! Oh, Will, I'm so glad!" Another light kiss, and she moved swiftly into the hall. Her voice floated back to him. "Kathy, your turn to set the table! Krista, help me with the vegetables!"

Sitting on the edge of the bed, he massaged his temples wearily. It wouldn't be easy to get away, but it was the best idea so far. The Soviets had nowhere near the troops to mount a surveillance like that. As soon as he left town, they'd find something else to do and forget all about him.

He didn't even bother to call Davis. That could wait until morning, and he didn't care if Davis objected or not. Once the idea lodged, he embraced it. Dinner passed in an excited babble. The girls couldn't believe their good fortune, at first, and poked at the announcement as if it might explode if jostled. Only after their mother reassured them did they squeal delight and argue for the place of their choice. Will overruled them.

"Mom picks the spot. It's her week."

Bobbie's eyes loved him. "Santa Barbara," she said immediately. "We never got back. We said we would."

"Never too late." He reached for her hand, and Kathy giggled. Nudging Krista, she rolled her eyes. Krista choked on her milk, barely avoiding a dinner-table catastrophe. When she was able to talk, she said, "Why can't we go to L.A.? There's nothing to do in Santa Barbara."

Will continued to look at Bobbie. "You'll think of something. And me and your mom'll walk on the beach and remember."

"Super," Krista grumbled halfheartedly, knowing the argument was stillborn. "We get out of school for a week and all we do is nothing."

Kathy asserted the authority befitting a two-year-older sister. "It's something romantic, silly. Even people like Mom and Dad get like that."

Will looked at her seriously. "I appreciate that," he said. "Elderly people's feelings are so often forgotten in our society." He stuck out his tongue and made a rude noise.

Kathy tossed her head, picking up her dishes, moving off to the sink. "I just wish somebody appreciated my position once in a while, having to explain everything to a baby sister,

251

trying to bridge an inconceivable generation gap." She let the phrase expire with a gusting, helpless sigh.

Boos, groans, and an irate younger sister chased her from the room.

Laughing, Will shook his head, then looked back to Bobbie. "We've been very lucky," he said.

She pulled her hand away as if his flesh burned her. "We *are* lucky. Why would you say 'have been?' "

"Jesus, Bobbie, lighten up. I only said—"

"I heard. You said 'have been.' Like it was over."

"That's crazy." His chair squalled protest as he shoved away from the table. "You really do need a break."

Her lower lip quivered. "I know. I'm being awful. I'm worried about you."

"Well, your worrying about me has me worrying about you. Can we both stop now?" He pulled a can of beer from the refrigerator and opened it, the sudden hiss scolding both of them. He took a drink and said, "When we get back, everything'll be back to normal, honey. I promise."

Traces of worry scribed razor-thin lines at the corners of her eyes, but she found an easy banter. "Normal's nothing to brag about around here, you know? Maybe you noticed?"

He bent to kiss the top of her head. "You're just frustrated because I haven't come home in the afternoon for a couple of weeks."

"It's been five, old-timer. Maybe your daughter's right about you." She pushed him aside, standing up to clear the table. "Not that I've been counting." Laughing, she ducked away from him. He pretended to be angry.

"We'll discuss this later," he said formally. His heels pounded the floor as he left.

The girls were in their rooms, the thudding rhythm of their stereo pulsing through the house, when Bobbie came to sit on the arm of Will's chair. He looked up from his book, and she said, "I'm going to take a shower, if that suggests anything to you. Concentrate."

Slipping an arm around her, he said, "No ideas. Simple, uncomplicated lust. Why are you dawdling here?"

In a few minutes the rush of water joined the steady,

almost subliminal throb of the music. He was wondering exactly what there was about the house that created that resonance when the doorbell rang.

It was ten minutes after ten.

He started for the bedroom to get the pistol but barely reached the stairs before the bell rang again. Torn, he looked up the stairs. Another ring might disturb Bobbie. He hurried to the door.

The entryway was well-lighted. Through the peephole, he examined the caller. Blood streamed down his face. A wound like an embarrassed smile split his forehead. The man bent to wipe his eyes on his shoulder. He cradled a dangling left arm, grasping it at the elbow with his right hand. Looking past him, Will saw the pickup truck nestled against the old cottonwood at the curbstone. A figure hung out the window on the passenger's side. There was a long, dark stain against the white paint just under the figure's dangling head. As Will watched, the man on the steps twisted to reach the bell button with his shoulder.

Will opened the door. "Come in," he said. "I'll call an ambulance and the police."

The man came erect, letting go of the swaying left arm. In his right hand he held a sawed-off shotgun that had been hidden behind the fake injury.

Like the girls submerged in their songs and his wife luxuriating in her shower and her life, Will never really heard the shotgun. The pain lasted no longer than the flick of red and orange flame that started tiny smoldering fires in his shirt and undershirt. The dread of dying was shattered in him by the time his body hit the stairs and sprawled awkwardly against the wall.

It was ten forty-five before Bobbie had the girls in bed and called down to ask Will why he hadn't come up.

She wore a white negligee that emphasized her lustrous dark hair and eyes.

When he didn't answer right away, she said, "Are you okay, honey? I thought I heard something."

CHAPTER 26

Davis said, "IT'S BEING HANDLED AS AN UNKNOWN-ASSAILANT case, Steve. It could be, for all that. There were a lot of flakes in Will's civilian business."

Black stared at the narrow office wall before peeling the look free to rest on the other man. After a bit, he said, "Marvin."

"I don't think so." Davis was very judicious. A muscle twitched irregularly in his cheek. Drawing the doctored photograph of Alex in a tuxedo from a fat manila envelope, he placed both items on the desk between them, the picture on top. "Will checked out a motel you thought might be a meeting site for Marvin."

Black ignored the familiar face. "I already knew Will was reporting to you."

Davis's eyebrows rose a tiny fraction. "He didn't know that." His determination to control the interview reasserted itself in the quick return to an interrogator's cool interest.

Black noticed the action and understood it. "What's the difference? You were jerking both of us. Why?"

"Surely you've already answered that for yourself. I gave you a shot at Marvin because I need you." He gestured as though ridding his hand of something foul. "Not this Black, the one rotting in self-pity. And not just for this operation. I'm moving up. I need my own people. Capable and dependable."

Black made a sound in his throat and shook his head. Davis nodded easily, then went on. "Without organization and support behind you, you don't have shit. You've never understood this is a business, like construction, or canning beets. I mean to be in control—management. You want to be where the action is—labor. I need you. But first I had to get you back on your feet."

"Fuck you. Will's dead, and all you can talk about is promotions."

"Don't lecture me. Not you. There's enough guilt here for everybody. You're all broken up because I was checking up on you, didn't know if you could still take pressure. So you put together an operation behind my back. Will went into that motel on your lead. He's gone. If I was wrong about you, it was for nothing."

Black blinked. "That's even dirtier than I expected from you."

"I do the job."

"At any cost."

Davis threw himself back into the chair. It complained in a tiny, polite voice. He said, "You'd never have taken help from me. Will knew it. Marvin was my operation. If it ever gets out I let you work his case alone, the organization'll eat me alive. He was our catalyst, mine and Will's, the thing that was going to get you up and moving. You weren't ever to know the details."

"God damn you. If I don't nail this Marvin for you, you'll take Will's name into the toilet with you."

"And yours."

"I've been there. It was better than this room, right now."

"Get me Marvin. You owe me. I was trying to help you. You can save my career. And Will's."

"Bastard. Rotten, using bastard."

"When this is over, you'll agree my way was the only way. The Steve Black I worked with before would've known."

"Oh, I've changed, that's a fact." Black got up, turned to the window. "I've lost and survived. God's special curse for people like me."

"So change back. That's what we wanted. You're a winner."

"Winners have to believe they're the only ones involved. You only know what losing means when you look up from the game and see into someone's eyes you care about, see what used to be there, only it's all black and burned. That's when you know you have to be alone to play our game, because if you care about anyone, they've stolen your invulnerability. I don't want to be alone anymore. So I don't care enough to win. I avoid losing. I survive."

Davis held his silence so long Black wondered if he was still in the room. When he turned from the window, Davis had his fingers knitted together, palms out. He stretched, cracked his knuckles, then said, "Good thoughts, my friend. Maybe even right. But speak of reality. You know I'm the best man to run the department because I'll do what I have to do. You also care about Bobbie and the kids. We could argue about which of us has the nobler reasons for keeping Will's connection with us secret, but we agree it's necessary. You have to get Marvin before that connection's made public. You need the win."

"You mean you do."

"Hell, yes. I said that. Look, I have to decide if I want to go to the Director and tell him what happened and take my medicine, or stick my finger in my ulcer and hope you can salvage this shithouse. You call it."

Black laughed sharply. "You don't even have any sympathy for yourself."

"I haven't turned into a breast-beating hermit, no. I won't quit. If I was half the field man you are, I'd wrap this up without you."

Again, Black turned to the window. A gull paced the roof across the street, discreet in soft grays and white.

"Marvin's mine. I'll get him," he said.

"Call me when you need help." Davis was out of his chair, moving toward the door. He stopped. "Two things. Your daughter and her boyfriend—is there anything you want done there? And the lady you're involved with, this Madeline Hosmer—do you think it's wise to keep her around?"

"You put anyone within a mile of Jane, I break his legs, okay? And don't even mention Maddy again. She'll be able to go home soon. I'm trying to convince her she should sell her store and move up here to be with me. Her name doesn't belong in your mouth."

"Jesus. You can be a real white-knight asshole when you try. There's one other thing you have to know. The night Will was killed, the motel owner was shot, the place robbed. It's all in the report, there in the envelope. Guy's name was Slidell. Shot three times. No witnesses. Will didn't really have anything. And this is what happens. Try to see it from the other guy's point of view." He smiled tightly at Black's quick shock, then went on. "It was a desperate thing. Stupid. You've scared Marvin, made him tell us he stays in the Bay area. That other business indicating he lives up here was a diversion. I expect you'll be spending a lot more time down there now yourself." Before Black could respond, he left.

Black sat down and waited for the letdown, the flatness that should follow such an emotional binge. Instead, his thoughts scattered like drops of mercury.

Eventually, with great effort, he formed coherence.

Davis was wrong.

Desperation came only when a man had run so far there was no pain greater than the next step, when exhaustion and the animal need to escape combined to scrape the organism free of all but raw instinct. Some broke. Some struck out with savagery that was wonderful in its innocent violence.

Marvin was in no immediate danger from Will's investigation. Even if Slidell could identify Marvin—and that was very doubtful—Will certainly couldn't. And Marvin would take a lot of pushing before he admitted fear, much less desperation.

Black stared at the blank geography of his desk, thinking of Marvin as a man.

He had to be hard, but not without sensitivity.

No. Perception, yes. Sensitivity, no.

Marvin would quickly perceive a person's emotional structure. In order to use it, he'd winch it out of the body with the callousness of a torturer pulling out ribs.

257

He would feel totally alone after years of living in the half-world of a different name and an alien environment. No hand could be allowed to touch what was truly himself.

That would be one of his strengths.

He was free of concern for anyone, anything. By accepting a unique, secret existence, he insulated his soul from the surrounding culture. It had no bearing on his interior truths. Whatever came to hand was used to advantage or discarded.

Nevertheless, Marvin's detachment couldn't be absolute. Even food and shelter carried dangerous obligations. Other things would be at him every minute, had already been at him for years. The rigidly ordered control that made him so successful was possibly eroding right now. And if it was true that the bigger they are, the harder they fall, then the collapse of an entity as cruelly rational as Marvin would be the disintegration of a flywheel, central to the movement of any number of satellite personalities, each as crowded with emotions as Marvin was void.

Black nodded unconsciously, certain of his conclusion.

Marvin wouldn't strike out until he was desperate, and if he did, it would be as destructive an attack as he could manage.

The deaths of Will and Slidell were not only unnecessary, they were counterproductive.

There was more. Black thought about the testimony that tied Marvin to the Pacific Northwest. It was too sparse, too understated, to be a planted diversion. Marvin had made some human errors, not superhuman ploys. The man was clever, not psychic.

An unconscious smile slipped across his face as he told himself to keep that last thought in mind.

So the killings weren't done by Marvin.

He cursed his sluggishness as he rooted out the file on the man who replaced Alex. He read and reread for over an hour, although he was satisfied with Nicolai within the first five minutes. Sometimes his lips moved, falling short of forming words. A massive hand worked reflexively on the desk, the clench and release like the ugly machines that mash car bodies into degraded scrap.

When he was finished he returned the material, plus the envelope Davis had brought, to the drawer with almost reverent care. The doctored photograph of Alex caught his eye. He moved to put it in with the other material, then shrugged and folded it in half. Balancing it on end in the oversized ashtray, he touched a match to it. He stirred the ashes into a heap before leaving.

Davis looked up from the microrecorder and smiled at the Professor. "I was just listening to a replay of my meeting with Black."

"It went well?"

"Quite well, thanks. He's got the bit in his teeth." He shook his head. "The stupid son of a bitch who killed Will is in a world of trouble."

"There's been talk—" The Professor dropped into a seat, features twisted in distaste. He drummed on the chair arm with two fingers, like an old-time telegraph operator. Davis waited, half-smiling. When the Professor realized what was happening, he shifted irritably. "You're going to make me say it, aren't you? Very well. There are people who think you could have prevented what happened."

"If I'd anticipated anything like this in my wildest scenario, I'd have stopped everything. Any operation involving Black is potentially violent. That's where he belongs, it's where he's assigned. Simple. But Will's always been an outrider, a man nobody sees."

"Someone saw him."

"Thank you. Nevertheless, it's all in the nature of an accident. A stupid, murderous accident. We're moving on it."

"You're putting Black in terrible danger."

"Whoever killed Will's in danger."

"Damn it, man—perhaps the best covert man in the business, not just exposed, but shot down in his home! Can't you see it? If they could uncover a man that good, what makes you think they can't trap Black?"

"Will made open contact with Slidell. Obviously, Slidell

informed Marvin. There was no great sleuthing involved. And Black won't be as easy to hit as Will was.''

"You know they'll try. If you don't reinforce him, make this a team operation, you're going to get him killed. I told you at the outset—''

"I remember. And I understood. You didn't understand me, however. I'm no different than Black, except I'm not as good as him. Not where it gets hardest.'' He stopped abruptly. His eyes lost their tight anger, their focus on the Professor. When he spoke again, it was with a touch of wonder. "I'm going to tell you a story. When I was a kid, I had an uncle out in Colorado, a hunter. He had a pack of dogs—good trackers, all but one, a big Airedale. The pack was friendly enough with him, but sort of reserved. I always figured it was because he looked so goddamned odd among those slick-coated others. Then I saw them catch up a bear. The hounds yapped and bawled and some even got in close enough to snap. The Airedale came up last, never made a sound. Just went in and fought. He knew he wasn't going to kill the bear by himself, but he knew he worked for my uncle, and the man meant for that bear to die, one way or the other.''

He pronounced it "t'other,'' which startled the Professor and made him suddenly aware he knew absolutely nothing about Davis's background. He determined to do something about that, then said, "You really admire that, don't you? Are you sure everyone does? Are the pack any less because they acknowledge a final, higher authority, hold the quarry, and wait for the man's verdict?''

Davis squinted, pulled his vision back to the present. For one fleeting instant his expression showed how he resented the necessity.

"You're goddamned right we're less. A man like Black is likely to die alone, no matter how many of us are dancing around while it happens. Listen to me. *Listen*! I'm sick to death of dealing with people who babble about the courage of their convictions and then go into our courts pleading innocent, hoping some asshole lawyer'll get them off on a fucking technicality. Black's a killer? There's a purity in him those people can't conceive. And us? We'll turn our backs on him. Watch us, and remember I told you.''

"You're standing with him." It came with an upward tilt at the end, an implied question, but sympathetic for all that. The Professor heard himself and repeated in his mind that these people had to be treated with total objectivity. It troubled him that he'd slipped.

Davis speared him with a look. "I told you once I'm the only friend he has left. I'll stand with him as long as I can. There. Are you happy, Professor? You've heard the indictment from my own lips. You poor bastard, haven't you seen it yet? He has to win or die. I'm all he's got, and I'll drop him before I'll go with him. I'm nearly at the end of the rope, Professor. Inches. A few inches. And then I sell him for whatever I can get."

Laughter broke past the chewed cigar. Davis dropped a hand on the Professor's shoulder, who tried not to recoil and failed. Davis either didn't notice or didn't care. "He thinks he's a survivor. Can you imagine that? The only one of us who's not afraid of dying, knows how a man ought to die, and he thinks he's a survivor! Christ, that's so funny it's tragic!''

The Professor knew better than to comment. Instead, he said, "It isn't pleasant for me, but I have to point out that this operation's not gone the way you anticipated at any point. There are simply too many variables, Bob. You said yourself your career's in the balance, and frankly, it's a very shaky situation. You don't even know if Black will go after Marvin, and you certainly don't know what he'll do if he catches up to him.''

"Yes, I do. Black'll do it, and he'll succeed. Picture a man who cares more about the people around him than he cares about himself, Professor. He doesn't have any choice. He *has* to fight for them. He sees his strength as a necessity to them, right?''

"A good point. Still, you're involved. He knows about you now, about your career?''

Davis nodded.

The Professor tossed off a weak gesture. "Well, then.

What makes you think he'll help you? He must be enraged at what you've done, or what he perceives as what you've done."

"That's my hole card. Even if Will hadn't been killed, it was time for me to expose my part in this thing. Black'll hunt down Marvin to protect Bobbie and her girls. He'll help my career because he believes I'm best for the job, and it polishes his self-image as hard and logical. But I needed hate. The man who killed Will guaranteed it, better than I could create it."

Plucking at an eyebrow, the Professor twisted his head so he was looking sideways at Davis. "Exactly what do you have in mind?" The voice said he already knew.

"Marvin suborned one of our people. He nearly destroyed my friend. He's a very good Soviet resident who's caused this country God-only-knows how much damage. I want him killed."

CHAPTER 27

THE RIVER MUMBLED CHEERFULLY AT SUMMERTON'S FEET. Warm sunlight danced on its small sharp waves and pierced the surface to spangle the jumbled rocks on the bottom. Farther out, perhaps fifteen yards from shore, a large branch drifted past. The foot-thick butt end was a splintered white scar against the roiled jade surface. Suddenly it rolled, tripped by a submerged boulder. A smaller, secondary branch broke the surface in a gleaming curve, shedding water like sweat from a straining arm.

Summerton shifted his attention to the country road paralleling the river.

He didn't like this location. Winter floods had carved a deep, wide bed, and the road on the top of the bank was a good ten feet above the present waterline. He felt at a disadvantage. There was no rational explanation, but it made him uncomfortable to have the river on one side and an uphill climb on the other. It gave him a trapped feeling.

Nothing disturbed the silence, and he picked his way up the cobbled beach to the grassy slope, then farther, up to his car. The magazine with the envelope hidden in its pages lay on the front seat. Glancing back at the river, he located the broken branch. When it rounded the curve, he decided, he'd be on his way. If Marvin didn't want to make the pickup in person, the hell with him.

He leaned against the car and studied the magazine cover. He couldn't identify the man pictured there, but the self-satisfied smirk he wore irritated him.

"Look at you," he said out loud. "A nothing. What've you ever done? Ever risk your ass passing off stuff to somebody?"

He stared out at the river. The glare hurt his eyes and he wished he had his sunglasses. There was no sign of the branch. Walking out to the road, he searched in both directions, listening. A goldfinch flew across the meadow opposite him, up, then down, then up once more before it dove out of sight in a brush pile.

He saw Martin's car before he heard it, simultaneously realizing his tactical error. There was a farmhouse across the river. The most disinterested watcher would know he was impatiently waiting for another party. Worse, Martin must have seen him by now. He'd know, too. That meant another tiresome lecture about not attracting attention.

Moving quickly, he took up a position beside his car again. The man on the magazine cover continued to taunt with his smug grin.

Summerton spoke aloud, practicing what he must say, wanting the reinforcement of his own voice. Nevertheless, he held his lip movement to the barest minimum. "Goddammit, I don't want to hang out in shadows all my life."

Martin was slowing down, pulling off the road fifty yards downstream. Summerton faced upstream.

"I'm not risking my ass so I can hide out and count my money, Martin. Sneaking around in the dark may get your jollies for you, but it doesn't mean shit to me. I want to enjoy what I've got. I want to *live*."

It was a good speech. And Martin was okay, under it all. He'd understand.

Summerton got the envelope from the magazine and tucked it in the back pocket of his jeans. He made his way to the river's edge, then strolled casually downstream. Martin moved toward the water similarly. Two cars passed while they performed their charade of approaching each other accidentally. When they were only a few feet apart, Martin said, "What

264

were you doing, standing up there on the road? Why don't you take out an ad in the paper, invite the public?''

Smiling, Summerton said, "So I got a little impatient. That's why I wanted to talk to you.''

"Impatient?''

The voice rose sharply, and Summerton, startled and elated, wished he could point out to Martin how another professional saw through him. That single break in the voice, for instance, tore a gaping rent in Martin's false composure. It exposed more than his usual wariness, more than the stress he'd shown in the hotel suite with Nicolai.

Summerton wanted to hug himself, to run in circles, shout at the sky. Martin afraid! He, Harry Summerton, was relaxed, sure of himself in every particular, and the teacher, the great leader, was afraid!

He said, "I've got excellent news, Martin, really super news.''

"Something you couldn't write? Why are we meeting?''

"I want to share this.'' Inspiration struck him. "I want you to be able to tell Nicolai you heard it from me, personally.''

He paused for dramatic effect, and Martin snapped, "Go on, damn it! What?''

"They've formed a study group to determine priority projects for the computer!''

Martin stared. "That's it? That's all?''

"Well, no. I can get at their work. That's important. But don't you see what it means? They're so sure they've got a product, they're turning their attention to the best way to use it. And I'll be inside! Here's the names of the people in the group and the first list of projects to be evaluated.'' Summerton reached for his back pocket.

"Stop! Get beside me, quickly! Walk with me!'' Martin's leisurely pace belied the brusque orders. Summerton did as ordered. When he looked toward the road, the other man's hand clamped on his wrist. "Don't turn your head! Look at the river! Look at the farmhouse!'' Martin released Summerton, who flexed the offended joint carefully.

"What the hell's wrong with you?'' He studied the

farmhouse, stumbling over rocks as he did. "What's going on?"

"A pickup truck pulled in behind your car. Two men."

"For Christ's sake, Martin, it's lunchtime! A couple of guys are eating their lunch!"

"Perhaps." The angry frown grew uncertain. "It could be the one I saw parked farther upstream when I got here."

"Ridiculous. You're getting jumpy."

Martin glared, and Summerton reminded himself that Martin was frightened earlier. This was merely more of the same, but he was still the next man up the ladder. If the good relationship with Nicolai was to improve, Martin would have to help foster it. Summerton hurried to smooth over the damage.

"I realize it's for my benefit, Martin, but you have to give me some credit. No one followed me."

They were almost to the bend in the river. Martin said, "Where is the information?"

"In an envelope in my back pocket."

"Okay. You're going to sit over there. Work the envelope out, stuff it between the rocks. I'll continue walking a while, then come back for it when you're gone."

Summerton asked, "What do you think Nicolai will say when he hears what's happened?"

Martin half-turned toward him. "Hears about what?"

"The assignment! What else? Why I wanted to meet you, remember?"

"He'll wonder if you have to pass another security check." Martin pointedly flicked his eyes at the truck. "We'll stop here for a minute, then you sit down where I told you." Summerton nodded. Martin added, "Don't leave right away. Walk around on the bank, then go sit in the car for at least five minutes. Even if the truck leaves right now. Understand?"

"Yes. But there's one more thing."

"What?"

"I want to know what Nicolai says. About the assignment."

"Don't worry—I'll see that everyone who should know is informed."

Summerton spun on his heel and headed for his position.

266

Martin's whisper leaped after him, a scratching, scolding rasp. "Straighten up! You're walking like a spoiled child!"

When he turned to retort, Martin didn't notice. He was already moving upstream, head to the front.

Grimly, Summerton delayed the operation, responding to Martin's impatient glances with the quickly turned head and slightly raised shoulder of an injured lover. He sat in his car a full ten minutes, leafing through the magazine, before setting out down the road. When he saw the truck in the rearview mirror, a tremor of doubt tightened his grip on the steering wheel, but the vehicle dropped off at the first crossroad.

On the freeway, his thoughts turned to Esther.

What must life be like for her, a vibrant, spirited woman, married to a slug like Ted Wade? It was obvious he'd never have done anything exciting without her impetus. He was just another worker ant, lost down in the tunnels.

With a woman like that—The Woman—an intelligent, aggressive man would establish a whole series of contacts. A network, by God. The Woman would be the perfect hostess, entertaining an endless stream of guests, charming the guts out of everyone. The right man would bring home other contacts. And all the while, they'd be protected. If things ever got the least bit chancy, it'd be over the fence and off to a life of ease. Not a bad deal.

The shattering blast of an air horn yanked him out of his reverie. A logging truck loomed beside him, so close his shocked mind focused on an individual pebble wedged between slabbed scales of bark. He twisted the wheel violently, pulled back into his own lane. A trembling foot backed off the gas. Two final wails of the horn floated back to him, their message perched on the driver's upthrust middle finger.

Summerton was thoroughly angry when he reached his apartment. He slumped in his favorite chair, steadily downing cans of beer. The softness of late dusk was hardening to night when he made his decision and reached for the phone.

Esther answered.

He identified himself, delighting in the cheerful ring of his voice. The thick, stunned silence that followed was wonderful, a rich sauce his boldness deserved.

267

At last, she said, "It's been a long time. Our friends all said we'd never hear from you again, and we agreed. Is everything all right?"

"Better than all right. You sound wonderful. I just decided I wanted to talk to you, like old times down there. I miss my friends."

"That's nice. Did you call for a particular reason?" Her nervousness came over the wire in jagged syllables.

"I have to see you." She'd wonder if he meant her alone, but she'd act as if the statement included the wimp, of course.

"Us? Impossible! What's wrong with you? Where are you calling from? Who knows about this call?"

Now she was plainly frightened. He paused, imagining her expression, her position, the strained, taut muscles. Fear would emphasize her color, draw one clenched hand to her breast. He said, "No one knows. Not yet. I'm here at home. I'm doing so well I think we have to get together to discuss things of mutual importance and advantage."

"What're you talking about? Are you in trouble?"

"Far from it." He laughed, low, confiding. "I'm in a position to make trouble, though, and I think together we'd have an even stronger position. Impregnable, in fact."

"Why don't you talk to our mutual friends and tell them what you have in mind?

"That won't do, I'm afraid. I'm more interested in us than them." For a long beat he listened to the hiss of the handset, finally saying, "I really have to see you. I don't want to be forced to bring in anyone else, you know?"

There was a quick intake of breath, then, "Wait. Wait just a minute."

Smiling, he sipped his beer, letting the muffled conversation from the other end roll without even trying to hear it. She'd be coming, and soon. Still, the can was empty before she spoke to him again.

"We can be there on Tuesday, next week. Where we talked the last time, right?"

"Fine," he said. "You won't be sorry. This is—" The dial tone buzzed in his ear. She'd hung up on him. For an instant his face twisted in an ugly fury. Just as swiftly, it melted to a tight, admiring smile. He hung up the phone, patting it gently. "You're a bitch, but a fascinating one. It's going to be great fun working with you. And on you."

It took a few seconds for his own pun to dawn on him. He laughed uproariously all the way to the refrigerator and back.

CHAPTER 28

Summerton strolled in through the side door of the Marriott. His reflection in the barbershop window was very much the spruce businessman. Coat and tie, shined shoes, creased trousers—he found no flaw.

And The Woman would be pleasantly surprised to see how well he'd learned his lessons. She'd expect him to come in from the front. No one but a professional would think of the side entry and the opportunity to search for opposition.

Not that there could be any danger, of course. She was too smart to be trailed, even if Teddy was stupid enough to be a constant hazard.

He loitered by the sauna entry until a brisk walk brought him to the restaurant exactly on time. He was seated, reading the menu, when the hostess approached.

"Are you Mr. Summerton, by any chance?"

The voice that finally responded sounded a hundred years old. "Yes, I am." He tried to stop there and couldn't. In his mind he saw himself falling, falling, too horrified to scream or close his eyes. "Is something wrong?"

"Oh, no, sir. There's a telephone call for you. The gentleman you're expecting couldn't make it."

Gentleman. No Esther? "Where do I take it?"

"Over there." She gestured. "I'll show you." As he rose, she extended a hand, inches short of actually touching him.

270

"Are you sure you're all right, sir? I didn't mean to startle you."

The way her voice ranged up and down reminded him of the goldfinch's swooping flight beside the river. It seemed impossible that meeting with Martin was only a week ago.

Steadying himself, he smiled. "I was daydreaming. Nothing to be concerned about." Following her, he pointedly waited for privacy before using the phone.

It was Ted. "Go directly to your car. Use the same side entrance. Drive north on Pacific Highway to the Thriftway store on the right. There's a phone booth outside. Wait there until you're called." The receiver clicked.

Summerton hung up deliberately. The handset gleamed with sweat, and he wiped it before walking slowly to his car.

It was about a mile to the phone booth, and he made all three traffic lights. He waited almost ten minutes before the ring came. When he answered, Ted said, "Don't use any names. Where did you come to the booth from?"

"Who is this? Is that you—?"

"*Shut up!*" The command was a scream, painful. "I told you no names! Tell me where you were fifteen minutes ago!"

"The Marriott! Don't shout! Jesus, you'd think—"

"Just keep your mouth shut. Drive directly to Southcenter. Park in the lot between the west mall entrance and the Doubletree Inn. Stay in your car. You'll be contacted. Understand?"

Summerton hung up hard enough to set off a soft, admonishing ring from the bell. In his car, he vented a string of curses. He was still talking to himself when he pulled onto the freeway.

"The goddamned nerve of it, the goddamned *nerve*. Watching me! He thinks he's playing with a fucking child, a moron! Son of a bitch!" He burlesqued Ted's tight, hard speech. " 'Between the west mall entrance and the Doubletree. Understand?' You'll get something to understand, motherfucker."

Taking a hand from the wheel, he massaged his cheeks, his temples. Under the skin the muscles were like planks. He

271

twisted the rearview mirror around to practice smiling and looking noncommittal.

He backed into a space at the very edge of the parking lot, which gave him a view of any vehicle approaching. As the Wades neared, he recognized Esther and stepped out to wait for them. The rear door flew open as they reached him. They stopped long enough for her to command, "Get in!" The car was already moving forward as he struggled into the seat. Before he could complain, Esther pivoted in her seat, glaring.

"Don't talk," she said, jabbing a finger at him. "Not a fucking word. We'll get to you later." She dismissed him completely, concentrating on everything around them that might possibly be surveillance. Ted drove with an electric, hunched concentration, darting glances from side to side. In contrast, the car moved through the traffic smoothly. Never speaking, they nervously proceeded to a group of picnic tables on the bluff above the Green River where it marks the eastern limit of the huge shopping and industrial complex. Ted parked and gestured Summerton to one of the tables. Esther stood beside the car, looking back the way they'd come, until the men were seated. Then she joined them. She sat beside her husband, across from Summerton, glowing with unvoiced rage.

In the past, no matter how provoked, Ted was invariably considerate to the point of diffidence. Now calculating eyes coursed every inch of Summerton's body. That searching gaze lingered on his neck, and Summerton was unable to ignore the sensation that Ted was looking through the knot of his tie, through the flesh, to center on the carotid artery. For one terrifying instant, he felt blood bulk like setting Jell-O in the constricting vessel, but the moment passed when he raised a hand to his collar.

Esther led off, as he expected. "Did you really think we'd stick to meeting arrangements made by you on a phone? Because of you, I spent last night in a nasty whore's-nest hotel on that goddamned strip. You'd like the Windmill, Harry. It's just your style." Her fingers writhed in knots. "Why're you doing this? What do you want?"

272

Ted said, "You can't blackmail us, you know. You'll only be condemning yourself."

Summerton spoke to Esther. "I'm working for us. For *us*, mind you."

Esther's harsh laugh cut across his explanation. He continued mildly. "I was recently promoted, both by my regular employers and the people we work for in common. Since then, I've been wondering why I shouldn't capitalize on my advancement. Because I owe so much to both of you, I felt I ought to include you in my plans."

"No, thank you." Ted maneuvered to get his legs from under the picnic table. "Leave us alone."

"Please, don't be impatient," Summerton said, chancing a direct look at Ted. He was elated to see the old, uninteresting expression back. He hurried on. "We're all in danger, you know. My contact's become erratic. In fact, his nerve's going. I don't have to tell you what'll happen if he breaks. Maybe your contact's someone else, but I don't think it makes much difference. If my man goes, he'll certainly take me with him. You may be next."

"Erratic?" Esther bent forward, demanding. A vein moved at her temple, insistent blue fluctuations suggesting electricity under the smooth white skin. "In what way?"

Summerton gave them a reassuring laugh. "He's done nothing unprofessional. It's his behavior—obvious counter-surveillance all the time, elaborate meeting schemes, hesitant approaches. In short, he's risking my ass every day with ridiculous restrictions. He can't appreciate how much good I can do him."

Esther glanced quickly at her husband, and Summerton's heart lurched with the hope she was going to admit to some doubt regarding their own contact. It would forge the bond he knew he must have. Instead, she said, "What's your contact's name?"

Something splashed in the river and they all started, puppets on the same string. Summerton had to turn to see where the fish had leaped. "Summer-run steelhead," he remarked absently, wondering what could spur it to abandon the water, even momentarily. The widening ripples it left behind were rapidly disappearing when Esther said, "Well?"

"Martin. He uses no last name."

Ted turned away. Esther's eyes narrowed, and she chewed her lower lip. She said, "What's on your mind? Briefly. However your contact's behaving, nothing could be more dangerous than our being together like this."

Summerton nodded. "Martin's superior is the one who made my promotion official. It was clear Martin resented it, and the superior's losing his respect for him. We're caught in a situation where the personal dynamics are breaking down and we've got to protect ourselves. My suggestion is that we prepare for Martin's departure—perhaps even contribute to it, but that's a thought I want to talk over with you—by creating our own stable of informants."

Ted swung back to stare at him. "You're insane! You'll get us caught—or worse." He spoke hoarsely, cords standing out in his neck. His hand sought Esther's incessantly twining fingers, clasped them. "You'll call CIA thugs down on us! You'll get us killed."

"The only way to avoid capture is to eliminate weakness. I saw your reaction to Martin's name. We're dealing with the same man, aren't we?"

Esther pulled free of Ted, smothered his answer with her own. "There's something in what you say. Are you sure of your relationship with Marvin's superior?"

The triumph was too heady not to be drained to the last drop. "You know him as Marvin, do you?" When she winced, he dismissed her concern with a wave. "Yes, my relationship is solid. The only real question is, how do we rid ourselves of Martin/Marvin before he goes under and takes us with him?"

Ted scrambled clumsily to his feet. Hands on the tabletop, he lowered his face to within inches of Summerton's. "You don't know what you're talking about. The man's survived in a hostile environment for years, with never a moment's trouble until you came along. *You're* the weak link!"

Esther said, "Now, Ted, you've said yourself, we take all

the risks and he's the one whose cover is practically holy. If his nerve is cracking, we have to protect ourselves."

"His nerve is not cracking! *His* is!" Ted's accusing finger glanced off Summerton's chest. "We should have demanded an emergency meeting with the new contact man, told him this back-stabber is endangering everything and everyone."

"Wait, darling." Esther touched his hand. "Remember the last phone call from the new contact? Remember what he said about that creep at the motel and the government agent? For our contact to know so much, there must have been a major breakdown somewhere."

"If it was Marvin—"

"That's just it. They never said exactly what happened. But the man connected with our meeting site was apparently ready to expose us to the FBI, or CIA, or someone. Thank God our friends eliminated him in time, along with the government man. Now I understand the full significance of what our contact was saying." Esther's manner was returning to normal, her speech losing its harsh, brusque accents.

Wade was adamant. "You've never seen Martin, Esther—not to deal with. We're leaving. Now!"

"No." His eyes widened at her single, thoughtful syllable. "We have to think this through."

"Think? Think about us in danger, Esther! Not from Marvin! From him, from Harry!"

"Harry has nothing to gain by consulting with us, Teddy, and we have everything to lose by not exercising constant caution. If there's the slightest truth in what he suspects, Marvin will be the cause of our destruction, if not the source. We have to protect ourselves."

"Against him." Ted pointed again, sighting down the finger at Summerton. "I wish I'd never seen you."

"Believe me, I understand. Your show of loyalty's wonderful. But I'm right. You'll see."

Ted stalked off to the edge of the bluff. Although he was sure the man was far beyond hearing distance, Summerton lowered his voice to a near whisper. Obligingly, Esther leaned into it, and he inhaled the intimacy of her presence.

He said, "I'm glad I can talk to you alone. What was that about 'friends' eliminating someone?"

She was suddenly wary. "You've heard nothing about it before?"

He shook his head.

"It was something down in our area." She spoke in the direction of the river. "Nothing to concern you. Forget I mentioned it."

Summerton looked at her expression and decided not to pursue the issue. Not now. He said, "Okay, then let's get to business. Ted's a wonderful man, but he's suffering terminal hero worship, Esther."

She looked at her husband's rigid back. Sorrow and affection lent her face a tender, childlike cast.

Summerton said, "I'll bet these meeting arrangements today were yours. What'd you do, make him come up yesterday?"

She looked away, nodded. He said, "See? You're the brains. We owe it to ourselves to profit from our own abilities. We cultivate people in positions like Ted's and mine. We bypass Martin, let his superiors arrange the recruitment and training. We make the pickups, handle liaison and control."

Esther's grin winked on, sly. "Eliminate the middleman. Safer."

"Right. We take the no-risk jobs, the ironclad cover."

Straightening, she reached to take his hand. "Before you even knew we were interested in you, I told Ted, 'That one's special,' but I never guessed how special." She squeezed before pulling her hand free, trailing a lingering touch across his palm, down the length of his fingers. "I'm looking forward to this different relationship with you." A minute flicker took her eyes to Ted and back again.

Summerton said, "That makes me very happy, Esther. Happier than I'd dared hope."

"It'll take me a while to talk Ted around. In the meantime, for everyone's sake, Harry, be careful. And keep us informed, every move. Will you do that?"

"Certainly."

276

"Wonderful. Now, please, just stay put until I get him out of here, all right?"

Summerton watched Ted's vehement argument as they got in the car. She nodded constantly as he spoke, never interrupting, but making points with a determined air when he paused for breath. They were still at it as Ted sped onto the boulevard that serviced the small park.

As soon as they were clear, Ted relaxed against the seat, flexing his hands on the wheel. "Well, what do you think?"

"The rotten bastard thinks he can make me."

Ted managed a grim smile. "I half suspected that. Marvin'll shit."

"We can't tell him, Ted."

"What d'you mean, can't?"

"Down, lover." She patted his hand, but the familiar, sensual humor fell flat. "What can Marvin do? Certainly not eliminate him and touch off an investigation. Our safest course is to play along with him."

"What? Play along?" Incredulity stopped the sentence.

Easily, Esther said, "Teddy, honey, he may actually be right about poor Marvin's condition. Obviously, he sees more of him than we do. But the major point is, we can outlast Harry, dear. This ridiculous infatuation will pass, and no harm done. Harry's promised to tell me everything he does, and he will, I'm sure of it. We're going to smile and nod and let Harry fondle his little fantasies. Meanwhile, we get in touch with our contact at home and tell him Marvin seemed nervous at our last meeting, but we didn't want to say anything. We finally decided we had to. No matter what Harry does, or Marvin's condition, we're covered."

"What about our coming up here?"

"No one but Harry knows about that. We build an alibi at home, and then it's Harry's word against ours—and Harry will always be the one on the defensive."

Ted was silent for a while, then, as they pulled into the rental agency to return the car, he slammed a fist on the steering wheel. "Miserable son of a bitch! I hope a truck hits him! I hope he dies slow and hard!"

Esther leaned over to kiss him on the cheek. "Silly. Not slow. Fast. Before he can speak."

Ted grinned in wry admiration. "My cuddly kitty-cat. Always purring, always ready to scratch and bite."

They were laughing when he parked.

Summerton selected a small pebble from the collection in his palm and tossed it in a high arc out over the river.

How very like her, he thought. Such an incredible combination of realism and romance, of logic and emotion. Without Ted to hold her back, there was no limit to her possibilities. How pathetic to watch her protect a loser.

She'd been so clever, pretending interest in the proposition. When he thought how she'd led him along, bitter tears seared his eyes like smoke. Now there was no choice. Sooner or later, Wade would break. The only way to protect himself was to make the first move. Esther would just have to adjust to the new realities. At least she'd have him to help her.

He threw the remainder of the pebbles at the river in a sweeping arc, their patter like the slap of machine-gun bullets in the movies.

CHAPTER 29

MADDY STOOD AMIDSHIPS, CLUTCHING THE LIFELINE, LEANING out over the water. The wind tugged her hair into a gleaming, swirling mist around her head. Black watched from the wheel as her features were revealed one moment, then hidden again. She leaned even farther outboard, the motion pulling her shorts high enough for him to glimpse the untanned first curving swell of her buttock. He shouted at her from the wheel. "Be careful, Maddy! One wrong gust, and you're in the water!"

She straightened, laughing, tossing the rebellious hair out of the way. "You'd come back for me." It was a teasing answer, inviting response.

"Well, certainly. It's almost impossible to get another crew when the word gets out you deep-sixed your last one."

"Aren't you the romantic thing." She wrinkled her nose, then moved aft, left hand clinging to the lifeline. He winced inwardly at the way she still favored that side. After she lowered herself into the cockpit beside him, he put his hand on her shoulder, kneading softly. "It still bothers you, doesn't it?"

Framing his face with her hands, she smiled up at him. "Only there, just a little bit. Really. You more than me, I think."

"It wouldn't have happened if you hadn't gotten mixed up

279

with me." He moved to kiss her hands, taking both of them in his. "You'd still have your shop in Frisco, too. I haven't brought a whole lot of your basic sunshine into your life."

Freeing her hands to cover his mouth, she grinned at him. "Are you fishing for reassurance again? How many times do I have to tell you? Of course I wish I hadn't gotten beat up, but I'm better now. And I'll get another shop here, soon. The important thing, though, is that I'm here, with you, where I want to be. If you'd just stop saying 'Frisco,' I'd have enough sunshine in my life, thank you."

His brief smile failed to dislodge the troubled expression. "I'm glad you're here, Maddy. Happier than I can tell you. But I can't simply forget what they did."

"They're gone, Steve. They didn't frighten me away."

"*I'm* afraid, dammit. Not only that—" He bit off the argument.

Maddy backed away, leaned against the cabin hatch. Heightened color lent a faint wash to remnant facial damage, the softly darker edges blending into the unaffected areas. The very delicacy of the healing only drew his attention away from her steady recovery and back to her vulnerability.

She said, "You did it again."

He looked at her blankly. She raised her chin, the gesture both defiant and indicative. "That. You said, 'Not only that,' and stopped. You keep me away from the deepest things. I love you, Steve. And I think you love me. But I don't know. You won't let me close enough to be sure."

Ruffling sails signaled a wind shift, and Black automatically altered course to draw them tighter. The rigging muttered, and the boat slapped a wave out of the way. As soon as they settled in the new track, he answered. "It's because I love you I won't let you into all the corners of my world. You wouldn't like what I do there."

"What you do doesn't—wouldn't—change how I feel."

He fixed his eyes on hers, probing, the unwavering gaze like polished metal. In a moment, she blinked, looked away. He stepped around the wheel, holding the course true with one hand. He said, "*I* don't like what happens there. People get twisted around."

"You haven't."

"What?"

"I said you haven't gotten twisted around."

Self-consciousness stained his laughter. An errant thought slipped through her mind—what if he secretly enjoyed the part of his work he refused to discuss? He looked out over the small, crisp waves, each burnished by the early sun. She said, "You've been fair with me. You lied at first because you had to. You told me the truth when you could. That's not twisted."

"Lying's wrong. I do it for a living."

Her silence outlasted his will, and he turned her way again. She dropped her eyes. "The boy who attacked me— Richie. I don't care if someone lies to him to arrest him. If that's what it takes—"

He cut her off. "Why bring that up?"

"I'd lie to him. Not because he hurt me. At least not just because he hurt me. Sure, I think he ought to be punished, but if he's not put away, he'll keep hurting people."

"There's no similarity. He's a punk, an animal."

"Are the people you're after nicer just because they're better educated, or because they have more important friends?"

"No, of course not, but—"

"What do you believe in, Steve? If what you do is so terrible, if it does such terrible things to the people involved, then what *are* your beliefs? Never mind what you do. Tell me why you do it."

Swaying with the motion of the boat, he could have been a part of it, a machine to mindlessly weigh forces and respond. When he blinked, it was like an awakening.

"I see people trying to gut this country, turn it into a blind cripple, ashamed of its own interests. We've got a new Inquisition, so bound to achieve absolute purity it's willing to destroy the one culture free enough to spawn it. Sometimes I hope I lose. I'd like to watch what happens to my American enemies when they wake up to a homegrown butcher like Castro."

"That's a terrible thing to say!"

"I know. I warned you." Leaning to one side, he sent the

281

boat into a harder tack. The vessel drove forward as if whipped, heeling over until the deck grazed the sea. Shattered waves turned to spray that stung exposed flesh almost like hail. Maddy ducked below the protective cover of the cabin. Black leaned into the assault, his face clenched in denial.

Over the increased pounding of the hull and the avid rumble of the sails, Maddy raised her voice to a shout. "What would you do to those people?"

"Do?" He was genuinely surprised. "What can you do? Make 'em listen to my speech, maybe." He laughed, a rich, honest amusement. "Nothing changes, Maddy—while the Athenians were sharpening their debating skills, the Spartans were sharpening their swords. My job's to stall the Spartans as long as the Athenians'll let me."

"I don't see how that's so twisted. I think you worry about it too much."

Black eased off the helm, and the deck swayed back to near level, the hull sighing deeper into the water with the sound of a weary runner. As their speed fell, the warming effect of the sun rose dramatically. Maddy moved out of her sheltered corner.

He said, "I probably do worry too much, but it frightens me when I realize my attitudes are exactly those of the progressives who despise me so—I reserve the right to break any law I deem inconvenient."

Maddy laughed before she saw the peculiar set to his jaw, the tense angle of head and neck. She moved to him, linked her arm through his. He continued to watch forward, although there was nothing closer than the distant coast. After a short silence, she said, "I think you're true to yourself. I think you'd never go back on your word."

Smiling down at her, he said, "Old saying in my business— 'Never say never.' But I try." Then he pointed at the wheel. "Enough of that. You want to handle her while I slice up some cheese and bread? I'm starved."

In answer, Maddy hurried below, shouting indistinctly about not wanting to compete with his first love. A few minutes later, they were side by side in the cockpit, washing down thick sandwiches with chilled San Miguel dark beer. He held up his bottle. "One of my major discoveries."

Maddy nodded. "I never would have thought to try it. Have you ever been there?"

Dismayed, she watched the subtle changes as he pulled away again. She jammed the bottle in the waste can and flung the half-eaten sandwich as far as she could. Then she struggled upright, clutching and staggering against the motion of the boat. The awkwardness added to her irritation. "No more, damn it. We've walked around this thing once too often. I'm not spending my life with some bozo who turns off like a goddamned light bulb every time I mention the past, or his job, or the price of peas. Forget it! Either we're together, a team, or I leave while I've still got some feelings left. I won't let you freeze me, Steve. I can't. I won't."

Carefully, handhold to handhold, she went forward, where she settled with her back against the rise of the cabin. It was almost a full minute before some spray flew up from the bow and drifted back to her, giving her a welcome excuse to wipe at her face and clear away the tears she refused to let him see. The action helped steady her, and she knew there'd be no more crying.

It would be better to lose now, if it had to happen.

They wanted each other, meant to be good for each other. Richie's beating had made the decision to sell the boutique easier, if not unavoidable, but she admitted she would probably have moved to be with Steve in any case. She had the freedom to move her earning capability, and he didn't. If that was a rationalization or a cop-out, so be it. But none of it meant anything if he continued to shield himself from anything more than surface contact. If he truly couldn't share himself, his loneliness was impenetrable.

When he touched her shoulder she started violently. His reassuring smile was incongruous under the concerned eyes. He said, "I lashed the wheel. She'll hold this course a while." He coughed, massaged one hand with the other, as though wringing courage from them. Maddy watched the thick knuckles bleach white with effort. Some were blunted

283

from battles she dreaded hearing about but yearned to share in some way.

He said, "I'm not good at what you want, Maddy. It's hard for me to say things from inside, as you said. I'll be overprotective. I'll try not to interfere with the things you have to do to be yourself. I'll tell you whatever I can about what my job requires. The one thing I can't do is involve you or break my word to the people I work with." He stroked her hair. "If that's not good enough, I'll leave the job as soon as this business is over. I love you. I don't want to be alone, Maddy. Not anymore. I need you."

As joyous as the words made her, she heard the amazement in the last sentence. It sounded almost disbelieving.

Black was making his final check of the mooring lines before leaving the dock when the approaching figure caught his eye. Something made him look closer. It was Davis. Unconsciously, he reached for Maddy's arm, and she reacted with surprise at the strength of the grip. She opened her mouth to protest but caught the direction of his gaze first. Rather than speak, she put her hand on his. He glanced sharply at the touch, then relaxed the hold. His expression remained unreadable.

Davis said, "When you weren't at your home or Miss Hosmer's, I guessed you might be on the boat. I've been waiting up at the restaurant."

Black said, "Maddy, this is my boss. Bob Davis, Madeline Hosmer. Maddy." Maddy extended a hand, and Davis held it momentarily. His smile blinked on and off like a signal. He said, "I've heard good things about you. I'm sorry about what happened. It's obvious you're recovering, though, and that's good to see." Then his attention was back on Black. "I've got bad news, Steve. It's Jane."

Black stammered. "Where is she?"

"On the way to Seattle. I—"

"Is she hurt?"

Davis swallowed. It made a ripping noise. He said, "Steve, there's no other way to say it. She's dead."

Maddy's heart pounded at her ribs.

Black stared at Davis, unmoving. Seconds dragged past. Finally, he said, "Tell me what happened," and an inexplicable chill slipped down Maddy's neck.

A small muscle jerked irregularly under Davis's left eye. Black could have been carved of stone. Davis said, "An accident. An overdose. Jane and her boyfriend."

"Richie? Heroin?"

"In L.A. Yesterday. As soon as the police had an identification, they—"

Black gestured, a hard, cutting motion. "Why did they come to you, Bob? What are you doing here, on this coast, with this news?"

Davis leaned away from the growing anger, but his feet remained in place. Maddy saw the movement and squeezed Black's hand. Davis said, "They couldn't reach you, Steve. The answering service forwarded the call to my office." A hand rose to rub a bristled jaw. "I got the word at five A.M., our time. I flew out here because I didn't want anyone else bringing you this kind of news." His eyes flickered, as if he wanted to look at Maddy but couldn't, and he added, "That's God's truth, man. I swear it."

There was a plea in the last words, and a suggestion of warning. The stench of hidden emotions and secret knowledge threatened to overwhelm Maddy. Once again the unreasonable chill touched her neck.

"Steve?" When she failed to break the concentration of his stare, she repeated herself, tugging on his arm. "Steve!" He turned reluctantly. "Don't take it out on him. Even if he'd known we were out on the boat last night, no one could reach us. He's done as much as a friend can do. More."

Ponderously, as if tired beyond endurance, Black nodded. His eyes glittered, unnaturally bright, and she was surprised to recognize unshed tears. For a brief moment, she was shocked, and then she remembered her own refusal to admit tears earlier. She wanted to tell him how foolish he was being. And how foolish she had been.

He said, "You're right. Thank you," and faced Davis again. "I wish I could feel some surprise, you know? I knew

285

it was coming. It hurts. It hurts like a bitch, but it's a pain I've expected for a long time."

Davis said, "I told them you'd want her buried here. It's all taken care of. She'll arrive tomorrow."

Black nodded. "Thanks." He shifted his attention back to Maddy. "Would you go on ahead and get the car, Mad, please? Bob'll stay with me, and I want to sort of get my thoughts together. Okay?"

She rose on tiptoe to kiss him. "Of course. I'm sorry, Steve. So very sorry."

"I know you are, Maddy. Just be close for a while, will you?"

"Try to get rid of me."

He managed a small smile before she turned to leave, then he faced Davis. Bleak control absorbed the smile, and he leaned forward slowly, nostrils flaring briefly. He said, "If you're lying to me, I'll come after you. You know that. You, whoever did it—anyone. I'll kill you."

Davis twitched. His lips barely moved as he spoke. "I knew that'd be your first reaction. You think I like telling you what happened?" He headed down the dock toward shore. Somewhere in the softly moving mass of boats a woman's voice rose in a surprised cry. A man laughed. Black walked beside Davis, continuing his silent scrutiny, and the smaller man spoke again. "I'm not into killing children, Steve. Even if I could consider it, this situation wouldn't force me to it. If Janie and her boyfriend ratted on you, you'd deny it, take your lumps, and continue to deny. Think about it—if I'm such a cold son of a bitch I'd have your daughter murdered to protect you, wouldn't I also be cold enough to know you'd go to prison before you'd expose us? That means I'd never do what you're thinking. I'm standing here in front of you, afraid of you, because I know you want to blame someone for what happened to her, and I'm the logical choice. Don't—"

"That fucking shrink."

They were at the ramp leading from the waterborne dock up to the parking lot. Pale, Davis stopped, one foot on the sloped walkway. He gripped the rail and straightened. "What?"

"That doctor. He laid this out. You *did* have her taken out."

"Jesus, Steve. No one set up anything! I'm talking common sense, that's all."

Black put a hand on Davis's shoulder. His thumb extended to rest against the other man's Adam's apple. When he talked, his voice was thick, almost slurred, with emotion. "I'll check. I'll find out. A hint, Bob—any suggestion that you did this to plug a leak, and that's it. I don't give a shit about proof. A whisper's all I'll need. You better be very, very clean, you hear?"

Davis tried to smile. "I know you'll investigate. There's nothing to find, Steve. No matter what you think."

"That's why I'm not breaking your neck. But I'm not sure you wouldn't eliminate *anybody*. I'll find out, though."

Slowly, Davis moved out from under the pinioning hand. "There's nothing to find. I give you my word."

Black's smile sent Davis hurrying up the ramp. He was opening the car door as Black came through the security gate. No one spoke as both men got in. Then Davis said from the back seat, "Miss Hosmer, I want to get to the airport as quickly as possible. Can you drop me at a cab stand, or something?"

Black reached into the glove compartment for a notebook and pen. "We'll take you there. You can fill me in on the way. I need to know time of arrival, what airline—all that. And I want to know anything you can tell me about the circumstances—who found her, and so forth."

Maddy winced at his calm decisiveness before she was able to turn and examine him more closely. Cruel downcast lines at the corners of his mouth and the crushed, despairing slump of his shoulders nearly made her cry out her own pain. Yet, when the full impression of him moved through her mind, she saw more than that. There was a sense of someone looking beyond the moment. She had the impression he was acknowledging injury and carefully surrendering only the resources necessary to restrict the damage. His logical processes were elsewhere, remembering, projecting, accepting and discarding.

Seeking to describe what she'd seen, she first described it as thinking, but the word was too general. Next she considered the look as calculating, but rejected it as suggesting something mechanical. The sudden appearance of the word "hunting" startled her, and she snapped the car through a gear change with sharp, ramming movements.

Angrily, she reminded herself that her primary responsibility was to help him, not to probe his mind. She resolved to concern herself strictly with what was important.

Two days later, she stood in brilliant sunshine with him and the strangers who accompanied them to the cemetery. Funeral-home employees moved the casket from the hearse to the platform spanning the open grave. Middle-aged, dressed in their proper business suits, they exuded solemn dignity and immense professionalism. Maddy wondered if one of them ever slipped, then tried to picture the four of them around a table in shirt sleeves, drinking beer and playing poker. She gave it up. They belonged where they were.

She had been surprised when Steve asked for a preacher to say something at the burial, and was surprised again at the studied attention he afforded the short, thick man and his well-meant homilies. When it was over, Steve thanked him and pressed a check into his palm as they shook hands.

Then, with a round of practiced condolences and the rumble of departing automobiles, it was over.

She took his arm while he continued to stare at the spray of flowers on the coffin. "Are you all right, Steve? I'll wait in the car, if you want to stay here alone awhile."

He turned quickly. "No. I'm ready to leave." He led off toward the car, turning a twisted grin to her. "I was thinking how much she'd hate this." He made a small, circular gesture. "If she ever thought about God, I imagine it was to curse Him, but I had a preacher here because I want Him to know someone loved her. Still and all, she's mad as hell right now. She'll never forgive me for the weather, either."

He opened the door for Maddy, and she settled onto the seat. "The weather? Come on, Steve."

When he was in on his side, he said, "She hated the

weather here. Burying her on a such a beautiful day must strike her as the ultimate revenge.''

Uncertain, Maddy laughed nervously. "I don't picture her worrying about revenge. Not anymore.''

"If there's anything to this business of another life and a next world, you can be damned sure that's what she's thinking about. This family knows all about getting even.'' The starter motor stuttered and the car responded with an out-of-place vigor. He eased away from the grave site.

Maddy turned on him. "I don't want to hear any more of that. You're not making any distinction between doing a hard job that needs to be done and simpleminded vindictiveness. You're a good man, damn you, and I won't let you destroy yourself because everything won't always come out the way you want it to. You can't make the world perfect.''

For a moment, he frowned, but the furrows in his brow smoothed out before he answered. "You're right, of course. But I have to try to make it better, Maddy. Isn't that what we all do, try to make a better place?''

"It's only better for me when we're sharing it, Steve.''

He reached for her hand. "A little time, that's all I need. A little more time, and it'll be just us.''

She kissed his cheek, settled her head against his shoulder. It was a discussion that could only create an argument neither of them could win. Let it rest there, she told herself, and smiled secretly.

A woman learned to clasp each moment at its birth, to treasure a present joy with the bittersweet awareness that it must pass. Men always talked of tomorrow, but they lived in their yesterdays.

CHAPTER 30

ONLY CARMODY'S BREATHING BETRAYED HIS ANGER AS HE swerved off Admiral Way and into the parking lane at the scenic overlook. Summerton stood with his back to him, looking at the city in the distance, spread out in an incredible mural across the arm of the Sound called Elliot Bay. Without preliminaries, Carmody demanded, "What is it this time? Why can't you understand this sort of thing is dangerous?"

Summerton turned slowly, looking hurt. "I almost didn't get in touch with you. I knew you'd be upset, and you'll be even more upset when you hear what I have to tell you."

Carmody stiffened. "What?"

"Nothing we can't handle." Summerton wanted to grip Carmody's elbow or shoulder—make a gesture of solidarity. A movement in the other man's eyes alarmed him, however, and instead of making contact, he took an involuntary step back. He went on, "This all started before I met you."

"What?"

"The lying. I always wanted to be honest with you, Martin, but they wouldn't let me. You're more than my teacher, my contact, you're my friend."

"What lying?" Muscles in Carmody's shoulder tightened. A minor pressure at first, it intensified and grew, radiating needles of pain. Pretending nonchalance, he massaged it.

Summerton said, "I couldn't help it, Marty. Alex made

me tell you I came here from Colorado. I haven't been there for years. I met the people who introduced me to him down in the Bay area. He insisted I never tell you that. I wanted to, but—''

"Shut up. Let me think." Carmody rolled the aching shoulder and continued to rub it. The muscle stiffened further, and he dug fingers into it. The accelerated pain cleared his mind.

So. Alex, the trusted friend. Another treacherous, ambitious fool. Of all people, Alex knew best that one lie about a human resource is like one infidelity from a wife. Suspicion taints every future event, reaches back to darken days and times thought forgotten. One never fully trusts the woman, hates the intruder irrationally, and usually winds up despising the informant.

What lies had Summerton told Alex that Alex accepted as truth? What other lies had they agreed on between them? What lies were known to Nicolai?

How can I use this information to defeat them all?

There was no more point in standing around damning Alex's stupidity than there was in mourning it. Summerton's continuing fidgeting could only mean he had more to confess.

"I know how you joined us," Carmody said. "That's not what's troubling you."

Blinking rapidly, Summerton half-raised his hands, as if expecting a blow. "They were here last week. The ones—the couple from the Bay area."

"Couple? What are their names?"

Summerton seized on the brief confusion in Carmody's manner, realizing it stemmed from the mention of a couple. Ted was his agent. Was it possible he knew nothing of Esther's involvement?

He said, "The man brought his wife as cover, I think."

"How long was he in town?"

A thrill so forceful it weakened his legs shot through Summerton. The fool didn't know about her!

"Not more than a few hours. Up in the morning, back in the afternoon."

"What flights?"

"I don't know."

"You should have found out! Why did he come here? When did you know he was coming?"

Squealing tires jerked them both around. A car rubbed along the curb, the abused rubber easing to a dry, crunching sound as an elderly woman parked. Grinning embarrassment, she offered a limp wave as apology for the disturbance. Carmody nodded sharply, training overriding instinct. He pulled Summerton to the far end of the overlook pavement and said, "I'm waiting, damn you!"

"I didn't know he was coming. He called, told me to meet him. I started to tell you, but we'd never have known what he wanted if I didn't meet him. And he sounded funny, like he was making a threat. Christ, Martin, I had to go!"

Carmody kept his eyes on a small boat, far, far below. From here it was a toy, a windup white plaything. "You broke compartmentation. You should have come to me immediately. It's been a week, you said. Plenty of time for you and your FBI friends to arrange an ambush." Without turning his head, he jerked a thumb over his shoulder. "Are they back there now? Or did they just put a microphone on you?"

"No! I didn't tell them. I didn't tell anyone. I wouldn't do that, Martin. I wouldn't!"

"It's too late for me to worry about it, isn't it?" He faced Summerton. "If you've turned on me, I promise you, you'll regret it. Terribly."

"I didn't! I wouldn't!" Sweat beaded Summerton's upper lip, glittered in the deep crevice between his eyebrows.

"Then why did you delay?"

"Because I was afraid of something like this, afraid you wouldn't believe me, wouldn't trust me."

"Afraid? We'll talk about fear sometime, you and me." Carmody's laugh was the quiet rustle of something hiding in dead leaves. "Let's hear the rest of it, then. Why did he come? What does he know of me?"

Again, Summerton wondered if he was hearing concern, a hint of confusion in the voice. He wished for it, wanted it so badly it triggered the acid bite of tears at the corners of his eyes. Carmody would kill him if he ever found out what

292

really happened. It was wrong, wrong! It was their fault, Ted and Esther's. He'd never have started any of this if they hadn't talked him into it!

He said, "All I know is he called you Marvin. There was some talk about you being replaced."

" 'Some talk'? How delicately phrased. Who would replace me? How?"

"He said 'superiors.' Like, 'His superiors may replace him.' "

"Exactly what did he say? Who did he quote?" The hand that closed on Summerton's arm above the elbow forced yielding fat aside, scissored into muscle.

Summerton's voice wavered. "He said one of your superiors questioned your ability to continue in your line of work." Inspiration struck, and he added, "He said a couple of men had to be eliminated in Frisco 'cause your net had some kind of breakdown. For God's sake, let go of my arm!"

Carmody relaxed his grip and returned his gaze to the view once more. The indifference of the release affected Summerton more than the pain.

It was some time before Carmody spoke. "Go home, Harry," he said, staring across the water at the city.

"You're not angry, Martin? Listen, everything—I only did it because they made me, you know, but all along, I was thinking, 'Marty's got to know all this shit,' you know?" After a pause, he dropped his voice. "No one really got killed in Frisco, did they?"

"Of course not. Now go home. Do absolutely nothing until you hear from me." He faced Summerton, eyes vacant.

"I got it."

Carmody looked away. Harry hurried to his car and drove off.

As Carmody walked to his own car, the adrenaline of a lifetime of anticipation flooded his blood, electrified the muscle structure, prepared it for a massive discharge of energy. The elderly woman ogled the scenery, unaware of his turmoil. Traffic went by on the boulevard. No one passed on foot. No one peered from the windows of the proper, middle-class homes. Still, he felt disapproval, as though the spirit of this unremarkable, ordinary neighborhood knew him and whispered of uncomprehending hurt. And fear.

It was an affliction of stress that logic should have rejected easily. Try as he might to dislodge it, however, the idea preyed on his mind. Finally, he told himself it was a simple thing, like a dream, and to worry about such things was foolish.

So many dreams had broken on his life he understood every nuance of their use and their impotence.

He elected to take the longer route back to the city. He wanted the time to think.

The multiple moves possible in the situation careered through his mind, each situation generating subschemes and counterplots.

If Summerton was doubled, he'd have been carrying communications equipment, and there would almost certainly have been surveillance, particularly since the meeting site was known in plenty of time to set up a stakeout.

There was no guarantee Summerton wasn't wired. And everyone missed a surveillant sooner or later.

There was still a chance to pull the emergency identity papers and simply run for it.

He gritted his teeth. There was too much at stake to run.

With that decided, he turned his mind to the rest of the puzzle.

Assuming Summerton was telling some form of the truth, Nicolai was making a move, and he clearly regarded Martin Carmody as expendable. But Summerton was nearing the heart of important discoveries. He could save the country years of its own time, possibly arrange the elimination of the Americans.

Damn Nicolai!

The difficulty wasn't what was happening, but that the board was so obscure. There was no integrity to anything.

None of them has an honest self, an identity. I lie—cheat, suborn, betray anything. But for a true cause!

A pedestrian shouted something unintelligible, leaping backward. Carmody belatedly yanked the car to the right, straightened it out again.

Imbecile! Run over someone and get thrown in jail like a common criminal!

So. If Nicolai was trying to bypass him, the pawn was Wade. It spoke poorly of Nicolai's skills that he'd choose such a peculiar weapon.

He found a parking place among the massed cars at Alki Beach. Closing his ears to the bellowing of radios and cassette tapes, he crossed the street and walked until he found a pay phone. His lips moved as he reviewed what he must say, and then he dialed direct, dropping in coins when the operator instructed. The man on the other end answered with a noncommittal "Yes?"

Carmody said, "Good afternoon. This is Jerry North. I'll be getting in tonight at nine. Later than usual. Not eight, nine. I want to talk about file number three-four-oh-two. Got that? Three-four-oh-two."

"You said three-four-oh-two? Coming in around nine? Who'd you say this is?"

"Jerry. Jerry North. I'm coming in, like always, only at nine."

"Mister, I don't know any Jerry North. You've got a wrong number."

"I can't have. I—oh, shit. What area code is this?"

"Four-one-five."

"God damn. Sorry." Carmody hung up and left the booth, knowing his message had been received and understood. Nicolai would run a fast security review on agent thirty-four, Ted Wade. That night, at precisely nine o'clock, he would call a prearranged number and report whatever he was able to learn.

Back at his car, Carmody stood for a minute, watching the crowd on the beach. Like flowers, the bright bodies clustered the grayish sand, masses of color surging with vitality. In contrast, the metal-hard blue of the Sound feigned indifference. It waited, insatiable, chopping waves licking the shore like unceasing cold tongues.

The blunt sexuality of the youthful mob sometimes of-

295

fended him. They were no less intense today in their clumsy leering and grabbing, but instead of being repelled, he was amused. In fact, an unknown pain wrenched his heart, and he wanted to shout at them to leap higher, run faster, love more—to taste life to its ultimate limit.

Then he realized he was staring at one girl.

In five years—maybe only three—Nina would look exactly like that.

Would she ever know the heedless enjoyment of a time like this? Or did she already have her mother's wise eyes, brimming with the awareness that she must spend her brightest years evaluating eligible males, counting their prospects like so many coins?

These people screamed their freedom, flaunted their accomplishments, their acquisitions, as if everything was their due. Pain was what they needed, these fleshy consumers battening on the world's production. Fire to cleanse them, starvation to instruct them in the suffering of others.

He twisted the ignition key viciously, speeding away from the scene. He went directly to Elise's apartment building.

She was unloading groceries from her car when he walked into the apartment garage. Smiling her greeting, she kissed him lightly and filled his extended arms with a paper sack. He made a face. "Some big hello—an old married kiss and this junk to carry."

"If I were paid better, I wouldn't be buying junk. You might even get better kisses."

He peered at the contents. "Quality stuff. You obviously have an understanding, progressive employer."

"Ha! He's progressive. I'm poor but honest."

"Ridiculous combination. However, as a generous man, I'll go out and buy something special if you feel my staying for dinner won't compromise your standards."

An angry buzz discolored her laughter. Handing him another sack and taking one for herself, she headed for the elevator. She said, "I'm already pretty well compromised."

"Don't ruin the evening, Elise. Please. We've talked about why we can't live together."

296

"I'm not afraid of your wife." She jabbed the elevator button impatiently. The cage groaned toward them. "You said the divorce is final. She's got no right to interfere with us."

"Rights have nothing to do with it." The elevator door closed shut behind them, trapping the rest of the lies in its small enclosure. "She's unbalanced. Why do you think I park away from here, leave so early in the morning, try to avoid establishing a schedule? I can't take a chance on her learning where you live."

Elise stalked out, onto her floor. "Call the police."

"I have. All it gets me is more trouble."

"Well, if it keeps up, I'm calling them." She unlocked the apartment, strode to the small kitchen and started slamming things into proper places.

Coming up behind her, he put down the bag and enfolded her in his arms. She stood rigid, unmoving, while he buried his face in her hair. He said, "We've got to be patient. She's leaving soon. I don't know when, but I know she's leaving. What we have is too good to risk. Isn't it?"

The force of his need for her stirred in him.

He strained against the admission, hated it.

Regardless, the need grew. Knowing he would inevitably leave her, he knew he had to be with her as long as possible.

"I can't breathe." She pushed his arms apart, turned in their circle.

He said, "I didn't realize. I was thinking about losing you."

Rising on her toes, she kissed him, matching her body to his. The embrace quickly became desperate statement, an attempt to compress all of life into physical contact. It was Carmody who pulled back. "I'll help you fix dinner."

"Okay." Her head on his chest, they clung to each other. Carmody closed his eyes, lowered his lips to the crown of her head. She made him think of Nina, always clean, untouched by the world around her. Her hair, too, smelled of sun and sky, of nature. They all went to the circus one evening, he remembered—he, Olga, and the girls—and when they stepped

297

outside, the moist evening air set the smells of the arena in their clothes as firmly as dye. Nina fussed in her tiredness, and he picked her up. Her little coat was full of strange odors that conjured clowns, jugglers, bears and horses. But her hair had smelled exactly as Elise's at this moment, like falling leaves and dark nights.

He wondered if he loved Elise as much as he loved Nina. The question shocked him. He stepped away quickly, went to uncork the wine.

Need had been grudgingly acknowledged long ago.

Love had never been considered.

They ate quietly, mutually denying the earlier tension. Still, it was there. Fork against plate took on the brisance of a skirmish. Conversation was short phrases. Implications hovered over the table like summer clouds, hoarding lightning that threatened and grumbled without ever truly revealing itself.

When the dishes were in the dishwasher, they moved to the miniature balcony, settling into the padded lawn chairs. He took her hand in his, reaching across his body with the other to stroke it. They leaned toward each other to kiss. Each watched the other's eyes at first, and when they closed them, it was simultaneous. It was a gentle exchange of vows, unlike the earlier hard meshing of wants.

It was too rich for Carmody. Awkward, clutching at the balcony rail, he got to his feet. His words tasted and sounded like brass. Nevertheless, he delivered the lines with accomplished skill.

"I can't stay any longer. Business." He gestured weakly. "I have to go."

Elise made no effort to hide her hurt. "You kiss me like that one minute and tell me you have to leave on business in the next? Like hell! What d'you think I am, something to turn on and off? What is the *matter* with you?"

Taking a backward step, he said, "Elise, I didn't plan on this." He repeated the earlier gesture, a limp waggle of one hand. "I promised to be somewhere to talk to a man. I can't miss the connection. There's nothing else to it."

She rose swiftly, charged with anger. "Enjoy yourself.

298

And find yourself another girl. I'm quitting you, here and in that damned store, too. Just get the hell out of my life.''

He raised his hands, and she stepped away as if threatened. "Go away. Just go, Martin. I don't need anymore.''

Wordlessly, he moved to the door, turning for one last word. She had her back to him, arms folded. He thought her shoulders were shaking, but it was too dim to be certain. He pulled the door shut behind him so gently the bolt went home with a barely discernible scrape.

It was two minutes to nine when he stepped into the prearranged phone booth. Three minutes later, the first ring came. He let it sound three times. It stopped, and he was fidgeting irritably by the time it started again. After the third ring, he picked it up. Very distinctly, he said, "This is Jerry North. I expected to be there at nine.''

Nicolai said, "Is everything all right?''

"I'm not sure. You checked as I asked?''

"What is it you want to know? Why are you asking?''

"You spoke to him personally?''

"Yes, yes. What *is* it?''

Carmody heard the routine irascibility, certain there was impatience there, a sense of anticipation. His mind raced, seeking reasons for this new development. There was no choice but to pursue the questions at hand. "Did he say he was out of town during the last two weeks?''

"What? No, of course not. I specifically asked him if he'd missed any work, gone on any trips on the weekends. What do you suspect?''

"I was in the airport nine days ago. I'd swear I saw him there.''

"Impossible. He volunteered that his wife went on a trip, but that was to San Diego. They're completely dependable.''

"I'm very relieved to hear that.''

"The result of my efforts to beat some discipline into our organization. They're aware of what happened to the two people who interfered with our operation. They were properly impressed.''

There it is! The bloodthirsty bastard wants to gloat over his killings!

299

"Fine. That's fine. Thanks for your help. I'll be in touch."

"If you have a reason." Disappointment warred with rebuke for dominance.

Carmody hung up and made one more phone call. An hour later, he was in an elegant restaurant, seated across a small table from Summerton. There were few other customers, and the waitresses gathered by the kitchen entrance, chatting among themselves. Their easy posture and small gestures contrasted with the hard chords of the rock group working the adjoining bar. Summerton ignored all of it, nervous eyes jerking from Carmody's face to some distant point, then back again.

Carmody repeated his first question of the meeting. "How do you know they stayed here?"

"She told me! Bragged about it! Came early to make sure they weren't being set up!"

Nicolai said she went to San Diego.

For another hour, Carmody made him repeat every word he claimed to have spoken to either of the Wades, every word he remembered their speaking. Summerton ran with sweat. He put his elbows on the table, linking his fingers. Carmody smiled to himself at the wasted attempt to hide the shaking hands, at the same time thinking of the terrible damage Nicolai had done them all by killing the two men in San Francisco. Traitors needed no harsh measures to frighten them into line. If they had character, they wouldn't be traitors. One needed only to shout, to squeeze, to stare into their eyes and let them know you had the moral upper hand. At base, they were all like Summerton. Alex knew that. Nicolai never would.

Summerton repeated his story. Carmody let him run, the slimmest thread of his attention tuned to the sounds, hoping to catch a pause, a sudden change of pace. His mind refused to focus on Summerton any longer.

Alex wasn't a traitor, nor was he a fool. He was my friend, but he destroyed himself and betrayed me. He lied to me. How could it happen? Men like Summerton do those things. People like Wade scheme and plot with men like

Nicolai and this piece of shit because they don't dare attack an honest man frontally. How can Nicolai align himself with capitalists to destroy me? Why? Why did Alex turn his back on everything we've all been taught? What can happen next?

"What're you going to do?"

He reached for Carmody, who jerked away from the touch and said, "What?"

"I asked you twice—what're you going to do?"

"Check with hotels. If we can't find them registered, we'll have to think of some other way of proving they were here."

Eagerly, Summerton accepted his inclusion in the action. He watched happily as Carmody paid the check, only to lose his enthusiasm when he learned that he would do the actual questioning at the hotel.

They were very fortunate. Esther's disgust for the Windmill had led to an honest slip.

Summerton described himself as her friend, helping her relocate a lost ring. He supplied the date of her arrival and departure with her lover, suggested the bill was paid in cash. She was no tramp, he emphasized, but the wife of an important politician. It was very important that she get the ring back. Her husband's influence was barely second to his jealousy.

The manager remembered. They paid cash. He knew nothing of any ring. However, he remembered the agency they called to rent a car.

The clerk at the car-rental agency also remembered the couple who paid cash. He balked at guaranteeing to recognize them again—dark glasses and hats made it difficult—but the description sounded right. Summerton raced to give the good news to Carmody, waiting in the car.

Carmody took it very quietly. "Positive identification? We have no photographs. How can you be sure?" He pulled away, into traffic.

Jerking his head at the rental agency, Summerton said, "You should have heard him. I gave him a basic description, and he ran with it. 'Sure,' he says, 'I remember them. Paid cash.' "

"Now I have to decide what to do about it."

Summerton smackd his lips before speaking. "We'll have to suspend operations, won't we? I hate to say it, with my position so improved and all, but it sounds like we're out of business."

Carmody continued to drive silently, exactly at the legal speed limit. Impatiently, Summerton said, "Well, what do we do?"

Starting, Carmody looked at him as if surprised to find him there, then, "Do? Oh, yes." Only when the oncoming lights of a truck splashed across Carmody's eyes did Summerton understand the depth of concentration he was witnessing.

Carmody went on in the same detached manner. "You've had the misfortune to get caught up in something no collection effort can stand, Harry. We're dealing with something much like mutiny, much like treason. It's up to me to put an end to it." He patted Summerton's shoulder. "I'll take you back to your car now. You'll go to work, continue normal living. Everything'll be just fine."

Later, Carmody knocked softly on Elise's door. She opened it slowly, just enough to reveal taut features and a robed arm. She matched his stare, waiting.

He said, "I don't want to be alone. I need help." He looked away, shook his head like a man getting rid of pain. "No. Not help. A friend. You. I need you to be my friend."

"You don't treat me like a friend. Am I really that easy?"

"That's not it!" His voice writhed while the body and face held firm. "Sometimes we don't have a choice, believe me. There are things we have to do."

"Are you a criminal? Is that what you have to do?"

"No!" He was shocked. "I swear to you."

"Your wife?"

"A detective. She's paying him to find you. I made a deal with him. He'll fail." He shrugged, half-smiled. "It makes me feel like I bought you, or something. I feel dirty. We'll talk about it tomorrow."

"Wait." She caught his arm as he turned. Her robe was satin, a dove gray. In the hard burn of the night light over her

302

door, it gleamed like metal. "You're a strange man. I hoped you'd love me the way I love you. I was afraid to hope we could be friends. Don't go. Not tonight."

He let her gentle touch lead him into the room.

CHAPTER 31

Down in the garage, a motorcycle blasted into action, bringing Carmody fully awake instantly. Elsie stirred languourously. Soft, smooth skin caressed his chest as she drew an arm across it, and the previous night was alive in his mind once again. He rolled out of the bed quickly.

He dressed rapidly, wasting no movement. When he was finished, he bent down to her, whispered her name. Her eyes opened in wide alarm before understanding settled into them. Then she frowned. "Are you leaving?"

"Just for a while."

Taking his hand, she said, "It's Monday. We don't work today."

"I know. I'll be back soon. Why don't we go on a picnic?"

"See? You can't wait to get away from me!" She flung herself facedown, shaking the bed with burlesque sobs.

Sitting beside her, he moved her hair aside, kissed the back of her neck, the hollow between the muscles of her naked back. "That's the dumbest thing anyone ever said."

She rolled over, reached to take him into her arms. "Stay."

"No." He got up, backing away. She grinned and sat up, letting the sheet fall to her waist, arms extended in invitation. Clumsily, he backed into the door and said, "Damn you," the words so freighted with emotional contradictions they

304

came out almost a growl. She blew him a kiss and snuggled back under the covers.

Smoldering reminiscence of their reconciliation lightened his step, made the humid morning air smell fresh, and transformed the rumble of the waking city to a song of beckoning. He whistled as he walked, a thin sibilance to accompany his brisk progress.

It was ten blocks to his car. Every foot took him away from fantasy and deeper into the real world.

He had no idea why he'd been singled out for destruction.

It was pointless to dwell on it. The state declared a man its enemy deep within its own councils. The declaration was conviction. He'd spent his life watching the accused whine of innocence, heard the cries sink into the oblivious stone of the Lubianka, the uncaring vastnesses of the north.

Nevertheless, a man didn't surrender abjectly. A man fought.

Summerton was the indispensable man, his access the single most important factor in the problem. Nicolai was undermining the net, using Ted Wade to suborn Summerton. The most rational solution—to report Nicolai's treachery to higher authority—was impossible. Nicolai controlled all communications. Indeed, there was no evidence to prove any allegations. Even if Summerton corroborated what they'd discovered—which was a chancey possibility—Nicolai and Wade would deny everything. Standoff.

There was a solution. Wade was Nicolai's only effective lever in the Summerton matter. Elimination of Wade would isolate Nicolai. It would also warn him that he was not the only man capable of drastic action. For as long as he remained in the San Francisco office he would be helpless to do anything but perform his mission properly.

Summerton would have to be convinced his own survival depended on aligning himself with Carmody. The weapon to use there was fear.

The first requirement was Wade's death.

Carmody arrived at his car at the same time it all fell into place for him. He placed a forearm on the roof, pillowing his head, exulting. He envisioned the net operating as it had, smoothly. Living with Elise would lock his cover. They'd be too typical for anyone to notice. Explaining absences would be simple—she was so trusting. The trips home would be a problem, but not insurmountable.

A voice called, "You all right, mister?" and Carmody straightened. Two small Oriental boys, brightly curious, poised ready for flight on the opposite sidewalk. A newspaper cart lay on the ground beside them. At Carmody's silent stare, one tugged at his friend's arm, chattering rapidly. The second one shrugged himself free. He grinned at Carmody. "My friend's new here. He don't talk no English yet. You sick, or something? We can get help."

"Nothing's wrong." Carmody unlocked his car and left quickly.

There was a principle underscored in the incident, he told himself, and he was lucky to be reminded so painlessly.

There were no neutrals. Anyone with eyes to see him was an enemy. There were no allies. There were assets under control. No more, no less.

Which made it imperative that Nicolai's teeth be pulled and Summerton completely reined in.

He deliberately called Summerton at work to startle him, to play on his fear. He wasted no time chatting, saying, "When you get off work, drive to the University District. Wait on the steps of Suzzallo Library. I'll see you there."

Summerton's voice strained through the earpiece. "What time? You shouldn't call— I'll be there! What time?"

"Six thirty-five. Be on time." He hung up, harder than necessary. His hand was trembling. Stuffing it in a pocket, he told himself it was right to be nervous. Not frightened, but alert, all the senses coordinated.

Stressing Summerton was risky, but it had to be done. The man must be brought to heel and kept there so firmly, so securely, there could be no thought of betrayal. Scheduling the meeting that close to quitting time left little opportunity for him to contact Nicolai, should the option occur to him. It was equally unlikely he'd run to the FBI, because he feared exposure as a spy.

There was a flaw in the plan, Carmody conceded. It was

306

the danger that Summerton might be tempted to become a double agent if promised some immunity.

Harsh control required ever harsher control.

Summerton must be stripped of options.

The phone in the booth rang shrilly. Carmody took it off the hook as if touching something dirty. "Hello."

Nicolai practically snarled. "Have you nothing else to do but call me? Are you completely out of your mind?"

"I must see the man we discussed the last time I called you—the one who handles account number three-four-oh-two."

"Impossible. See him on schedule."

"There are gaps and flaws in his report. Do you want to take responsibility?"

"Control is your problem."

"And I say he's lax. Training is your responsibility."

"I disagree. He's done excellent work."

"There are technical journals full of information he's failed to produce. If he's not lax, he's withholding. Why? You are assuming a great deal of responsibility already, my friend." It was the coldest warning Carmody could muster.

"He knows what happened to the last two—"

Carmody interrupted harshly. "Perhaps he's sharing his new fear with our competition."

"Impossible!" Nicolai wrenched the word from his guts.

Carmody let the silence between them hang empty, knowing the tight-featured little man's memory filled it with the sounds of slamming iron doors. When Nicolai spoke again, he was composed. "I will contact you. He will be told to report to you for additional training and tasking. Determine the cause of his failure and report to me. You are to take no further action. Do I make myself clear?"

"Perfectly. I'll wait to hear from you." Carmody hung up and stepped out into the humid night air. Headlights approached, passed, uninterested in him. He thought of a nature film showing ants in a tunnel dashing past a beetle, ignoring it because it had learned to mimic them so well it was completely accepted. Before, he thought of the beetle and himself in his professional context, and was amused. Tonight, however, he watched the hurtling cars and longing nearly gagged him. He wanted to step off the curb and strike one of them, attract some attention to his existence.

What was it he wanted, exactly? Why was it important to be noticed?

On the way to his car, he thought about his conversation. Two points stood out. Nicolai initially defended Wade, although, in fact, he should know practically nothing about the man. Wade had been recruited, trained, and utilized long before Nicolai appeared. Whatever he knew of him was from the files, which indicated simply that Wade produced information. Quality was unmentioned. Yet Nicolai insisted he'd done "excellent work." Interesting.

More interesting was the instruction that Carmody was to do nothing about Wade.

The terrible possibility, that Wade was indeed doubled—and Nicolai knew of it—fell on Carmody like a weight. He leaned against a convenient brick wall, calming himself, telling himself such a thing was even beyond Nicolai.

Or could it be that Wade and Summerton were both working against Nicolai and himself, leading them farther and farther into the grasp of the FBI in order to uncover the rest of the net?

Sweat slid down his neck, formed a loose, uncomfortable seal between shirt collar and flesh. He rubbed it away roughly.

The tremor left his hand. The sweat lost its greasy texture, became the product of heat, not emotional excess. He continued up the street, crossing to the fire station, past the miniature park and the rough music of its waterfall. He was calm when he reached the parking lot.

Ten days later, Carmody initiated the final phase of his plan.

Shortly before five o'clock on a Wednesday evening, he entered Kane Hall, on the University of Washington campus. To his front stretched a huge courtyard, perhaps ninety yards across to the building on the south side. Suzzallo Library, separated by only a few steps from the left end of Kane, loomed in that direction as the base of a U-shaped formation of buildings, its major opening about one hundred and twenty yards to the west, on Carmody's right. In the early evening light, the architecture of the massive Gothic library was transformed to shifting tracery and gentling shadows. The roof was a melange of black and green random patches, the latter a chemical tint unlike any he knew in nature. Tall, narrow windows, countersunk in the reaching wall, appeared to turn inward, as if denying the world in arrogant certainty all wisdom dwelt behind them.

The Kane Hall entryway provided the vantage point Carmody needed. Auditorium-style classrooms ranged down one wall, while the windowed doors on the opposite side faced the bricked yard.

He got comfortable near the door closest to the library, drew a paperback book from his jeans pocket, and pretended to read. Ten minutes into his vigil, a spare, brisk woman stepped out of a classroom. From the corner of his eye, he saw her staring at him. Eventually she'd ask him his business here.

The woman sniffed audibly before moving off to the stairway, rubber soles squeaking indignation.

Few people moved out front. The students called the brick-paved area Red Square, a tongue-in-cheek allusion to the myriad speakers and demonstrators it hosted. Since the inflammatory sixties, the students had returned to a calmer attitude, treating the various spectacles with amused interest.

Americans were especially addicted to that response, Carmody knew, and it was perhaps the most infuriating facet of their character. At times he saw them as a race of superintelligent apes, afraid of nothing, attracted to everything. No matter what crossed their path, they examined it with the same maddening tolerance, trying to figure it out, learn how to use it, apply it to their personal needs or wants. Idea, object—it made no difference—the thing was held up to the light, dunked under water, bitten, rolled on the ground. And all the while, they smiled. They enjoyed wringing what they wanted from the world.

Worse, they expected everyone else to do the same. They recognized no proper restraint, refused to understand the fundamental fact that anything that isn't controlled is, by definition, out of control, and the state has an obligation to exercise control. Even when they did cooperate with someone else, they insisted on their stupid, inquisitive, acquisitive individuality.

The chirping shoes interrupted his musing. The woman was returning, a graying, tightly bound rope of hair down her neck bouncing at each step, tart eyes fixed on her personal stranger. Carmody returned to his observation of the Square.

The irritating sound of her walking stopped too quickly. He knew she was watching him. One final note from the shoes preceded the closing of the door.

Two students passed within two feet of him, chattering. He doubted they even saw him.

Outside, a lone man walked across the yard, his shadow wavering across the prim bricked surface. Suddenly, the solitary figure dropped his books, lifted his arms horizontal to the ground, then executed a series of sinuous, gliding dance steps. When he was done, he hurriedly retrieved his materials and searched to see if he was observed. Carmody drew back quickly, and the man jogged into the library.

The Square turned bleak with his departure. The emptiness made Summerton's shambling appearance all the more emphatic. When he stopped to turn, slowly, as if admiring the buildings, Carmody groaned. The swinging head only served to broadcast the search for surveillance, and the supremely casual turn to scan for a follower was as blatant as a bonfire.

Pitching the paperback in a trash can, Carmody moved toward the stairs. He was perhaps fifteen feet from the nervous woman's door when it popped open. She looked directly into his eyes, and her hand flew to her collar, bunching itself in the material. His smile apparently irritated her. She said, "Are you waiting for someone?"

He waved vaguely. "Had some time to kill."

The back-exit from Kane Hall afforded him a shielded approach to the library until he was forced to cover the open ground of Red Square between the two buildings. He intercepted Summerton and said, "Follow me," leading him away at a fast pace.

Summerton puffed, keeping up. "What's the hurry?" he said, the words coming like little explosions.

Carmody slowed immediately. "No hurry. Excitement, that's all. You have tomorrow off?"

"They didn't like it. What's going on?"

"We're meeting your friend Wade. You're renting a motor home. We're all going up to the mountains for a short training course."

"Motor home? Training? For what?"

"Emergency measures."

Summerton slowed, suddenly nervous, and at the appearance of Carmody's easy smile, a terrible calm moved through his veins, the crystallization of an awareness denied until now. What he saw was a face uncomplicated by any purpose other than survival.

CHAPTER 32

Tᴇᴅ Wᴀᴅᴇ sᴛᴇᴘᴘᴇᴅ ɪɴsɪᴅᴇ ᴛʜᴇ sᴍᴀʟʟ ᴍᴏᴛᴏʀ ʜᴏᴍᴇ ᴛᴏ sᴇᴇ Harry Summerton lounging on the built-in sofa. Wade made an unintelligible sound and paled visibly. His canvas duffel bag slipped noticeably in his grasp. Summerton grinned broadly, beckoned him forward. "Good to see you again, Ted. How are you?"

Wade continued to stare. He repeated the strange sound, as if his surprise was a physical obstruction in his throat. Carmody's firm shove from behind nearly cost him his balance.

He searched Summerton's features for a signal. The muscles in his own face fell slack.

Summerton exulted at the raw fear. He hoped he was capable of hiding his feelings, afraid Wade might penetrate the forced geniality and understand how much he should be afraid.

Summerton moved to the refrigerator, busying himself with ice and Scotch. "A drink to celebrate your safe arrival," he said. Wade took it cautiously. Carmody forced his way past, taking a glass from Summerton as he did. He drained it in large, gulping swallows and handed it back before sliding in behind the steering wheel. Wade watched blankly, his untasted whiskey glinting in the sunlight that burst through the window.

The vehicle lurched forward, staggering both Summerton

and Wade. Once it was moving steadily, Wade sipped slowly, determinedly calm. Speaking to the back of Carmody's head, he said, "I don't understand what's going on."

The depth of the understatement brought an honest chuckle from Carmody. "You and Summerton are acquainted. You've destroyed our compartmentation. You were directed to take a cab here so I could perform a long countersurveillance on you. It's one way I can hope to protect the remains of our security. Also, we'll meet less frequently, for our mutual protection. We have some new equipment—radio transmitters—to teach you. Since there's no longer any extra risk in training you two together, that's what we're doing."

Wade blanched. "Radios? They can be intercepted!"

"Not these. State of the art. You punch a button and it selects a random cipher. Compose your message on the typing keyboard, then punch another button. That tells my receiver what your transmitting frequency will be, and both sets switch, automatically. Hit the button again and the signal goes out at such speed it sounds like a squeak, enciphered by the on-board computer chip. When my receiver gets the message, it reads the cipher your equipment has selected and automatically deciphers it. Even if the signal's picked up, it'll take months of computer time to break the code, and we won't use the same frequency twice in a year. Piece of cake."

"Good God! The thing must be huge!"

Carmody chuckled. "I told you, state of the art. It's about the size of a brick, weighs about three pounds, complete with hookup wire. We won't be using any juice today, of course, although it comes with a battery system for short-range work." Summerton watched, uninterested in the words. The important thing was to see Carmody's delivery, his behavior. As expected, it was flawless. No nervous twitch, no hesitancy.

When Wade learned what was actually going down, he'd have a fit.

Thinking about that scene displaced the conversation, turned it to a pleasant background buzz.

Wade had it coming. Esther was the one who was going to suffer needlessly.

She truly cared for her husband. When she saw him humiliated, she'd feel some pity, of course. When she saw him revealed for the loser he really was, the mistaken notion that she loved him would wither fast.

The thought of the favor he was doing her made Harry feel wonderful. She'd made a typical woman's mistake, but with his help, he knew her natural intelligence would work things out.

It wasn't as if Wade never had a chance. All he'd had to do was agree to the original plan, and it would have been Carmody on his way down the toilet. Wade could've had a good position in the new structure. Now he'd be on the outside for good.

It was all going to work out quite well. Even if Wade did the unthinkable and confessed to their clandestine meeting, he'd merely be convicting himself. Going to Carmody first effectively killed that problem. Now if Wade brought the matter up, Carmody would never believe it was anyone else's idea.

Idly, Summerton returned to listening until he heard enough to understand the conversation was trivia about Wade's work in the laboratory. He dismissed it, once more allowed the voices to blend and sink into the background noise of the highway.

It was mid-afternoon when the sudden turn and the immediate change from smooth pavement to ruts and potholes pulled Summerton to attention. Wade had changed clothes at some time during the trip and now wore well-used hiking garb. He sat beside Carmody, silent, oblivious to everything but the meandering dirt road ahead.

Summerton sighed hugely, looking out the window. Scorn for Wade's lack of appreciation moved him to study his surroundings with greater interest than usual. A gently rising valley climbed out before them until it was eventually part of the mountain wall. Logged years ago, now it was covered with clumps of alder, firs, and heavy scrub. Multiple hues of green created an overall hard, industrious color. Wallowing bulbous clouds tumbled overhead, spreading sheets of light and shadow across the slopes and the valley floor. A stream as brightly clear as living crystal hurried parallel to the road.

When Carmody stopped the vehicle and cut the engine the living, vibrant silence of the mountains poured over them. Summerton and Wade sat immobile. Their ears, accustomed to the idiot babble of civilization, missed the breeze sliding among the fir boughs above them, failed to register the distant laughter of the stream. Tiny, insistent insect voices had no presence for them.

Carmody heard it all, begrudging the rasp of the window as he rolled it down to let in more of the outdoors. He tasted the air, noting the hint of snow-mantled ridges, the resinous tang of evergreen. Nose-stinging heat made the naked rock shimmer, but in two hours—three at the most—the exhausted sun would decline. The stone would return to sulking massiveness.

Meanwhile, there was work to be done.

Scanning the area, Carmody sought out the point where he'd crossed the ridge with Elise.

Their valley.

It would always be their secret. No matter who knew of it before their discovery or who else would eventually learn of it, it belonged to them because it was part of their discovery of each other.

He hated the two men with him because they made it necessary to share the place.

"We have to hurry," he said, thrusting himself out of the seat. "Harry, get the daypacks out of the cabinet over the sink."

Jerking the equipment out, Summerton sneaked a quick peek inside one. The object inside, wrapped in aluminum foil and glass-fibred packing tape, looked as if it held a real radio. He chuckled, remembering Carmody taping together milk cartons and filling them with sawdust to create his dummy electronic marvels. It troubled him that the attached instruction manual looked like something typed in someone's home and duplicated on a cheap copier. Fortunately, Carmody said all that was needed was an excuse to isolate Wade and make him talk.

Summerton's amusement continued. Wade would try to blame his problems on the one man who was outsmarting both of them. Carmody would be convinced Wade was selling him out and dump him, and Nicolai would be pissed off out of his mind at everyone but good old Harry.

He turned his attention to the packs, maneuvering outside with them. As large as an average shopping bag, they were made of a tough dark-blue material. The shoulder straps that suspended the load against the wearer's back were well-padded, and the narrower band that secured around the waist featured an easily adjusted buckle. He noticed a partial store tag on the cloth of one. Curious, he examined it, and an idea struck him, so brilliant he was shaking as he pocketed the scrap of paper.

There was no chance to dwell on the new thought. As soon as they were out, Carmody locked the door and set off at a demanding pace.

Wade kept up with little apparent effort, but within a half-mile, Summerton was red-faced, breathing hard. Forcing a light tone, he called up to the others, "It's a good thing these packs are light, you know? I'm not used to this shit."

No one responded, and Summerton's color darkened. Hitching the pack higher on his shoulders, he leaned forward, counting paces, telling himself a break would come before he reached a hundred. After several hundreds, he quit counting.

When they started downhill, he heaved a sigh of relief but then realized Carmody was taking advantage of the slope to increase his speed. For a moment, he considered simply sitting down. Aching knees and burning lungs begged for rest. As he slowed, anticipating the luxury of immobility, Wade casually hopped over a branch in his path. Muttering curses, Summerton hurried after them.

Carmody suddenly stopped. The downhill gradient increased sharply directly in front of him. On his right, a sparkling-clear stream angled toward him from farther up the hill, then changed course almost at his feet to leap down the steeper slope with the glee of a child on a playground slide.

He watched the others relax. Wade settled against a tree, throwing his head back, inhaling deeply. Summerton's drop

316

was more like an angry surrender, and Carmody smiled to himself. He was secretly surprised by Summerton's gritty performance. It was the first time a surprise from Summerton had been pleasant.

He stepped to the bank of the noisy little stream, affording himself a better view of the downhill course. There was a break about twenty yards beyond his present position, an almost flat space where the flow lost some of its exuberance for perhaps another ten yards. A plump gray bird a bit smaller than a robin stood on a rock in the middle of the rushing water. Carmody recognized it as a dipper. It bobbed up and down with a peculiar, unhurried rhythm, fluttered its wings briefly, and dove into the stream. The current snatched at it until it reached the bottom and gained a foothold. The clarity of the water allowed Carmody to make it out, although the roiled surface mangled the image so that his mind, unaccustomed to birds walking on creek beds, readily argued against what his eye reported. The dipper faced upstream, angling its body to move left or right, poking under rocks and litter for creatures that had every right to anticipate life safe from birds. When it popped through the surface and onto a different rock, Carmody was, as always, entranced by the carefree wonder of the thing.

At Summerton's crashing approach, the bird fled. Skimming along the surface to where the smooth stretch of water once more broke away down a steeper grade, it flared dusky wings once, pumped, and was gone.

"Now what?" Summerton's voice still carried the rasp of exertion.

"We might as well get on with it." Carmody continued to look at the spot where the bird had disappeared. "Tell Wade."

They withdrew a short distance from the stream, stopping where a huge tree lay toppled. The trunk pointed downhill toward the lake in the heart of the valley. Carmody leaned against it, facing the others. At his instructions, they sat down and opened the daypacks.

"Don't unwrap the radios yet," he said. "Study the instruction manuals."

317

Wade waved the package like a teacher's pointer. "Why are we doing this out here? We used a room before."

Carmody moved past their backs. "Three of us checking into a place would be cumbersome. This'll only take the rest of the day, anyhow. You'll be home in a few hours."

Nodding, Wade said, "I told Esther I'd call her this evening."

Stopping abruptly, Carmody asked, "She knows you're here? What'd you tell her?"

The criticism in the questions startled Wade. He turned to look up at Carmody. "I told her I had to come up here on business. I had to tell her something, didn't I?"

"Of course." Carmody took two more steps. The move put him a body's length from the two seated men and partially hidden behind a huge tree. His eyes remained on the men at their reading.

Carmody opened his shirt and withdrew a pistol. The curved handle melted into his grasp, while the long, thin barrel extended away from him, seeking. There was a sinister beauty to the piece, a wicked esthetic of form wedded to function. The grace disappeared when he screwed the lumpish tube of the silencer on the end. Disfigured, the weapon became no more than a tool.

Tucking the pistol under his belt at his back, Carmody moved to a position behind Wade, slightly to the seated man's left. He said, "Ted, what did you and Nicolai say when you told him I wanted you to come up here?"

Wade hesitated, then, "I'm in the middle on this. He said I should report to him exactly what we talked about." He twisted to face Carmody, so intent on the standing man that he failed to notice Summerton's pale nervousness. Continuing, he said, "I don't know what's going on. We've worked well together. I don't like Nicolai. He frightens me, to tell you the truth. He keeps talking about some private detective who got killed because he asked too many questions about what he called 'our people.' "

It was hard for Carmody to avoid smiling. Nicolai's stamp was so clear. Of course Wade was told to confess he was in

318

frequent contact with Nicolai. That was to ingratiate himself with Carmody.

He said, "You're working with him to undermine me."

Wade's eyes bulged. He saw Summerton's quiet triumph. Furious, he leaped to his feet. "There's your traitor!" Carmody watched how the accusing finger changed Summerton's expression to a hatred so complete it couldn't be artificial. Summerton made as if to rise, and Carmody gestured him down.

"Explain that," he said.

"He made us—" Wade swallowed, started again. "He made us get together, called me, said I had to come up here. Said we could get rid of you, take over your function in the effort."

"You lying son of a bitch," Summerton growled, subsiding at Carmody's irritated gesture.

Looking from one to the other, Wade was suddenly calm. Colorless lips drew back in a slashed smile. "So that's why we're out here, away from everyone. This fat bastard's convinced you I'm working against you. He's sold me. What d'you think you're going to do, beat a confession out of me? You're wasting your time. I've already told you the truth. He's your enemy, not me."

"Neither of you is my enemy, Wade, any more than you're my friends. We work together. Or we did. You and Nicolai have broken that arrangement. How can I trust you anymore?"

"What trust? You never trusted me. Or him. Or anyone else. And I learned from you. Believe me, I learned."

Cautiously, Carmody said, "Learned what? What's that mean?"

"Every meeting we ever had, Esther was there, somewhere, with a camera. We've got pictures of Alex, Nicolai. You, too. Plenty. If you rough me up, she knows what to do with them."

"I see. You've planned this for a long time. You meant to stick a knife in my back from the start. Probably even poor Alex's, too. And Nicolai himself, if you feel like it. Does he know about your photographs?"

"Of course not. You wouldn't either, but you're forcing my hand."

"Yes. I see that." Carmody pulled the pistol from its hiding place.

Summerton said, "Jesus," with such quiet awe it was almost prayer. He scuttled backward on his haunches until he stopped against a tree.

Wade looked at the weapon as if he'd never seen one. "What are you doing? Are you crazy? Esther—"

"You make it easy." Carmody spoke quietly. "I don't believe your pictures exist. If they do, you're a greater threat than I feared. Not just to me. To our work."

The silenced .22 made a spitting sound like a frightened cat. The bullet's impact on Wade's forehead was much sharper, a brisk crack combined with the solid thump of a struck melon. A small dark-rimmed hole appeared. His head snapped back and he staggered, wild-eyed. He collapsed, all at once. Stolidly, Carmody walked the four steps to where he lay, his hands and feet drumming the earth. Lips already losing color moved in imagined speech. Carmody bent over to put another bullet directly between the staring eyes. The reflexive flutterings exploded in one last collective spasm and stopped.

Far away, a jay scolded. The forest's heavy, imperfect silence eased through the trees to immerse the two men.

Summerton interrupted the scene with a moan that rapidly escalated into a drawn-out retch. Still seated, bent slightly forward at the waist, his eyes remained riveted on Wade. He emptied his stomach between spread legs with the mechanical detachment of a pump. Only when he'd reduced himself to dry heaving did he scramble to his feet to lean on a tree.

"My God," he said, the words rasping out of a strained, raw throat, "so fast. Gone. You *killed* him!"

Carmody stopped in the act of replacing the weapon, studiously avoiding looking at Summerton. "We killed him," he said, accenting the first word. "He was a danger to everyone." He glanced slyly out of the corner of his eye and added, "I'll personally see our superiors are aware of your invaluable contribution. Now help me get rid of him."

"How? What'll we do?" Brassy hysteria rang in the words.

Carmody was beside him in an instant, grabbing a flaccid arm, dragging him to the body. He said, "Just over there's a cleft in the rock. We drop him in, throw leaves and dirt over him. They'll never find him. Get his arm."

Staggering back, Summerton said, "Oh, God," and swayed, eyes closed. "This isn't what I wanted! What'll I do now? What'll I do?"

Carmody slapped him. Snuffling, mumbling a singsong dirge only he understood, Summerton took Wade's wrist, carefully keeping the shirt material between the dead flesh and his own.

Their passage through the supple brush and rustling ground litter produced a rising and falling sibilance that Summerton tried desperately to shut out. It made him feel the very forces of nature were whispering of what happened.

Wade's body dropped loosely into the narrow notch. In a few minutes, he was out of sight under the leaves and branches his companions dumped over him. Carmody indicated the job was finished by walking away, calling over his shoulder for Summerton to get the daypacks and follow. Summerton rushed to do so and hurried after.

Carmody set a relatively easy pace. He needed time to quiet the chaos blasting through his mind.

Wade's incredulous face appeared. He dismissed it, but only with difficulty.

Next, his imagination pictured Elise's reaction had she seen Wade's body tumble into its rock-walled grave. It was a totally inappropriate consideration, he told himself, forcing it aside a little more easily than the previous problem.

Then he was wondering what would be an appropriate consideration. According to the storybooks of his youth, he should have been seeing thrilling visions of socialism's progress. He thought back over the day, couldn't remember thinking of anything but each next step and the necessity for doing what he must do. He never even thought about Nicolai's frustration. Protect the net, protect freedom of movement—that's what spurred him on.

And during the actual killing, nothing. Even now, there

was an easy, clean detachment. Wade died so the man named Carmody might live.

He stopped so abruptly Summerton stepped on his heel. The nervous spew of apologies registered as a distant mutter.

Leading off again, he realized he no longer thought of Martin Carmody as a phantom. Martin Carmody was becoming disturbingly real, frighteningly secure in his own existence.

He shivered, wondering if he was sinking into schizophrenia.

Would a mind forced to serve two identities turn on itself? Would one personality drive the other to suicide? Martin Carmody murdered a man today. Wade's death guaranteed Carmody, too, had to die. Could the man calling himself Carmody be forcing himself to break away from his creation and run for his life, his real life?

He slowed to another stop, settled onto his haunches against a convenient rock. His head hurt terribly, and he shaded his eyes. Summerton's grunting collapse reminded him he wasn't alone.

They rested directly above the parked motor home, visible through the thinner growth at the base of the intervening bushes. Clouds had rolled in, unnoticed, bringing a thin, soft mist with them. The sun was no longer visible. The combination created a damp wash across the valley that blurred objects and colors.

Craning about, Carmody enlarged his field of view and discovered a gray Chevrolet parked on the valley's dirt road. He estimated it to be a half-mile away. A man leaned on the driver's side, smoking a cigarette.

At first, it merely irritated Carmody. The only way out was past him, and there was no point in taking a chance on being seen for possible later identification.

His interest was drawn to the smoking. Something about the man's movements was unusual. They were too quick. He was nervous. Carmody leaned forward. The cigarette rose and fell, smoke wisped away. The man's head moved in a rhythm of observation. He watched the highway for about ten seconds, then slowly scanned the flanking hills on both sides of the road. Lastly, he watched in the direction of the motor home. His gaze lingered in that area.

The back hair on Carmody's neck tickled.

"Stay right here," he told Summerton. "Don't move until I tell you, understand? And don't let those daypacks out of your hands!"

"Where are you going?" He saw the man in the valley for the first time. "Oh, Jesus, no! Could they hear? Do they know? What have you gotten us into?"

Carmody said, "Shut up, or you'll ruin everything. Stay here. Leave this to me."

Carmody moved swiftly, confident in the cover afforded by the brushy growth. Closing on the motor home, he was out of sight of the man beside the Chevrolet, which was now only about a quarter of a mile distant. Still, he moved with greater caution.

He was no more than twenty yards from the second car when he saw it. It was a scruffy brown Toyota sedan, and someone had pulled off the road and hidden it well behind a stand of scrubby alders. The two looters had found it, nevertheless. Their backs were to Carmody. One, holding a crowbar, leaned into the open trunk and handed out something to his partner, who dumped it into a burlap bag. The latter said, "We get the stereo now?" and the other answered, "Piece of shit. Couldn't get nothing for it." He swung the crowbar and shattered the rear window. The one with the bag laughed. "That'll teach the cheap fucker. Want to hit the motor home or split?"

"I didn't come all this way up here for nothing. C'mon."

Carmody drew the pistol. He had no idea he was smiling. *Blacks. Bastards. They damage the motor home and the owner reports it. Police.*

He stepped out of the brush to face them when they were ten feet away. Carmody felt time freeze around him, knew the next few moments would be preserved forever in his memory like ancient insects in amber.

The man with the crowbar moved first, raising it to a striking position.

The silencer-equipped pistol appeared between them, level with Carmody's eye. It filled him with the mingled joy and amazement of perfected sorcery. His first awareness that he

323

was firing was the sharp yelp from the other man. The weapon was drawn to the sound, terminated it with three sharp, commanding snaps.

They were quite young, Carmody noted, probably not yet twenty, and they fell in loose, soft mounds like toddlers asleep on a picnic in the woods. A trickle of blood from the taller one's ear and the bloody ruin of the other's eye added a macabre touch to that impression.

Two quick rounds assured the job was finished. Carmody reloaded the magazine as he hurried toward the lookout, grateful for the foresight that had him carry an extra twenty bullets loose in a pocket.

He passed the battered Toyota and paralleled the road until he also passed the Chevrolet. The lookout's cigarette glowed in the increasing darkness, while the mist padded the drifting smoke, making it thicker. Circling back, Carmody stalked from the least likely direction, the highway. Tall bushes were scarce, but high, grassy weeds provided good cover. Their dampness soon had him wet and cold, a discomfort he accepted gladly because the same moisture muffled the rustle of dry stalks that might have exposed him.

Moving, pausing, he felt the first twinges of unease. The lookout was younger than the others, probably no more than sixteen, and his nervousness made him formidably alert. At this range, his eyes were a constant flickering in the dark face. Anger displaced concern, and Carmody slid forward with grim caution until he'd closed to less than five yards. The next time the youngster looked in the direction of his dead companions, Carmody rose and charged.

His quarry turned only far enough to see someone approaching before he broke and ran.

Carmody's first round slapped dust from the boy's right side, midway between belt and armpit. He yelled, a shout of surprise, with pain only an undertone. When he saw the blood, he yelled again, terrified. He turned so quickly he was still moving backward while he raised his hands. The mouth moved, but Carmody didn't hear. He fired again, twice, watching the dust fly from the grubby shirt. Staggering, the boy stumbled in retreat. Understanding flashed in his eyes, a

324

visible admission of unimaginable death. He turned to run again. The pistol spat at his back.

A rattle of rocks brought Carmody running to where the boy disappeared, and he almost toppled over the small cliff after him. Face down, blood staining the crystalline water, the youth lay in the stream. Carmody allowed himself one last shot at the back of the head. Water splashed in a derisive column. Carmody cursed, amazed at the loudness of his voice in the after-action silence, then ran for the motor home.

He felt good.

CHAPTER 33

"It was the CIA," Summerton said. He spoke huskily, staring at the carpet of the Wade living room. The warm brown suggested a perfect match with Esther's eyes, but when Carmody looked up to check, she'd closed them in a grimace of pain. She rocked in her stark modern chair, moaning softly, as she had throughout the whole story.

Carmody looked away, reminding himself that this woman and her husband were enemies of the worst kind.

He scanned the room again, finding it as unredeeming on second look as the first. The entire house was a monument to pretension. He remembered choosing hard, bright furniture like theirs for his own apartment because it appeared to typify the shallow glitter Americans considered quality. Gloss *was* America, and no one could be more firmly entrenched in that consumer society than these two. The proof was everywhere, cold, repellent stuff.

Carmody coughed gently. She gave no sign of hearing, and he hesitated, mouth half-open. Suddenly, she was staring at him, a fierce grief twisting her features. "If you escaped, why didn't he? Where is he? Why isn't he with you?"

Carmody said, "Harry told you, Mrs. Wade—Ted's perfectly all right. The CIA apparently followed him, hoping to capture us. Only Harry's countersurveillance avoided a catastrophe."

"Avoided?" She turned her fury on Summerton. "My husband's missing! Anyone else would have saved him!"

"We did save him. He's already in a safe house in Canada. He's on his way to a place where his contribution to world peace will be appreciated."

"Take me to him. I have to be with him."

Summerton smiled gently, leaned toward her confidentially. "That's exactly what he told us you'd say." He leaned farther, patted the unresponsive knee. Carmody felt a chill drift up his back, almost missing Summerton's next words. "He said to tell you he understands, but you have to understand as well. Our friends are protecting us. They know how it's done."

This was the moment Carmody feared, and fear was the only word for it.

The pistol in its holster weighted at his shoulders.

Now was when she must falter. There had to be a sign she knew she was beaten. The trick was to recognize it.

The perversion of it bothered him. In nature, where truth lived unrestrained, a show of strength could mean continued life. If Esther didn't indicate, however subtly, a surrender, she would prove herself too dangerous to live. Her death would tell the police Ted's disappearance was no accident, but it would tell them nothing about Carmody.

Unless she released the photographs. If they existed.

She said, "What happened?" and Carmody locked his throat against a pent-up exhalation of relief. He didn't answer, deferring to Summerton, according to their plan, and an expression he couldn't identify passed over her features. As Summerton went through the quick, glib lies of CIA shadows and a high-speed chase, Carmody tried to reconstruct that image. He failed, and it troubled him. He was sure there was something she was deliberately leaving unsaid, but there was more.

He shifted in the chair, absently rubbing at the pressure of a binding holster strap.

Summerton said, "Let Martin tell you the rest," and Carmody tucked away the puzzle of Esther's odd look. He said, "When no police helped out in the pursuit, I knew it was a CIA covert operation and not a legitimate FBI arrest attempt. They meant to murder us. They were so afraid of Ted they wanted him killed at all costs. They must have known he was meeting someone else involved in our effort, but they were too anxious to eliminate him to even care about us.''

It was such a silly story. Could she be so stupid?

Nodding, she said, ''It's what we've always expected. He always called them thugs. What did you do?''

Affecting embarrassment, Carmody said, ''As soon as I was sure we'd lost them, I insisted our people activate my emergency departure plan. It's been ready for years, examined, tested, foolproof. We'll create a new one for me. The point is, it worked perfectly, and Ted's safe.''

''When can I go to him?''

''A month, give or take a little. Occasionally in the past when couples have rallied to us, we've tended to surface the first partner too quickly. The sensationalist press and brutal officials can make life very difficult for the remaining one. We'd prefer to get you out as quietly as possible, and before the world knows of your husband's courageous gesture.''

''I have to communicate with him.''

Carmody extended his hands, palms down, fingers splayed. ''I'm sorry. Absolute secrecy—''

''You said a month. That's it, then.'' She interrupted sharply. ''I'll be with him in a month. At the very least, I'll be in contact. I insist.''

The thing I saw before! There, in the eyes! What is it?

''I'll do everything I can, Mrs. Wade. We've already done a great deal, just getting him out of the country. These things aren't easy.''

''It's not easy being alone!'' Shrillness ripped at Carmody. ''All I have is your word! I don't like any of this!''

With her increasing excitement, Carmody felt his own person strain to draw apart into separate beings.

The logical part of his mind insisted it was time to state some facts and get out while she was in his hand, under control.

328

Simultaneously, something feral and cruel demanded he put questions to her and see her reactions.

He chose the logical course. "If I had any way to make the situation easier for either of you, I certainly would. Now all I can do is assure you your husband's in no danger. We'll take care of you just as carefully, when the time's right. Just cooperate, please."

From the corner of his eye, he caught Summerton's look. Forestalling anything untoward, he rose quickly. "The CIA will refuse to reveal its hand in this. Most likely, they'll simply go to work trying to identify Harry and me. It's no triumph for them to confess they failed in a murder attempt. Report Ted missing on a hiking trip. Tell the police the exact truth, simply omitting any mention of his real mission. Add nothing. If anyone asks questions about his other work, you must convince them you have absolutely no idea what they're talking about."

"Do I strike you as someone who breaks down? I know what to do. But one thing you didn't mention is my contact with you. I should have rapid access."

She was good, very good. Carmody wondered exactly how much of Wade's operation had been hers. He said, "You will report every approach by anyone who says he represents us. Stall until you can reach me. You call Harry, he calls me. I'll tell you who you can talk to. Is that clear?"

Her eyebrows moved a fraction of an inch. "You think the CIA will try to trap me?"

"Perhaps."

"Who else? The police? Why would they—?"

"I'm not concerned about the police. Or the CIA. I've seen enough to convince me you'll handle them, as you said. But some peculiar events have taken place lately. I mean to see there aren't any more."

"Peculiar?" Her eyes betrayed her, darted to Summerton and away before returning to Carmody.

"Mrs. Wade—Esther—I only tell you this because I respect you and your brave husband. Furthermore, what I'm saying is painful speculation. Aside from us, my local representative was the only one who knew Ted was meeting me.

329

Fortunately, he didn't know I'd have Harry providing countersurveillance. I have to tell you, the men following Ted got off the plane with him. The tail originated here.'' He gestured quickly, a vigorous dismissal. "It's possible there was another reason for that. Until I know what happened, no one moves unless I approve.''

Her nostrils pinched inward above thinned lips. Shocked disbelief strained her words. "An informer?''

Carmody looked to Summerton. On cue, the heavy man said, "It's the only explanation, Esther,'' and Carmody added, "I've taken steps to neutralize the man I suspect. He's being watched constantly. Once Ted is perfectly safe, we'll scoop him up.''

Esther was on her feet, quivering. "Get him now! Make him talk!''

"Not yet.'' It was Summerton's turn. "Ted's vulnerable while he's being moved, and Martin says the man under suspicion knows the entire route. Remember, it's the one they planned for Martin. Now they're arranging one for you, unknown to him.''

"Kill him! He's ruined us!''

Carmody was properly indignant. "We have only suspicion. We aren't the CIA—we act on evidence. Furthermore, you can be sure a traitor like that has protected himself well. All we can do is quarantine him until Ted's safe. Then we'll confront him.''

"Why would anyone do such a thing?''

"Power. There have been rumors about my capability. My representative here apparently thinks he can get me recalled, even use some of my own people to help move me out.'' A look of naked guilt sparked between them, and he told himself he would have to probe deeper into their relationship one day. In the meantime, they should have some rope to play with.

He moved to Esther, took a cold, limp hand in his. "Don't lose faith, Esther, please. This is a bitter blow, but it's time the world knew of your devotion to peace, your years of sacrifice. I've been instructed to say you and Ted will be taken care of in better style than you've ever seen.'' He

330

waved carelessly at the expensive furnishings. Then, "And there are other benefits. Someday the world will learn how one patriotic American—Harry—saved another—Ted—from the CIA gangsters, and be forced to face the truth about this government as seldom before."

He stared into her eyes, imagined he could see the thoughts growing there. "Another thing you have to know is, Ted told me about your photographs." At her instant withdrawal, he knew they existed. He shook his head sadly. "A terrible thing, terrible. But it may work to our advantage. There may be a clue in them. They have to be kept secret until we're ready to examine them in safety. Take care of them. And remember, if anyone but me asks for them, you'll know you're dealing with our informant."

The thought of her having pictures of him and his people almost made him ill, but she was too shrewd to simply surrender them, he was certain. Letting her keep them built trust. When she thought she was leaving to rejoin Wade, that would be the time to claim them.

Slowly turning to Summerton, he released her, saying, "We can't leave together, Harry. You stay here for five minutes. Turn left when you leave. I'll pick you up in a block or two. Okay?"

Carmody was moving before Summerton could answer, leaving them standing in front of each other, awkward as two teenage lovers.

Signaling Esther to silence, Summerton rushed to the door, listening closely before cracking it open to peer down the street at Carmody's departing back. Satisfied, he hurried back to where she stood, frowning. He put his hands on her shoulders, practically forcing her into her chair. He sat in one facing her.

"We've just got a few minutes. You heard what he told me, and he's parked only a couple of blocks away. I had to tell him you knew about Ted's activity, Esther. It wasn't my fault. I didn't want to. Carmody was going to let you go on believing Ted really got lost in the mountains. I said I'd tell you everything if he didn't. It was the only way Ted agreed to go without you. I wasn't going to see you suffer needlessly, no matter what.''

Some of the pain and anger drained from her features. He thought of the hard green knot of a bud unfurling to reveal delicate petals. He said, ''We're between a rock and a hard place, you know. I still don't completely trust Martin, and this Nicolai he works with is very, very tough. We're going to have to help each other.'' He pointed at her phone. ''Call me any time, but never use that damned thing. Use a phone booth. We'll exchange alternate numbers as soon as I get home, okay?''

She half-smiled. ''You're being very helpful, Harry. I was a little worried about you, after our meeting in Seattle. What does Martin know about that?''

Summerton frowned, unsure of the right answer. ''He learned you came up, but he didn't know how much you were involved with Ted's action. He thought you were just cover on the trip. I had to tell him we knew each other, that Ted recruited me. I swore we hadn't been in touch again until the trip. I think he checked up on it.''

''He did. Nicolai asked Ted about trips out of town. Ted said there hadn't been any.''

''Shit. That means Nicolai passed the lie along to Martin. That's bad for us.''

She shook her head. ''No, you tell Martin Ted confessed to the trip, too. Let Martin think Nicolai's the liar. I'm sure the rotten bastard burned my Ted. He'll suffer for it.'' Her hands drew into knotted fists. Eyes slitted, she looked past Summerton into a future he couldn't see, but the implied ferocity of it made him shiver. He imagined his arms around her, showering kisses on that smoldering fury. He yearned to savor her vengeance, taste her rage.

Her voice pulled him to reality. She was saying, ''—time you were leaving. If you're late, he'll be furious, and we have to keep him sympathetic to us.''

He moved to the door, surveying the empty street. Turning back, he was surprised to discover she had silently joined him, was so close they were almost touching. She put a hand on his bicep. ''It's not my style to carry on and make scenes,

332

Harry. Don't misjudge me. I'll cry about Ted when I'm alone and no one can see." She looked away, making a small gesture of confused irritation, then returned a dense, penetrating gaze to his eyes. "I want you to know I'm not all politics and brittle lines. I want you to know how much the part of me you've never seen appreciates what you've done for me. And Ted, of course. You're much more than I thought. Thank you." She brushed his cheek with her lips, stepping back quickly.

He was down the walk and onto the sidewalk before real coherence returned to his thoughts.

Terribly, it wasn't her face that surfaced. It was Wade's, the expression of hopeless terror as the bullets struck. And there was the way Martin looked at the two men he'd killed for trying to rob the motor home.

That was what life had brought Harry Summerton.

His throat constricted with the injustice of it. All he ever wanted was a normal relationship with the most exciting woman he'd ever meet.

It wasn't enough she was married. Oh, no! Harry could work around that. For Harry, it had to be worse than anyone could imagine. A clever move to discredit the stupid-bastard husband had to be turned into a massacre, a disaster.

Now if Harry tried to get close to Esther, Martin might suspect the original motive.

Summerton lurched, rudely torn from his thoughts by the snarling barks of a fenced-in dog. Heart hammering, he continued on with stiff dignity, only once peering back over his shoulder.

At least, he decided, there was one good thing to come out of all this. He knew exactly how dangerous Martin was.

Cruising the street in the rental car, timing his pickup of Summerton, Carmody suddenly jerked to attention behind the wheel.

He remembered exactly where he'd seen Esther's troubling expression before, and cursed himself for not recognizing it.

Interrogations.

Sometimes they gave you one to work on who had connections, or information, or some other supposed bargaining chip. There was a look in their eyes, a desperate wanting to believe he could turn off the pain before it got too great. Fools, all of them. And now this one, this Esther, thought she had some surprise that would work for her. There were those damned pictures, of course, but she retained the expression even after he forced her to acknowledge they existed. Further, they were as incriminating for her as anyone. Something else was propping her up, something between her and Summerton, something more than his fawning revealed. She probably hoped to seduce the simple bastard. Bitch.

So, then—the look meant her bag of tricks carried a bullet for the man named Carmody.

He smiled.

CHAPTER 34

Bᴌᴀᴄᴋ ʟᴇᴀɴᴇᴅ ʙᴀᴄᴋ ɪɴ ʜɪs ᴏғғɪᴄᴇ ᴄʜᴀɪʀ ᴀɴᴅ ʀᴇᴀᴅ ᴛʜᴇ article again, telling himself he was grabbing at straws. People got lost in the Cascades all too frequently. For the most part, they were fools, as this man appeared to be. Anyone who thought he could simply go for a solo stroll in that country was in trouble before he put his boots on. A challenge to those mountains demanded experience and preparation. This man had a bare minimum of both.

What made him very different was his string of degrees in physics and his job with a company on the leading edge of radar technology.

Speaking softly, Black said, "Did you really come up here just to go hiking in our mountains? What about it, Theodore Wade?"

Black stared at the name until the two words swam in his vision, turned into meaningless symbols.

He slammed his hands together, crushing the paper. Neck bowed, he glared at it, swinging his head back and forth like a tormented bull. Dropping the wadded remains, he stood and turned his back on them, staring out the window. A lovely day smiled back, refused to share his frustration.

In a few minutes, he was smoothing the paper on his desk so he could read it while he talked to Davis. He called immediately, and when Davis answered, got to business without preamble. "I need information." Reciting the sparse data on Wade's background and disappearance, he added, "It's hardly a lead, but I'm desperate. Call in some markers if you have to. I want to know every move he's made for the past two years. Income. Expenses. Contacts. Other trips."

"What else have you got?"

"That's it. I said I'm desperate."

"I don't know, Steve."

"Goddammit, who does? The guy we're after isn't going to walk in off the street! We dig him out or forget him!"

"You said it's hardly a lead. You know how much time and money's involved."

"And if we don't catch him—what's that cost us?"

Davis's silence meant he was making a decision. Black shifted nervously.

"I'll get what I can. And don't call here trying to rush me."

"Send everything as soon as it comes in. I'll enter it in a computer out here, so I can juggle it around. And thanks."

"Sure."

Black hung up quickly, dialing a local number. At the answer, he identified himself as Arthur Bronson, and asked to speak to Mr. Hall. Again, his luck ran good. Hall came on immediately. Black said, "I need your services again. A missing persons' report has been filed on a Theodore Wade from San Francisco. My only information is from the newspaper article in today's *Post Intelligencer*, which I'm sure you have. I want the following: time of arrival; if he was met, by whom; if not, did he rent a car or take a cab or bus; if he took a bus, did he talk to anyone on board; if he took a cab, what did he say to the driver; in any case, where did he go, and was he met when he got there. I want anything you learn about him. Nothing's unimportant. Get me any information the police have as well."

"I'll start with them. They may already have most of the other details." Hall spoke carefully, the words stiff with considered selection.

"If they do, you're just that much ahead."

"That's why I mentioned it, Mr. Bronson. You're a special customer. I don't want you thinking I'm taking advantage of you."

"Just get me the information and save me dealing directly with the police. We've got a good arrangement, haven't we?"

"Excellent."

"Good. I'll have a certified check delivered to your agency. Your rates are the same?"

"Yes, sir."

"Fine. I'm expecting a picture of Wade. I'll enclose it with the check. I'll call you around quitting time tomorrow." The electronic reproduction device facing the filing cabinets blinked on. Davis was already transmitting something from back East. Hall's voice carried over its soft hum.

"So soon? That's—"

"It's important. Do your best."

"Yes, sir. Anything else?"

"That's it. Good-bye."

It wasn't like working with Will. Nothing ever would be. But Hall didn't ask questions, and he was fast.

It wasn't time to think about Will. Not now, not yet. The pain of losing him was too fresh. The right memories would come in time.

Everything took time, especially blunting pain.

The major problem in the business was time. The worst of it was waiting, when you saw your present cannon-balling out of reach and the future dawdling off on the horizon, like it was hoping you'd have an accident so it wouldn't have to show up for work in the morning.

Even time's ruthlessness was imperfect, though. If it weighed so heavily on Dina she tried to kill it with alcohol, it had also brought Maddy.

He pushed his chair back from the desk, rose swiftly.

As for Will, it wouldn't do any good to mourn him.

Don't get mad, get even.

The electronic reproduction device switched off, finished with Wade's picture. It was good stuff, front and profile, almost mug shots. Probably from a job application, Black decided, studying it absently. He ran the images through the copy machine, holding out two for Hall. He decided Wade was probably a likeable man, although there was a suggestive curve at one corner of his mouth. Black turned the picture to an angle, imagined the expression amplified. He was surprised to see how unpleasant it became.

He slipped the pictures in an envelope and addressed it to Hall. There was barely enough time to get to a bank to buy the cashier's check, but if he hurried, he could have a messenger deliver everything that day. Pocketing the envelope, he scooped up the rest of the papers on his desk and stuffed them into a filing cabinet. There was nothing there but routine, and it would damned well wait.

On his way to the elevator, he grinned at himself, admitting he had no intention of coming back to the office because he meant to swing by the new shop Maddy was readying for her grand opening. It was probably hopeless, but he wanted her to knock off early today. The thought of her feeling good enough to work so hard was warming, but the place ate into time he'd rather spend doing something important. Sailing. Or whatever.

When he called the private investigator the next day, he was unprepared for the cold reception. Bluntly, Hall said, "You put me in a bad spot. I used up a lot of brownie points getting your information for you."

Black's heart sank. Was it possible another agency was after Wade? Could Davis be moving on him? He coughed, steadied his voice, and said, "How come? Wade's a missing person—what's so bad?"

"You said you got your information out of the paper. Did you read the front page?"

"No. Not really. Nothing I remember." His voice trailed off as he cast back. There was something—a shooting, in the mountains. Why would that affect Hall's investigation?

Hall said, "Two guys from here in town got killed and a third got the shit shot out of him. It happened way up toward Chinook Pass, but we already had two serial killers in this area, and that gambling-joint massacre in the International District, remember? The cops are jumping through hoops to

338

come up with a suspect on this new deal, and when I went to the courthouse to ask about Wade, they leaned on me hard just for being around.''

Some of the details came back to Black. ''They were thieves, weren't they? Didn't I read they found the loot on them?''

''That's right. The cops figure some guy caught them going after his car and blew them up. He made real sure two died, but the third one fell down a bank into a stream. The killer must have thought he was done for, 'cause he left him.''

''Well, I'm sorry if I steered you into a hornet's nest. But you said you got my information for me.''

''Sure did.'' Pride damped Hall's injured tone. ''Wade came in on PSA Flight seven-oh-one, nothing but hand baggage. He caught a cab from the airport south on old Highway Ninety-nine to a supermarket lot in Midway, out by a community college—Highline. That's where he disappears.''

''No one recognized his picture?''

''No, sir. We canvassed the place.''

''The cops have anything?''

''They didn't even have what we got, and there's something I haven't mentioned. I think Mr. Wade may have meant to disappear for a while.''

Carmody half-rose. ''Why do you think that?''

''He had no return flight scheduled. He paid cash, and I take that to be an attempt to avoid signing his name to anything. There's a motel he could've walked to from where he got out of the cab, but they never saw him. There's no place else close by where he could get a room, so somebody must have met him in that parking lot. I could try again, maybe catch somebody who saw him leave.''

''No, I don't think so. You've done a more than thorough job, Mr. Hall. I think we can arrange a small bonus.''

''Well, thanks. I appreciate it. You want those pictures back?''

''Burn them.''

''You got it.''

''Fine. And just to satisfy my morbid curiosity, did you hear if there's a suspect in those shootings that got you in such trouble?''

Hall made an apologetic sound, then, "Not that much trouble, really." Enthusiasm crept into his voice. "I did hear one thing. They think the piece might have had a silencer. The guy that owned the car that was vandalized wasn't very far away, and he didn't hear anything. And the shooter's *hard*. The two dead ones got it a couple times, close, and then he shot each of 'em in the head, just to be sure. The little one in the creek's one lucky sonofabitch. If he makes it."

"Sounds that way. Terrible business. Thanks again, Mr. Hall. Good-bye."

They hung up simultaneously. Black glanced at his watch and drummed impatient fingers on the desk. Lunch with Maddy was going to have to be canceled. This wanted attention.

There was a chance the dead men were caught by a vigilante type who'd acquired a silencer. Anything was possible.

He grimaced. It was such a slim chance.

Still, several bits of knowledge about the man identified as Marvin indicated he was an outdoorsman. More than that, he had a known *modus operandi* of picking a rural resort as a training locale for his agents. It would only be a variation on a theme for him to alter that MO, to train people in a secluded place outdoors. There were certainly things that could be taught in that situation.

And if Marvin intended to get rid of someone, the forest would be his most likely choice. And the arrangements for meeting Wade were ideal for such a trip.

If there was anything to any of it.

But it was something—some*one*—to hunt. Like a quick miss in an engine, a signal had broken free.

Inexplicably, Dina's image was before him, the angry, suicidal eyes that probed with manic determination for the weak spot that would make a victim of the survivor, the eyes that assumed his very life to be a crime and allowed no answer but confession. He heard the rote accusations.

You don't love me. You can't. It's the job. Your family doesn't mean a thing to you.

The image wavered, faded. When it returned, she was in a

340

hospital bed. Everything was white. Her dark hair was a black flame against a colorless void.

It was the worst memory of all.

She laughed at him, knives of laughter.

The man who's so good at his work! The man who loved his friends more than he loved his wife! Now you know what they think of you! Shit-canned! You've been dumped on all your life, and now you've been dumped! Asshole!

No more words. Shrill, incoherent screaming. A nurse.

A blond. More white. God. God.

The needle, glittering promise of peace, however false.

Then it happened. He turned to leave, and something tore in his guts, and all the frustration erupted. He rounded on her, undeterred by her sodden, shuttering eyes, the downturned mouth.

All I wanted was for you to be there, help me believe everything would be all right. Why couldn't you share my life instead of trying to own it? I loved you, and you killed it! You've killed yourself!

Understanding fought to the surface of her drug-clouded features. He stumbled out of the room.

And when he stepped into the hospital hall, there was Jane.

He was sweating when he broke free of the memory. Damp clothes chilled him. He shivered, massaging his arms and torso. Moving quickly, he headed for the door, yanking his coat from the rack with a carelessness that nearly tore it on the hook. He fidgeted impatiently in the elevator until it stopped, then hurried into the sun. Even that warmth glanced off the frozen memory.

At least now there was Maddy, who was helping. Perhaps that was what made this attack so virulent. Perhaps the memories were fighting to retain their grip on him, as Dina had.

That was fanciful. Cruel, as well. Better to try to remember an earlier Dina, the one who said she wanted nothing more than to be a good wife.

CHAPTER 35

THEY DROVE TO MADDY'S HOUSE IN A SILENCE RICH WITH shared comfort. Thinking about it, the word that came to Black's mind was "uncomplicated." Neither felt an obligation to entertain the other.

No one else blended with his silence. Davis understood his need for it, tolerated it as best he could. Will Walters had understood, too—well enough to go along easily, riding the depth of it the way a ship breasts water, using it, not genuinely part of it.

Maddy joined with his inward-turning mind, and he thought of a road with two views. Only rarely, deliciously, would they ever see the same view simultaneously, but their direction, their speed, matched perfectly. In those silences he possessed her far more completely than during any physical union. He also felt more exposed, more vulnerable, than ever before in his life.

They were in the driveway of her newly acquired house before he realized it. He wished the trip had taken longer, but when Maddy reminded him of the fresh ling cod in its newspaper wrapper on the floor behind them, his stomach growled approval before he could speak. For a moment, she stared at him, wide-eyed, and then they were laughing uproariously.

The amusement slowed gradually, until they were sitting

looking at each other with smiles that had little connection with the incident itself. Black leaned on the steering wheel, turning to face her more directly. He said, "How I love you, Maddy. You make me so very happy. You make me laugh."

"I'm glad. I want you to love me. It'd be a shame for me to be the only one of us who felt that way."

He grinned widely. "Not satisfied just to be a sex object, huh?"

She burlesqued heavy consideration, extending a hand to turn it palm down, then palm up, in an Italianate gesture of indecision. "A little of this, a little of that—you have to have some balance, you know?"

He moved to kiss her, and she returned it briefly before breaking away. "Not now, you don't." She opened the door, slid her legs out. "How can you think of that when your stomach's rumbling like a cement mixer? Men!"

Posed in front of the car, he said, "Steve Black, Man of a Thousand Appetites."

Shaking her head, she led the way inside.

They'd picked the place together, and he was proud of the choice. The sale of the store in San Francisco had totaled almost enough to get her reestablished in Seattle. He'd loaned her the difference, and she insisted that since her store was her responsibility, his money must go toward the house.

An older building, it was still solid, although it needed work to bring it to the appearance it deserved. There was a sense of solidity in the bulky stone fireplace and the thick, dark-stained columns of the doorway separating the living room from the dining room and kitchen area.

Maddy was wringing more life out of the place every day, painting, polishing, cleaning. Her color sense brought light to the formerly dull walls, her eye for furnishings offset the unimaginative configuration of rooms and windows.

They hung their coats in the vestibule, and he followed her to the kitchen. She gestured at a cabinet. "You make the drinks. I'm going to start dinner."

When he finished pouring two Scotch-and-waters, she was frowning at the fish, stretched out on the counter. "How can anything that tastes so good be so utterly ugly? Poor thing! Look at those teeth. An orthodontist's dream.''

Taking the knife from her, he said, ''I'll fillet it.''

She reached past him for a paperback cookbook. ''I've got these Hawaiian recipes—one's for fried ling cod, but it has to marinate for at least two hours in honey, brandy, and grated lemon peel. Then you make this beer batter, see, and—''

''Jesus!'' Black leaned heavily on the counter. ''I'm starving! Mercy!''

''How about I fix up some burgers and you get the fish ready for tomorrow night?''

''Anything! Quick!''

She made a slight noise behind him, derisive, and he turned suspiciously. She was smiling. ''Five minutes ago you were all lathered up about one of your other appetites. Fickle, fickle.''

He waved the knife. ''Don't trifle with me, woman. The beast is dangerous when hungry.''

She laughed at him, moving to the refrigerator, and he fell to cutting the fish.

Dinner passed quickly, a homely, ordinary meal, exactly like thousands of others taking place at the same time. To Black, however, it turned from pleasure to trial as soon as they started picking up the dishes.

It was a time he dreaded.

He had a choice of two evils. If he made the telephone call now, here, Maddy would have to see him at work. She'd never know what it was about, but there was a chance the conversation could go bad.

She knew he lied sometimes. After all, he'd done it to her.

What if he had to lean on the other man? How would she take it?

They walked to the living room, where she turned on the stereo before settling onto the sofa next to him. She smiled up at him and turned to look over the night-shining wedge of Puget Sound visible from her window. He put his arm across her shoulders and drew her close.

The other choice was to ask her for complete privacy. She'd go along. That wasn't the problem. The problem was

344

the act of putting one more step between them. They seemed to have found their way, even if it was along a razor's edge. They could move forward or backward, but if he shared too much or became too secretive, that was a step to the side. Either way, they went down.

He said, "Maddy, I have to go to the hospital tonight and talk to a guy. I'm going to call and let him know I'm on the way. It's business. Just so you know."

Speechless for the moment, she watched as he walked to the telephone. Before he finished dialing, she was beside him, pressing the disconnect button.

"Hold it! *Talk* to me! Are you in trouble?"

Surprised, he gestured helplessly. "I told you—business. I wanted you to know. I could've just gone out, or something."

"I *love* you. Tell me what you do's legitimate, and I'll believe you. Say it's too secret for me to know about, and I'll trust you. But I'm entitled to some idea *why* you do things."

He went to a chair, plodding, and she had to steel herself not to run and comfort him. He sat down as if very tired, but his voice was firm when he spoke. "My everyday work is trying to frustrate people who want to destroy what we are. I can be as ruthless as they are. In this country, that makes me outcast. I don't want that, so I hide—from strangers, from the people I love. From me."

"Why do you put up with it?"

He looked into her eyes as he had earlier. Something small and scratchy walked her spine. He said, "I'm not sure. It's not exactly like being a detective, or a soldier." He smiled suddenly, a twisted scar. "A mechanic might understand. He sees more of the thought and beauty in a machine than anyone else, but he's the one with the bloodied knuckles, the one who wears the dirt while someone else enjoys the ride."

"Why are you ashamed, then?"

Heaving out of the chair, his momentum carried him an extra step before he controlled it. Violence crackled in the air around him. He shuddered, still standing, withdrawn to a place she couldn't follow.

Reluctantly, the chiseled planes of his face softened. He said, "No one else ever had the nerve to ask me that." He

345

shook his head. "I'm not ashamed. Afraid, maybe. Am I so much different than my enemies? If I do what I believe I must do, is it enough if I feel remorse?" Quickly, he was defensive. "Not remorse for the act, remorse for the necessity of it."

"I could live with it if that were the case. I said I love you, Steve." Quick laughter shielded embarrassment. "Not the 'he's-my-man-and-can-do-no-wrong' kind of love, but something that makes me want to help, to contribute. I want to be part of you, Steve, not just a spectator. I won't be baggage."

When his arms rose, she fled to them. He enclosed her, and although she felt herself smothered in his grip, there was a sensation of outgoing power, of providing him a strength he needed desperately.

So softly it was like intercepting a thought, she heard him say, "Help me, Maddy. Please."

She stepped back. "I'll try. I'll try my best."

He nodded, turning away abruptly. He said, "I'll call from a booth. I'll be back as soon as I can, okay?"

"You'll be careful?"

"Certainly." He kissed her, then left with the peculiarly soft tread that always surprised her.

The detective was waiting in the hospital lobby when Black arrived. He gestured Black to his side. "How come you people are interested in this?"

"I'm the only one asking."

The detective shrugged. It had the look of practice. "If that's the way you want it. Just curious. What do you want to know?"

"What kind of leads do you have?"

"Jack-shit. The kid says the guy's white. Says there was a motor home there, too. That's it. We thought we had something. One of the boys found a folder—a little booklet thing, you know?—from a backpack. New. An odd make. So we traced it to the only store that sells them. Naturally, the owner can't remember any special customer. Probably not the fucking shooter, anyhow.'' He held out a closed fist, opened it. ''Empty.''

Black said, ''Anything on the motor home?''

Laughing, the detective said, ''Good luck. The kid says it's green and white.''

''He going to make it?''

''He'll live to get hanged. The way he hates cops, you'd think we shot him.''

''Can I talk to him?''

The detective looked at him a long time, then lit a cigarette. Exhaled smoke carried his words. ''You guys have done us some favors. I'm glad to help you out. Don't crowd us, okay?''

''Ten minutes. I'm not a cop. Maybe he'll talk to me.''

''You're white.'' He took a drag on the cigarette, then, ''What the hell, being white's only one strike. Maybe he'll give you the other two. But I want to know what he says.''

The detective escorted him to the room, pointedly stopping so Black entered alone.

The patient looked incredibly small against the stark white of the hospital bed, his face no more than a receptacle for defiant, frightened eyes. A bottle of clear fluid dangled from a bright metal holder beside him. Plastic tubes snaked down to a pad on one scrawny arm.

''Who're you?'' Sedation slurred the words.

''I'm new,'' Black said.

''Why you ain't lookin' for the motherfucker shot me, 'stead of hasslin' me?''

''That's why I'm here. I need help.''

''You fuckers got two dead black thieves and one live one. I see you bustin' your ass to catch the honky did it.''

Black stared for several heartbeats, only leaning forward when he saw the first blink. He said, ''I think I know who shot you, kid. I want him. I don't give a shit if he wastes you. I think he killed a friend of mine, and that's important. *I want him.* Now you tell me exactly what happened.''

''I ain't scared of you!'' A hand as thin and quick as a whip reached for the nurse signal.

Black pinned it to the mattress, never taking his eyes from

347

the boy's. "If you're not, you're a real asshole," he said, then, "Tell me about the man."

The crushed face looked out the window, swallowing one more defeat. "I never seen him good. White. Light brown hair. Blue eyes." He winced. "He fuckin' *aimed* at me, man. Them blue eyes lookin', aimin'—" His voice trailed off, vibrating from the shiver that moved him under the sheet.

"Tell me about the motor home."

The boy frowned. "White, green top."

"You want this guy nailed, or don't you? *Think,* goddammit!"

Black moved to the window, waiting, feeling the eyes on his back. The boy said, "You ain't no real cop, are you?"

Black sat down again. "Never said I was."

Moving quickly enough to force a wince, the boy propped himself up on an elbow. "You ain't shittin' me—you really after him?"

"Right."

Exaggeratedly confidential, he whispered, "The first letter on the license was an 'E.' And there was a one and a seven in the numbers."

"Got it. Why didn't you tell the cops?"

"Shee-it." The scorn was bone-deep. "They wouldn't do nothin', but you remind me of the fucker shot me." He made a face at the door. "They just takin' care o' business. You don' care about me, but you care about somethin'. You get him, you think about me. And *my* friends. Okay?"

It took so long for an answer the boy reached to tap impatiently on Black's forearm. "Hey. Okay?"

"For what? So it'll be safe for you to go out stealing again?"

"I got four holes in me—is that a clue? No more, man."

Rising slowly, Black extended a hand. They exchanged a slapping five. "I'll get him, kid. And maybe I do care about him trying to grease you. A little bit, anyhow."

"Bullshit." A bright, contradictory grin flashed and was gone. "Listen, you and me, right? You won't rat on me about not tellin' them about the license?"

348

"I don't forget my friends." Black paused, and added, "Either." He walked to the door. When he turned, he saw uncertain bitterness battling friendliness in the pinched features and turned away quickly, not wanting to know which won.

In the hall, the detective said, "You learn anything?"

"Only what you said."

Maddy opened the front door as soon as he finished knocking. She said, "Is everything all right?"

He tried to make light of her concern. "Never. But things aren't bad."

"Tough. Too ignorant to be anything else." He put an arm around her, headed for the kitchen. "Whoever said ignorance is bliss was dead-on. It's the really clever ones who can't see right or wrong, black and white. They're never really happy or sad, either."

"And you're so sure? You always know which is which?"

"Of course not. But I'm not afraid to be right or wrong, as long as I know I'm something." He kissed her forehead. "Being sure means always having to say you're sorry. It also beats hell out of not having anything to say."

"God knows you'll never have that problem."

Laughing, he tilted her head back, kissed her properly. Pulling back, he said, "I met someone who made me think of you. You'd like him. Both of you make me look inside myself." He stroked her hair. "God, Maddy, how I love you."

She said nothing as he swept her up in his arms, let herself be carried silently to bed. She gave herself wildly to the heat he kindled in her, exulted in her ability to rouse him and sate him.

When he slept, she turned on her side, facing away from him, wondering if he thought of their lovemaking as she did.

It was her refuge. She treasured those minutes. They were the only time he was totally hers.

The more she thought about it, the more she was certain that was enough. He'd been honest about wanting to be the man in her life, and confident enough of her character and ability to let her enjoy the freedom of seeking self-sufficiency. In fact, she didn't want to own him, no more than she wanted to be owned.

What they had went beyond possession. There was sharing. There was understanding, and friendship. Most of all, there was trust.

She smiled to herself in the darkness, tugging the sheet up under her chin, wriggling backward to rest against his solid warmth.

CHAPTER 36

Black cruised the street slowly, checking house numbers. A spiral notebook lay on the seat next to him, opened to scribbled notes. One line identified the agency that rented a motor home to Harry Summerton. Another indicated a telephone call to a number in the Bay area. Penned in next to that were the names Ted and Esther Wade, underlined several times. Immediately below was the Wade address.

There had been no time to properly investigate Summerton, but the link between him and the Wades was too good to pass up. Black reviewed the bluff he intended to run. If it worked, Summerton would be clearly identified, and the lead to Marvin would be solid. Better, neither of them would have any reason to suspect there even was an investigation.

On the other hand, if the connection was innocent, all hell would break loose.

Black identified the house. A familiar jolt of energy, a kind of psychic shock, passed through him. His senses strained for greater acuity.

The place was unremarkable among its equally expensive neighbors. Immaculate, landscaped, the entire complement of Sunny Acres Estates brooded across tailored streets at each other.

Wade's house had a perfect lawn and a dry birdbath surrounded by yellow flowers that looked like molten gold against the rich grass. Black had a sudden image of people who needed color but refused to fill the birdbath and attract creatures with bodily functions.

At the end of the block, he debated a return pass and decided against it. Despite appearances, people lived behind the blind windows, and the police would be quick to respond to complaints of a suspiciously behaving driver in Sunny Acres Estates.

Black looked up at the grim overcast and smiled.

A few minutes' drive took him to a shopping center, where he found a restaurant and a bookstore. Reading was a failure, however. He ended up sitting in the bar, fitfully watching boxers on the sports network while he composed a note for the woman and waited for darkness. It took forever to arrive, and then suddenly it was on him, and it was time to move. In the men's room, he took one last look at the memorized names and numbers before flushing the paper down the toilet.

He drove directly to the Wade house and parked in the driveway. There was no time to be subtle. When she peered through the chain-locked door, he said, "I was in the neighborhood and thought I'd drop by." He held up the note for her to see, extending it carefully, keeping well back from the suspicious, wary face.

She held the note so she could see him while she read it, then said, "Come in, come in. It's so good to see you." Opening the door, she led him rapidly, almost at a trot, to the living room. The piercing colors and hard-edged, avant-garde furniture complemented her feverish tiny gestures, the abrupt starts and stops. The earth tone of the carpet was the sole object in the place that gave his eyes any rest.

She was scribbling on the notepaper as he sat down. He looked at what she'd written: *Where is Ted? How is he? Why did Harry send you instead of coming himself? Are you sure this house is bugged?*

The handwriting was prim, correct, with no tremor in the sweeping cursive script. Even the sentence structure was exact. He examined her carefully as he touched the last question with his pen and nodded.

His first impression had been of a woman repressing stress.

352

That was a mistake. She exuded the primed tension of a scholar ready for exams.

Now he knew how to break her.

Writing as he spoke, he said, "I've been out of town. I just heard the terrible news about Ted. I came over right away." He showed her the written instructions: *Offer to make coffee. I'll inspect the room.*

"Would you like coffee? It'll only take a minute."

"Thanks, I'd enjoy some."

Her departing steps were quick and sure. He was certain she was waiting for someone, someone she didn't know. That anticipation had to be tied to Marvin, but she'd accepted him without any exchange of recognition signals.

Something was very much out of line.

The search for listening devices was originally a ploy to frighten her. Now he wondered if Wade's control might not have actually bugged him. He bent to the search with increased interest while she watched from the doorway. As he inspected the bookcase next to her, her impatient movements made small, rustling noises in the leather skirt and cotton blouse, spiced the air with scent he knew would be expensive even though he could never name it and didn't particularly like it. He stole a quick look at her. She watched with deep-set analytical eyes. Translucent skin stretched over long, slender facial bones, so delicate they made him think of wings. Her lips were too thin under a nose a shade too long for elegance, although hardly outsized. She was not attractive, he decided, but an artful construct that achieved a maximum efficiency from its components.

She would be very susceptible to a suggestion of disfiguring damage.

He moved away, and she disappeared momentarily, returning with a coffee service on a tray.

Over-loud, she said, "Here we are. Sorry to be so long. I can't remember—sugar and cream?"

"Just cream." The woman was impressive, responding naturally, feeding him cues. She poured as he sat across the low table from her, then signaled for him to look at the paper again. She had written: *How is he? When can I go to him?*

He wrote: *Has anyone from the government contacted you?*

She shook her head. He nodded. "Good. We can talk. The place is clean."

Bending toward him, she said, "Are you to take me to him?" There was no grace in her position, her whole body drawn to sharp, aggressive angles.

"Your husband was taken into the Cascade Mountains by Harry Summerton and the man known to me as Marvin, where he was murdered."

The fine facial bones seemed to tremble under flesh that remained unaffected, save for the instantly drained lips. Her eyes lost focus, taking on a deep, soft gloss, like well-polished stone. She swayed to the side and Black stayed his hand, unwilling to catch her unless she threatened to pitch forward onto the table, where she might be injured. If she fainted, he'd give her some time to revive by herself. The shock of waking into an unwanted reality could be very helpful to an interrogator.

She didn't faint. Slowly, with the tremors of mental catastrophe, she got to her feet, said, "Excuse me," and moved toward the door she'd used to go to the kitchen. He rose to follow, but she changed course, lurched to the fireplace. Dropping to her knees, she leaned inside and vomited. Black got her coffee and sat on the arm of a chair while waiting for her to stop. Tearing, pulling sounds echoed in the chimney, resonated throughout the house. When she stopped, she sat back, hands splayed on the hearth at her sides. Black held the cup to her lips, wiping her face with a napkin from the tray.

"I'll get you a drink if you tell me where it is."

She shook her head, then recoiled from his presence. "Who are you?" The words were agonized.

"My name's Black, and I'm with the government. Our government, specifically. I'm after Marvin."

"What you said about Ted—"

"He's dead. I don't have a body, but it's certain. Marvin killed two other people and tried for a third, just to cover things up."

"Summerton. That slimy motherfucker!" She was on her

354

knees, striking at him. "He killed my Teddy!" The last syllable built on itself, started to keen upward. Black slipped one hand behind her head and clamped the other around her throat. The sound died instantly. Her eyes bulged grotesquely, and she clawed ineffectually at the strangling grip.

"You were doing fine," he said. "Don't spoil it with a lot of hysterical crap. We've got a lot of things to iron out." He relaxed some of the pressure. "You understand?"

Tears suddenly welled as she managed an affirmative nod. When he let go, she grabbed his wrist and screamed. With ridiculous ease, he slammed her hand into her mouth. The hand behind her head pressed forward. She struggled for a moment but quickly realized she could do nothing against his strength. The attempt to scream was forgotten. He continued to hold her immobile, expressionless. Without warning, he increased the pressure on her hand, mashing her lips, pivoting her head up and backward. Straightening fractionally, he spoke down at her, impassive as ever.

"I don't know if I can break your neck or crush your skull like this—there's not much leverage. I *can* force your teeth through your lips. Maybe the teeth'll break. If you make any more trouble, I'll do it."

He released her, and she rubbed her mouth with the other hand. "When I tell the press—"

He raised a hand and she stopped, twisting away. Angrily, he said, "You'll never tell anyone I was here. Listen to me. I'm going to catch Marvin. You're going to help me. You're going to keep your mouth shut about it, and be glad to do it. I'm the only one who knows about you, the only one who knows Marvin killed your husband."

"What're you going to do, offer me a deal? Get me twenty years instead of life?"

"I can't believe you're as stupid as you're behaving." He slapped her, a sudden crack that was more sound than power. Patiently, he continued. "Marvin—who he is, what he is—is more important to me than my life. If you don't give me what I want without any more trouble, I'm going to go to work on you. If I have to mark you up too much, you won't be able to hide the fact that I was here. I'll have to kill you to

355

guarantee you don't do that. I'd rather not, but that part's up to you."

By the time he finished, Esther had a hand raised in front of her, the palm outward in a defensive posture. She said, "My God, what are you? Kill—?"

"I'm exactly like the people you'd sell me to, bitch. The ones who killed a friend of mine and snuffed your husband." He leaned forward quickly, forcing her to back away. Small animal sounds squeezed past her compressed lips. Remorseless, he went on. "Marvin blew away your husband for screwing around in his operation, and I may have to kill you for screwing around in mine. Funny, isn't it? Marx's iron laws of history squashing both of you from opposite directions. Does that amuse you?"

"Marvin is a good man! He'd never do a thing like that! Harry did it! He killed Ted!"

"I doubt it. But what's the difference? If this Summerton did it, you can be damned sure your good man Marvin knew all about it." Black folded under the fingers of his left hand with his right. Knuckles popped ominously. "Why is it, every time I deal with someone like you, no matter how hard I try to be objective, I end up hating you? At least this time I don't have to hide it."

Her eyes fastened on his hands. A pink sliver of tongue sped across her lips. She said, "If I tell you what I know, will you leave?"

"Like a shot."

"You won't tell the FBI or the CIA about me?"

"I won't tell them. If they catch you, I'll speak to some friends of mine."

"I want more than that! What I can tell you is worth plenty more! I don't want Harry and Marvin getting away with what they did!" She panted in her anxiety, her throat pulsing with the effort.

"You know how it's going down. You're wasting my time."

Gathering herself together, she pulled her knees to her chest, wrapped her arms around them. Her eyes flashed. "Harry's the one you want. He—"

356

"Marvin."

"But—Harry's onto something very big. He was trying to cross Marvin."

"For the last time, how do I find Marvin?" He rose, putting a hand on her head. Slowly, gently, he twined the dark hair around his fingers.

"I've got pictures," she said, her voice several levels higher. "From meetings. Pictures of Marvin, Alex, Nicolai, even Harry. Places where we met. Dates, too. Everything. Don't hurt me, please. I'll tell you."

"You have the pictures here?" He let her go.

"Upstairs."

"Jesus H. Christ. Show me." He pulled her to her feet, holding on to her arm as she led him to the bedroom. Lifting out a section of wainscot, she rolled back the carpet and pad. A series of manila envelopes lay exposed. Black picked up the closest and opened it. There were two photographs with accompanying negatives. In the first, Alex stood on a motel balcony, surveying the pool below. A red circle was drawn around the room number on the door behind him. Another door on the first floor was similarly marked. "What's this one?"

"That's where they met," she said, pride breaking past the circumstances. "Look at the next picture."

It was good, clear enough to identify the bus-stop sign as a Los Angeles route. The man leaning against the post was wonderfully clear. The body appeared completely at ease, but the eyes were alert with a predator's scrutiny. They were fixed on something to his right.

Black wished he knew what it was. More, he wished he knew the man, knew that in the same place at the same time, he, too, would be staring at that unknown thing. The knowledge burned across his mind like a grass fire. "Marvin," he said.

The woman gasped. "You know him?"

"In a way. Is this everything?" He indicated the other envelopes as he folded the photograph and put it in his pocket.

357

"That's everything, I swear it. Except something I learned a while ago. He lives in Seattle. Harry knows where."

Not trusting his voice, Black nodded briefly. He gathered up the envelopes before speaking again. "One more time. Is this everything you've got? And do you understand what I'll do to you if you ever even suggest I was here?" He reached for her, and she cowered against the wall. A spasm of loathing jerked at her features.

"I'll remember you. I hope you do kill him. I hope he kills you. You're all alike." Then, defeated, she said, "I don't have anything else. Nothing." She stiffened and shuddered violently, as if the act of uttering the last word impaled her on its full meaning. She remained standing there, rigid, while he quickly scanned the contents of some of the other envelopes. They were all of different places. Some featured Alex, some Marvin, some a small, tight-eyed man Black disliked intensely on sight.

When Black touched Esther's arm, she shuddered again. Her eyes found his. There was no answer in them for her, and she sagged against him, sufficiently beaten to look for support from any source. He led her down the stairs, back to the sofa, seating her. She kept her eyes fixed on the fireplace.

"I'm leaving," he said.

"Yes."

"Don't make me come back."

"No. Never." She hugged herself.

It took him no more than ten minutes to reach the freeway, where the headlights turned the evening fog into a glowing, seething mass with a life of its own. The billows pressed against his car, reaching for him, soft, lying caresses. Five minutes later, he rolled to a stop on the shoulder and cut his lights. Stepping outside, he walked away from the road. Afoot, the fog revealed itself as chill and invasive. When his progress was blocked by a barbed-wire fence, he felt his way to a post, leaning on it for support. The sound of his heaving rolled into the night, where the misting droplets wrapped themselves around it, muffling the noise. Only in his ears did it sound like drowning.

CHAPTER 37

As HE HAD THE PREVIOUS EVENING, BLACK WATCHED HARRY Summerton stroll across the parking lot and climb into the sports car. The heavy rain that had spread random puddles over the macadam graced the crusted dirt on the vehicle with a liquid gloss. Like the standing water, the wet metal caught the afternoon sun and returned it in a dazzle of light. Harry reached in the glove compartment and slipped on sunglasses.

A few cars away, a man in the driver's seat of a standard Plymouth did the same thing. His partner drummed the sill of his open window, obliquely watching Summerton at all times. Black gave them good marks. They blended well, almost invisible. The Plymouth's engine started, expelling a wad of blue exhaust that swayed listlessly in the heavy, hot air, like a confused beast looking for escape. It dissipated slowly.

Summerton ground gears mercilessly, lurched backward into the departing traffic.

The evening crush made it easy for Black to drift in the wake of Summerton and the surveillance, although by now he knew the way to the apartment. In fact, he was already intimate with Summerton's apartment, having let himself in to inspect it. Inching uphill past banks of apartment buildings, observing the set jaws and weary expressions of the commuters around him, Black allowed himself to feel a bit smug.

An old VW scuttled into the minute gap between Black's

359

car and the one in front. In his benign mood, he merely edged back, creating a safe interval between them. Ahead, Summerton signaled a left turn. Black tensed. This was the wrong intersection. He scrambled to follow, noticing the team ahead forcing their way over as well. Horns blew irritated discord.

The sports car led them into a shopping-center parking lot, and Black groaned aloud. Summerton didn't have the appearance of a man aware of a tail, but there wasn't a better place to lose one or burn one than a mall. There was no opportunity for discreet work when the quarry could literally move in every direction but vertically. You closed up on him and you hung tight.

As if reading Black's mind, Summerton reached the end of a row and paused, making up his mind which way to go. The surveillance team jerked to a pointless stop, caught in the middle of a saw-toothed row of unmoving cars. Black, farther back, immediately stopped in the fire lane, as if awaiting a passenger.

Summerton suddenly swung out and around an approaching camper that blundered into the aisle, completely blocking the surveillance vehicle. Black reversed, earning hard looks from several pedestrians. He ignored them, cursing Summerton steadily, fighting to parallel the new course.

If Summerton continued two more lanes over and turned right, out of the mall onto the boulevard, he was away clean.

He turned right, and Black yanked the shift lever, preparing for a hopeless attempt to get to the boulevard before the dirty little car disappeared in the flow.

The surveillance team broke into the clear with a squeal of abused tires, hurtling recklessly in pursuit.

Summerton slid casually into a parking place.

The team raced past with nowhere to go, suddenly faced with a need to park and a long row with no vacancies. The car stopped and the passenger leaped out hurriedly, only to slow to a nonchalant stroll as he closed on Summerton.

Black debated chasing after them. There was more at stake than he believed at first.

It had been almost too easy to pump Davis about the man suspected of falsifying his employment history, the one who

360

substituted California for Colorado. "Nothing to it," Davis had said, enjoying shop talk. "His name's Summerton, a design-planning specialist. The Feds are running routine spot surveillance on him, but that's only because he's new, in a very sensitive job."

Black asked how sensitive. The summary of Summerton's position rang in his ears.

Most sensitive information in our defense structure. Access to anything dealing with the nation's capability. Could even distort primary programming. Possible to target our own missiles against our own cities.

He told himself it was practically impossible that Summerton was making any kind of contact now. If he was, it would be observed and reported. If he passed something off, it would be staked out. He had to be allowed to run free. The important thing—the imperative thing—was to let Summerton expose Marvin.

Black swore under his breath, massaged away the pain of clenched jaws.

He eased away from the curb, cruising the lot, passing up several parking slots until he found one that enabled him to watch Summerton's car.

When the paunchy figure came into view again, he carried a grocery bag. The man behind him stopped at the curb, searching for his partner. When the car stopped in front of him, he flung himself in brusquely.

Black grinned. He knew the feeling. Playing peekaboo with a suspect while he shopped for such sinister material as day-old bread or kitty litter tended to make one question the allure and romance of the intelligence trade.

The three cars quietly paraded the remaining couple of miles to Summerton's apartment. Black continued on down the hill and into the valley, noting where the surveillance team positioned themselves as he passed them. It was a very long two blocks to the sprawling apartment complex where he stopped in a visitor's slot and walked away.

A small bar on the opposite corner gave him a place to kill time while he waited for Summerton to settle down for the evening. The thought that the man might have social plans created a brief flutter of nervousness, but Black decided to think positively about the matter. There was little else he could do.

He studied the faces around him, envying the youth, pitying the features welded in expressions of anxious happiness. For each one truly enjoying the loud laughter and shouted exchanges, another peered out through a mask. Black saw disappointment, dissatisfaction, and, in the haunted eyes of a handsome, well-dressed man at the center of things, a startling raw pain. It so shocked Black he stared, and that aching gaze met his. They held each other long enough for the younger man to realize the older one saw, knew. For an instant, his smile cracked. It was Black who looked away, shaken, reminded of his own vulnerability.

A long swallow disposed of his drink, and Black looked outside. It was impossible to identify faces across the street, which meant it was dark enough to get moving. He paid his tab and headed up the hill in steady, solid strides, enjoying the unusually warm evening. Traffic was light now, giving the air a chance to purge the stink of burned oil. The night asserted itself, spiced by the aroma of landscaping cedar bark, the fat sweetness of cut grass, and once—piercingly, rising from the darkness with the fervor of a flute—a burst of perfume from banked roses.

He wondered if Maddy liked roses. Most women did. There was something about the complexity of the flower, as well as the scent, that suggested a natural affinity. Another image closed out Maddy and the roses, and he was seeing the woman in the Bay area again. Her complexity demanded intrigue, treachery.

He remembered the soft strength of Esther's hair, coiled around his hand.

Maddy's was no different.

He wondered if Maddy's eyes ever looked like those of the stranger in the bar.

He rounded a corner slowly, shaking his head like a wet dog, dislodging all the images, all the distractions. He kept close to the deodar cedars, blending in with their dark bases.

The surveillance team was where he left them, waiting patiently for Summerton's lights to go out.

Making his way back around the corner, Black went to the side entrance and up the stairs to Summerton's floor. It was about a two-minute walk to the apartment through the hallways. A woman's shrill anger boiled through a wall to his right once, and at another point someone's stereo pounded rhythmically. When he arrived, he looked at the blond surface of the door for several thoughtful seconds before knocking softly. Then he rolled his shoulders and waited.

Summerton had changed to jeans and tee shirt. He regarded Black with mild curiosity, left hand still on the doorknob. Black was surprised to see him holding a book in the right. He said, "Mr. Harry Summerton?" and Summerton essayed a faint smile with his acknowledgment. Black smiled back. "My name is Steve Black. Esther Wade sent me," he said, and was rewarded with the sight of the book falling to the floor. The pages rustled noisily and it bounced when it hit.

Dazed, Summerton's suddenly watery gaze shifted to the less-threatening disturbance, and he bent slowly to retrieve the volume. His movements were contained, and when he straightened, stunned disassociation lingered in his features. Black remembered other men who looked like that, men who felt their mortality oozing away.

He stepped inside, pushing the door shut, leaning against it. Summerton offered no resistance but finally found his voice. "Who are you? Why are you here?"

"It's payday, Harry." Black stepped forward, and Summerton made a small sound in his chest, retreating. Black moved forward steadily, shepherding him toward an easy chair in front of drawn drapes. He already knew no silhouettes formed on the material. "I talked to Mrs. Wade. I talked to the people who rented you the motor home. I've got the records of your telephone calls." When his legs contacted the chair, Summerton looked around, startled, and almost fell into its embrace. A tall glass of ice and amber liquid jangled as his arm jarred its table. Black pulled up a straightbacked chair. He moved it close to Summerton and sat on it with the back

363

to him. He went on. "I've got you made for murder, Harry—twice."

Summerton moaned. Saliva trickled from the corner of his mouth. He wiped it absently with the back of his hand. "I want a lawyer. I don't have to listen—"

Black jabbed with his right hand, the fingers joined, rigid. Like a spear, it dug in immediately under Summerton's ribs. For one heart-stopping moment, Black thought he'd struck too hard, that the man was going to die. The frightened face collapsed like a pricked balloon, falling forward. The pudgy fingers scrabbled at the arms of the chair and the feet thumped on the floor in uncoordinated twitching as he tried to rise. It was several moments before a full breath wheezed in his chest, and more yet before he lifted his head to look at Black again.

The larger man was waiting. "That was to get your attention, Harry." He feinted another jab at the heaving stomach, making Summerton squeal and double over. "You're going to answer questions and do what you're told. You need a friend, Harry, and I'm the last chance you've got. And even me, your newest, best, and only friend—I'll hurt you if you disappoint me. Have you ever had to deal with pain, Harry? I mean, professional pain?"

Continuing to suck air in hungry gulps, Summerton spoke from his semifetal curl. "I didn't do it. I didn't even know what was going on." He bobbed his head. "He blackmailed me, made me work for them. I'm a good American, good as the next man."

"Sure, Harry, and I'm here to help you."

Blinking rapidly, Summerton waited. Black said, "Come here," and led the way to the bedroom. In the darkness, he pulled the curtain aside. "See that car? That's the FBI, Harry. They're checking you out because you're a new man in a very critical job. They don't suspect you're a spy, but they're watching, getting your moves down, writing a book on you. They don't even suspect you helped kill Ted Wade. *I know*. And you know where Marvin is. You help me get him and I'll help you with them." He jerked a thumb at the car outside.

Even in the sparse light of the darkened bedroom, he saw the hope and treachery flare in Summerton's eyes, and for the first time he savored what was coming. Harry moved a bit more confidently leading back to the living room, settling in his chair. Black returned to his.

"Why shouldn't I make my deal with the FBI? I don't even know who you're from. I guess you're CIA, but you haven't shown me any credentials or anything. What's to stop me calling in those guys outside to get rid of you?"

Black grinned, hoping Harry could see it as he felt it. "You're a rotten spy, Harry. A traitor. I *want* to kill you. Look at me. You really want to check me out?"

"Big talk." Harry sneered, but his arm found its way across the more vulnerable part of his stomach.

"Try me. Or do it my way, and give yourself a chance to beat the system." He lowered his voice further. "Did you know Esther has pictures of you? Couldn't we convince the FBI she was part of the blackmail plot against you?"

"She has a picture of me? Me? From where?"

"Right outside the Marriott, Harry—counting money."

"Conniving, lying bitch! She did all of us!"

Black rose, leaning the chair forward. "That's right. Wouldn't you like to turn things around, dump on her? We'll take care of all that later. But first, Marvin."

Summerton was silent, a fingertip buried in the soft flesh of a cheek while he thought. Black chuckled softly. "You're thinking there's another possibility. You're thinking Marvin may guess what's coming down and run."

Tentatively, Summerton returned the smile, eager to find some bond. "Yes, that's true. Martin's good. And he's ruthless." He fell silent.

"Don't concern yourself with that. First, he can't run. His government'll let him get caught rather than take a chance on losing what you're supposed to produce. Second, if he gets rid of me, you're home free, aren't you?"

"I never thought that! Listen, don't think like that about me, you hear? I want out. He killed two people, man. I'll help you, but you have to promise to protect me!"

Black laughed shortly. "You never quit, do you? I said I

had you made for a couple of murders, so you're feeding my line back to me. I was talking about the two thieves. You're going to help me prove he killed Wade, too.''

"If I do, you'll protect me? I didn't have anything to do with any of it, I swear! You've got to help me!'' Desperately casting for escape, he suddenly remembered the store tag he'd taken from the daypack the day Martin killed Wade. He said, "There's things you don't know about him! He runs—'' Something stopped him, an instinctive cunning that warned him he needed secrets. If he told this man he'd watched the store and discovered it was Martin's cover, it was wasted knowledge.

"He runs what?''

"A net. Other people.'' Summerton tried not to babble. "Like Wade. Get one of them to do what you want. They *wanted* to do this stuff! I couldn't help myself!''

"I don't want anyone else, Harry. I've got you.''

"Oh, God! Promise you'll protect me?''

"Done. All you have to do is help me set up a meeting where I can take him.''

"Just like that?'' An argument swelled up from the parking lot. The angry sounds clashed furiously, then trailed off. Summerton twisted in his chair, staring at the drapes as if his vision could penetrate the material. When it was quiet again, Summerton said, "If he catches on, he'll kill me. Both of us.'' There was a child's sadness in the observation.

When Black answered, he found himself instinctively adjusting his thinking to use the name "Martin,'' accepting Summerton's knowledge as more intimate, and therefore more accurate. He wondered if he'd ever know which name Martin/Marvin preferred. He said, "Then we'll have to be very careful, won't we? Especially you. Sooner or later you're going to think you can go to the FBI and they'll protect you from both Martin and me. Wrong. See, Martin compromised one of my men. He destroyed my man and my career. Cheat me out of my chance at him, Harry, and I'll be after you as long as I live.''

Resigned, Summerton waved languidly. "What do we do?''

"I'm leaving you alone to think about Martin and me. And the lovable Esther. Don't forget you're under surveillance. Your phone's tapped, here and at work. If they lose you, I'll know about it in minutes, and I'll have to assume you've run off to tell Martin about me. Poor Martin'll find out he can't run away, and if he can't go, guess where that leaves you?"

Sweat appeared on Summerton's upper lip and at his temples. Black was fascinated by the way the droplets grew from no visible source, melding one to the other. Agonized, Summerton said, "What if they screw up? You can't blame me for that!"

"I will. Are you to contact Martin tomorrow?"

"No. Not for the next week."

"Good. I'll contact you before then. The sooner we set him up, the better."

"Esther. She knows about me. Will she keep her mouth shut?"

"Yes. Now get to bed, so our civil servants can get their rest." Black let himself out.

For several minutes Summerton sat alone, eyes unfocused, while he tried to think. Thoughts, images, memories—all swirled out of control.

Esther. In the parking garage, in the hotel, lying to get away to take pictures of him.

Ted. The stupefaction when he comprehended what Martin was doing.

Martin. A prisoner, the same as himself. A government that let him think he might escape, exactly like this ape talks about helping with the FBI.

Black. So sure of himself. So big. Mean, cold. "—as long as I live," he said.

Liars, liars, all of them. Lying bastards taking advantage of everyone, profiting only themselves! Whatever happens to them is what they deserve, damn their souls!

A lopsided smile split Summerton's face. He giggled, clapping a hand over his mouth as it threatened to fly open in hysterics. Grabbing the glass, he poured the drink down, ignoring the weak, melt-water taste. The act calmed him more than the whiskey, but he continued to laugh to himself, reveling in relief and salvation.

They were all so stupid, so wrapped up in their own self-images! That was how to get rid of them!

Standing by the deodars, Black watched Summerton's light go out. He held his position when the surveillance team rolled slowly out of the neighborhood. The passenger was already slumped over, catching a nap on the trip home.

"Think," Black said, looking at Summerton's dead window. "You want us both, don't you? You have to see us both go down. And that's why you'll mark him for me."

CHAPTER 38

"WHAT'S WRONG?"

Standing naked a few feet back from the window, Carmody continued to stare into the sunrise, not ready to answer Elise yet, not sure he had an answer. The bedclothes rustled behind him, and then he felt her approach.

She made no sound on the carpet, and even as she pressed against his back and wrapped her arms around him, he was preoccupied with the knowledge that he'd known she was coming. What created an intimacy that profound?

Maybe he wished it so. Maybe he wanted someone to come to him so very much he'd created the fact, willed someone, anyone, to come to him. What if she was merely handy, an object to be used?

If that was so, why couldn't he remember what Olga looked like? Why, when he thought of Nina and Zoya, did he mourn?

He stroked the encircling arms, smiling softly. Warm, soft skin, but an underlying strength. Beyond physical capacity, she had a psychological strength, a complete confidence in the eventual satisfactory outcome of everything.

Sometimes it maddened him. Typically American, it was one of the things that put his teeth on edge. Americans could be hurt, they had a capacity for sadness, but they refused to learn what every Russian knew at birth—the world is made for misfortune, and happy moments must be created or stolen. Elise, more than most, turned that concept upside down.

Of course it was impossible to discuss it. It was impossible to discuss most things. Many others he resolutely refused to even think about. He tightened his grip. There was another power in her. Looking at the slim arms, he saw them as delicate. His own, slabbed with muscle, could snap them like sticks, but that had nothing to do with anything important. The truest strength in her was the thing that robbed him of everything that made him strong.

She left him his independence but took away the wanting of it. Her presence made him joyful in his own manhood, and made him aware he was unable to be himself. Every time he touched her, the man who had created Martin Carmody died a little bit.

The creation was slowly strangling reality.

If he invented a phantasm, a paper man who appeared genuine, how could he doubt that any love he kindled in a woman was equally illusory? No magician believed in magic. Why should he believe her love to be any more real than Martin Carmody? But if that man actually lived, *became*? Would her love prove to have the substance of his name, his face? Or would the magician find he had tricked only himself?

"What's wrong, honey?" She squeezed him as she repeated the question, her voice still unsteady with unexpected waking.

He said, "Woke up and couldn't get back to sleep." In the distance, Rainier speared a glowing dawn, swathed itself in softened reds. Eternal snows accepted the change gracefully, the pure white showing through as an underglaze. A single cloud stretched westward from the crest, a banner of imperceptibly altering colors, writhing through subtle shape changes.

Elise said, "You never did that before. You sleep light, but you sleep well. Is something bothering you?"

Laughter ripped out of him before he could stop it, and he extended it, feigning an amusement he hoped she'd hear even if he didn't. "Can't I even enjoy a little insomnia without you worrying, little mother?"

She released him, moving away, speaking from the bathroom door. "I can't help it." A current in the words made him turn to look at her. She held a towel in front of her, an inadequate covering that left one breast partially exposed. Her hair was still mussed, and when she lifted a hand to it, the soft mound was fully revealed, only to retreat as she returned to her original position. The complete naturalness of her actions was so erotically exciting his groin stirred with demand, and he twisted away, continuing to look at her from an angle. Elise looked at him almost sadly. "Am I in love?" she asked him.

Startled, he forgot about sexual stimulation. "You're asking me? How do I know something like that?"

"One of us ought to be sure. I don't know if I'm in love, I don't know if you are. I want to be with you. I worry about you. I feel safe with you. Are we just sleeping with each other?"

"No!" It was more forceful than he meant, and he thought of the laughter that had escaped him. He damned her for both events. She dangerously eroded the layers of decision between thought and speech.

He said, "We're more than that to each other. I worry about you, too. I care about you."

"We're very modern about us, aren't we? We can talk about fucking and caring, but words like love and marriage are too embarrassing." The rush of the shower followed the close of the bathroom door so quickly he feared it might be covering the sound of crying.

Resentment burned in his stomach. She had no right to talk like that, use that language. There were no promises, no suggestions of anything more than the simplest of liaisons. He never asked for love.

Nor had she.

The cloud at the mountain's peak was torn free, a tattered splash across an incredibly blue sky. The wind clawed at it, ripped off strips and flung them away. The sun, too, revealed its other nature, searing the moisture from it, literally eating it alive.

He put on underwear and trousers slowly, and was lacing his shoes when she came out. One towel encased her body,

371

another was wrapped around her head in a turban. She moved to him quickly, bending to kiss him lightly.

"It's your own fault," she said, smiling. "If you'd slept properly, I wouldn't have started worrying about you, and then I wouldn't have started saying dumb things. Blame yourself."

Standing, he took her in his arms. The towel was laden with moist smells of soap, water, herself. He pushed the thickness of the turban aside to kiss her neck. "We don't deal with blame, not even in fun. We've got something very special. Words are nothing. If we worry about them, we'll start worrying about what they mean, what *we* mean. Please, Elise, let's just enjoy. It's so good it frightens me, like if we talk about it, something bad will hear us and take it away."

"I know. I understand, Marty, completely."

He leaned back, smiled down into her eyes. "Really?"

She nodded, serious. "I haven't told any of my friends about you. You're my secret. My secret lover." She looked away shyly, suddenly very young. "That's how I think of you when I'm alone, or when things get a little rough in my mind. I've got a lover who'll come to me and make everything all right. He's mine, someone no one else knows about."

A small, fierce flame leaped in the pit of Carmody's stomach, a thumbnail-sized focus of anguish. He continued to smile, years of experience fixing the malleable flesh. "You constantly surprise me. No matter what I think I've learned about you, you find a way to show me I've learned practically nothing."

Elise shook her head. "You make me sound complex. I'm not. More romantic than I ought to be, I guess, but I don't care. People think it's silly, but I think a person needs something like that. It's just my way of getting away from the world for a little bit. That's not really silly, is it? Wanting to have a small, safe world, away from the real one?"

"Silly? It's wise, sweetheart. I hope you can do it."

"You have to help. If you're not there, there's no point."

"I'll always be there." The flame soared, triumphant with new fuel. He stepped back, mumbling something about shaving.

372

When he came out of the bathroom, she was already dressed and had his breakfast waiting. She hummed to herself, pouring coffee, and his mind flashed back to his childhood. No two places could be more dissimilar than the dark, demanding rooms where his mother had worked so hard to provide meals for her family and this bright, airy room full of machinery. He remembered with pride and love, dismissing the fragrance of bacon and coffee, suddenly yearning for the rough, harshness of boiled turnips, of tea so sharp it tickled the nose like dust. As he sat down, he wondered what triggered that burst of nostalgia.

The singing. Insight shattered the pleasant sensation, left it dreary. Mother's singing made him happy, but he also remembered approaching the house, listening. If there was no melody, he always hurried, hoping against hope she wasn't involved in one of the hushed, dispirited conversations with Father. Those low, unintelligible rumblings spilled out of the house and filled him with the vague unease of an animal waiting for a storm. It was worse when there was neither song nor speech. The conversations excluded the children. Her silence included everything. It was Russian to the core, the wasted antithesis of joy. It trapped souls. Caught in it, one was bled dry, drained of light and heat.

Elise said, "You're not eating. Is something wrong?"

"Stop fussing over me, all right? I was thinking. People do."

"Don't snap at me! You're not the only one with things on your mind!"

"What's this, temper? What happened to sweetness and light?"

Her mouth opened as if she would speak, and just as quickly snapped shut. Color flooded her face, but her expression faded to complete neutrality, a withdrawal that brought to his mind her comment about a private world. Awareness that he'd forced her there did nothing to improve his irrational, grating anger. Looking away, his gaze was interrupted at all points by diamond-bright glints from appliances, metal trim, shining enamel. Even the kitchen plants seemed to glow from within their leaves. He shoved away the untouched food

373

and rose. Elise turned off the stove and left, slamming the door behind her.

He expected to catch up to her in the parking area, but she was nowhere in sight when he reached the car. Feeling ridiculously petulant, he decided she could drive to the shop herself. He drove to his apartment, wanting to change clothes before going to work. By the time he arrived, he was worried, unsure how badly he'd offended her, wondering where she'd gone. The phone rang as he reached his door, and he nearly snapped the key off in the lock in his hurry to answer.

At the sound of Summerton's voice, his fury returned, redoubled. That disappeared, replaced by professional attention, when he caught the trembling excitement in the words.

"I've only got a few minutes," Summerton said. "I'm calling from a phone booth at a gas station. I have to see you, right now."

"Where are you?"

"Bellevue Square."

"Drive to the U District." Carmody checked the time. "Be in the lobby of the medical center in forty-five minutes. Act as if you're waiting for an appointment. I'll be there."

"It's really important. I'm sorry to call—"

"Be on time." Carmody hung up. He moved to the kitchen, poured a cup of leftover coffee, putting it in the microwave to heat. He selected a light-blue shirt and levis, nondescript attire that would blend in reasonably with a campus background. Back in the kitchen, faint bull's-eye circles danced on the steaming surface of the coffee when he lifted it to drink. The hand tremor was a mild surprise. He hadn't expected his body to key in the chemical and emotional factors required to deal with emergency so quickly.

He arrived in plenty of time to park in the pleasant neighborhood across the Montlake Canal from the medical school and the towering hospital. Halfway across the bridge, watching a cruiser gliding through to Lake Washington, a shadow distracted him, and he looked up to see a vee of Canada geese, nine of them, sweep by in perfect formation. Quiet gabble drifted to him through the noise of traffic as they flew

374

away. He slowed his pace, dawdling, wishing they'd come back into view, but they never did.

Approaching the hospital, a feeling of detachment seized him, so strong he actually stopped to wipe his brow. The sensation refused to be dislodged, and he continued his advance with wooden legs. It was as if he drifted through his surroundings, immune to the increasingly hot sun, the dangers of betrayal, or the consequences of failure. He was not carefree so much as unconcerned, brimming with the certainty of victory a man feels when he sees his enemy stagger.

Summerton entered the lobby exactly on time, betrayed in his nonchalance by a tongue that couldn't stop wetting the fleshy lips. Carmody complimented himself on his choice of meeting site. Knowing Summerton was sure to be agitated, he'd selected a place where agitation was the norm.

He moved in on the heavy figure, steering him unobtrusively by the elbow toward the long hallway. At the first exit sign, he guided Summerton into the stairwell and started up. At the next landing, he gestured for continued quiet and watched to see if anyone followed. He checked his watch until they'd been in place a full three minutes, then indicated they should leave the landing and go into the hall. Once inside, he turned to Summerton. "This better be very important."

To his amazement, Summerton smiled disbelief. "I don't think so. I've learned exactly how important I am to you. No—not to you." The smile changed, became almost coy. Carmody's amazement grew. Summerton repeated. "No—not to you. To your government. And you know how I found out? From a man in my own government."

"I'm sure you mean to explain all this." Carmody gestured toward another staircase, outside the building, and they walked down the steps. When Summerton spoke, the first sound echoed in the cement well, and Carmody waved him to silence.

As soon as they were on the sidewalk, Summerton could wait no longer. "Some time ago, you compromised a man who worked for the government."

Carmody's breath caught. He stopped, watching Summerton carefully. "Go on."

"You brought the roof down on the guy who was his immediate superior. That's the man who checked out Ted Wade's disappearance. Darling Esther gave him our names. He came to me. He wants you pretty badly."

The peculiar detachment returned as Carmody pretended to massage his neck, surveying the area. They were completely alone on a large raised courtyard that jutted from the flank of a waterfront campus building. Carmody leaned on its riverstone wall to check below. A research vessel, the *C.E. Miller*, rocked lazily at dockside. Across the small expanse of Lake Union stood some luxury houseboats, all primly at right angles to the floating boardwalks linking them, like stylized fruit on branches. Without Summerton and his news, it would have been idyllic.

"Why didn't he take you in? Are you supposed to talk me into surrendering?"

"No way. He wants you for himself. The FBI doesn't know about Esther, and he's got her scared out of her mind to keep her from talking. No one else knows what he knows. *No one.*"

Carmody turned back at the suggestiveness. He forced himself to return a smile at the sly, sweaty grin. "You're sure? He means to apprehend me personally? Alone?"

Summerton shrugged. "You bought one of his men, blew away his career, made him look like an idiot. He said he wants to grease you."

"And exactly where do you fit in?"

"We're friends. I want you to know the deal he offered me, so you can figure out our best move. He wants me to believe he won't arrest me or turn me over to the FBI if I help him kill you. Also, he'll 'help' me with the FBI 'if' I'm arrested. You hear that? *If.* He doesn't mean to kill you. I didn't fall for that shit. Anyhow, how the hell could I not be arrested if he caught you? I mean, you'd never tell them I worked for you, but there're records and stuff. And even if they never catch you or me, you know Esther's going to break and go to the Feds sooner or later." He shook his

376

head, stared out to the lake, where a trio of windsurfers slipped across the surface, sails jewel-bright in the sun. "He means to blow you up. Even if I was willing to burn a friend, what good would it do me? He'd kill me too, likely."

"He's out of his mind."

"Fixated, maybe. Obsessed. Crazy? Not a bit. And he's not stupid, either." He dropped his chin, peering upward as if squinting over the top of eyeglasses.

"You're certain he's operating alone? You haven't been followed, your car's clean, everything?"

Hands out, palms up, Summerton said, "I thought about it a lot, myself. And you know what made up my mind he's not bluffing? I asked myself what you'd do if you were in his place. He's not talking about politics or causes or any other goddamned thing. He's after a guy who screwed him. He's willing to die to get you. I think we could trick him, set up an ambush."

"Exactly what have you told him? What does he know about me?"

"All I said was that I could get in touch with you, that we had an emergency signal. He said he wanted to plan where I should meet you, because he doesn't know this area. He said he'd get back to me."

"And he thought his orders would be obeyed? No surveillance, no observation of your schedule?"

Summerton looked down at his shoes. "He said he'd kill me. I think he would, too. I'm sticking my neck way out on this, Martin. Be careful, please."

The greasy camaraderie hurt Carmody's ears, but he continued in his role. "I appreciate what you're doing. Someday I'll get a chance to prove it."

He understood the feeling of ultimate victory that had refused to leave him earlier. It wasn't a premonition of the destruction of enemies, but a sign he would accomplish the mission and disappear.

A thin smile worked its way across his face. Summerton. *An ambush*! The man was an imbecile. He rolled the idea through his mind, seeing it as a movie, silly and pointless. Blazing guns. Even if everything the American told Summerton were true, killing him wouldn't solve anything. There was still Esther Wade. Although she could be eliminated easily, if it came to that.

He coughed, forestalling a growing urge to laugh. There was an undeniable excitement to the thing. Especially for a man who enjoyed the hunt as much as he did.

But there was no time for games, even mental ones. Things were at a head.

Summerton must be squeezed for the last bit of information he could produce, be directed to grab everything available in one final raid. If Nicolai wanted to salvage him after that, he could have him.

And himself. Nicolai must be informed of his resident's imminent compromise, his likely apprehension. He would be extracted immediately.

Carmody looked to the right, his mind's eye soaring, rising above the bridge, the lake shore with its homes and businesses. Beyond those, beyond the Sound, hulked the forbidding Olympics. They were no barrier any longer.

He was going west beyond them, going home.

Home!

CHAPTER 39

"ELIMINATE HIM."

Nicolai delivered his decision with an abrupt turn of his head, suddenly intent on the cloud-studded sky outside the hotel-room window. It was the ingrained camouflage of a bureaucrat, an immediate first step in the retreat from possible association with failure. The move separated him from the words before their echo died in the room. Across the table from him, Summerton managed to hide most of a smile.

Carmody, between them, felt no surprise. Throughout the entire argument—it had started out to be a presentation, but Nicolai's hot stare had cleared up that misapprehension almost immediately—the pinched little face had registered badly suppressed excitement. It was not the expression of a man anticipating a complex, delicate operation.

As a matter of form, Carmody said, "I must disagree." Logical argument came to his lips automatically, the result of a sleepless night thinking of nothing else. Nevertheless, while he talked here, in this ultra-modern hotel room, he could smell the soaked forest.

He remembered lying in his tent one dawn, deliberately keeping his eyes closed to concentrate on the minor-key breeze in the trees and the sporadic dripping from wet branches.

Then he heard the scuffling sound, a tiny noise, tight with desperation.

Without moving, he looked out of the tent. Only feet away, a rabbit abandoned the thick, weedy cover of the meadow for the open forest floor. It was clearly fleeing something it dreaded, creeping close to the ground, exuding terror touching on mindless panic.

The weasel slid out of the grass no more than ten seconds later. Quick, stumpy legs drove it forward in a humping motion that covered ground with astounding speed. The slick nose quivered furiously. Carmody tried to think of it as snakelike and failed.

A snake struck in deadly silence, but if it missed, the game was over, the prey reprieved. The weasel pursued. There was lust in it. And joy.

An atavistic energy pulsed Carmody's spine. *Empathy? For which animal?*

Perhaps it was that infinitesimal reaction that halted the weasel. It rose on sleek haunches, black diamond eyes fixed on Carmody's. It twitched once, the entire body jerking as if electrified. Screeching, chattering, it warned the man, dared him. When it was satisfied there would be no interference, it dropped back on all fours and resumed the chase. Carmody was astounded at the level of his relief.

Shortly afterward, the rabbit's dying shrieks keened out of the dark forest.

Nicolai said, "No. I will see to the woman. You eliminate the man. There are no loose ends."

"Loose ends?" Carmody wanted to laugh, wondered if he was getting hysterical. "You've already killed one of their counterintelligence people. Now you want to kill another, plus a woman connected with us? Can't you see what you're doing? They'll hunt us down like rats in a warehouse. We won't be able to recruit anyone. You'll destroy us!"

"These people need teaching, and so do you! *I* didn't eliminate Wade. I didn't kill even one *chernozhopy,* much less make a massacre." He broke off with an abrupt smile for Summerton. "That means 'blackass.' " When he looked back to Carmody, the friendliness blinked off. "You get rid of this man who approached Summerton. I'll get rid of the Wade woman. Everything will be over."

380

Carmody shook his head. "It's only a matter of time before someone else makes the assumptions he made. And he's probably left written records of everything. We must take what we can get and run." As soon as the phrase was past his lips, he knew he'd sealed his own fate.

Nicolai paled. His voice turned reedy. "Harry's project is first priority. First! You will protect him. It is your soldier's duty. We will never run from it."

"Of course." The surrender came easily, the totality no more painful than a partial concession. It wasn't even important that his humiliation was witnessed by Summerton.

Men went into the camps for lesser failures than what loomed ahead.

The rhythms of his body slowed, laboring under a constrictive pressure like wet sand. Unable to resist the impulse, he stretched his legs under the table, not caring that he kicked the others' out of the way. Simultaneously, he lifted his arms from his sides and flexed his shoulders.

Moving to the small refrigerator, Nicolai poured himself a fresh glass of vodka. He raised his eyebrows inquiringly at Summerton, who held up two fingers about an inch apart. Carmody shook his head, and Nicolai returned with two glasses, touching his to Summerton's in a brief salute before draining it. Summerton followed suit, and Nicolai patted his shoulder approvingly. He said, "The next time I come to Seattle, I'll bring Russian vodka, the best. You'll see the difference."

Carmody asked, "You feel I should agree to meet with this American and kill him, is that it?"

Muffling a small belch, Nicolai said, "Absolutely. The man is a problem. Fortunately, he's also a fool." He clapped his hands behind his back, pacing in his tight-stepped stride. "This is like the old days. We knew how to treat pigs then. Any bastard who raises his head, knock it off! They feared us, then."

Summerton's mouth was open in a wet smile.

Carmody said, "We'll get together later to plan things out, Harry. I have to speak to Nicolai for a minute. We can't leave together, in any case, so would you excuse us now?"

He poured himself a drink while they said their good-byes. Summerton tried to be as Russian as Nicolai, embracing the slight man, clapping him on the back. With the American gone, Carmody planted himself in the center of the room. Nicolai faced him irritably.

Carmody said, "This man is no fool. He's done what no one else has. Summerton said he might want to kill me. I'm certain he does."

"You are afraid?"

Carmody laughed bitterly. "We know all the fears, people like us. Right now, I'm afraid you're risking me and Summerton to insure your promotion. If we succeed, you'll be scolded, but with good humor. If we fail, you'll claim we told you nothing of the present circumstances."

"You accuse me? You dare—"

Carmody took two fast steps toward the bristling little man, interrupting the impending tirade. "When I get back to the Square, we'll sort this out. Meanwhile, your 'old days' don't mean shit. You won't find me as easy as Alex. For the first time in your miserable life, you're dealing with a man who can hit back. And I will."

His hand was on the doorknob before Nicolai found his voice. "You'll pay for this."

This time there was genuine amusement in Carmody's laughter. He turned around. "Where'd you hear that? You've been watching too many old movies." The smaller man's eyebrows rose, and Carmody's laughter pealed again. "That's it! Depraved capitalist fairy tales! You're catching up on all the films we don't show at home." He was still chuckling when he reached the elevator.

Leaving the parking lot, however, his thoughts returned to Summerton and the nameless American.

Perhaps there was some advantage in eliminating the American, he thought. That death would break off the only living investigative link between the net and the Wades. And Nicolai would take care of Wade's wife soon.

He breathed deeply, pulling onto a freeway ramp, heading north.

Yes, the Wade woman—*Edith? Esther. That was it. Funny,*

382

another zhid *name*—would be out of the picture very quickly. Even if the American left material indicating every step he'd taken, only Summerton could physically identify the man who called himself Carmody.

Another person to eliminate? Would that be the end of it?

He blended into the roaring stream of traffic, wondering if Nicolai fully realized the gravity of Summerton's knowledge and weakness. After all, he could, and would, identify Nicolai, too.

It was unlikely that little man would overlook that fact. Summerton might very well be already dead in Nicolai's view of things. That would certainly have contributed to his grimace when the sloppy American embraced him.

He decided to put together as much of a plan as possible that night. For now, there was some time to visit the snow leopard. He wished it were winter, when there were fewer people. It was impossible to commune properly with the cat if anyone was around, and it'd be good to talk freely, to feel safe and understood.

Elise would like the cats. She'd probably prefer the female. After this mess was over, he'd have to think about taking her to see them. Maybe there'd be time for some hiking, too, before the real cold set in up in the mountains.

Angrily, he jerked the car into the right-hand lane. He turned off, changing direction away from the zoo and berating himself. There was no time for syrupy dreams of romantic weekends or leisurely afternoons in the park. There were things that demanded attention.

There would be time to think of pleasure later.

Summerton was bent over in front of the refrigerator when the voice demanded, "Where the hell have you been?" He straightened so quickly he hit his head and dropped a beer can. Spinning, he started a yell, but a huge hand clamped over his mouth. He pawed weakly at the grip, fright blinding recognition. Black shook him roughly. "Calm down! It's me!"

Shuddering, Summerton nodded, and Black slowly released his grip. Only then did Summerton notice the pain in his arm.

Black continued, "This is the second day you've missed work since I talked to you. You're lucky you didn't have a team on you today. What the hell d'you think you're doing?"

Massaging his bicep, Summerton picked up his beer and put it back in the refrigerator, selecting an unshaken one. "How'd you get in? How long—"

"I got in. That's enough. Answer me!"

Summerton extended a beer to Black, getting only a glare in response. Shrugging, he replaced it and popped his own as he leaned back against the sink counter. "If I knew how to get hold of you, I'd have told you," he said. "I got a signal from Martin that he wanted a meeting. I had to lose the tail or lead them to him, and I remembered what you said about wanting him for yourself. Look, man, I'm working for you!"

"What about today?"

"The same thing, I swear it! At the last meeting, he told me to meet him today. In the Olympic, in a room. I'm trying to *help* you. I mean, you caught me, and I'm cooperating. I'm not going to fuck with you."

"Fine. Now what?"

Summerton drank, smacking his lips. "Sure you don't want one? Hot as a bitch out there today." Black ignored the ingratiating invitation, and Summerton went on. "Martin's getting very nervous. The cops won't give up on the niggers he shot, and he's afraid someone's going to find Wade and put it all together. I think he's almost ready to run, and if he does, I'm left here all alone."

"What'd he want with you?"

"First he wanted to know if I could clean out our safe. I told him no way. Then he got real buddy-buddy, said he'd never let anyone know I was around when he killed those two. He's in bad shape. If you're going to take him, all I can tell you is, you better move quick."

"You're being goddammed good to me."

"Hey!" The voice demanded, but the body attitude was servile. "I'm doing everything I can to take care of you. What choice do I have, for Christ's sake?"

384

"Martin likes the woods a lot, doesn't he?"

A confused frown darkened Summerton's features. "I guess so, yeah."

"Good. Come on, we're going for a ride."

Gripping the counter, Summerton resisted the tug on his arm. "Where? What for? What if the FBI checks? I mean, I didn't call in or nothing, and—"

"They're too undermanned to cover everything. We're going out the side door, and we're leaving your car here."

Mumbling concern, Summerton let himself be led to Black's car. They were out of the city, past the creeping extensions of suburbia, and into the mountains in an hour. Summerton made halfhearted tries at conversation, but Black responded with little more than grunts. Only when he turned off the main road and pulled to a stop on the shoulder did he speak an entire sentence.

"You're going to get Martin up here the day after tomorrow." He smiled at Summerton's raw shock. "I don't care how you do it, but I want him up here between nine and noon. Remember this turnoff."

"What if he sees you first? What if he runs? I—"

"I'm not completely crazy, Summerton." Black proceeded up the narrow road. "There's a chance something'll go wrong up here. I'll have a radio with me. As soon as I see you two arrive, I'm calling in the FBI. If Martin gets away from me, he'll hit the roadblocks on his way out."

"Swell." Summerton grabbed the dashboard as Black swung off into a tiny parking area. A large rustic sign listed points of interest and distances. Summerton read the names with an increasing sense of surrealism. *Lake Ray. Miles Creek. Michael Peak Trail. Annie's Meadow.* He turned to Black. "If he gets away, I'm left to wear the whole fucking deal. What if something happens to you? What happens to all the good shit you said you'd do for me, huh? What about that?"

Black got out of the car, tapped the sign. "The secondary trails to these places branch off this main trail." He pointed uphill to his left. "He won't want to talk here at the trail head, so you lead him away from the car and give the FBI time to set up those roadblocks. I'll intercept you where the path to Annie's Meadow breaks off. If you have to get out of here on your own, you take that trail and keep going downhill till you hit the highway. You can thumb back into town. No one'll know you were here. You may get away clean, Harry—no FBI, no me, no Martin.''

There was no sound in the surrounding forest, not even the sibilance of wind touching the curtained fir needles. Around them, the lowering sunshine picked out haphazard spots on the deep-fissured pillars of trees, gilded sprays of leaves. Something pulled at Summerton's mind, something important about the woods and Martin's hanging out there all the time.

Black said, "You have something to say?''

Summerton shook his head.

When they drove back to the main road, neither man saw the lone figure standing behind a clump of brush beyond where they'd turned off. Hurrying, the watcher retreated to a waiting car and moved out slowly in their wake.

CHAPTER 40

MADDY'S HOUSE WAS DARK WHEN BLACK PULLED INTO THE driveway. He cut the engine and lights, letting the cassette tape play on. Twisting the volume knob, he reduced the final sounds to the edge of hearing. The selection was a random one, a fumbling pick in the dark. It turned out to be Mahler's *First,* with its suggestions of camp fires and starred skies. Now it grew to its climbing, demanding climax. Keeping the volume soft created distance, matching Black's mood.

It troubled him to find Maddy not at home. What he had to say was going to be difficult. Waiting might break his resolve.

The music ended, the last flourish an affirmation. He flicked off the player and walked inside.

"Who's there?" Maddy's greeting shout came from the back of the house.

"Where are you?" he called.

"On the deck. Come on out." She got up from her chair when he arrived, put her arms around him and kissed him. "It's a lovely night. I've been watching the lights and the stars. There's wine in the cooler, and a glass waiting."

He hugged her tighter, then stepped back. "We've got to talk."

She put her hands on his chest. "I know. That's what I've been thinking about out here." He started to speak, and she touched his lips gently. "Me first," she said, then returned to her chair and waited for him to be seated. When he was still, he saw her torso move, the slow rise and fall of her breathing silhouetted against the glow of the distant city.

"That man Davis called here today. He doesn't like me."

"He's hard to know. Give him—"

She talked across his protest, not raising her voice, but determined. "He's jealous of me, afraid I'll influence you more than him." In the darkness, her dismissing hand was like a soft white moth. "You're all in some tight little club, and women never come in. You come out when you need us, and then you go back there. You tell each other that's where you belong." She stopped abruptly, then began again. "Anyhow, he called, and he was upset. He hasn't been able to get in touch with you, either at your apartment or your office. You're supposed to call him, no matter what time you come in. You know where to reach him, he said."

She stopped, waiting, and when he failed to answer, she shifted in the chair. "That's his message. I've got one, too. If I've got to share you with that sonofabitch and whatever you two do together, I'll do it, but I'll never pretend I like it. And don't lie to me."

He watched a ferry steam across the bit of Sound they could see, a mass of light carving the water. The screws left a filigree wake that danced carelessly, unconcerned at being left behind. At the bow, however, the sea clawed at the hull until forced back in cold sheets that had the cruel edge and brittle-cold sheen of steel shavings. He watched it, almost mesmerized. It was the blackwater of his nightmares, frigid, beautiful water, greedy for the life of those foolish enough to slip.

The boat cruised out of sight, and he turned to Maddy. "He's been trying to get hold of me because he's afraid I'm about to make a fool of myself. He's probably right. A long time ago, a man hurt me so bad I thought I wanted to die, but I didn't have the guts, you know? So I compromised, died a little bit every day, stayed alive enough to feel sorry for myself. The day after tomorrow, I'm going to meet him. I don't know how it's going to work out, Maddy, but I can tell you I'm scared as hell.''

She reached for him, her hand like ice on his arm. "For God's sake, Steve, don't go! Whatever happened, it's over! Let it be!''

"I wish I could, I really do. I've gone over all the arguments, and nothing works. It's more than professional, it's more than personal.'' He covered her hand with his. "Maddy, he's my enemy. I can't let go of this thing.''

She flung herself out of the chair, walked to the rail and faced away, hugging herself. "Jesus, Steve, more *macho* idiocy? If he's done something wrong, the law'll take care of him. You just want to play soldier, or cop, or whatever you do.''

"You oversimplify it, but there's enough truth in what you say to hurt. God knows enough people have said men like me are no better than men like him. Maybe that's why we look for each other.''

Whirling, she faced him, wide-eyed. "Look for each other?''

He rose, walked to her, took her face in his hands. In the night it was indistinct. He said, "Men like us have to stand up. We're not leaders. If we're union, we're the guys who turn off the machines and carry the goddamned signs in the rain. If we're soldiers, we get the scut jobs because we don't know how to do anything except our best. We're so dumb that even when we know we're being used, we try. If you can't understand that, Maddy, at least believe me, because I'm defining my life. Next to you, the most important thing in this world is dealing with this man this way. I could believe we were put here to test each other.''

"But what you said—you look for each other—that sounds like—'' She shook her head, refusing the words. Black kissed her.

"If it comes to that, it comes,'' he said. "I avoided challenge for years because I thought of myself as a failure. I'm sure he'd be happy as hell to get away from here if he could do it and think of it as honorable. He and I, we've tried to do what our individual worlds require of us. He almost destroyed me. I've trapped him. One of us is going to lose. For the other one, this is redemption.''

"I could lose you." She pulled back from him. Her arms remained raised, forgotten. In tableau, she could have been reaching to him or pushing him away. Wearily, the arms dropped to her sides. She repeated the sentence, heavy with wonder, a discovery too monstrous to be considered. Then, suddenly, her head tipped to the side and her chin rose. "You're risking me, too. This—this *showdown*—means you're gambling with my life, too. If I'm the most important thing in your life, how can you risk losing me for the second most important thing? Does that make sense?''

"What I'm doing makes sense to me. It's not all that complicated.''

"Not for you. You just bull ahead, always being right!''

"I don't believe that. Neither do you.''

"I don't know what I believe. You're being a damned fool! Don't tell me what I believe!'' Stepping back, she slumped against the deck rail, head lowered. "None of this is happening. Not to me, not today. Men don't go out and face each other anymore.''

"Maybe not enough.''

She made a flaccid gesture with one hand, shook her head. "Don't. My God, Steve, you're thinking of killing a man, and I have to want you to do it, just to be sure you stay alive. Can't you see what you've done to me?''

"Of course. Would you believe me if I said I wish it could be different?''

"No." She looked at him from under hair falling across her forehead. "No, I wouldn't. I think you're delighted to be what you are. Proud of it.''

He put his hands under her arms, and she allowed herself to be half-lifted, pulled into his embrace. He said, "No matter what else is true, and I'm not really sure what is and what isn't, I know I love you, Maddy. That's where everything starts and ends.''

She reached around him, squeezed as though she would make them one by main force. "I love you, too.'' Her

390

laughter was quiet, tinged with resignation. "We're stuck with it, aren't we?" Held-back tears glittered in her eyes, a spurious brilliance, beautiful and misleading. His mind went back to the gleam of the devouring sea, but when she lowered her head to his chest, he forgot why the connection had occurred to him in the first place.

CHAPTER 41

Maddy's alarm clock clicked before making its harsh buzz. As usual, Black woke with the first noise, silencing the thing before it even got its proper start.

Getting up, he twisted his head from side to side, pleased at having slept so soundly. Today would require his best.

He looked at Maddy. She was wide awake. The faint dawn was enough to expose the concern in her eyes. He bent down to kiss her, and she remained cold, unresponsive. He pulled back stiffly, making his trip to the shower a retreat. When he came out, the bed was empty, and noise from the kitchen told him she was fixing his breakfast. He hurried into his clothes and joined her.

"We agreed," he said. "You weren't supposed to get up until I was gone."

"I was wrong," she said, working hard at buttering toast. "This is the way it should be." The bread flipped out of her hand, striking the sink edge. Grabbing reflexively, she hit the toaster. The toast landed spinning, ran across the room. "Damn it!" She stamped, hard, the vibration dislodging the off-balance toaster. Black lunged, caught it before it could fall. Maddy stood stock still, hands wadding her robe at her sides.

Black took her in his arms, soothed her with the quiet

nonwords of understanding. Little by little, she relaxed. In a minute, she gently freed herself. "I'm okay."

Nodding, he took a plate and helped himself to just-finishing poached eggs, sliding them onto waiting toast. A sizzling slice of ham went with them. She watched him, shaking her head. "I'm too nervous to butter toast, and you're putting away breakfast like it was another day at the office."

An unsure smile worked its way across his features. He said, "I don't want to insult your cooking, honey, but I'm taking on fuel. I can't afford butterflies, you know?"

Something like a wince moved under her skin, a deep, secret reaction she fought to hide. He went on eating.

"Is Davis still coming today? Will he be as angry as he was yesterday, when you called him?" she asked.

"He may be. He suspects I'm working behind his back. He'll be in around eight this morning. When he asks where I am, tell him you don't know."

"Wonderful." She swirled back to the sink.

Black finished the meal quickly, chased it with a fast cup of coffee. Maddy walked to the door with him. They stood together, awkward. At last, she said, "I'll be here when you come home."

He kissed her, quickly, then trotted to the car. She was waving as he turned into the street, and he waved back.

High above the gold-green of the meadow, Carmody inhaled deeply, pulling the freshness of the day into his body, feeling it speed through him. He held the breath, releasing it through his nose in a slow stream, reveling in the stressed muscles of chest and diaphragm. Blood pounded in his temples. He felt enriched, alive to the point of exaltation. He traced the scribed line of the rising sun on the peaks across the valley, anticipating its heat with a welcoming shiver.

A movement disturbed him, and he glanced down at the untidy lump that was Summerton, burrowed into his sleeping bag. A whiskey bottle lay cuddled up against the material, most of its contents gone. He wanted to laugh at that symbol of the man's unending inadequacy, but the sound might wake

393

him, and watching day claim the earth was too important to share. Especially with Summerton.

Still, what was to come must be shared with him. That was an unavoidable pity.

It would be a difficult stalk, but there was the advantage of surprise.

His mouth formed a humorless grin as he thought of his decision to follow Summerton back to his apartment after the meeting with Nicolai. It sent a chill up his back. He'd been very fortunate. If the man Summerton had identified as Black had waited another twenty minutes to leave the apartment and drive Summerton into the mountains, no one would be the wiser.

There was more to it than luck. Skill, experience, determination—those things made one man better than another.

That was why Black was walking into a trap, instead of the other way around.

Carmody pursed his lips, telling himself it was exactly like any other hunt. Man invented weapons to establish superiority through better mind-power. Squeamishness about ambushing a man had no basis in reality. The smarter man won. Black was big, and the way he moved indicated the weight was muscle, but he would never have a chance to use it.

He looked at the softly snoring Summerton and smiled ruefully. Perhaps it was simply the most devious man who won.

Slightly to the left, a little more than a hundred yards down the mountain from the camp site, the near-level sweep of Annie's Meadow glowed pale and soft against the harder green of the huge expanse of forest cloaking the rest of the steep slope and surrounding mountains. The trail from the meadow angled slightly uphill and to the right to intersect with the main trail. From his present position, Carmody could look down on that junction, which was also approximately a hundred yards away, and farther down to the trailhead. The latter was somewhat more than a mile off in a direct line, but the walking distance from there to the Annie's Meadow cutoff was a bit more than twice that.

Far below, looking past the meadow, the black slash of the

394

road appeared sporadically through breaks in the trees. The glint of metal in one of those gaps caught Carmody's eye. An approaching car beetled along from the direction Black must come. Carmody tensed, yanking large binoculars from a case, stealing a glance at his watch while he fumbled with the catch. It wasn't even eight o'clock. Too early.

He quickly focused on a stretch of road ahead of the vehicle, waiting. Even with binoculars, a car was barely large enough to permit identification. He was glad he'd had a good look at Black's. This one swept into view, and he tracked it past the clearing, where it changed to a blurred object hurtling along in a welter of intervening branches and tree trunks. Carmody strained for a clearer image, got another look.

It wasn't Black's.

Replacing the glasses in the case roused Summerton. He stirred sleepily, rheumy eyes surveying the surroundings with infantile disapproval. Suddenly, he bolted to a sitting position, head swiveling. He actually missed seeing Carmody on his first pass, then swung back to find him grinning at his antics.

"I can't believe I finally slept," he said.

Carmody grunted, indicating the almost-empty whiskey bottle with a thumb. "That much'd put a horse to sleep."

Summerton pouted. "I needed something. This isn't my line of work, okay?"

Carmody swallowed a retort. "There's hot coffee in the red thermos, hot chocolate in the blue. Granola's in my pack. Help yourself."

Summerton looked around glumly. "No fires, I imagine."

"No fires."

Puffing, wheezing, Summerton pulled himself from the bag. Carmody shook his head at the crashing sounds of departure into the brush, and a few minutes later, wrinkled his nose at the even louder sounds and almost staggering odor. He moved away, putting distance between himself and the problem.

Twenty minutes later, he watched another car, lost it, then leaned forward with excitement when he caught it turning

395

onto the dirt road leading to the trailhead. The vehicle stopped, and he studied the man getting out.

Glasses still to his eyes, he called back to Summerton, "He's coming."

Summerton choked on his coffee. Carmody went on, undisturbed. "It's started. If he still believes you're bringing me up the main trail to Annie's Meadow trail, I'm sure he'll set up to wait for us in that heavy growth just above the turnoff. When he does, we'll surprise him by coming at his back from up here."

Creeping up beside Carmody as if Black could hear him even at this distance, Summerton whispered. "Are you sure it's him? Maybe it's not."

Carmody snapped back an answer. "It's the right kind of car. If I hadn't followed you back to your apartment when we left Nicolai, I wouldn't know that, would I? I'd be up here blind."

"Damn it, I've told you a dozen times, I was too nervous to remember what kind of car Black drove. Anyhow, I didn't know he was going to be there. How could I know?" Indignation lifted Summerton's voice back to normal.

"You should have."

"Shit." Summerton scuffled back to the food.

Carmody turned a smile on him. "If I hadn't followed you up here, were you going to tell me all about your conversation with him?"

"Well, hell, yes. What do I have to do to convince you, Martin?"

Carmody continued to smile as he faced away. "I don't know, Harry. I'll think about it." He raised the binoculars and swept the lower mountainside.

There was no sign of human activity, no cars parked along the stretch of road leading to the trailhead. Black adjusted his small backpack and set out up the main trail at a brisk pace. About ten minutes into his climbing walk, he stopped to open his camouflage jacket, pumping cool air in, then set out again. A crow called up ahead and to the left, a series of hacking caws—*Ah! Ah! Ah!*—that sounded like an excited child making a discovery. Black stopped immediately, sheltering behind a tree. He held his breath, listening, searching.

The crow made no more noise. Nevertheless, Black took the Browning 9mm automatic with its tubular silencer out of the shoulder holster and checked the chamber to be sure it was loaded. He flicked off the safety before replacing the weapon.

In another twenty minutes, he was at the turnoff to the meadow. There was nothing in this part of the forest that hinted at a grassy field. Huge firs loomed in every direction, massive branches forming a dark canopy that spanned out to glean precious sunlight. Smaller growth strained upward in the dim glow, entwined in a death struggle for the pale energy filtering through.

The path to Annie's Meadow angled off downhill to Black's right, a less-traveled scar than the main route that continued uphill. He moved into the brush opposite the intersection.

The heavy undergrowth wasn't difficult to move through but very difficult to penetrate silently. He thought of that as his major advantage, and possibly his only one, if it became necessary to actually pursue Martin. Ruefully, Black admitted to himself that Martin was the better woodsman. Anything that slowed the Russian, or gave away his location, would be a blessing.

Black had chosen his observation point carefully. It provided good concealment and was practically impossible to approach, unheard, from any direction. Almost exactly twenty-five yards from the trail junction, and slightly higher, it afforded a good view and acceptable handgun range.

He took off his pack and settled against a jagged stump, wedging himself between it and the shattered, decaying trunk lying on the ground. Raising the pistol, he sighted through the branches at the trail junction, then walked down to snap off some twigs that interfered with a clear shot. Working on the assumption that Martin and Summerton might parallel the trail and approach from an angle, he aimed at three other likely points where they might come into view. He cleared some branches out of the way to improve those views as well. Satisfied, he worked back and forth, fixing himself comfortably for a long wait.

Once more, he checked the weapon, giving the silencer a twist, brushing lint from the barrel and slide, reinspecting the brass gleam of the loaded round. He ejected the magazine, testing the spring tension of the stacked soft-nosed slugs with his thumb, then replaced it.

Far away, a plane broke the silence. High against plodding clouds that now smothered the sunlight, it growled defiance at the wilderness and was gone in a minute. As he watched, it occurred to Black that the sound might be completely uninteresting to any of the myriad creatures that heard it except himself.

Daydreaming!

He shook his head violently. Stress, and the retreat from stress.

Men went to sleep on ambush, fell out for a break on patrol and got lost within feet of their unit. He'd seen it, marveled at it, and almost fallen victim himself.

Stress.

Not because he was afraid of Martin. Because he'd admitted something to himself, driving up here, praying that Davis knew nothing of Esther Wade, Harry Summerton, or Martin, nothing that would bring him pounding out here to interfere.

He wanted Martin to resist. He wanted to fight him.

To kill him.

Steadying the binoculars against the trees, Carmody moved his head in minute nods of approval. The man was good. He'd be literally invisible from the trail, and the business of checking the aim was markedly professional.

"You remember what I told you?" he said, continuing to watch his quarry.

"What if he hears me and comes after me?"

"He's supposed to hear you, you fool. You distract him to be sure he doesn't hear me, so I can get a clear shot at him."

"But if he comes—"

"Then I'll get an even better shot because he'll be standing up. Stop whining! If he wanted to kill you, he'd have done it already. Remember, you go down on the left side of the main trail, with the meadow on your left. I'll go down the right side, Black's side. I'm starting now. You get over that way and start down in two minutes. Keep far to the left, understand?''

"*Far* to the left.''

Carmody glared at the bald cowardice of the answer, but Summerton went without looking back.

"—would have killed you already.'' The words pumped through Summerton's head with the rhythm of his already-heaving heart. He wiped sweat from his forehead, barely choking off a curse as a branch got between his forearm and his face, scratching him.

"—*would* have *killed* you al-*ready.*''

There had been the other line, too. Summerton sat down for a breather, remembering. He'd asked Martin what he had to do to prove he was loyal, and all Martin could say was, "I don't know. I'll think about it.'' Jesus. A partner in three murders, and it didn't count for anything.

What if Martin missed, and Black got away?

He knew exactly where to find good old Harry.

Or what would happen if Martin bought it, and Black survived?

Harry still went to jail, but with a friendly pat on the ass. Provided anyone believed he was forced to help with the ambush.

At best, if Martin were the one to survive, it meant more spying, more risk.

And as soon as Black turned up missing, every government man in the world would be looking for somebody to drop on. Nothing would stand up long under that kind of pressure.

The only real chance he had was if they killed each other, and that was no chance at all. Black didn't have a prayer.

Nowhere to turn. And in minutes, no hope.

Nicolai.

Nicolai would take care of him. If Martin died, he'd have to.

A picture began to form in Summerton's mind.

He started down the hill again, careful to make just the right amount of noise.

The first of Summerton's thrashings came to Black as he was opening his pack. Puzzled, he cocked his head, listening like an old dog. Moving more urgently, he thrust into the pack, coming out with a small watermelon, the kind advertised as "refrigerator-sized." Next he drew out a pair of stout garden shears, and then he stripped off his jacket. Quickly, he cut two thick saplings, lacing them together with a short cord, forming a cross. Jamming the butt of the longest sapling in the ground, he draped the camouflage jacket over the structure. He adjusted the shoulders quickly, then speared the melon on the crown before pulling the hood over it.

From six feet away, the decoy was indistinguishable from the man who'd been there.

Black forced himself to sit still long enough to search for Martin, wondering if he was being watched. His skin crawled.

Finally, he crept away, cursing his bulk, working himself backward under a patch of thick-leaved salal. He could see a little to his left, where the trail was, hardly anything to his right, but he had a good view of the dummy and several yards uphill from it.

Another bit of noise trailed through the forest from high up on the other side of the trail. A small bird scolded, a thin rasp, and then the forest was still.

Carmody paused under the intertwined branches of two vine maples, listening to Summerton's distant efforts. Another sound jerked his head around, almost cost him his balance. Holding the branches to stifle their action, he rose swiftly to full height. What he saw pulled his lips back in an angry snarl.

Three hikers strode up the trail toward the Annie's Meadow junction. Kids, full of energy and shouting. He lowered himself into the foliage, sinking into the cover like a creature in the sea. Summerton rustled some more leaves, and Carmody pulled the silenced .38 out of the inner pocket of his jacket.

From this position, he couldn't see Black, but he was

400

certain the American heard Summerton by now, and must be equally aware of the newcomers on the main trail. There was a chance he'd feel trapped, and break for better cover.

The two boys and the girl advanced with carefree grace, bare legs flashing, smiles like semaphores of good health.

They stopped at the trail junction, debating, with much waving of arms. Moving uphill, the friendly argument continued, a boy pointing back to the meadow path, his two friends determined to proceed up the mountain. Adjacent to Black's hiding place, they stopped. The one boy started back. His friends each grabbed one of his arms. Wrestling, yelling, they stumbled off the trail, staggering dangerously near Black's position.

Carmody heard himself whispering, "Be strong! Be strong!" cheering for his enemy to hold fast, to wait for him.

The playful brawl ended as quickly as it began. The three left Black undiscovered, continued up the trail, happily chattering past where Carmody lay hiding. When they were gone and Summerton moved again, his false racket profaned the lingering memory of their presence.

Carmody moved forward.

Something moved at the extreme edge of Black's vision. His heart pounded so violently he was sure Martin would hear it. He rolled his eyes in that direction, strained so hard everything blurred. Leaves trembled, moved steadily, slowly, like smoke floating on a draft. A hand came into view, then an arm, forcing a gap. The movement had the smooth muscularity of a swimmer in slow motion. A foot moved out, settling with a lightness that brought a rush of perspiration to Black's forehead.

No man moved like that, he thought. There was immense danger in that silence, a power of control.

The sweat collected in his eyebrows, glittering like ice on eaves, waiting to blind him. There was nothing he could do about it.

Gently, easily, he began the long process of bringing the pistol to bear on the stalking man.

Across the trail, something made more noise. Black was sure it was Summerton. He didn't care.

Martin took another step, emerged into full view.

As carefully as he moved the leaves, he raised the pistol.

Black watched the articulation, the total control of the body. Keyed to Martin's rate of movement, he continued to bring his own weapon into position.

Holding the pistol with both hands, Martin sighted it on the hooded figure.

Suddenly, Black saw Summerton lean from behind a tree, uphill from Martin. Unbelieving, he watched the streaming face contort with effort and fear, saw him lob a rock. It was still in the air, sailing past Martin, when he crouched, whirled and fired, the silenced weapon slapping nastily. Summerton made a noise like an uncertain dog's bark and fell thrashing in the brush. Almost too quickly to follow, Martin came full circle. Before Black could get off a round, he shot again. Black saw his lightning realization that his primary target hadn't moved because it wasn't real. He was turning Black's way, wide-eyed, seeking, while pieces of melon still flew through the undergrowth.

Black's first bullet spun Martin around, lifted him off his feet and dropped him facedown on the forest floor.

Martin snapped off an answering shot in Black's direction, close enough to make him scramble for cover behind a tree. By the time Black peered around the trunk, Martin had clawed his way upright and was off uphill. He moved rapidly but carried himself in an odd, bent-forward posture. Black's second shot glanced off a sapling next to the scrabbling figure. Martin turned, pistol rising. Black dodged behind another tree, but as he did, he saw the bloody smear midway between Martin's armpit and waist.

The bullet hit the tree shielding Black with the thud of an ax. The silence afterward filled his mind with the repeated image of Martin's stalk.

He forced himself to move out.

Martin was gone. Small scraping sounds, the telltale frictions of disturbed leaves and twigs, gave him away. Black followed, patient. He smiled with satisfaction at blood on a bush in one place, on the ground in another. Wounded, pursued, Martin was less magical.

Black made a long dash between two large trees. An eruption of bark just in front of him and the demented scream of a ricochet sent him sprawling for the ground. He forced his body against the earth, unsure where the round had come from, dreading the next one. He listened to sly, quiet noises that hinted of someone retreating. Then the forest was silent, completely silent, and he knew Martin was at bay.

He came to a narrow gully and felt the presence ahead of him. Lying immobile, gathering himself, he was convinced Martin was waiting for him, hidden somewhere on the other side. Nevertheless, he didn't *know*.

He lowered himself to the gully floor, then moved several yards away in order to climb back up. If Martin saw him disappear on the way down, he'd expect him to come out directly opposite that point. That was to be avoided.

Black came out in a clump of young vine maples, and the tight cover pleased him. He was almost through it when Martin rose into view no more than two body lengths away. Expressionless, left arm clamped down on the wounded side, he fired.

A sledge-hammer blow seemed to kick Black's stomach up into his throat. He heard his own shocked yell, and then he was flailing, tumbling backward into the gully. His right knee crackled under his weight, and an electric pain burst in it.

He managed to get up on one elbow, the gun pointed roughly in Martin's direction. Dazed, he waited, hoping for one last chance to shoot before he was put down.

Nothing happened.

Almost fearfully, he began to accept that Martin was gone. He explored his body gingerly, unwilling to see the damage that must be there. He found some slivers of wood protruding from the right side of his shirt. When he tugged one, it hurt. They were buried in his skin, and after he jerked them free, he was astonished to find the blood from those small holes marked his only open wounds. When he lifted the shirt, the imprint of the branch that absorbed the major shock of Martin's bullet was tattooed across his lower ribs.

He struggled to his feet, limping back down the mountain.

CHAPTER 42

SUMMERTON'S GROAN STOPPED BLACK. HE LEANED AGAINST a tree, listening, trying to think clearly, remembering this as the place from which the fat man threw his rock.

Why? The fool was winning, until then.

It made little difference to him if Summerton lived or died. He was void of hatred, of revenge. At the same time, he felt no particular compassion, not even much interest.

Like himself, Summerton had played his cards as he thought best. Now the hand was over. Martin was gone. Wounded, likely to be captured, but not by the man who had the most claim on him. He might even manage to escape.

It had all come down to two losers, alone.

Summerton groaned again. A bush stirred, flagging his location. Black pushed his way to him.

The puffy face was the cold gray-blue of death, twisted in pain. Labored breathing whistled through puckered lips. The wound soaking him from the waist down oozed slowly, the obvious ebb of a flood. Both his hands were red from his efforts to staunch the flow. He had difficulty focusing on Black, and gave up easily, appeared to sleep. He said, "You kill him?" disbelievingly.

"He got away. I hit him. They'll catch him."

A movement that might have been a smile moved Summerton's lips. "No way." He opened his eyes, sighed. "He

405

killed me. Son of a bitch.'' A sudden tear trickled free, glistening. It swept up a tiny piece of dirt, carried it down the trembling cheek. ''Nothing ever works out, you know?'' He sobbed aloud, triggering a quick surge from the wound.

''Where'll he go?'' Black asked. A touch of hope, a wisp, stirred in his mind.

This time Summerton did smile. ''Got a woman. Works his store. Star Sports. He's hurt? He'll go to her.''

Black straightened. Summerton's hand clutched at him, missed. ''Don't leave me?'' It was question and plea.

''I can't do anything.'' The words clashed in his own ears.

''No! No, it's not my fault!'' The flabby figure strained to rise. There was horror and protest in the eyes that cleared briefly, saw with childlike clarity. They looked at Black, through him, and, as quickly, lost interest. The glow of life fled, left behind a lying sheen. Flesh settled wearily, aging him decades in a second.

Black rose and left.

Carmody drove with exaggerated care, acknowledging his unsteadiness, determined to avoid being stopped. Even though the wound was hidden while he was seated, anyone looking down through the window couldn't miss the welter of blood. Driving wasn't too difficult—the left arm was useful if he was careful, but he needed no doctor to tell him he was terribly broken up inside. Every breath burned like being shot again, and there was a tearing, heavy feeling deep in his gut.

The route from the freeway off-ramp to the store almost finished him. Sweat poured from his face as he nosed into the parking slot off the alley. For a full minute, he slumped forward, head on the steering wheel, mustering strength. Disorganized thoughts whirled through his mind. Questions. Eventually he felt strong enough to face reality.

Wadding his jacket, he tucked it under his arm, covering most of the bloody shirt. Quickly, biting his lip, he made his way in the back door, certain he was unobserved. In the office, he almost fell into the desk chair, heard Elise's hurrying steps approaching. He pulled the chair forward, turned his wounded side away to spare her that first sight.

406

She read his face and ran to him, framing his head in her hands. "What's happened to you? My God, Martin, what's wrong?"

He gritted his teeth and pushed her back. The jacket fell to the floor. She screamed and wilted but caught herself. "I'll get a doctor." Her hand was already feeling blindly for the phone, her eyes unable to leave the damage.

He caught her wrist. "I have my own doctor. I need to get rid of these clothes, bandage the wound."

"I'll be right back."

He smiled at the door when she was gone. Repairs first, then explanations. Wonderful.

Elise ran back into the office, trousers and shirt and underwear over one arm, first-aid kit in the other hand. She flung the load on the desk, then rushed out again to return with the office coffee pot full of water. Her lips were drawn to a thin slash across her face, pink against the stressed white skin around them. She squinted, although the room was quite dim. When he stood up and pulled the shirt away from the puckered hole in his side, she grabbed his arm but made no outcry except for a sharp exclamation deep in her chest. Releasing him, she bent to wash the blood away while he continued to strip.

In a few minutes, he was bandaged and dressed. Stained water rendered the chair unusable, so he sat on the desk. She huddled against the wall, watching him with her chin tucked in, a fearful attitude. It angered him.

"Don't look at me like that. This is something I was prepared for."

She remained silent, stared accusation. He gestured widely, careful to use only the right hand.

"I'll send for you. When it's over, when we're together again, I'll explain everything. I'm not a criminal, Elise. Please believe that."

"I don't care about that. You still have the bullet in you. It has to be taken care of."

He said nothing.

"Who shot you? Why are you running?"

"I don't have time to explain. I'll send for you. Say you'll come!'' He reached out to her, and she took his hand, moving forward to hold it to her lips. When she spoke, it was as if the words entered his body, strengthened it.

She said, "I would always come to you. You know that."

Nina. Zoya. My babies. Forgive me.

"I love you, Martin. Whatever you've done, I know you did it because you believed it was right. I'll help you any way I can."

Olga! Damn it, why won't you be still, let me see you, instead of clouding my memory with this shifting, smoky image? Where are we? Oh, yes—Moscow, the Kremlin wall. Winter, you bundled against the wind, the flesh-burning cold. You touch your new fur hat, stroke the pelt of the new coat, face my camera. Now you are fading, changing. Don't! You cannot be Elise. But you are, smiling, pointing. Such a lazy, languid finger, just like Olga. I see your tongue, red as a coal, as you lick your lips. What are you saying? "You lying, murdering son of a bitch. I was free!"

"Martin? Say something!" She tugged at his arm, gently insistent, pulling the hand down, away from his ear. "Come on, I'm taking you to your doctor right now. Marty, please!"

He jerked his arm away, grunted with the painful effort. "You can't." Turning, he took her inside his good arm, kissed her. At first, he crushed her to him, exulting in the force, the pain, the overwhelming possession. Then, slowly, he released the pressure, continuing to kiss her but with a lingering tenderness, burning the memory of her into every part of his mind and body.

He hurried out, hating the pain that brought the tears.

Fifteen minutes later, she finished cleaning up. The fouled clothes hung heavy in a plastic bag as she stepped out of the office, imagination adding weight and dimension to the burden. The large man standing silently in the middle of the store startled her, and she stopped abruptly. When he advanced, he limped very badly. Closer, she saw his eyes, and was afraid.

"I'm just closing up," she said, stepping back. The sack

408

bumped her leg, and she dropped it, shoving it out of sight behind a counter.

"I want to speak to the manager."

"He's gone. I'm just closing up." Her voice grated. The man continued toward her, hands dangling loose at his sides. A clamor in her mind told her to run, to scream, but another, soothing voice said there was no need. The violence in him was aimed elsewhere.

He said, "Tell me where he's gone. I have to find him."

He was after Martin. He was the one.

"I don't know. I haven't seen him today."

Towering above her, his words rumbled like the departing thunder of a spent storm. "His blood's on the back doorknob outside. I think those are his clothes in that bag."

"You tried to kill him! You can kill me—I don't know where he went!"

The man lowered himself to a counter. "I wanted to kill him. I don't anymore." He shook his head, looking past her, talking for his own benefit. "Not because I'm hurt, or because there's been enough killing. Just because there's no point. He did his best. It was goddamned good, but it came up short. Let him put together whatever pieces he can find." Abruptly, he glared. "He's a Russian."

"I know." She looked away. "He talks in his sleep. I memorized the words and found them in the dictionary. In the library."

"Did you know he's a Soviet resident agent? A spy? His mission's a wreck, lady. If he ever gets home, they'll eat him alive."

The slow assurance infuriated her. "You know he's almost helpless! You want to kill him!"

He shook his head. "No. I told you. If I get to him first, he has a chance. I'm about out of time. In a few minutes—*minutes*—I have to tell everyone he's wounded and running. He'll die without medical attention. He's involved in killing one of us. My friends won't work hard to take him alive."

"You're the one who shot him. Why would I believe you?"

"Because he would. We've walked the whole mile to-

409

gether, done everything we're supposed to. Now we can quit. He doesn't want me to kill him, and I don't want to do it. He's got one chance to ever be free, and I'm it. You can help him or throw him away. It's up to you." He limped toward the back of the store.

"What're you doing? Where're you going?"

"To the office phone. That's how long you've got to make up your mind." He walked on, spoke without turning.

"Wait! Wait, please!"

He faced her. "Quickly."

Weaving her fingers together, she twisted them mercilessly, forcing the blood from the knuckles, revealing the patterns of veins and ligaments under the skin. "He said he had a doctor."

"Maybe there's a doctor he can trust. That's not enough. You saw him. He needs a hospital. He knows it. Tell me where he'd go to die, lady, 'cause that's where he's gone, and if I don't get to him soon enough, that's what he'll do."

"The zoo." Her voice cracked.

"What?"

"The zoo. He loves it. In his sleep, he said it all the time. The word for zoo. And leopard. And another word I'm not sure of—cold, I think it is."

"That's all?"

Pulling her hands apart, she lifted her chin, met his eyes. "Some names. Olga, Nina, Zoya. I didn't understand anything else."

He said, "I'll do everything I can for him. I promise."

"Sure."

"Listen, don't quit. There's hope." He headed for the door, the cliché stuck to the roof of his mouth.

"For you, maybe."

He stopped, looked at her over his shoulder. She was picking up the bag of clothes.

Carmody parked across the street from the zoo's entrance, a few doors down from the Norwegian Retirement Home. He got out of the car slowly, hissing in pain. Changing to old, comfortable clothes and downing a handful of aspirin while he stopped at the apartment wasn't proving to be much help. He pulled himself erect, telling himself to walk like a man, not all bent over like some cave creature.

It was only a few steps to the intersection. Crossing the street, he paid in his money. The young woman who took it looked at his drawn features curiously, but dismissed him at the approach of the next customer. Carmody walked slowly, feeling rather like a drunk trying to appear sober. He wondered if the aspirin might be making him giddy.

A lassitude came over him, further deadened his pain. Unlike the feeling of detachment when he realized he was trapped by Nicolai—*Ah, Nicolai, you little whore's mistake, look what you've done to your country, to me! And we deserve you*—this was a communion with everything around him. A bird cried from inside the aviary building as he passed, an exotic sound like struck metal. A few steps farther on, a pair of blue and gold macaws hung from their wire cage-front and squawked wildly. The rank, fetid smell of the primate house struck him.

Passing the tropical house, he came face-to-face with a young mother escorting her two daughters. The sight physically staggered him. Fortunately, she was busily wiping ice cream from the face of the youngest and didn't see him. When she looked up and caught his eye, she smiled and he returned it with a warmth and kinship that put a lump in his throat before openly admiring the children once again.

The bears watched him, huge, calculating.

The Chinese call us polar bears. The Europeans see us as brown bears. They would all put us on a chain, make us dance. They hate us. Bastards. Bastards!

Huge, lumbering, one of the Kodiaks suddenly rose on hind legs, barrellike head raised to test the air. It sought eagerly, centering eventually on Carmody. It remained erect, following his progress until he was out of sight.

The snow leopards were out, lounging in the shade. The female dozed lightly. The male, higher, stared west.

West. Home.

The male looked at Carmody, twitched its tail. The female

411

opened her eyes, instantly alert. Carmody said, "It's me, cat. Once more."

The male cocked its head, listening. Its eyes picked a spot in the distance over the man's right shoulder.

Looking around, Carmody was surprised to see how few people were in attendance. Luck was running with him.

That was as it should be. A man was entitled to a little luck.

He said, "I brought liver today, special. Bigger piece than usual."

The cat curled a lip in a silent snarl.

Carmody said, "That's right, put on your little show. We all do, don't we? But there's no time for that. No more time." He pulled the liver from his pocket, unwrapped it. Throwing it made him gasp. The animals both leaped toward the meat. The female, closer, was there first.

When she tried to eat, the male shouldered her violently from behind, sending her stumbling past the offering. She whirled angrily, but he faced her down easily and bent to the food, sniffing.

"Good." Carmody clapped his hands together with pleasure, ignoring the jolt of pain in his side. "You tough son of a bitch, you understand everything. How I wish you could talk! Or I had eyes to speak like yours."

At the gate, Black showed the cashier the picture of Carmody. "Do you recognize this man?" he asked. Frowning, the woman looked closer.

"Maybe. There was a guy looked like that, but thinner, you know? I thought he looked kind of sick, actually. I can call security if you want, or have him paged?"

"No, that's not necessary. Tell me, are there any leopards here? Ones that live where it's cold, maybe?"

The woman brightened. "Our snow leopards. We're especially proud of them." She pointed over her shoulder. "There's a map—it'll show you how to get there."

He thanked her and paid. He felt an urge to hurry, and despite the pain of the knee, forced himself almost to a trot.

Coming around the corner, he saw Carmody apparently

412

applauding the larger of the two cats. Black assumed it was the male, and it appeared to be bullying the smaller female.

The male snapped up something from the ground, swallowed it in one bite, then leaped to a simulated stone shelf. He looked out, away, through space and time, the eyes flame-bright, even at that distance.

Black's breath caught in his throat.

The larger cat turned to the man. For several seconds, their eyes were locked, immune to the world. When Carmody's hand went to his mouth, Black's aching lungs cried to him that it was time to breathe.

No air ever tasted, felt, so wonderful.

He walked toward Carmody as the Russian backed away from the cage to sit on a bench. The leopard on the shelf lay unmoving, his head on his paws, withdrawn in contemplation of something in the distance. When the female came to nuzzle him, he licked her face briefly before resuming his position. Obviously troubled, she paced rapidly, making a strange, rolling growl.

Carmody looked up at Black, surprised. Then he smiled and indicated the seat next to him. "Sometime you must tell me how you learned all these things about me," he said. "My security went very sour."

"Not your fault," Black said. "Who pushed you so hard?"

"No, no." Carmody waggled an admonishing finger. "People like us cover up, even for the shits of the world. You know it's a waste, in your case. You're going to lose."

"You're in a pretty poor position to be talking like a winner."

Carmody winced. "I had that coming." He indicated the leopard, lying now with his eyes tightly closed. "You saw?"

"I think so. Your stuff?"

Smiling again, Carmody said, "Painless. The heart just stops—baf!—and it's over. Irreversible. In case you're interested."

Black spread his hands. "Not at all. Is there anything you want to tell me?" At Carmody's instant twist of scorn, Black waved the hands defensively. "I meant about the cat. To help me understand. It was a strange thing to do."

Muscles melted in Carmody's face, and he reaffirmed them with a visible act of will. His hand crept up to his chest. "Sorry," he said. "Not quite as painless as the lying bastards said." His eyes drifted to the cat, which looked at him for an instant, then resumed its sleeplike pose. Carmody said, "We're going home, my friend and myself."

"They have them where you come from?"

Half-coughing, half-laughing, Carmody said, "Hell, no. I hoped you'd understand. Especially you. We're going to the home we never had. Look at him! He's not afraid of us! He knows he's the better animal by far." His voice strengthened to a quiet authority. "Stupid shit! You know everything about men but the truth! Man is the beast with weapons!" He breathed heavily, looked to Black again. "He'd never make it in the real world. And I can't go home to a world that I died for, a world that never was. So we'll make a new one. Somewhere."

Carmody clutched his chest, eyes widening. Black grabbed his upper arm. Desperate to reach him, he searched his mind for some way to keep him talking. He said, "I read these cats are really mild. Inoffensive. Is that why—"

"No!" Carmody struggled upright. He made no effort to remove Black's grip. "He's fierce! Vicious! But I made him my friend, and now I've freed him. He's mine!"

He gasped. His back arched and his hands clamped on the edge of the bench hard enough to make a knuckle pop. Then he went limp. There was a faint, erratic pulse at his temple, and Black bent to his ear. "I do understand!" he said. "Don't go without knowing! I understand."

There was a movement, and then Carmody's head came to rest against Black's shoulder. Black told himself he'd seen a nod of acknowledgment. When he felt for a pulse, there was none.

They were still in that position—Black had no idea how long they'd been that way—when the small voice brought him back to the present. He looked down at a boy he guessed to be six or seven. He was very thin, with bright, dancing eyes. He said, "Is that man asleep?"

414

Black said, "Sort of. Are you here with your mom and dad?"

The boy pointed. "They're over there. That leopard's asleep, up there on the rock."

"Yes. Like this man. Can you—"

The boy ran to the guardrail, looked back to Black. "My father says we have to protect the animals. The zoo's the only place they're safe."

"He's right. Can you tell him I have to talk to him, please? I need some help."

"Sure." The boy set out immediately, stopping as he came abreast of Black. "If the animals in the zoo have enough babies, and we can teach people who live where the animals come from to stop killing them, then the babies from the zoos can live in the forests like they want. Wouldn't that be great for everybody?" He ran off, calling to his father about the man who needed help.

Black looked at the man lying against his shoulder, so confiding in his last gesture, and at the dead leopard. He said, "Great for everybody."